Portage Public Library
2665 Irving Street
Portage, IN 46368

The Collected Short Works 1920–1954

DISCARD

University of Nebraska Press
Lincoln and London

Bess Streeter Aldrich

The Collected Short Works 1920–1954

Edited and Introduced by Carol Miles Petersen

PORTER COUNTY PUBLIC LIBRARY SYSTEM

Portage Public Library
2665 Irving Street
Portage, IN 46368

AUG 26 19

pabfi POR
ALDRI

Aldrich, Bess Streeter, 1881-1954
The collected short works, 1920-
33410005292729 01/21/19

Publication of this volume was assisted by The Virginia Faulkner Fund, established in memory of Virginia Faulkner, editor-in-chief of the University of Nebraska Press.

Sources and permissions for the use of previously published material appear on pages 319–21.
© 1999 by the University of Nebraska Press
All rights reserved
Manufactured in the United States of America

⊗ The paper in this book meets the minimum requirements of American National Standard for Information Sciences—Permanence of Paper for Printed Library Materials, ANSI Z39.48-1984.

Library of Congress Cataloging-in-Publication Data
Aldrich, Bess Streeter, 1881–1954.
[Short stories. Selections]
The collected short works, 1920–1954 /
by Bess Streeter Aldrich ;
edited and introduced by Carol Miles Petersen.
p. cm.
ISBN 0-8032-1052-3 (cl.: alk. paper)
I. Petersen, Carol Miles, 1930– .
II. Title.
PS3501.L378A6 1999
813′.52—dc21 98-19283
CIP

Contents

Introduction

"To my mind, there are three essentials in the making of a good short story writer: Imagination, a good English foundation, and a desire to write so keen that there are no obstacles which you will not surmount to attain that desire." Bess Streeter Aldrich penned these words in 1921 and lived by them throughout her long writing career. Aldrich felt that if any one of those elements was missing the writer could not be successful, just as she believed that a writer must interpret life with sympathy and understanding, must see, feel, and think with his heart, for " 'out of the heart are the issues of literature.' " As you read the stories in this volume, you will see how deeply Aldrich believed these tenets and how she incorporated them into her work. Aldrich further noted that one must write with an "imagination so vivid that it becomes sympathy," and, along with her good English foundation and the keen desire to write, the sympathetic imagination is the keystone of her writing. She wrote what she called "clean" stories, wanting every member of the family from the youngest reader to the eldest to be able to pick up her stories and read them without embarrassment or distress.[1]

Knowing Aldrich's writing values allows us to understand why the major magazines of her era purchased her work, why she was one of the most highly paid and widely read authors of her time, and why we are reading her short stories and articles today, more than three-quarters of a century later. Few short story writers are able to claim such longevity. We also continue to read her novels, all of which remain in print. Her continuing readership indicates that she has created a permanent place for herself and her works among the most noteworthy of women frontier writers.

Aldrich's audience was astounding; by 1920 the circulation of *The American Magazine* alone was over 125 million. It was to that magazine that she sent the series about the Masons and the Cutters, which later became the books *Mother Mason* and *The Cutters. The American* also purchased many of her other stories, for the editors were eager for her entertaining fiction. The hallmark of *The American Magazine* was editor John M. Siddall's policy of presenting upbeat stories in the belief that readers of the magazine would thus reflect similarly positive attitudes in their daily lives.

Aldrich stories were in demand by other publications as well, and editors often wrote to her requesting that she send them her next story; her name in the table of contents meant increased readership and magazine sales. Aldrich's work appeared in such highly regarded magazines as *Cosmopolitan, Colliers, Bookman, Century, Christian Herald, Delineator, Good Housekeeping, Ladies' Home Journal, McCall's, Saturday Evening Post, Story World*, and *The Writer.*

Aldrich wrote of reality and rejected the sentimental. John Neihardt wrote that "her appeal is not through sentimentalism, but through a genuine understanding of the common life and a warm human sympathy."[2] I have described Aldrich as a romantic realist, a term I believe she would have accepted. With her usual light touch, she once told a writing seminar that you can no longer be "leading your heroine to the altar and leaving her there, safe, safe at last, the harbor past—as well as all interest in her future. That is not all of life. We who have lived past our youthfulness know that life does not forever arrange itself in well-defined patterns, nor always arrive at solutions."[3] For example, in such stories as "What God Hath Joined," the main or guiding character is most often a woman who is strong without being domineering and is wise but not didactic—traits that also describe Aldrich the person. Her women rear their children, work at household chores, have common sense, rarely feel sorry for themselves, and, although they may have problems, solve them and go about the business of living with zest and humor.

By enrolling in a correspondence school, Bess Streeter Aldrich found the encouragement that confirmed her determination to write: its founder, Dr. J. Berg Esenwein, hailed her as "a born writer" and declared that "there is little I can teach you."[4] In submitting her stories to magazines, Aldrich relied upon their editors as her teachers; they knew the market best, and rejections that were accompanied by their suggestions for changes became lessons in writing for that market. Aldrich also studied the contents of magazines to determine the kinds of stories a given magazine would purchase, which helped her to know where a particular story might find a home. In the early days as she was learning her craft, Aldrich said of one of her stories that it "was like a weaver's shuttle, flying back and forth between the postoffice in Elmwood and editorial sanctums in the big cities."[5]

One story that must have seen much reworking, "The Man Who Caught the Weather," went out twenty-nine times before being purchased and published by *Century Magazine;* it then went on to be included in the O. Henry volume of the best short stories of the year, *Prize Stories: The O. Henry Awards.* Thus, Aldrich's "lessons" from various editors, her own analysis of magazines, and her willingness to rewrite and retype (when a manuscript no longer looked fresh she would retype it so that the next editor to see it would believe she or he was the first to see it) was the process by which she honed her art.

Small towns in Aldrich's short stories contrast sharply to the small towns described by her contemporaries such as Sinclair Lewis, Hamlin Garland, and Edgar Lee Masters. She saw the positive side of Main Street, knew the bankers who loaned money that saved farmers, knew the grocers who still supplied food even when a bill could not be paid on time, knew the neighbors who were there when help was needed. She wrote, "I want to portray the better side of the small town because the better side does exist." Aldrich's vision of the small town was that it contained "warm-hearted hospitality, loyal friendship, and deep sympathy."[6] She interpreted life as she saw it, and she wrote, she said, of "clean, decent, and law abiding families. . . . I suppose the idea is that there isn't any drama in that sort of family. But there is birth there, and love, and marriage, and death, and all the ups-and-downs which come to every family in every town, large and small."[7] Her stories do not contain headline-making characters; as letters to Aldrich affirm, she wrote about ordinary lives and demonstrated the drama and reality of ordinary people. One correspondent wrote that she was "refreshed and happy" about Aldrich's "perfect" understanding of the small town, while a woman from Texas wrote how much she had enjoyed "Welcome Home, Hal!" saying that it was the best short story she had ever read because Aldrich had created such an accurate picture of life in a small town that the people were as real as they were on her own Main Street.[8]

Aldrich continues to be popular today in part because we so often recognize our own dramas, our own sensibilities in her stories. She also continues to be read because she evokes the sense of an era that was secure and relatively safe, a world to which a part of each of us would like to return. In the 1920s, '30s, and '40s, she reminded readers of the days when America was a country of rural life: towns were small, everyone knew everyone else. In the 1920s this was fact; in the '30s and '40s, however, rural life was becoming a memory as more and more people moved into the cities.[9] She caught memories webbed with nostalgia.

Aldrich worked hard at her writing, all of which was in the

short story genre until 1925 when she published her first novel, *The Rim of the Prairie*. Until then she had considered her field to be strictly that of the short story, but John M. Siddall, editor of *The American Magazine*, suggested she try writing a novel. Aldrich at first hesitated—a novel seemed a huge undertaking. However, she enjoyed challenges, and this was an exciting and new one. She later said that at various times she almost broke *The Rim of the Prairie* into eight or nine short stories. After this first novel's successful publication in 1925, Aldrich moved into a loose pattern of writing short stories one year and a novel the following year. By 1947, however, when she had been living for about two years in Lincoln, Nebraska, next door to her daughter, son-in-law, and their children, she slowed her writing to not more than one short story per year—she was having too much fun being grandmother to her two nearby grandchildren.

Throughout her life, Aldrich enjoyed the work of Charles Dickens, and her characterizations and humor have been compared with his. Helen G. Masters notes that "Humor . . . matched with sympathy, makes a combination that stands firm in the winds of criticism. In Dickens these qualities met. . . . [T]hese two properties characterizing Mrs. Aldrich's style . . . can be depended upon." Perhaps even more of an influence on Aldrich's writing was James M. Barrie, author of *The Little Minister* and *Peter Pan*. The sense of whimsy found in so many of her short stories reflects the sense of "a sort of laugh under the surface" that she found in Barrie. One reviewer of Aldrich's work wrote that "much has been said, justly said, of Mrs. Aldrich's humor—her kindly, spontaneous humor. It is the flavor, the salt, the yeast" of her writing. The "laughter under the surface" was an important part of the Aldrich personality; Donna Greene Rueter of Elmwood remembers Mrs. Aldrich's smile and her warm laughter; Aldrich's daughter, Mary, speaks of her mother's light-hearted, self-directed humor; and writer Lillian Lambert described Aldrich as having a "buoyant personality."[10]

While including a running laughter in her stories probably made writing more pleasurable for her, she nonetheless contended that writing was hard work and that finding ideas for stories was hard work. She wrote, "fresh ideas do not flock to a writer's head (not to *this* head) like birds to a martin house. . . . A few times . . . I have visioned the skeleton of a story in its entirety or have been haunted by some theme which would not down. For those few times I have thanked the gods and hastily sketched the outlines of the stories. But for the most part I have worked hard . . . trying to get hold of an idea which would only elude me."[11] Aldrich wrote that when she saw or read something she was emotionally disturbed about, she knew that she "should look for a story germ. . . . That, of course, is because my type of story is largely a story of emotion. . . . I try to make the reader *feel*."[12]

Aldrich knew that for the reader to "feel" there were other necessary elements as well. Aldrich wanted her reader immersed in the story, and she believed for that to happen the author must incorporate "a myriad of small deft touches [to] compose its fabric. The things seen and felt, smelled and tasted and heard. Those hundreds of references which quicken the reader's senses and which bring him a feeling of living the story almost unrealized to him. Characters protrude themselves, atmosphere surrounds them. It is the writer's achievement when the reader is unconscious of the two and knows only the effect blending."[13]

Aldrich expected her audience to be literate. She added layers to her story and to the reader's involvement by invoking quotes or near quotes from Shakespeare, mythology, or paraphrased lines from the King James Bible. This is an added enrichment for readers who are aware of such references, but no story is lost on those who do not recognize them. An illustration of her use of the Bible may be found in "What God Hath Joined," published in October 1922 (*The American Magazine*), the story of a woman whose decision is swayed when she thinks that "it was as though all the kingdoms of the world were to be hers." Troubled, she realizes that another had been shown the kingdoms of the world "*and been tempted.*" Such quotations resonate in the reader's mind and add both depth and texture.

The people of Elmwood, Nebraska, liked and looked forward to Aldrich's stories. The town librarian had lists of patrons who wanted to check out Aldrich's latest work. One rural Elmwood farm woman could go to town only when her husband took her in on Saturdays to sell her butter and eggs, a day when the library was closed. She was a dedicated Aldrich fan and had a sub rosa agreement with the librarian (whose husband was the rural mail carrier) that when a magazine with an Aldrich story or a new Aldrich book arrived at the library, it would be wrapped in brown paper and sent to the farm, read quickly, rewrapped, and returned by the mail carrier to the library. Only then would it be put into circulation.[14]

The people of Elmwood not only liked their best-known resident's writing, they also liked and enjoyed her as a person. Aldrich was a woman who smiled at people, who spoke to everyone—adults and children alike—and who took off her shoes when they were muddy before going into someone's home. Aldrich fit into her village life much the way any of her neighbors did: she went to church and to Women's Club; she wore her shoes as long as she could before having the local cobbler repair them; her slip sometimes showed; she did not "put on airs." As far as Elmwood and its residents were concerned, she was, she said, just a woman who bought her groceries there. And that was the way she wanted it.[15]

Nationally, Aldrich was also a well-loved author. Readers from all over the country wrote to her; in 1921 alone she received over twelve hundred letters from fans and replied to every one, a practice of responding to fan mail she followed throughout her life.[16] After *A Lantern in Her Hand* was published in 1928, her work was so sought after that first, second, and even third printings were sold out before the books reached the shelves (book dealers often purchased large stocks in preparation for the rush of customers, who, the dealers knew, would want her newest work immediately). *A Lantern in Her Hand* and all of her subsequent novels became best sellers, with *A White Bird Flying* reaching third in sales for the entire country in 1931, even though it was not in bookstores until well into August of that year. (Pearl S. Buck's *The Good Earth* was first, and Willa Cather's *Shadows on the Rock* was second.)

Chesla C. Sherlock, who as managing editor of the *Ladies' Home Journal* had published several of Aldrich's stories, declared in an article about Aldrich's career that "her strength has been in the fact that she has not lost contact at any time with *the real people in this land!*" These comments remain true. Bess Streeter Aldrich knew and understood the community of Americans; she wrote to them and for them, and they responded eagerly. We continue to do so today, for her stories remain as insightful about the hopes, the dreams, and the complexities of life as when they were first written.[17]

Publication of this volume rounds out Bess Streeter Aldrich's short story writings and ensures that her fiction will remain available to both old and new readers. These stories, some of which appear here for the first time since their original publication, were selected to complement other volumes of her work that remain in print. For example, the books *Mother Mason, The Cutters,* and *Journey into Christmas* are available under the Bison Books imprint of the University of Nebraska Press; some of the Mother Mason stories are included in *The Collected Short Works, 1909–1919* by Bess Streeter Aldrich, the first of two volumes of her short stories. Rather than repeat works that you may have in your own library or have read in a public library, I have included only one of the Mother Mason stories and none of *The Cutters* or the *Journey into Christmas* stories. However, for those who might have missed the Aldrich flavor of those first Mother Mason stories, one should be included, and for this reason you will find in this volume "Last Night When You Kissed Blanche Thompson," one of my favorites and a fine example of her humor as well as of her ability to see the world through the eyes of her main character. Aldrich may have had this particular story in mind when she commented that in writing about a boy, she thought about what it was to be a boy, and then she became that boy, seeing what he saw, smelling scents that he smelled, reacting as he reacted.

When Aldrich wrote about a banker, she did not have to think about what it was to be a banker, for, in a sense, she was one—although not an active one: she and her husband, Charles, shared ownership of the American Exchange Bank in Elmwood with her sister and brother-in-law, Clara and John Cobb. Aldrich illustrated her warm regard for those in the banking profession in her Mother Mason stories (the character Father Mason is a banker), in *The Rim of the Prairie*, and in *The Drum Goes Dead* (originally written as the *McClintock's Magazine* story "The Cashier and Christmas"). Aldrich wrote seven brief stories or articles that were generally about bankers, sending them to her friend O. B. McClintock, who owned a banking supply company in Minneapolis, Minnesota, and who published *McClintock's*. However, because she wrote so sympathetically of bankers and could more fully develop them in the longer works mentioned above (the Mother Mason stories, *The Rim of the Prairie*, and *The Drum Goes Dead*), I have included only one related item from her *McClintock's* publications, "The Story behind *A Lantern in Her Hand*," although it is not typical of her banking tales. As with all of her publications in *McClintock's*, the piece was quite short. In 1951 she rewrote and expanded "The Story behind *A Lantern in Her Hand*," and it is this version that appears here; Aldrich retained the original title when it was published in the *Christian Herald* in 1952.

For those who would like to read the *McClintock's* pieces, including the original of "The Story behind *A Lantern in Her Hand*," they can be found in the Bess Streeter Aldrich archival material at the Nebraska State Historical Society in Lincoln, Nebraska. The titles and dates are, in order of publication, "A Message to Mrs. American Banker," May 1921; "The Cashier and Christmas," December 1922; "The Cashier and the Little Old Lady," January–February 1923; "The Cashier and the Business Woman," June 1929; "The Story behind *A Lantern in Her Hand*," October 1929; "The Cashier and the Children," March 1930; and "The Cashier and the Old Man," April–May 1930.

Aldrich reworked some of her ideas, as most writers do,

and, for inclusion in this volume I have chosen those pieces that seem to me to be the most representative (omitting two articles on writing and one short story). Aldrich's best comments on writing are found in "How I Mixed Stories with Doughnuts" and "Working Backward," both of which appear in this volume. Thus, "Advice to Writers of the Future," from *Story World* (April 1924), and "The Story Germ," from *The Writer*, 45:355–57 (December 1941), have not been included. I also felt that others of her class reunion stories were stronger, and for that reason decided not to include "Fagots for the Fire," from *Today's Housewife* (January 1924).

When I reached this part of the introduction in my original draft, I wrote: "One work that I would like to have had in this volume is 'The Outsider,' which Aldrich sold to the *Christian Herald* and which was the last story she wrote. The reason it is not included is that no copy of the May 1954 issue of the *Christian Herald* could be found, even in the files of the Library of Congress. Many of Aldrich's stories have been elusive and have taken much time and searching to find, but they *have* been found. 'The Outsider,' however, remains a frustrating problem. The search continues." However, a month or so after writing these words, I *did* find "The Outsider," and it does appear in this volume. Perhaps it was the Aldrich persistence at work, or perhaps it was the Aldrich belief in "Fate." Whatever it was, I am pleased this last story was found and could be included here.

I hope you will enjoy reading the work of Bess Streeter Aldrich as much as I do.

Notes

1. Bess Streeter Aldrich, "How I Mixed Stories with Doughnuts," *The American Magazine,* February 1921. All quotes in this paragraph are taken from this story with the exception of "out of the heart . . . ," which was taken from Dr. J. Berg Esenwein, Box 8, Manuscripts and Notes, Nebraska State Historical Society, Lincoln, Nebraska, hereinafter NSHS.

2. John G. Neihardt, "Of Making Many Books," *St. Louis Post-Dispatch,* 24 September 1933.

3. Bess Streeter Aldrich, "There are two viewpoints," Box 10, "On Writing" file, NSHS.

4. Bess Streeter Aldrich and J. Berg Esenwein correspondence, Box 3, Series 6, Manuscripts and Notes, advanced short story correspondence course letters 1917–21, NSHS.

5. A. B. MacDonald, "Nebraska Mother Tells How She Writes 'Best Sellers,' " *Kansas City Star,* 22 October 1933, NSHS, C-1.

6. Bess Streeter Aldrich, *The College Eye,* Cedar Falls, Iowa, 18 June 1926; *Ladies' Home Journal,* 50:21, June 1933.

7. Bess Streeter Aldrich, quoted from a press release dated 19 March 1986, NSHS.

8. Both letters may be found in Box 3, "Fan Letters, 1934," NSHS.

9. *Statistical Abstract of the United States,* Government Printing Office. In 1920 the United States population was 105,710,610, with urban and rural populations of 51.3 percent and 48.6 percent, respectively, or a 2.7 percent difference. In 1930 the population was 122,775,046, with urban and rural populations of 56.2 percent and 43.8 percent, a 12.4 percent difference. In 1940 the population was 131,669,275, with urban and rural populations of 57.5 percent and 43.5 percent, a 13 percent dif-

ference. The population jump of almost 26 million between 1920 and 1940 makes the sheer number of people in urban areas even more significant.

10. Helen Geneva Masters, "Nebraska Authors, Bess Streeter Aldrich," *Nebraska Education Journal,* February 1928, 60; Bess Streeter Aldrich letter to James Hearst, 30 April 1927, University of Northern Iowa Archives; Blanche Colton Williams, "Bess Streeter Aldrich, Novelist," review for Appleton-Century, no date, no page; Donna Greene Reuter, interview with editor, 23 May 1997; Mary Aldrich Beechner interview with editor, 9 February 1989; and Lillian Lambert, "Bess Streeter Aldrich," *Midland Schools,* April 1928.

11. Bess Streeter Aldrich, "The Story Germ," *The Writer,* December 1941.

12. Bess Streeter Aldrich, Box 10, File Misc., 4.

13. Bess Streeter Aldrich, note card, no date, no page, Box 10, NSHS.

14. Shirley Wenzel, conversation with editor, 5 May 1997.

15. Elmwood Mothers' Club, May 1994. Bess Streeter Aldrich, "Why I Live in a Small Town," *Ladies' Home Journal,* June 1933.

16. Bess Streeter Aldrich letter to Grace Simpson Bailey, 22 December 1921, Julie Bailey files.

17. Chesla C. Sherlock, "The Place to Begin Is Where You Are," *Opportunity* 29 (August 1938), NSHS.

The Collected Short Works 1920–1954

Ginger Cookies

This story was originally sent to *The American Magazine* to be the Junior Mason story, but the editor didn't feel it was strong enough for the Mason family, returned it, and asked for a new story. Because Aldrich did not believe in "wasting all that work," as she described any unaccepted story, she did some rewriting and sent it to the editor of the *Ladies' Home Journal,* who promptly accepted and published it in their January 1920 issue. Aldrich later was asked to write a series of six stories about a boy or boys for the *Journal,* but, despite having three boys of her own as well as a daughter, she was not comfortable with the assignment and did not fulfill the request.

Aldrich, who understands children, provides in "Ginger Cookies" an excellent example of the workings of their minds, of the kinds of food they like to eat, and of the ways in which adults sometimes frighten children. She used a similar scare for Emma-Jo of "How Far Is It to Hollywood?"

As there is no word in the English language with which to describe adequately the boiling caldron of Georgie Billings' mind on this Saturday morning, it becomes necessary to use several feeble terms: He was hurt, scornful, resentful and angry. This was not an unusual state of mind with him, for Georgie was twelve; and twelve is the age when a boy's hand is against every man and every man's hand against him, the term "man" being used in its generic sense as including women—in fact, in Georgie's case meaning mostly women. Georgie's world was full of these disturbers of the peace: Mother, Aunt Ann, Sister Margaret and Hannah-in-the-kitchen.

As he sat now on a pile of cement blocks just back of the garage looking wrathfully out upon a gloomy world, he reviewed these feminine autocrats in a mental roll call: Mother; she was the decentest of the whole outfit, but even she was awful silly about some things. Like to-day. She had gone with father in the car to Bluff City to a funeral, and she had said as she left: "Be sure and do just what Aunt Ann and Margaret and Hannah want you to." As if he was a baby!

Margaret—he just wished Dick Kingsbury knew what kind of girl she really was. You bet Dick would never marry her if he knew. He'd a good notion to tell him what a smart Aleck she was.

Aunt Ann—at the memory of Aunt Ann and her treatment of him that morning, his wrath grew. He'd only been hunting for pins in her dresser and her old hand glass had busted. It was just a plain old thing with a white back anyway. He'd just like to do something to Aunt Ann to pay for what she did to him. He'd seen a girl in the movies get choked. Her eyes kept getting bigger and bigger. He'd like to—to do that to Aunt Ann.

Hannah—the wrath in him spouted afresh, geyserlike, at the thought of Hannah. Georgie and Hannah had just participated in a particularly lively row about cookies, fresh ginger cookies. It is not necessary to go into the lurid details of the argument that had taken place in the kitchen. It had ended with Georgie throwing the objects of the violent discussion onto the table and saying: "Take your old cookies. I'll never eat one of the rotten things again."

Hannah's voice, stern and uncompromising, had followed him to the door with "Georgie Billings, as sure as you're alive, you'll be sorry before night you said that sassy thing to me."

Well, he wouldn't! Nothing could happen to *him* to make him sorry for one word. He'd say it right over if he got a chance. Next time he saw her he'd tell that old girl a thing or two. He'd tell her she was as homely as Al Smith, who brought the coal—he'd knock her old false teeth out—he'd—

His rage led him to rise and shake off the dust where all these self-righteous, feminine monarchs trod, and started him down to Jim's and Bertha's. Jim was his only brother and the proud possessor of one wife, one baby and one bungalow.

As Georgie passed down through the alley, whacking viciously at the scattered clover blossoms, a window was raised in the Billings home and the voice of one of his self-appointed guardians called: "Georgie Billings, where you going?"

"Bertha's," he called back briefly, sourly.

Bertha, too, was just starting to bake cookies. The kitchen was hot, and the baby, sitting in her cab by the window, was fussy.

"Oh, Georgie, I'm just real glad you've come," Bertha greeted him. Here, indeed, was sweet welcome, balm to a sore heart! "Can you take baby around the yard in her cab until I finish?"

So Georgie and his youthful niece started up and down the walk and around the house.

Tiring of the monotony in a few moments he picked a dandelion that had seen brighter, yellower days and held it to the baby's nose. "Want to smell it, old top?"

The baby rubbed her diminutive nose in the fuzzy white ball, sneezed, and the seeds flew far and wide.

He picked another and held it to her nose. To his delight she sneezed again and the seeds scattered. He was suddenly, deeply interested in her. She was as good as a little machine. He picked another. With charming regularity she carried out her part of the program, but with an additional act. She puckered up and howled, long and vigorously.

Like a mother hen, Bertha came tearing out from the house with "Did 'e hurt dis sweetie lambie?" and a great deal more jargon that Georgie thought disgustingly silly. At the continued wail that gave every evidence of going on forever, like the brook, Bertha turned to Georgie with "I guess you'll have to go on home, Georgie. When she gets started she cries every time she looks at the person that scared her. Old man Smith was here working yesterday and she cried until he left."

As Georgie started around the house, she called: "I'm sorry, Georgie. You go on in the house and get some cookies and come again another day."

Glad to escape, he went into the kitchen and filled his pockets with warm ginger cookies, which proved upon sampling to taste enough like Hannah's to remind him of the late unpleasantness, so that his rancor returned.

He retraced his steps through the alley, and at the corner of the next street ran onto Slim Higgins. Slim was Georgie's Huckleberry Finn. Young Mr. Higgins displayed an animation that verged upon jubilation. He held in his hands a box. He removed the cover in a silence that was more dramatic than words.

In the box were multitudinous packages, most of which were decorated with pictures of gaudy pumpkins. A mere half dozen unadorned packets modestly proclaimed that they were cucumbers and turnips and hailed from no less substantial a source than the United States Government. One fly-specked package of larkspur and one of poppies, equally dog-eared, concluded the display.

"Wha'd ya think o' *them?*" Georgie's friendship with the speaker was of such a familiarity that he could detect that Slim was swollen with the importance of some mysterious plan. His association, moreover, was not of that familiarity which breeds contempt, for Slim's plans were usually of an astonishing brilliancy.

The conference developed that Slim was the possessor of a round-trip ticket to Westwood, which he had "found" at home, that he purposed to exchange it for the pleasure of being transported from Centerville to Westwood, and that he had conceived the glittering scheme of taking the seeds along and selling them in Westwood for fabulous prices.

The Higgins household was not run on the same type of greased wheels as the domestic system of the Billings home. At one time in a past that had seen Mr. Higgins change his occupation as often as his shirt the family had been encumbered with a collection of seeds from a store that did not flourish as Mr. Higgins had anticipated. The shiftlessness which had allowed the left-over seeds to collect in divers corners was one with the carelessness with which an unredeemed railroad ticket lay around the house. By a master stroke of the genius for which he was dear to George's heart, Slim had correlated the two and was going to Westwood that very afternoon on Number Six and back on Number Nine. Westwood was fourteen miles away, and there were four hours between trains.

As Georgie listened life seemed a very stale, monotonous thing, as flat as a punctured inner tube. "I—I wish I could go, Slim," he said wistfully.

"Well," said Slim in that snappy, right-off-the-bat manner so characteristic of the merchant prince, "tell ya what I'll do, Georgie. You go with me 'n I'll hire ya to sell. I'll pay ya half when we've sold 'em."

Georgie opened his mouth to say that his father and mother were not at home, that Aunt Ann and Margaret and Hannah wouldn't let him do a dog-gone thing, but he didn't say it. There came a great plan to his mind, as fascinating as it was daring. It suddenly occurred to him that they thought he was at Bertha's, and Bertha thought he had gone home. As a result of this combination he was not really anywhere.

Georgie was not a bad boy. His wickedness for the most part consisted in formulating wild and wicked schemes that never materialized. Always something held him back. He did not know that it was the good angel called "Conscience." But now he turned his back on the good angel and informed Slim that he would probably be over to his house as soon as he had eaten dinner.

Arrived at home, he waited by the alley fence until he could see Aunt Ann and Margaret sitting at the table. He was hungry, but he would have to forgo dinner if he got away with Slim. So he went around to the front door, took off his shoes on the porch and crept upstairs to his room. There he grabbed his best coat, tucked under his arm a little china pig, whose snout was open enough to admit nickels and dimes, and slipped downstairs again.

He stayed in the empty garage a sufficient length of time to cover the dinner hour, and then went to Slim's. There he spoke carelessly of having forgotten to wash his hands and black his shoes. So Slim laid out a toilet equipment, lent him the shoe blacking, and even charitably contributed some saliva when Georgie's source of supply ran low. The china pig, upon patient shaking, disgorged from its inwards the sum of ninety-four cents.

Georgie's sense of propriety would not allow him to ask Slim for something to eat, but just as they were leaving the house he casually wondered if they shouldn't have taken a little lunch along. It seemed to strike Slim favorably, for he ran back and came out with one pocket bulging.

At the station Georgie bought a round-trip ticket for eighty-four cents, which left him ten cents for all overhead expenses. It seemed very queer to be getting on the train instead of watching it go through. Georgie's pleasure was somewhat marred by the butting in, so to speak, of the good angel which has been mentioned before. But, being firmly of the opinion that if one has already practically hanged oneself for both a lamb and a sheep, one might as well try to get what enjoyment one can out of the sensation, he entered heartily into the experience.

When they had passed Dry Run Bridge and the dairy farm, Slim took out his package. It consisted wholly of ginger cookies. That was "kinda funny," thought Georgie. First Hannah's that she'd howled about, then Bertha's and now these. Slim's were not large and golden brown like Hannah's or Bertha's. They were small and dark and hard, belonging to the species known as "boughten ones." Georgie ate his, but not enthusiastically.

When the long and perilous trip of fourteen miles was completed, they alighted at the Westwood station and walked over to the shade made by towering piles of lumber to plan their campaign. Details of the preparation included the equal division of the packages of pumpkin and Government seeds, while Slim took the poppies and Georgie the larkspur. Slim, as business manager, gave final instructions to his salesman. Territory was divided. Prices were fixed, but not inexorably. They took opposite sides of the street and started out.

The houses near the station were small and scattering. Families seemed poor. In fact, they seemed not able to buy pumpkin seeds. Georgie was surprised, but not alarmed. He was desperately hungry. The atmosphere was humid and terrifically hot. Sturdily, doggedly, he trudged up the blocks into every yard. He was not discouraged, for the first sale was always just ahead of him, a dancing, beckoning will-o'-the wisp.

In vain did Georgie dilate upon the merits of these particular seeds. In vain did he show the Government seeds. To him the word "Government" had a magic sound. The difference between mere "seeds" and "Government seeds" was as the difference between "chairs" and "mahogany chairs." But no one seemed impressed by the word. Some people told him their pumpkins had all been planted long ago. Some told him nothing at all, merely glared at him and shook their heads. Some frankly laughed at him, which was, of course, the unkindest cut of all.

Far ahead of him on the opposite block he could catch glimpses of Slim going monotonously in and out of various yards. After a while Georgie came, according to the pre-arranged, circuitous route, to the first of the stores in the business section. It was small and dingy, a book store. An old man sat in front of it with an open volume on his knee.

Georgie approached and asked whether he could sell him any garden seeds. The old man closed his book and took off his glasses with the deliberate movement of the old. He was slender, clean, courtly. Upon seeing him one would think immediately of the phrase, "a gentleman of the old school."

"Well! Well!" The old man spoke kindly. "So you're going to sell me some seeds." It was the first kind word that had been thrown to Georgie, so he felt a sudden rush of emotion toward the old gentleman. It was akin to seeing a light in the window of home after a long journey. "Yes, sir, I'd like to."

"Well! Well!" It would have been aggravating if it had not been so kind. "So you're out on a selling expedition? Then I know who you are. You are a ship laden with shimmering silks and priceless arabesques. You are a sled loaded with walrus tusks and costly furs. You are a caravan bearing golden-brown figs and aromatic spices." This last was, of course, the most apt metaphor of all. George was, indeed, a caravan laden with spices—mostly ginger. But since the old man did not know it and Georgie's sense of humor was not deep enough to recognize the joke, neither laughed. "Ah, yes! I know you then. Your name is Spirit of Trade."

Georgie, who was becoming fidgety, said: "No sir; it's Billings."

The old man smiled. "What kind of seeds have you?"

Georgie nearly choked with his hasty answer: "Punkins 'n' cucumbers 'n' turnips 'n' larkspur."

"Larkspur? My! My! I haven't thought of larkspur for years. Once I walked in a garden with a girl whose eyes were the color of the blue-velvet larkspur that grew there—she was very lovely—we were not to see each other for some time and we were sad. And what"—he looked whimsically at Georgie—"what more sad than that do you think happened?"

Somewhere, from vague, undeveloped depths of understanding, Georgie drew the answer: "I guess she died."

"No—no; she did not die. We met again years afterward in a crowded hotel lobby—it was in Berne—and the sad thing happened: *We had ceased to care!* . . . Well! Well! And what is the market quotation on larkspur to-day?"

"Quotation" had just one meaning for Georgie. It was a nauseous thing to be committed for opening exercises, so he looked stupidly at his customer, who immediately said: "The price, sir?"

"Oh, ten cents."

The old man took from his pocket a few small coins and looked at them ruefully. "There are not many, but surely I would not begrudge one for a memory. I will take the larkspur, my friend. See! I will put it here between the pages of 'Leaves of Grass.' I shall not plant it. It might not grow. So many things in this world are disappointing. But all afternoon I shall dream. I shall walk in an old garden—by the side of a girl who is very lovely."

As Georgie hurried up the street he looked back at the old man and, for some reason too deep for him, a lump came in his throat. In a moment, however, he was whistling for Slim, who joined him. It seemed that Slim had not sold anything. Then Georgie displayed his dime with a just pride and suggested their getting it changed so each might share his lawful dividend.

Thereupon ensued a discussion over which one could wish to draw the veil of darkness. By an intricate process of reasoning, Slim proved that the dime was all his.

"I said *half* when we'd *sold* 'em!" he bellowed. "Well, we ain't sold 'em *all,* have we?"

Disgusted but subdued, Georgie, whose stomach was craving something besides spices from the West Indies, made straight for a bake shop. With his own dime in his hand, he hung gloating so long over the array that the white-clad clerk looked his impatience.

"There!" said Georgie at last, even as Bassanio may have chosen the casket. "A dime's worth."

He indicated with a slightly soiled finger some delectable-looking white cakes with pink frosting. Then he turned quickly at an excited call from Slim and joined him outside of the shop.

Slim had discovered what looked to be a movie house in the next block. So Georgie got his sack of cakes and together they walked down to explore. There on the billboard was the fascinating likeness of the Knight of the Mustache.

"I'm goin'," announced Slim with that alacrity for changing plans so characteristic of the senior Higgins.

Georgie looked ruefully at the sack of cakes for which he had bartered his worldly goods. "It don't—don't—seem just fair, Slim."

"Oh, I guess it's fair, all right. Ain't I got the money?"

Georgie admitted that this was true, but his heart was sore within him.

So Slim went into the Abode of Bliss, and Georgie, with his sack of little cakes and both boxes of seeds, went over to a park bench. He opened the sack and peered in. Then he started up wildly and tore the bag half open in his haste. Where were his little pink-and-white cakes? These were cookies—ginger cookies! Suddenly he remembered that the tray of ginger cookies had stood next to the one of white cakes. The clerk must have thought he pointed to the cookies. He rushed over to the bakeshop intending to ask the man to change them, but several customers were in and his nerve failed him, so he went miserably back to the bench.

Georgie did not know what retributive vengeance meant. But in a vague, boyish way he began to feel that something spooky was following him all day, that some mysterious power was exacting satisfaction for a wrong. He and Petie Eberhardt had read a story like it in the Eberhardt barn; it was called "The Old Man's Curse." Had—he looked nervously around—had Hannah cursed him?

For a little while he sat quietly in the park under the shadow of the thought. Then his eyes fell upon the seeds. If he could only surprise Slim by selling them all! So, with sudden energy, he rose and crossed to the other side of town, where seemed to dwell the aristocrats. Because the proletariat had not purchased seeds, it did not follow that the patricians would do likewise.

For one solid, hot, perspiring hour he worked harder than he had ever done in his life. At the end of that time he turned wearily into a yard where a woman sat in a garden seat. She was old. She looked like a coiffured, manicured, bejeweled Witch of Endor.

When Georgie announced his errand she said sharply: "Have you got a license?"

Georgie did not have one. Moreover, he did not know what one was. But he was suddenly, intensely alarmed.

"Then," she said fiercely, her permanent wave bobbing up and down on her wrinkled old forehead, "you get right out of here or I'll call the town marshal. And what's more, you try to sell Government seeds in this town and I'll report you to the Federal authorities."

Georgie left hastily, aided in his flight by visions of President Wilson coming through the park to collar him. He dropped breathlessly down on a bench. All was lost save honor—and the seeds. He did not know whether he was a communist, a socialist, an anarchist or a bolshevist. He only knew that he was something he had not been before.

For another wretched hour he loafed around the park and waited for Slim. Occasionally he nibbled at a cooky, but it was not pleasant to his palate.

He was glad when the show was over, glad when they got on the home-bound train. Slim, full of enthusiasm over the picture, kept up a running dissertation on its merits, but Georgie was strangely silent. The old lady who sat across the aisle tried to draw him into conversation. Under ordinary circumstances he would have told her, unbidden, who he was, his place of residence, the make of his bicycle and his favorite color, but now he only responded with "Yes, ma'am," "No, ma'am."

She was a lady who bulged out in many places. Her cheeks, her body, her hands, all seemed to have been pneumatically blown up. The little, gray-whiskered man next to the window was almost hidden by her. The two spread out their lunch. Georgie's greedy eyes fastened themselves on some huge slices of bread and butter and pieces of fried chicken. There was a leg all crisp and—The old lady caught his look, so he turned his head away quickly.

"Here, little boy," she spoke in halting English. "Here iss somedings for you."

As he turned toward her he felt, intuitively, that he knew what it was going to be. Yes, it was just as he thought. They were huge and thick and ginger colored. He was not surprised. He had reached a state of calm despair, a sort of mental ennui, as though it would not do the least good to fight against this uncanny, nightmare thing. Mechanically he put out his hand for them. He gave one of the loathsome things to Slim and squeezed the other down in the crack of the plush seat. Whenever the old lady looked at him he wiped his mouth vigorously with the back of his hand.

When they were nearing Centerville, with that necessity for confession so essential to some souls, Georgie said: "Say, Slim, the folks didn't know I come."

"Didn't they?" Then he added consolingly: "Gee! I'd hate to be you."

Georgie half expected that Margaret or Aunt Ann would be at the station to meet him. There was no representative there, however—only Al Smith for the mail, and a dozen hangers-on. As the two walked up Main Street they spoke wonderingly to each other of changes in town. One would have thought they were old men returning to the scenes of their boyhood.

On the far edge of town they parted, Slim to go whistling cheerfully down the street, secure in the knowledge that there would be no reward and no questions asked, and Georgie to turn in at the Billings' driveway and saunter silently, albeit nonchalantly, toward the house. It was somewhat disconcerting to see the garage door open and the big car inside. Father and mother were home.

For a moment he paused to decide which of the entrances to the house looked less forbidding. He chose the dining-room door. His entrance could not have been more dramatic. For he opened the door directly upon the family sitting at the supper table. As they turned and looked at him, it seemed that there must have been seventy-five seated around the table.

There was a vast silence. It closed in around him like water over his head. It was his father who broke the long, chilly stillness. Rare indeed were the occasions when his father took the steering wheel of government from mother's hand. This was evidently a rare occasion, for he said in tones that partook of the qualities of lemon ice: "Young man, you can go up to your room."

As Georgie passed the table he caught a fleeting vision of cold sliced ham, pinkish white, of light rolls and blackberries. Lucifer might have gazed upon such a scene just before he was cast into outer darkness. Georgie carefully closed the door of Paradise Lost behind him, tiptoed up to his room and seated himself quietly in a chair by the window and waited for the Great Mystery.

Stoically he repeated: "Scoldin's don't hurt you; lickin's don't last long; and kill you they dassent."

For ages he sat there while outside in the great world people were born, married and passed away. He was the only person in the universe to whom nothing happened, whose functions were paralyzed, whose life was at a standstill. After a few years he heard someone coming up the stairs. His door was opened. He did not take his eyes from a small, green bush on the side lawn. The someone behind him spoke. It was his mother.

"Georgie," she said quietly, "we are all surprised beyond words that you would do a thing like that. Father says to tell you to go to bed. You're not to have any supper." Her chin wobbled suspiciously, but she went steadily, Spartanly, on: "But I didn't want you to go absolutely hungry to bed, so I've brought you just a bite." Georgie heard a tray being placed on his dresser. Then mother withdrew lingeringly. At the door she paused. "Don't forget to say your prayer, dear."

Georgie, who had thoughts of his own on this subject that did not in the least accord with the orthodox creed of the church of which he was a humble attendant, made no answer. He waited until he heard her going down the stairs, then turned hurriedly, avidly, to the dresser. On the tray stood one glass of water and two ginger cookies!

With a groan he hauled off his shoes and clothes, put on his gown and got into bed. A few lingering rays of sun were still stretched across his prison floor. He could hear the family laughing and the tinkle of dishes in the kitchen. Cars began going by with merry loads. Slim was whistling out in the alley—Slim, who was free.

For a long time he lay looking out toward the tree-grown hill behind the pasture, reviewing the miserable afternoon. He was glad he had hidden the seeds in a bush in the Westwood park, glad he had purposely neglected to remind Slim to bring them home. He hoped they'd take root and grow all over the park, thick, so thick that the Westwood folks couldn't ever walk through it, darn 'em!

The moon swung slowly into view. It was large and round and yellow, golden yellow. It leered at him. It looked— The perspiration broke out on Georgie's forehead. Then he shivered a little, pulled the sheet up, and turned his face to the wall. It looked like a huge ginger cooky.

Across the Smiling Meadow

The woman in this story is probably suffering from influenza, the disease that became an international epidemic in the years following World War I; by 1920 over twenty-two million people worldwide had died from this plague. Thirteen years later, Aldrich returned to the subject in "The Silent Stars Go By," a story that was made into a Christmas program for public television, renamed "A Gift of Love." It stars Lee Remick and Angela Lansbury and continues to be broadcast seasonally.

Aldrich knew her Bible well, and the last line of "Across the Smiling Meadow" (*Ladies' Home Journal,* February 1920) is one occasion in a short story in which she echoes or paraphrases a Bible verse. Aldrich ends "Across the Smiling Meadow" with the words *"But the woman kept all these things and pondered them in her heart."* Luke 2:19 of the King James version of the Bible, the version with which Aldrich would have been familiar, reads: "But Mary kept all these things, and pondered them in her heart."

The woman in the hospital bed lay quite still except for an occasional weary tossing of her head from side to side. It seemed to her befogged mind that she was constantly burning, but only when the heat came into her throat—to scorch and close it—could she endure the condition no longer. Then someone in white would put fresh, cool cloths on her head, and she would feel better for a few moments until the Heat Monster found the cool things and set fire to them too.

How nice cool things were! One of the doctors sometimes held something small and cool against her arm. Edward, her husband, was always there with the doctors. Edward, she thought wearily, must be ill, too, for his face seemed to look drawn and white.

Through what long period of time had she been hot? Months, weeks, or just days? Suddenly, in vivid memory, she could remember the day. She had been waiting for Riggs, the chauffeur, to come with the car to take her to a Woman's Club committee meeting. She hadn't gone to the meeting. Something had seized her—a torturing pain—and Natalie had been frightened and telephoned for "papa." Edward had come in the car with the doctor.

Up to that point she could clearly remember the circumstances. After that there was a blank space of time, and then this white room, and the white curtains, and the white nurses—everything was white excepting herself and the little black-and-gold crucifix on the wall.

It was queer about that crucifix. Of course it was really Christ hanging there, thirsty and heat-tortured too; but the strange part was that the face of the Grieved One looked like her mother. The resemblance about the eyes was marked. Again that old, troublesome question that had been haunting her returned to tap, tap at the door of bewildered memory: Why didn't mother come to the hospital to see her? Mother's hands were the coolest hands she had ever known. She would surely come soon.

For a time the woman fixed her flaming eyes on the doorway, watching intensely for a straight, white-haired woman with a calm, gentle face to come in and move quietly and placidly up to the burning-hot bed. Then, in a sharp flickering flash of memory, it came to her: mother had passed away last winter.

For a moment there was a swift, poignant sensation of grief and loss that as quickly left. Mother might come anyway, because the day she went away she had said: "Don't grieve, Jennie; maybe I can help you when you need me just as I have always done. The Father is so kind; I think, dear, if you ever want me He would let me come back to help you." The woman held her mind obstinately to the thought until she grew stupid again and heard only the roaring flood of fire going by her head.

She roused to notice that the doctor had come in again. It was the fleshy one with thick glasses. Someone out in the sun porch—it sounded like Natalie's voice—was whispering loudly: "What's a crisis mean?" She herself was going away now on the long journey. She knew that. And the queer thing was that *she didn't care.* People called it "dying." They seemed to fear it. *She* had feared it, had lived in dread of it, up until now. It was nothing, after all. It was just dropping all responsibility. There were others to look after things. She wouldn't have to be responsible for the big house out on Sheridan Avenue, nor church work, nor club work, nor Edward's comfort, nor Natalie.

At the thought of Natalie her mind paused and began vague, laborious searching for something she wanted to do. Groping in dark mental wanderings, she finally came upon the definite desire and held tenaciously to it: *She must take Natalie with her.* Why, Natalie was only eight; that was too little to be left.

The doctor sat down by the bed. The heat in the woman's ears poured constantly over a dam of molten steel. Somewhere on the other side of this dreadful heat mother would meet them, Natalie and herself—would put out a cool hand—and—show them—the way.

The doctor was moving away from the bed and beckoning to the nurse. Now was the time, the woman thought craftily. If she could only step out on the sun porch and get Natalie! She seemed to slip quietly out of bed and into the hall, only it proved not to be the hall of the hospital at all, but the lower hall in her own home.

She sped noiselessly up the wide, mahogany stairway to her little girl's room. Yes, Natalie was there just as she felt she would find her, lying across the pink-and-white bed.

The mother called to her softly: "Natalie!"

The little girl sat up, surprised. She had been crying.

"Come with me, Natalie," the mother called, "I'm going to take you with me, dear."

"I can't," the little girl shook her brown head. "My mamma's awful sick at St. Catherine's Hospital. I can't play."

The woman felt no shock at all that Natalie did not know her, for on the way down the hall she had realized that she was a little girl herself. She had a blue gingham dress with bands of white braid on it. How well she remembered it! Her yellow curls hung around her shoulders just as they had done years before.

At first she hesitated, wondering how best she could explain this unusual phenomenon to Natalie, that, after all, they were the same age. It seemed so difficult that she did not make the attempt. She only said: "Your mamma is better. She said you could come."

So Natalie got up, shook out her dainty skirts, and came quickly to the door, for childhood is ever glad to thrust sorrow aside.

"What's your name?" she asked the woman who had become a little girl again.

"Jennie."

"Why that's my mamma's name too."

Jennie laughed at that and, taking Natalie's brown hand in her own fa*ⁱ* one, led her to the stairway. There she paused. "Your doll!" she said, "Go get it. We may want to play."

Natalie ran back to her room and returned with "Baby Bumps" carefully wrapped in a soft, silk-lined blanket. Then the two little girls went down the back stairs and out into the warm, early-afternoon sunshine of May. They saw old Jane, the cook, sitting idly by the window with her apron over her face, and Emma, the second girl, frankly crying on the back porch. "What's the matter with them?" Jennie asked.

"They're sorry about my mamma; just about everybody likes her."

They passed the rose house, rounded the garage and climbed a fence that led into a cool, green pasture.

"I never knew this big, grassy place was out here before," said Natalie.

"It wasn't," Jennie informed her, and laughed at the other's incredulous expression.

There were sunny dandelions and honeysweet clovers. Little brown rabbits hopped away through the grass, and a meadow lark stood on a fence post and sang to them.

Jennie took the lead always, walking quickly along with Natalie's hand in hers.

"Where are we going?" Natalie asked. "Papa wouldn't like me to go far."

"We're going across the Smiling Meadow," Jennie answered. "I've never been there, but I've always wanted to go. I think I can find the way. I'll try and explain it to you, Natalie, but it's just a little hard to understand. You know how time keeps going on and on, and how children always grow up?"

Natalie inclined her head.

"Well, nobody ever turns around and goes back the other way, gets little again, you know. But every little girl *wishes* she could go back to play with her mother." She came closer to Natalie and drew her head over to whisper: "Listen! *Crossing the Smiling Meadow is going back.*"

If Natalie failed to comprehend fully, it did not matter, and she smiled trustingly at Jennie.

So the two little girls went on through the green grass under the friendly sky where the white clouds sailed low. They passed clumps of wild crab-apple trees in blossom and marshy places where dogtooth violets grew. After a while the path merged into a village street that lay basking sleepily in the pleasant spring sunshine.

"There it is!" called Jennie excitedly. "I'm for sure on the right way. My home is two blocks over there. You stop at the house with me while I get my doll."

They walked up the street past comfortable old houses until they came to an upright-and-wing house, white with green shutters, set far back from the road. Jennie opened the painted picket gate and together they passed up the brick walk bordered with petunias and sweetbrier.

"It isn't half so big as my house," Natalie announced with the naïve frankness of eight years.

"No, it isn't," Jennie agreed; "but it's my home and I love it."

She opened the door and they went into a big sitting room. A glisteningly varnished organ stood in one corner, a three-cornered whatnot of curios in another, and in the center of the room was a walnut table holding a fat, blue-flowered lamp, a stereoscope, and a red-plush album. While Jennie ran up the narrow built-in stairway to her room, Natalie looked at the queer people in the plump album. When Jennie came down, she held lovingly in her arms an old-fashioned doll with pink-tinted cheeks and neatly waving china hair.

"Now, I'll show you my playhouse before we go on," she told Natalie.

The two little girls went out through the pleasant kitchen, through the clean back porch with its wooden pump and shining dipper, and down the back walk where scarlet-flamed poppies grew.

Jennie led the way to the carriage house, where a big, clumsy, canopy-topped phaeton stood. Natalie's eyes were shining and she clapped her hands in ecstasy. "It looks like my mamma's playhouse used to. I know because it's just like she's told me, the funny carriage and the old, brown cupboard with the broken dishes! And oh! there's the rusty stove to cook on and the blackboard her papa made her and the cradle that rocks!"

Jennie smiled and laid her cheek lovingly against Natalie's for a moment. "Come on, now," she urged; "there's something else I want to show you."

They went out into the yard, where Jennie showed her companion the stout hammock under two trees. It was made from a barrel staves and held together with ropes. "She's told me about this too," Natalie kept saying.

Jennie, who was swinging Natalie, looked wistfully at the small weather-beaten house next door and the big red brick across the street. "I wonder where the girls are, Minnie and Belle. I wish they'd come out and play." Then she hastened to add: "Oh, I forgot! They're not there. They've gone on, you know—up the other way. Come now. We must hurry. We're going on farther back—farther back than this."

Natalie did not want to go anywhere else. She wanted to stay and play with the delightful old playthings that had been her mother's. She even pouted a little about it. But Jennie was firm. She took Natalie's hand, went down the sweetbrier path and out of the white-picket gate. They passed down the pleasant village street where no children played, and out again into the Smiling Meadow. As they walked along, the grass began to be coarse and high and sprinkled with gay-colored flowers.

"It's wild land," Jennie decided.

"What's that?" Natalie wanted to know.

"It's never been turned by a plow. Nothing ever grew here except just the things God planted."

Once they saw, afar off, a wagon drawn with heavy, plodding oxen. "Look!" Jennie pointed. "It's a prairie schooner."

After a time they came through the mass of bright-colored wild flowers to the end of the Smiling Meadow, for a fence was before them. "What a funny fence!" said Natalie. "It's looks as if it was made of big toothpicks."

"It's a rail fence," Jennie told her.

They climbed over it, catching their dresses on the rough bark, and turned down a narrow lane. At the end of the lane stood a little brown house in a clearing of timber.

"There it is!" called Jennie triumphantly. "I never saw it, but I know it."

"How queer it is!" said Natalie. "It looks like it was made out of tree trunks."

"It is," Jennie explained. "It's a log cabin."

A little girl came from the door of the house. She bounded down the path and came, laughing, toward the two girls. She had on a rough dark dress that reached to her ankles, and her sleek black hair was braided and wound round her head.

"There she is," laughed Jennie excitedly. "I never saw her, but I know her."

"How queer she is," Natalie whispered.

"You'll love her," answered Jennie stoutly. "She's Mary—Mary Burdick."

Mary put an arm around each girl. "I knew you were coming," she welcomed them joyously. "I put on my best linsey-woolsey dress, only I mustn't tear it. We'll play together all afternoon, won't we?"

They walked slowly up the path, the three heads close together, the sleek black braids, the yellow curls and the brown bobbed hair tied with a huge scarlet bow.

"I'm eight," volunteered Natalie.

"So'm I," said Jennie.

"Me too," echoed Mary. And they all laughed at the joke of it.

Then they showed one another their rings. Natalie's held a row of little seed pearls. Jennie's was a plain gold band. Mary's was made of beads.

"How funny it is," said Natalie frankly.

"It's real pretty," consoled Jennie, patting Mary's hand.

"What shall we do first?" Mary wanted to know.

"Where's the playhouse?" asked Jennie. "The one under the pine trees." Jennie seemed to know all about it.

So Mary led the way down to the playhouse and showed them the cupboard in a hollow stone and the acorn cups and saucers and the pine-needle baskets. Then she ran into the cabin and came back with her doll. It was made out of a corncob. The corn silk was braided like hair, and the dress of husks stood out stiff and full. "What a funny doll!" Natalie's amazement was genuine. "Is that the only one you have?"

Mary nodded and hugged the stiff little body close. "It's lovely," comforted Jennie. "You must think lots of her."

So they set the three dollies in a row—the corncob doll and the china one and the "Baby Bumps."

For a long, long time they played house with the acorn dishes under the sweet-smelling balsam boughs. Then, because they grew tired of that, Mary took them into the deep woods and showed them the mourning dove's nest and the rabbit's burrow and the damp, dark place where the bluebells grew. They went to the spring for water and drank out of a hollowed gourd with the long neck for a handle. Then Mary took them back through the garden that had been planted in a little, rail-fence inclosure.

"Oh, what big tomatoes!" Natalie reached for one of the huge scarlet balls.

"No! No! You mustn't touch them," called Mary excitedly. "They're love apples. They're poison."

"Pooh! We eat them," Natalie retorted, but she hastily took her hand away.

Then they went into the cabin. There were bright, oval-shaped rag rugs and a spinning wheel and tallow candles stuck in shells. There was a great, open fireplace with a kettle in front, a flintlock musket above the door and a cow's horn that would blow.

"How queer things are in here," whispered Natalie.

"It's a dear little home," Jennie whispered back loyally. "It's cozy and nice. I like it."

Mary gave them each a lump of hard brown sugar.

"My! That is good," Natalie told her. "Where did you buy it?"

Mary gave a gay little laugh. "From Mr. Maple Tree. My father taps the trees in the spring. That's the only place you *can* get sugar."

When they went out again the sun was getting low, the chickens were flocking around the door to be fed, and the cows, tinkling their bells, had come out of the woods.

"I must go right away," said Natalie. "I mustn't worry papa."

But Mary held onto the two girls' hands. "I wish you'd stay here all the time."

Some vague premonition of the return of torturing discomfort made Jennie say: "I'd love to. Let's stay, Natalie."

"Oh, no!" Natalie insisted. "I have to get back. I have to go to the hospital to see my mamma. And tomorrow I have to take my music lesson."

"*You* stay." Mary clasped Jennie's hand tighter.

"I will. I like it here. I'll stay with you always, Mary."

"Well, good-by, then." Natalie turned abruptly. "I'm going back to mamma."

She started down the green lane sturdily, "Baby Bumps" held close to her.

The other two, still holding hands, stood looking after the little, brown bobbed head.

"She seems awful little," said Jennie. "She might get lost."

"You'd better go," sighed Mary. "Something might happen to her."

"But I wanted—I planned to stay here with you."

"No, no, dear! I'd love to have you; but you must take care of Natalie."

"Yes, I guess I'd better go. You're right. She's so little; I must take care of her."

So Jennie kissed Mary good-by and ran in a panic down the lane.

"Wait, Natalie!" she called. "I'm going with you." She caught hold of her hand and held it close within her own.

The two turned back and waved to Mary. She was standing on a stump, the corncob dolly in her arms.

"I wish I could stay with you," called Jennie. Tears were in her eyes.

Mary nodded and smiled. "I know. You can come back again. But Natalie needs you now. You go with Natalie and take good care of her."

The two went on down the narrow green lane until they came to the rail fence. They climbed to the topmost rail, and then turned and waved again to the little figure, standing lonely at the edge of the clearing.

The woman slowly opened her eyes. The first thing she saw was the little gold-and-black crucifix; but the agony was gone from the face of the Broken One. He seemed to be smiling down at her. And suddenly she realized that she was cool, deliciously, refreshingly cool, like the soft wind that blows from balsam boughs across smiling meadows.

The two nurses were standing near. The doctor, the big, fleshy one with thick glasses, was sitting close by the bed. Ed was standing by the doctor's chair. They all seemed to be bending breathlessly toward her. Thoughts in her mind did not seem obscure and vague any longer. She knew exactly what she wanted. She looked up at Edward and asked the question definitely—only her voice sounded very faint and far away: "Where's Natalie?"

Everyone seemed released from paralysis. The nurses, Edward, everyone seemed trying at once to get Natalie in from the sun porch. They brought her to the bed, half frightened and shy, her brown bobbed hair tied with a huge scarlet bow. The mother gave her a faint, wan smile. "Did you—like—going back—with me—to Mary Burdick's?"

The little girl stared stupidly. "What, mamma?"

With one arm the man drew his little daughter close to him. He leaned over the bed and with the other hand patted his wife awkwardly. Great tears rolled down his cheeks. "There, there, mamma, never mind!" he said brokenly. "You're all right now. You're going to get well. You gave us a scare—but you're fine now. It's Natalie you want. Here's Natalie."

He turned to the doctor. "Mind must have been wandering, I guess, doctor. Mary Burdick was her mother's maiden name."

But the woman kept all these things and pondered them in her heart.

Last Night When You Kissed Blanche Thompson

"Last Night When You Kissed Blanche Thompson" (*The American Magazine,* August 1920) is the only story from the Mason series published by *The American Magazine* that appears in this volume. As with all the Mason pieces, it was included in the *Mother Mason* book. It is reprinted here because it is not only an excellent example of how much Aldrich enjoyed youngsters but also an example of her sense of humor. Aldrich once commented that when she wrote of a boy, she mentally became that boy, seeing the world he might see, smelling the scents he would know; here she invites the reader to become one with her and her character.

The editor of *The American Magazine* felt that "Last Night When You Kissed Blanche Thompson" was a story worthy of being the Junior Mason story in the Mason family series, believing it was stronger than the "Ginger Cookies" story he had previously rejected.

Junior Mason was twelve. The statement is significant. There are a few peevish people in the world who believe that all twelve-year-old boys ought to be hung. Others, less irritable, think that gently chloroforming them would seem more humane. A great many good-natured folks contend that incarceration for a couple of years would prove the best way to dispose of them.

Just how Springtown was divided in regard to Junior and his crowd of cronies depended largely upon the amiability of its citizens. But practically everyone looked upon that crowd as he looked upon other pests: rust, sparrows, moth-millers and potato bugs. As the boys came out of school tearing wildly down the street with Apache yells, more than one staid citizen had been seen to cross the road hurriedly, as one would get out of the way of fire engines, or molten lava rolling down from Vesuvius.

There were a dozen or more boys in the crowd, but the ringleaders were Runt Perkins, Shorty Marston and Junior Mason, and the only similarity between charity and Junior was that the greatest of these was Junior.

At home, by the united efforts of the other members of the Mason family, he was kept subdued into something resembling civilized man. Mother ruled him with a firm hand but an understanding heart. It is a fine old combination. The girls made strenuous efforts to assist in his upbringing, but their gratuitous services were not kindly looked upon by the young man, who believed it constituted mere butting-in.

Katherine it was who took upon herself the complete charge of his speech. Not an insignificant "have went" nor an infinitesimal "I seen" ever escaped the keen ears of his eldest sister, who immediately corrected him. Mother sometimes thought Katherine a little severe when, in the interest of proper speaking, she would stop him in the midst of an exciting account of a home-run. There were times, thought Mother, when the spirit of the thing was so much more important than the flesh in which it was clothed.

For arithmetic Junior showed such an aptitude that Father was wont to say encouragingly, "You'll be working in the bank one of these days, Son." At which "Son" would glow with a legitimate pride that quickly faded before the sight of a certain dull red book entitled "Working Lessons in English Grammar." Katherine labored patiently many an evening to assist in bringing Junior and the contents of this particular volume somewhere within hailing distance of each other. Painstakingly she would go over the ground with him in preparation for his lesson, to be met with a situation something like this:

"Now we're ready. Read the first sentence, Junior."

And Junior would earnestly and enthusiastically sing-song: " 'He *took* his *coat* down *from* the *nail* with*out* a *word* of *warn*ing.' "

"What's the subject, Junior? Now think!"

"Coat," Junior would answer promptly. Then, seeing Katherine's grieved look, he would change quickly to "Nail." And when the look deepened to disgust he would grow wild and begin guessing frantically: "Warning? Took? From?"

Of the three girls Eleanor was his best friend. Rather boyish herself, she was still not so far removed from the glamour of ball games in the back pasture, the trapping of gophers, and circuses in the barn, but that the two held many things in common.

It was Marcia who was his arch enemy. Not that she committed any serious offenses. It was her attitude that exasperated him. She had a trick of perpetrating a lazy little smile on his every act, a smile that was of a surpassing superiority. And she had a way of always jumping at the conclusion that he was dirty. "Go *wash* your *hands*!" was her sisterly greeting whenever he approached. She used it as consistently toward him as she used "How do you do?" to other people. Junior would jump into a heated argument over his perfect cleanliness, a discussion that consumed more time than an entire bath would have taken.

Junior's other enemy was Isabelle Thompson. The Thompsons were the Masons' nearest neighbors, the two yards being separated by a low hedge. The family consisted of Mr. and Mrs. Tobias Thompson, and two daughters: Blanche, who was a little older than Eleanor Mason, and Isabelle, aged eleven.

Mrs. Thompson was a little thin woman who reveled in her reputation of being the neatest housekeeper in Springtown. Why do those characteristics so often go together? Does the thin, wiry condition of a woman's body beget neatness? Or does she keep herself worn thin by her energetic scrubbing? Is it a physiological or a psychological problem?

However that may be, Mrs. Thompson continued to lay strips of rag carpet over her best rugs to keep them clean, and then a layer of newspapers over the rag carpet to save that, too. Andy Christensen declared that she came clear out to the gate to meet him whenever he brought up the groceries on a muddy day.

Her neatness extended to the other members of her household. Tobias was proprietor of a combined grocery and meat market; and no pig, dizzily hanging head downward from its peg in the back room, looked more pink or slick or skinned than he.

"It is certainly nice to think our meat comes from such a clean place," Mother often said.

"Yes," the frank Marcia agreed, "if you don't mind a little thing like underweight."

"Believe me!" Eleanor added, "Tobias would pinch a weenie in two if he dared."

Mrs. Thompson's mind was as neat as the rest of her. It, too, was a prim, tidy place with symmetrical shelves on which were stored a few meager but immaculate items, such as cleanliness being next to godliness, dancing a device of the devil, and that the only route to heaven was via the particular church to which she belonged. Yes, everything in her mind and heart was small and neat and necessary. Those organs were not all cluttered up with a lot of unessential rubbish like Mother Mason's. There were no tag-ends of emotion over the moon swinging out from behind a swirl of silver clouds, nor messy scraps of thrills because a thrush was singing in a rain-drenched lilac bush at twilight. Mother's was the soul of a poet. Mrs. Thompson's was the soul of a polyp.

She was one of the few people who riled Mother through and through. She would say, "*I* won't quarrel with any of my neighbors," as though the others ran around seeking trouble. Or, "*I've* always said honesty was the best policy." It was as though she felt she had invented honesty. You know the type? And even now, some Mrs. Thompson will read this and say, "Doesn't that for all the world remind you of Aunt Abbie?" After all, it is probably a good thing that some power has never yet decided to give us the gifting mentioned by Mr. Robert Burns.

The Masons, among themselves, always spoke of the elder Thompson daughter as "Blonche," in imitation of the broad and stilted pronunciation her mother used. As for Isabelle, Junior's crowd of boys had a pet name for her also. There is a portion of the human anatomy that is never mentioned in a drawing-room. The said section is bounded on the north by the lungs, on the south by the hip-bone sockets and on the east and west by the ribs. Although it is never spoken aloud in polite society, far be it from anyone to accuse Junior and Runt Perkins and Shorty Marston of constituting polite society. So in the privacy of their own crowd they always spoke of the younger Thompson girl as Is-a-Belly. It was not gallant nor was it kind, but twelve-year-old boys are quite often neither gallant nor kind.

As a consequence of their mother's narrow attitude, the two Thompson girls were self-consciously engrossed in their own attainments. Their mother believed that her daughters, like the king, could do no wrong, a view that was thoroughly shared by the girls themselves. They were perfect in their manners, immaculate as to their persons, flawless in their conduct. But, lacking a sense of humor which would otherwise have been their redeeming quality, they were excellent specimens of that despicable creature—a prig.

The fun-loving Mason girls spoke always of "Blonche" as "The Perfect One," and Junior continued to use that nameless, ungallant appellation for Isabelle whenever his boyish disgust of her faultless record grew too deep.

Boys of this age live on the border between childhood and adolescence. It is a sort of No Man's Land in which they seem not to know just where they belong. In this they are not unlike the maiden with reluctant feet. They are such a queer mixture of Youth and Childhood that one hour, with developing mind, they seem to be reaching out into the future to wrestle with man-sized problems, while the next hour, with no conscious understanding of the change, they abandon that mood to drop back into the trifling plays of babyhood.

This was an hour, this particular warm summer evening, when Junior had slipped back into babyhood. With all the inanity of which he was capable, he had pried off a loose slat in the trellis-work under the back porch, and, with much grunting and wiggling, had managed to crawl through. His reason for doing it? Ask the wind or the stars or the morning dew. No, the motives of a twelve-year-old boy are not always governed by a rational cause. He just did it.

Scrouging under the porch, he looked around in the semi-darkness. His eye lighted on an old, battered, rusted tin street-car, a relic of younger if not happier days. He succeeded in pulling off one of the tin wheels. There was a hole in the center of the wheel left by the withdrawing of the hub. He held it to his mouth and blew. It gave forth a weird, plaintive sound like the mewing of a cat. Immediately, with that ability to become all things to all men, Junior felt himself taking on the characteristics of a cat. Fur seemed, in some miraculous way, to spring out on his body. With the erstwhile street-car wheel between his teeth and emitting continuous purring sounds, he pad-padded out from under the porch. With that capacity for sinking himself in an imaginary character, he felt in his heart all the sly, treacherous attributes of a cat. Nay, more, he *was* a cat.

Out on the lawn he crawled through the grass of the side yard to the hedge, stopped to rub a pair of invisible whiskers against a weed, nibbled daintily at a stalk of catnip, and, settling back on his haunches, laid the street-car wheel aside to lap a presumably clean tongue over a slightly soiled paw. Then, with half-human, half-feline promptings, he cogitated plans for the rest of the evening.

Across the hedge at the Thompson home, someone was sitting in the hammock behind the vine-covered lattice-work of the porch. Junior could hear the steady squeak-squeak of the swaying ropes. It would be Isabelle, curled and beribboned, daintily holding her big doll, likewise curled and beribboned. Just what there is in the contemplation of an immaculately clean, piously good, little girl to rouse the ire of a semi-soiled, ungodly little boy is one with the mysteries of the Sphinx and the Mona Lisa smile. Junior, at the thought of Isabelle sitting placidly in the hammock, was seized with an uncontrollable desire to startle her out of the state of calmness into one of sudden agitation.

So he crept through an opening in the hedge into the Thompson yard, pausing with an imaginary distended tail, to crouch and spring at a robin in the grass. Failing to capture his prey, he crawled noiselessly toward the porch, placed his forepaw on the lattice-work, and emitting a low whining purr peered through the vines.

It was not Isabelle. It was Blanche. In the hammock with her sat Frank Marston, his arm casually thrown across the back of the hammock, his face in close proximity to hers.

The cat did not purr again. Open-mouthed, he took in the little scene before him, which spectacle included the placing of a hasty, boyish kiss on Blanche's cheek. Then the leading man and lady both giggled rather foolishly. They were very young.

Once again in the annals of history had curiosity killed a cat, for all feline characteristics immediately left the onlooker, and he became a twelve-year-old masculine biped.

He slipped noiselessly away, waiting until he had turned the corner of the Thompson house before he allowed the pent-up laughter within him to trickle forth. It was too rich for words that he had witnessed it. Wouldn't everyone laugh when he told them! He ran down the Thompsons' side terrace, walked nonchalantly across the street and around the next block. On the way, he told the joke to three people, Runt Perkins and Hod Beeson, who delivered coal, and Lizzie Beadle, the town dressmaker. The reason he told no one else was the very simple one that those were all the people he met.

Reaching home by this circuitous route, he burst in upon the family with the tale.

"With my own eyes I seem 'em," he finished breathlessly.

"Saw them," corrected Katherine, didactically.

"Saw 'em," Junior repeated.

If Katherine was concerned with Junior's manner of speaking, Mother was immediately concerned with the moral aspect of his spying, but Marcia and Eleanor thought only of the news.

"*What* do you know about that?" It was Marcia.

"Mrs. Thompson would have a fit and fall in it." Katherine, too, was growing interested.

"I wonder if Frankie was all scrubbed and sterilized," Eleanor put in.

"Girls! Girls!" Mother remonstrated.

"Young folks are 'most of all fools," was Tillie's affable contribution. At which Marcia and Eleanor wrung their hands and pretended to weep.

"Junior!" It was Mother who spoke severely. "You probably meant no harm, but let this be a lesson to you about sneaking up on anyone. Promise me you'll not tell a soul."

"I promise," Junior said glibly. But even as he spoke he cast a guilty thought at the gossip he had left behind him like the long tail of a Chinese kite.

The next night, the Mason family had just finished supper, for in Springtown one eats dinner as the sun crosses the meridian and supper as it sinks down behind the elms that line the distant banks of old Coon Creek.

Chairs were pushed back. Tillie had begun to pick up the dishes. Father was opening the evening paper. The white ruffled curtains swayed in and out. The girls were humming in concert "Somewhere a Voice is Calling." It was as peaceful a scene as the Acadian village of Grand Pré.

Just then The Voice called, but it was neither tender nor true. It came in clicking, indignant tones from Mrs. Thompson at the dining-room door. She came in like a hawk in a chicken yard. In angry tones she told them that Blonche had just heard what Junior had been telling around town about her, that there was not one word of truth in it, and that she wanted something done about it. On and on she went, delivering vindictive verbal uppercuts to Junior, making a self-righteous speech on the excellent quality of her girls' upbringing, and finished with "Neither one of *my* girls would allow a thing like that."

For one brief, fleeting moment, Mother had an unholy desire to retort, "Oh, of course, I've *taught my* girls to spoon."

During the onslaught the members of the family had remained rooted to their respective places like the king's family during the curse on the "Sleeping Beauty." When she had finished, the spell broke. Father was the first to stir. He stirred himself so thoroughly that he slipped quietly out of the dining-room into the kitchen. Do not be unduly harsh in your criticism of him. There are so many good American fathers like that. He could have diplomatically refused a loan to the governor. He might even have unflinchingly faced a masked bank robber. But he could not face his little angry neighbor. Mother, in exasperation, sometimes wondered how so successful a business man could be so helpless in domestic crises.

So it was Mother who took the stage. She questioned Junior. The latter, very red and visibly embarrassed, wanted nothing in the world so much as that the painful scene should end, even as that older masculine member of the family. So he did what almost any little boy would have done, what George Washington might have done, had there been twelve feminine eyes gazing at him in grief or anger or concern. He lied.

"I was just—" he mumbled, "just jokin'."

"You mean," Mother asked coldly, "that you made it up?"

Junior nodded his head. And his guardian angel in sorrow, probably made a long black mark in The Book.

"Then," said Mother calmly, "you will go to every person you told and try to make right your *very poor* joke." She assured Mrs. Thompson that they would do all in their power to rectify matters, and that Junior would apologize to Blanche. Mrs. Thompson was mollified. She simpered a little. "You know *me*, Mrs. Mason. *I* don't like neighborhood quarrels."

"Neither do I," said Mother dryly.

Mrs. Thompson, in a state of mental satisfaction, wrapped her mantle of self-complacency about her and left.

"The old pole-cat!" Tillie remarked sweetly when the door closed. Although Tillie found plenty of fault with the Mason children, herself, let some outsider do it and she was immediately on the warpath.

Everyone was perturbed. "Who did you tell?" Katherine demanded, and the fact that she did not say "whom" was proof positive that she was upset.

"I happened to tell Lizzie Beadle," Junior whimpered.

"Good *night!*" Eleanor threw up her hands. "You might just as well have put it on the front page of the Springtown 'Headlight.' "

They all talked to him at once. Katherine gave a hurried résumé of the poem that concerns shooting arrows and words into the air. It was all very hard on his nerves. So he got his cap and started to the door. Action, even if it were attempting to pick up spent and scattered arrows, seem preferable to the society of the critical women of his household.

Strangely enough it was Marcia who followed him out onto the porch.

There were tears in her eyes. Careless, tender-hearted Marcia had impulsively erred so often herself that she felt more sympathy for her little brother than anyone else did.

"Junie!" She threw an arm around his shoulder. "You're like a knight of old—why, Junie, you're Sir Galahad. You're going on your white horse in search of the Holy Grail, only this time the Grail is Truth."

It pleased Junior's fancy. His drooping head lifted a little. He ran down the steps, and by the time he had unhitched an invisible white charger with gold trappings, mounted him and started down the street, he was quite impressed with the nobility of his journey.

Sustained by the thought of the character he was impersonating, he stopped at the Thompsons' and mumbled a hasty apology to the red-eyed Blanche. It was noticeable that neither the maker of the apology nor the recipient looked directly at the other.

He went next to Hod Beeson's. It was rather trying to explain his errand to him, Hod not knowing what Junior was talking about, as he had let the scandal go in one coal-grimed ear and out the other. Eventually, Hod closed the rambling confession with "All right, Sonny. That's all right."

So Junior rode next to the Beadles' little weather-beaten house and told fat, untidy Lizzie his message. Lizzie looked disappointed over the news. Perhaps she was thinking of a few arrows about it she, herself, had shot into the air. But she said, "You're some kid, Junie, to take all that trouble for a smartie like Blanche Thompson. Have a cookie."

Junior, further impressed with his praiseworthy conduct, rode on to the Perkinses, where he made known his errand to Runt and his mother.

"Now, look at that." Mrs. Perkins turned to her own offspring. "What a gentlemanly thing for Junior to do!"

After this Junior hated to give up his holy mission. It seemed uninteresting to turn around and go home after so few visits. So he began telling other people what he was doing. He told several of the boys of his crowd and Mrs. Hayes and the Winters's hired girl. He stopped Grandpa McCabe on the street and explained his self-abasement to that deaf old man. Grandpa couldn't sense it, but gathering that something was wrong at the Thompsons', he stopped in front of their home and leaned a long time on his cane, looking anxiously toward the house.

After that, with sudden inspiration, it struck Junior that no one had mentioned his apologizing to Frank. Surely that was an oversight on his mother's part. Did not one owe an apology to the kisser just as much as to the kissee?

So he rode up to the Marstons' Colonial home, dismounted and went in. The Marstons were eating dinner, as Springtown people do when they have company from the city. There was a rich uncle there and his pretty daughter, to say nothing of a charming friend she had brought with her. Nicky and Frank and Shorty all sat at the table, clothed in their best suits and manners.

Junior, standing humbly just inside the dining-room door, cap in hand, felt that here, before so appreciative an audience, was opportunity for the grand climax of his self-humiliation. So, in the polite tones of a well-bred boy, he respectfully apologized to Frank. It could not have been done with more deference or Chesterfieldian grace. Junior had a swift desire that his sisters might have witnessed it.

A dull brick-red color surged over Frank's long, lean face. "What you talkin' about, kid?"

Junior dropped the rather formal, stilted tones of his former speech and dropped into his own familiar boyish-ones. He seemed deadly in earnest. Anyone hearing him could not help but be impressed with his sincerity. "You know, Frank, last night when you kissed Blanche Thompson—you thought you heard a cat mew? Well, Frank, it wasn't a cat. It was me. I'm around to all the neighbors apologizin' for sayin' I seen you."

Amid smiles from the guests, an embarrassed laugh from his mother, and unrestrained shouts from his dearly loved brothers, Frank got up. Junior sensed the fact that he was to pass out with Frank also. Not everyone is gifted with as delicate and acute sensibilities.

Out in the hall Frank grabbed his caller's shoulders in a crab-like pinch. Words hissed through his clenched teeth. These were the words: "I'd like to make *you* into *mincemeat.* You hike out of here and keep your mouth shut. Ja understand? Now, *scoot!*"

It was trying to Sir Galahad to have his high mission so misunderstood. He started home a little wearily, trying to forget Frank's baleful attitude and remember only those who had praised him. Of such is the kingdom of optimists.

The entire Mason family was ensconced on the front porch. They greeted him rather effusively. Everyone seemed in a softened mood toward him. The truth was, the brave way in which he had faced the results of his ill-advised joke appealed to them all.

He sat down in the hammock by Katherine, who put her arm around him. It made him hot and uncomfortable but he stood it. Marcia threw him a smile and Eleanor gave him a stick of gum. He preferred the latter. Smiles are fleeting, but gum, with proper hoarding, lasts a week. Mother spoke to him cheerfully. Even Tillie neglected to look for dirt on his shoes. Father, his feet on the porch railing, gave a long rambling speech about veracity, a sort of truth-crushed-to-earth-Abraham-Lincoln monologue.

The family went to bed with that light-hearted feeling which comes after a painful domestic crisis has been passed. It was apparent to all, that Junior, in spite of the poor taste of his joke, had vindicated himself.

And the evening and the morning were the third day.

The members of the family straggled into breakfast one by one. Mother sighed as she saw them. She knew that the ideal way was for all the chairs to be pushed back from the table simultaneously. But she could remember just once when it had happened—the Sunday morning the Bishop had been there.

Junior was the last to arrive. Several drops of water, creeping lingeringly down the side of his face, proclaimed to all who were inclined to be pessimistic that he had washed. He sat down with great gusto.

"Well, I hope old lady Thompson feels better now. Ya, I sure hope she does." He chuckled, spreading eleven cents' worth of butter on a griddle cake. "The old lady was purty excited, she was. 'N' so was Blonchie, till I fixed it all up fine about her 'n' Frankie. Ya, I fixed 'em. But don't you fergit it, no matter what I said last night, just the same, I *seen* 'em."

There was silence in the Mason dining-room. Everyone looked at Mother. Mother looked across at Father, sitting there in all his financial capableness and his domestic inability. Father looked helplessly back. Mother knew that she was expected, as usual, to take the steering wheel, but she felt like a skipper on an uncharted sea.

A son of hers had spied upon his neighbors, gossiped, and then lied about the truth. Was the falsehood of last evening a double-dyed sin? Or was it the spirit of knighthood—that gallant thing that has been handed down through the ages—the traditional honor with which a gentleman protects a lady's name? Mother gave it up. For the life of her, she did not quite know.

Junior, conscious of the impressive silence, decided that he was making a hit. And as it was not often given to him to create that kind of stir in this particular circle, he waxed visibly in pleased importance and genially reiterated, "Ya, no matter what I said, you can put this in your pipe—I seen 'em."

"Saw them," corrected Katherine mechanically, from pure force of habit.

"Saw 'm," repeated Junior, also from force of habit, and again a pregnant silence descended upon the breakfast table.

It was broken by Father. The assembled Masons looked at him expectantly as he cleared his throat, preliminary to speech. It was a desperate situation that could rouse Father to grip the domestic steering wheel. In Mother's expression, relief struggled with anxiety as to just what he was going to do. If he was going to thrash Junior—She half opened her lips, as Father gave another preliminary cough. Then he spoke.

"Looks a little like rain," he said. "Hope we don't have a wetting before the haying's over."

How I Mixed Stories with Doughnuts

In this article (*The American Magazine,* February 1921), Aldrich employs a conversational tone, an easiness, that at times has the "running laughter" that she found so appealing in the work of James M. Barrie, author of *Peter Pan* and *The Little Minister.*

John M. Siddall of *The American Magazine* asked Aldrich to send him a story about herself, a personal story, aware that his readers would enjoy getting to know her as an individual as well as a writer. This is the first biographical information that Aldrich provided to her readers. However, in responding to Siddall's request, Aldrich did more than simply follow his suggestions for recording information about her life. She also outlined her views on how to accomplish one's goals, which, in her case, meant writing; her comments provided guidelines for other kinds of work as well.

Aldrich firmly believed that there are three major components needed to become a selling author, and here as in other articles and talks she refers to them; "How I Mixed Stories with Doughnuts" is the first time she records them. Perhaps the fact that she had been a teacher prompted her to try to help beginning writers, perhaps it was the memory of her own struggles. Similar articles such as "The Story Germ," a part of "The Story behind *A Lantern in Her Hand,*" and "Working Backward" also offer suggestions, not rules. Aldrich gave numerous talks on the art of writing to college students and to organizations of writers.

It is going to be hard to write a personal article without working the little pronoun "I" overtime. But if it will help anyone to do something he is not now accomplishing, I shall proceed to clamp down the "I" key on my typewriter, and tell how I have found time in the past few years to write and sell nearly sixty stories, while raising my babies and doing a great deal of my own housework.

People seem to think that if you write, you do it *all* the time. Somebody probably brings you a bun and a piece of cake and a cup of coffee, and then tiptoes away, lest the Muse, or the Spirit, or whatever it is be disturbed.

As a matter of fact, I make that bun and that cake and that coffee myself. As for being disturbed! . . . I once fondly thought I would have a secluded, private writing-room. So I turned a bedroom into it, had bookshelves built in, and bought a typewriter desk and a filing case. When, lo! friend husband began keeping his daily papers and his law magazines and his slippers there; my little daughter established a family of dolls under the desk, and my two little sons secreted kite strings and tin soldiers in the sacred pigeonholes. Thereupon I decided that *my* writing, at least, could never be separated from the family life.

I am a most ordinary person, tucked away in a tiny Nebraska town, where we have to count the section men, temporarily living in box cars down by the "dee-po," to make a thousand inhabitants. I have never been in an editorial office in my life, and I have never even been in New York City, where those editors reign.

I have had enough rejection slips to fill an old-fashioned bedtick. I have sold a story on its twenty-third trip. I was five years hammering on the door of *The American Magazine* editorial office before my Mason Family series proved the open-sesame.

So when I get a letter from a would-be writer saying, "I have sent my story to three different magazines and they have all sent it back. What would you advise me to do?" I write a very courteous and encouraging letter; but what I feel like saying is, "Oh, go and buy a meat market!"

There is no macadamized road to Fictionland; not even a blazed trail. Just woods! And neither can you sit down and enjoy the view after you do arrive. "In the sweat of thy face shalt thou eat bread" still holds its own after all these centuries.

These people seem to think I have "found time" to write because of some lucky stroke whereby the hours of my day are longer than theirs. But their clock ticks off the same sixty seconds to a minute that mine does. There is no truer axiom than that we will find time to do the thing we want most to do.

There are a great many things I have not found time to do—crochet, or make a suffrage speech, or play bridge whist. I believe sincerely in equal suffrage, but I have never turned my hand over to help obtain it. Crocheting is no sin; and neither is bridge whist if taken in homeopathic doses. I am just naming some of the things I have *not* found time to do.

So when someone says, "All my life I have longed to write more than anything I can think of," it sounds to me like a whopper. These people think they have wanted to write; but their desires have not been anywhere nearly so huge as they fondly dreamed them to be, or they *would have written.*

Everyone can think of something he has always been going to do. I have been married thirteen years, and I have always been going to set out an asparagus bed. Just now, for the life of me, I can't think why I have never done it, for I have talked about it every spring and fall for that number of years.

When I was a little girl, the joy of my life was to visit at the farm homes of my various relatives. One of my uncles used to enliven his early morning chores with singing. Lying there in bed up under the eaves of the old farmhouse, I would be wakened in the cool of the summer dawn by the robins in the maple windbreak, the crowing of the roosters, the creaking of the old pump, and my uncle's singing. John McCormack can sing pretty well, but you should have heard my uncle! The song that made the greatest impression on me was:

A child sleeps under a rosebush fair,
The buds swell out in the soft May air,
Sleeping, it dreams, and on dream-wings flies
To dum—dum-ty—dum—dum—Paradise.
And the years *glide* by!

He used to make two syllables of glide. "And the years ga-lide by."

I have never quite made out whether the person in the song ever moved away from the rosebush during her entire lifetime or not; for in the second verse, as a child, she plays under the same bush; and in the third, as a maiden, she falls in love beside it. As a bride, and as a mother, she is still there by the same old long-lived bush. As an old lady she is buried there. And all the verses ended: "And the years glide by!"

As I listened to the doleful strain I could not sense the steady flow of the years. Wasn't there a whole day before me? A day of sunshine and meadows and orchards—an eternity of pleasure? But I know now! They glide by, and leave in their wake the dreams of so many things unaccomplished, so many promises to ourselves unfulfilled.

I was born in Cedar Falls, Iowa, in 1881, in the same house from which I was married twenty-six years later. My father came from good old Revolutionary stock. In fact, there seems to be a conviction in the family that our ancestors *swam* here, and were drying their clothes around a bonfire when the Mayflower docked. My two sisters wear a pound or so of long dangling badges at D.A.R. meetings, but I have never even joined. Just another one of those things that I have not found time to do.

It is from my father's side of the house that has come to me a trait of seeing the funny side of things. My grandfather, Zimri Streeter, who represented Black Hawk County in the first Iowa legislature, was as gnarled and weatherbeaten as the native hard timber in which stood his first primitive cabin. He was droll; but to appreciate his wit one must also have known Grandma. She was fretful, energetic, humorless, intolerant of wasting time in fun-making. With no disrespect to the dear old dead, they were like a vaudeville team.

A malignant growth made it necessary to amputate the old man's hand—but they could not amputate his sense of humor, for he promptly made a bet with a stranger that he hadn't worn a pair of mittens all winter. When the disease crept upward and they took off his arm, he merely chuckled and wanted to know when they were going to amputate his head.

There came a day when he could no longer get out to the room where Grandma sat by the west window darning stockings. To the daughter beside his bed he said, "We never could get her," nodding his shaggy old head toward Grandma, "to see much fun in life, could we?"

A little later he asked, "How do you reckon it'll be? Psalms and harps and prayer meetings? No—no *fun?*" And then, with his fading eyes on the little old bent figure by the window, "It'll be mighty lonesome . . . settin' around . . . waitin' fer her."

My mother's people came from Scotland. Grandmother was a country girl, wooed and won at sixteen by Basil Anderson, of an aristocratic Edinburgh family. I have an old aunt in her nineties who remembers the distress with which the family viewed her mother's occasional lapses into peasant ways and speech.

The young couple came to America, where my grandfather, unused to hardships, sickened and died, leaving Grandmother, still young, with eight children. She moved with them on to the new, raw country of Iowa, brought them up carefully and prayerfully, and died at eighty-four, a widow for over half a century. It is from these people that I choose to think I have inherited a love of romance and of all things beautiful.

My first (so-called) literary experience occurred when I was fourteen. I won a small camera as a prize for a child's story in the old Chicago "Record." It was then that I first tasted blood; for the intoxication of seeing my name in print was overwhelming.

When I was seventeen, one of my high-school classmates, who had entered Woman's College, sent me a clipping from the Baltimore "News" announcing five prizes for short stories. I wrote one, and with the sublime fearlessness of seventeen called it "A Late Love." It was as heavy as a moving van. It oozed pathos. It dripped melancholy. And it won the fifth prize—five dollars. I have always had a sneaking notion that there were only five manuscripts submitted.

I cashed that five-dollar check the day it arrived. Did I buy some writing paraphernalia, a thesaurus of English words, or a textbook on story-writing? I did not. I bought a parasol that had chiffon ruffles from stem to stern. To be sure, I had nothing whatever suitable to go with it; but, oh! if there is a heaven for dead parasols, that one surely has gone there.

After high school I finished Iowa State Teachers' College. Then I taught in public schools; among others, those of Marshalltown, Iowa, where I met the man who keeps his slippers, etc. In the meantime, I burst out in various epidemics of children's stories, wrote professional articles, and produced one adult story that was purchased by a magazine so insignificant that I can't even remember its last name. At any rate, having paid me ten dollars, it curled up its toes and died.

I was married and had one little child when my husband and my sister's husband purchased a country bank here in Elmwood, Nebraska, where we have lived for eleven years, and where my other children have been born.

I might insert here a statement concerning my most hard-hearted critic—my husband. He leads a double life. He is of a genus known only to country towns: a combination banker and lawyer. He greets you affably at the grated window of the bank and smilingly deposits your hard-earned cash. But if you want a contract or an abstract or a divorce, he assumes a solemn expression and leads you silently and pompously into a back office.

Comes now the account of the time when a well-known magazine announced a prize offer for short stories. I wrote "The Little House Next Door" in a few afternoons while the baby slept. I had to go down to the bank to copy it on a typewriter, laboriously picking out the letters with one finger. When one of the boys on the force wanted to use the machine, I had to take out my manuscript and stand aside until he was through. So my husband, in sheer self-defense, bought me a second-hand one. Later, of course, I purchased a twelve-cylinder, sixty horse-power affair.

In a few months a letter came saying that the prize offer had been withdrawn; but that my story had been found worthy of purchase, and that a check for one hundred and seventy-five dollars would follow soon. Immediately there was great excitement in camp. Grandma told me to look again; it must have said a dollar and seventy-five cents. But it didn't. And there was no guesswork this time about the number of manuscripts entered. There had been over twenty-two hundred submitted, and six purchased.

That proved it! I could write! I had arrived! It was all very lovely. How easy! Just a few afternoons of writing, just an accidental twist of the wrist, as it were. So I sat down and wrote another story, much better than the first. Already I had the second check mentally invested—it would probably be for two hundred dollars this time.

It was like a slap in the face when that story came back. I began trotting out all the excuses that disgruntled writers use. I felt sure that the editor himself had not read it. But it seems that he *had* read it. The letter said so. And right then and there I received my lesson; that you have to *work* to be a successful writer, just as you have to work to be a successful groceryman, or to be a successful anything else.

I wrote story after story, beginning a new one soon after each had been sent out.

If all the ships I have at sea
Should come a-sailing home to me—

Well, they came all right! They had their decks washed and their masts straightened, and were sent out again and again. And one by one they found harbors. So, to-day, if I cannot begin to turn out all that I am asked to do, if I have on my desk letters from a half-dozen well-known magazines asking me to send in something, or to do a series for them, call me persevering if you will, but don't call me lucky! For it has come from sheer labor.

To my mind, there are three essentials in the making of a writer: Imagination, a good English foundation, and a desire to write so keen that there are no obstacles which you will not surmount to carry out that desire.

Imagination! And by that I mean more than is usually expected of the word; more than mere plot building, a cold thing whereby characters are moved about like checkers. I mean an imagination so vivid that it becomes sympathy. When you can figuratively crawl into another's skin and button it around you, sink your personality so completely in his that you think his very thoughts, then you have the imagination which is sympathy.

To use a homely illustration: Can you think how it would seem to a little, hard-working woman, the mother of five children, to have a bathtub with running water installed in her home after twelve tubless years? You, yourself, may have been born and brought up in a bathtub, so to speak. But can you see that family standing around that tub as the plumber finishes his work? Can you sense the ecstasy of that mother's thoughts as she realizes there will be no more aching trips to and from the well, no more dragging of the heavy washtub into the middle of the kitchen or splashing of the floor?

Can you hear her saying shyly, as the plumber begins picking up his tools, "Is it all connected? Will the water turn on now?" And the plumber's "Let 'er go!"

The children, you know, would all run pell-mell to the faucet with, "Let me turn it!" . . . "No!—me!"

If that tub is to you like Wordsworth's primrose by a river's brim, just a tub and nothing more, you are hopeless. But if—when the father grabs the youngsters, and says gruffly, "Here! Let Ma do it first!"—if you can sense the accumulation of unspoken wishes, of dumb, unuttered desires that in all these years of heavy toil he might have been able to do more for Ma—then you have imaginative sympathy.

The second requisite is a good English foundation, and I have no quarrel with anyone as to how he may have obtained it: university, college, day school, night school, correspondence school, or the school of experience. You can get an M.A. degree from any of them: Master of Arts from some, Mental Acuteness from others. But a good English foundation from some source there must be.

The third is a desire to write; a desire so keen that nothing will stand in your way. I have literally written those sixty stories, like the person who learned the seven languages, while the kettle boiled. The hand that rocked the cradle was often the left one, while the right was jotting down a sentence or two. I have had the first draft of many a story sprinkled liberally with good old sudsy dishwater.

And if, by any chance, you think that because I was writing light and airy fiction, my pie crust was *not* light, let me tell you that I am very humble concerning my stories, but quite chesty about my cooking. When I overhear a feminine voice at a woman's club picnic luncheon saying admiringly, "This must be Mrs. Aldrich's cake!" I get a warm, swollen, fluttery feeling under my fifth rib.

Imagination, a good English foundation, and a "desire-so-keen"—these are the three essentials; and no two of them will get you anywhere. I can illustrate by three persons, each of whom possessed two of the points. My mother had, to a wonderful degree, both imagination and the desire to write. But, like most of the pioneers, her schooling was meager, although she herself taught in the first little log school in the county. She has left dozens of manuscripts, faulty in construction, but replete with human sympathy.

Then there is a woman I know who possesses the first two essentials, but not the third. She has a university education, has traveled, and has all the finer qualities of imagination. But that little dynamo, the keen desire, stands uncharged, although for twenty years she has been saying that she has a great longing to write. Her excuses are something like these: This winter she has had no help in the kitchen; this year she has had to take Aunt Amanda into her household; this summer she has been to Yellowstone Park. Next fall she will begin to write.

And the years ga-lide by.

Now, I happen to know how she could have solved the help problem. I'm sure she could have written more than one story while Aunt Amanda was taking afternoon naps. And no little upstart Yellowstone geyser could have kept her from writing if her desire to do so had been as keen as she fondly dreamed it to be.

Another friend of mine possesses the good education, and she really does write. Day after day she struggles with her stories and once in a while a third-class magazine surprises her by accepting one. The first-class ones send them back with monotonous regularity.

Some day I'm going to cut loose, like Tillie, and tell her what is the matter with them. She, herself, has not the right attitude toward life. She has not cultivated the imagination which is sympathy. Like me, she lives in a little town; but she has nothing in common with it or with "common" things. She has written me more than one letter sympathizing with herself and with me because, on account of our respective husbands' very good businesses, we are "tied down" to two such little towns. Like Tillie, she wants to stretch her soul! And she doesn't know that she could get out in her yard and stretch it.

No, my friend has not the attitude that will bring her stories to life. If there is anyone in the whole wide world that ought to live in a "house by the side of the road and be a friend to man," it is the person who aspires to be a writer.

I talked with another friend not long ago about a magazine article which told of the lack of fiction whose scenes were laid in the Middle West. The article said the majority of settings were New York, the far South, the Southwest desert, Pacific coast country, or the Northwest.

"The reason is plain enough," said my friend. "There is no section of the country so lacking in sentiment as the Middle West. We just raise corn to feed more hogs to buy more land to raise more hogs. We're a community of statistics."

Fiddlestatistics! Sentiment doesn't lie in soil or climate or latitude or longitude. It lies in the hearts of people. Wherever there are folks who live and work and love and die, whether they raise hogs in Iowa or oranges in California or the sails of a pleasure boat at Palm Beach, there is the stuff of which stories are made.

I am glad I am contented in my Mid-West, hog-raising, corn-bearing, small-town environment. I am glad I like common folks and wild flowers and hash and babies, as well as Browning and Chopin and Shakespeare and Corot. My husband once had a note from a foreign-born farmer who wrote, "We want you and your family to come out to our place to spend Sunday. My woman has met your woman, and she says she's just as common as anything." I liked that.

I do not believe that the people of my community ever think of me first as a writer. If you were to get off at our "dee-po," and ask for "the writer who lives here," I can imagine our local Hod Beeson scratching his head and trying to figure out whether you meant the correspondent for the state paper, or the editor of the "Leader-Echo," or me. I am glad I am first of all a wife, mother, friend, and neighbor.

I have a little creed pinned above my desk, and I hope never to wander away from its teachings. Dr. J. Berg Esenwein wrote it:

> Out of the heart are the issues of literature. The writer who interprets life with sympathy and understanding sees, feels, and thinks with his heart. And so, too, they who read him aright must be heart-minded and not merely head-minded.

How is your imagination? Is it strong enough, vital enough, to merge into sympathy so that you can see life from another's standpoint? Whatever you aspire to be, is not this trait worth cultivating?

And what sort of excuse are you making for not doing the particular something you have been saying, for, lo! these many months or years, you wanted to do? Right now, start that story, or clean the kitchen clock, or write that letter to your old Sunday-school teacher.

As for me, I am going to shut my desk now and set out that asparagus bed! . . . Still, come to think about it, I would have to walk two blocks to get the roots—and it looks a little like rain—and I haven't looked over to-day's paper—and, well, I guess I'll wait till to-morrow.

And the years ga-lide by.

The Man Who Dreaded to Go Home

Aldrich enjoyed writing stories—such as this one—that involve light deception. She used similar ideas in the earlier "The Cat Is on the Mat," "Miss Livingston's Nephew," and "Marcia Mason's Lucky Star," in each of which a young woman attempts to mislead others. Deception, however, must be tempered with honor as far as Aldrich is concerned, and here, as well as in the three abovementioned stories, honor plays its part.

In "The Man Who Dreaded to Go Home" (*The American Magazine,* November 1921) Aldrich illustrates for the first time her understanding of older people, a sensitivity she may have acquired from her mother's living part time with the Aldrich household. Aldrich recognized that as people grow older they often no longer choose to have "better" or "fancier" things. Here Aunt Net does not want the new house they can now afford. This theme will recur in other short stories as well as the novels *The Rim of the Prairie, A Lantern in Her Hand,* and *Spring Came on Forever.*

Teachers, like verbs, are divided into two classes: regular and irregular. A regular teacher is one whose present tense is formed by adding extra time and thought and care to her school work. An irregular teacher is one whose present tense is formed by adding all the fun to her otherwise monotonous existence which the law (meaning the school board) will allow.

Jerry Hammond was an irregular. The responsibilities of the primary profession rested lightly upon Jerry's smooth brown head. She stayed conscientiously at the schoolhouse every afternoon, and worked diligently until four-thirty, for the excellent reason that there was a ruling to that effect.

Everybody liked Jerry. Even her landlady did; and that is proof positive of her good nature. On this particular Saturday afternoon Jerry had taken a few minutes after lunch to help that landlady, Mrs. McCloud, get her best room in readiness for the Parlor Reading Circle, which was to meet at two o'clock.

Ellen, her room-mate, was a regular. Her main object in life was to get several classes of students to speak English instead of high-school dialect.

As Jerry finished her task and was half way up the stairs, Mrs. McCloud came hastily from the stiffly arranged parlor. "Oh, Miss Hammond," she called, "I wonder if you would do one thing more for me sometime this afternoon. I was over at the old Maynard home part of the morning, overseeing a woman get it in shape for Doctor Maynard. He's arriving home from England to-morrow afternoon. . . . He's a nerve specialist, and a *way-up* one, too. I was a schoolmate of his mother's. I'm so afraid I left a rug on the back porch. . . . I may not, but I may; and I haven't time to go over. I thought maybe you'd take the key and look. . . . "

"All right, Mrs. McCloud. And for payment, you invite the gorgeous creature over here sometime to eat."

"Bless your heart, he wouldn't come. He doesn't go out in company. Poor boy! He's had a very sad life. His only sister was drowned and his parents died. There was a girl, too, . . . some sort of affair. I guess it just naturally soured him."

Jerry took the key and went on to her room, where she was repeating this information to Ellen when Mrs. McCloud summoned her down to the telephone.

When Jerry arrived at her room again, it was to announce disgustedly: "Here's where my afternoon hike goes up in smoke! It was Uncle Amos. He's at the Union Station, he and Aunt Net. They're on their way to California for the winter, and they're coming here to rest for three hours between trains. Rest! Imagine! With you under snowbanks of papers and the Poller Feeding Circus about to arrive! I wish there were a decently quiet place to take them."

Suddenly, dramatically, Jerry held out the key. "*Quiet!* Could anything, I ask you, be more quiet than the Maynard mansion? The key! I hold in my hand the *key to the situation.*"

"Jerry, you *would not?*" Ellen was frankly appalled.

"Oh, wouldn't I?"

"If you're in earnest, you certainly have your *nerve.*"

"I'm a nerve specialist, Ellen dear. . . . Doctor Maynard and Jerry Hammond, Nerve Specialists!" She was characteristically gay, enthusiastic. "Aunt Net can lie on the Circassian wal-*hog*any davenport. Uncle Amos can sit in a chair and rest his whiskers for fair! I merely tell them that the family is away. And it is, isn't it? Then a nice, quiet three hours' rest for those old folks, after which we lock the door and slip away to the station. And, presto! the whole incident is sunk in the sea of oblivion."

The next ten minutes Jerry spent in wheedling the protesting Ellen into meeting the old folks at the station and delivering them at the Maynard house. This accomplished, she tucked her samovar under her arm, crossed the alley, pressed through the hedge and into the large, grassy back yard. Around the house and onto the porch she went briskly, unlocked the front door, and stepped in. For a moment the gloom and silence of the big house clutched at her throat so that she stood irresolute. Then she turned to her right into what was evidently a huge living-room.

Although the air was close, there was that indescribable sweet odor that comes after a thorough cleaning. Snapping the shades of all the windows up to the full height, so that the sun sprang in like a joyous child, she looked about her. The furnishings were luxurious, if a bit old-fashioned. There were soft rugs whose half-faded tints ran together like the blending of a watercolor. A grand piano stood at one end of the room; and in front of the fireplace, dead and cheerless now, was a big tapestry davenport.

Here in this very room had been gay, sunny people. The father and mother had been here, the lovely young girl who was drowned, the son who was arriving tomorrow from across the sea, the girl who did not care . . . all had been here together. There had been soft summer nights when young folks strolled in and out. There had been Christmas trees and garlands, and stockings in front of the fire.

Jerry brought herself up with a cheerful "This will never do," and went quickly in the other rooms, letting in the light. Through the somber library she passed, where hundreds of wise, silent books stood shoulder to shoulder, through the dining-room, out to the back porch, where she found and brought in the rug. Then she set to work to give the house a more lived-in appearance. Remembering the perennials blooming in the rear yard, she flew out and snapped off some of the tall, nodding asters, cloud-white and queen-purple and shell-pink.

These she arranged hurriedly in vases, even placing a huge bunch of them in the umbrella stand in the hall. Into the cold grate she put a great armful of scarlet salvia, where it flamed out vivid, fire-red. Then she opened the piano, and, finding music in the bench, placed several sheets on the rack.

Back into the dining-room she hurried, and standing before the doors of a deep china cabinet look critically over the cups and saucers. "Nothing's too good for Aunt Net," she declared.

Then, as if it were a play, with people awaiting their cues, the taxi rolled up, and Jerry ran down the steps to greet the two old folks with impulsive kisses. Old? Why, she had not dreamed they would look so aged! The last time she had seen Uncle Amos he had been heavy, strong. But this Uncle Amos was using a cane; his clothes were baggy; the flesh above his newly-trimmed beard was ash-white. And Aunt Net was still more pathetic. She swayed a little as Uncle Amos tenderly helped her from the taxi.

Swiftly, with a rush of tears to her eyes, Jerry knew that this was to be her last visit with these old folks. Why, she had spent weeks with them when she was little, weeks that were filled with some of the dearest delights of her childhood: gathering little windflowers and wild oxlips, dreaming under the lazy shimmer of the silent cottonwoods, thrilling at the sight of a scarlet tanager against green pines. For a brief, poignant moment she could hear the call of the bobwhites in the wheat, the lilting plaint of the whippoorwill, the haunting heartache of the mourning-dove. What had she ever done in return for the happiness of those childhood days? Nothing, just nothing. Of late years not even a post card to them. Youth not only must be served, but after that it forgets. Into these three hours, then, must she crowd all the love she owed these kinsfolk.

"What a beautiful home, Jerry!" Aunt Net's eyes glistened at the sight. No woman ever gets so old that the sight of a lovely house will not quicken her pulse. "Where are the folks that you stay with?"

For a fleeting second the enormity of the thing she had done descended upon and enveloped her. Two old people, whose very lives were grounded on principles of honesty, were being made by her heedlessness to do unknowingly a dishonest thing.

"We're all alone," she announced.

She flitted around them, pulling out a huge tapestry chair for Uncle Amos, and settling Aunt Net on the great davenport with numerous pillows.

"Ain't this nice, Pa?" Aunt Net wanted to know. "My! To lay here on this couch is the best thing that could happen to me."

"Ma ain't very well these days," Uncle Amos volunteered. "But we're goin' to get her all right again Out West."

For half an hour they visited about old friends and places. Uncle George lived on the next farm now. There was a new iron bridge across the creek. Did Jerry remember the creek? And the bridge of logs?

Then Uncle Amos said, "Jerry, I been achin' to see you settin' at that *piano* and singin' to me."

So Jerry went to the piano, the one that had not been touched for years, and sang a little modern ditty with a catchy tune.

"That's nice," Uncle Amos told her. "But you know it don't take hold like the old ones. What's come o' 'Ben Bolt'?"

Aunt Net spoke up. "It ain't the songs themselves, Pa. It's 'cause we sung 'em when we was young. Jerry, now, she'll like that one she was singin' when she gets old."

So Jerry looked through the music and found a yellowed book, from which she sang "Ben Bolt" and "Sweet Belle Malone," and "Hazel Dell."

Jerry's voice snapped. Her hands hung suspended above the chords. Her head was up like a startled deer.

"Someone is coming," said Aunt Net pleasantly from her cozy nest of pillows.

Quite so! Someone *was* coming. In fact, to be explicit, he had already come. Wide-eyed, white to the lips, Jerry stared toward the hall.

A man stood in the doorway. He was both tall and broad. His face was grave. Unsmiling, he stood, showing neither surprise nor annoyance.

Obviously, something must be done. Jerry's mind seemed frozen, paralyzed. It functioned only in regard to one thing: Doctor Maynard was standing in his own house where he had every right to be, looking at *her.*

From complete inactivity, suddenly her mind sprang into action like a soldier to duty. Those two innocent old folks! Though she burned at the stake, she would save them, if possible, from embarrassment and disgrace. Trapped, frightened, but keen-witted, she rose from the piano bench. Nerves taut to the finger tips, she crossed the room.

"How do you do?" she said bravely.

She took the last few steps toward the passive looking spectator in the doorway as she gave him her hand, her cold, trembling hand.

"How do *you* do?" said the man.

"I didn't hear . . . hear Maggie let you in," she said firmly, and almost laughed at the bright thing she had thought to say. With that same passivity the man merely inclined his head courteously and made no answer. If she could only rouse him to the necessity of playing the game!

"Doctor Maynard," she said brightly, "I want you to meet my aunt, Mrs. Hammond . . . and my uncle, Mr. Hammond. They're on their way to California, and they're stopping *here with me* between trains . . . leaving at four-thirty-six."

On and on she chattered about the trip, as Doctor Maynard, still passive, apparently cold-blooded, shook hands with the two.

"Is this your young man, Jerry?" Uncle Amos wanted to know.

"Now, Pa!" Aunt Net remonstrated.

Jerry's cheeks were flying vivid, flame-colored flags, which in Youth's signal code is a variable sign, meaning almost anything.

"Oh, no!" She forced a laugh, a two-per-cent laugh of mirth. "Just a . . . friend. Doctor Maynard has been back from England only a short time."

Introductions over, still Jerry chattered on. "Now, let's all have tea together . . . a little farewell party for the folks." Anything to keep the steering-wheel in her own grasp! The reckoning must come, but by warding it off until the taxi arrived she would be saving the honor of these two old people. So, never meeting the eyes of the man, she indicated a chair for him. He took it with deadly calm. Talking gayly on she busied herself with the samovar, poured tea for Aunt Net, for Uncle Amos, pressed a dainty cup of it upon the uninvited guest.

"When you come in,"—Uncle Amos turned to the doctor—"Jerry was singin' to me. I like Jerry's singin'."

Doctor Maynard, composed, lounging easily in the big chair, looked at the girl through quizzical, half-closed eyes, then carefully considered the design on his teacup. "So do I," he said evenly. "Sing again . . . *Jerry!*"

He was playing the game!

So she sang "White Wings" for Uncle Amos, and "Lily Dale" for Aunt Net, and "Spring Hath Many a Rose" for the doctor. Then sitting on a low stool by the fire of salvia blossoms, she told the little group about her primary pupils, funny anecdotes that brought a laugh from each of them. That made Aunt Net think of something that happened when her children were little, which in turn reminded Doctor Maynard of a queer neurasthenic patient. Then Uncle Amos had to tell about an Indian scare in the pioneer days.

While Jerry took the tea things away she could hear Aunt Net on the davenport telling the doctor, "I had to sell two dozen of my best Plymouth Rocks to pay for them treatments."

It was all very cozy, apparently very friendly. No one seeing them would have dreamed that the ax above Jerry's head was suspended by a hair.

After all, there are only sixty minutes in the most nerve-racking hour of our lives. The last sixty were up. The taxi came. The old folks got their things on.

"I 'most hate to go and leave this nice, comfortable house," Aunt Net sighed.

"Ma's queer," Uncle Amos complained to Doctor Maynard. "Always wanted a new house when we didn't have enough money. Got the money now, and she don't want the house. Women's queer."

"No." Aunt Net shook her head. "Not now. I like my old settin'-room where the children played."

For the fleeting fraction of a moment, Jerry and the strange doctor looked at each other. There was a deep sympathy in Jerry's eyes. There was a world of understanding in the doctor's.

Then Uncle Amos was saying, "Get your hat and come along, Jerry."

"We don't need hats," said the doctor.

So they all went to the station in the shabby taxi, the two simple-hearted old folks, the strange doctor, and the girl who had done a dishonorable thing. Jerry saw the doctor almost carry Aunt Net into the sleeper, saw for the last time Uncle Amos, a pathetic old figure in a baggy suit, turn and wave his cane to her. A lump in her throat, she waved gayly back and smiled. Then she turned, ran around the corner of the station, and walked rapidly home.

With ominous quiet she slipped in.

"What's the matter, Jerry?" Ellen asked "You look sick."

"I *am* sick . . . sick and nervous."

"*You* need a nerve specialist, *you* do."

"Oh, stop!" Incoherently, then in self-condemnation, she told the whole tale. "I was too worn out to face him just now," she moaned. "Think, Ellen, *think* of something for me to tell him."

"It seems to me," said Ellen dryly, "there's nothing to tell."

"I need a guardian," Jerry raved. "Why didn't you stop me?" She was walking up and down the room. In a moment she laughed hysterically. "My samovar is still over there and twenty cents worth of perfectly good tea." Then, astonishingly, she burst into tears.

At Mrs. McCloud's call to dinner, Ellen went down-stairs, leaving Jerry at her writing-desk, commencing notes which were never finished. Some said,

"My dear Doctor Maynard." Some said, "Dear Sir." Another said simply, "Sir." And one had no heading. It merely began: "As I will never see you again. . . . " Finally, she put them all in the waste basket, rose, freshened herself, and went down.

On the first floor, with its subdued tinkle and chatter, Jerry was met at the dining-room door by Mrs. McCloud, who was smiling mysteriously. "Where's the key?" she whispered.

"I . . . I left it in the door."

"Well, it doesn't matter." Mrs. McCloud nodded toward the long table.

Across the table from Jerry, three places down, sat a recent sojourner in the land of King George.

Mrs. McCloud beamed. She slipped her arm around Jerry. "Doctor Maynard," she said importantly, "this is another one of my dear girls . . . Miss Hammond."

The other one of Mrs. McCloud's dear girls gave a frigid little nod and said, "How do you do?"

"How do *you* do?" said the doctor.

Jerry sat down and kept her eyes on her plate.

She spent a sleepless night and a wretched Sunday morning.

She did not go to church. Instead, after dressing for dinner, she went out in the side yard, and sitting down on an old bench under a clump of bushes thought out her own sermon. And the text was this: "The way of the transgressor is hard."

"I can see that you are distressed," said a voice abruptly near her. "Why not tell me about it?" And the man sat down unceremoniously by her.

"Distressed? It was terrible!" Jerry's words were tumbling over each other. "First, I want you to know that I'm one of those selfish people who do just anything they want to. But yesterday I grew up." The relief of getting the horrible thing off her mind was immeasurable. She told him all about it. She spared herself not at all. "The worst part of it is," she finished honestly, "if you hadn't come until to-day . . . if I had gotten away with it . . . I'd have gone on thinking it was a good joke . . . probably bragging about it to my room-mate."

Gravely the man heard her through. "Now, it's my turn to talk," he said quietly. "I'll have to tell you that the last few years of my life have not been very pleasurable. The only thing I have experienced that approached contentment has been a small amount of professional satisfaction. But I have had very little personal happiness, and I had about come to the conclusion—" He broke off abruptly, and then went on: "I was dreading to come home. There's something about old scenes . . . to turn the key, and open the door to memories. . . . As I went up the steps yesterday, steeling myself for the ordeal, I was thinking how typical of my life that old house was, with its empty rooms. Then . . . I walked in to receive the old gentleman's warm welcome . . . to see that frail little lady holding out her hand to me from the very place my mother used to— To tell the truth, I didn't give a great deal of thought as to how or why you were there. A vague notion ran through my head that Mrs. McCloud had rented a room or two without writing me. At any rate, I want you to know that something which had vanished"—the doctor turned to Jerry—"something beautiful and fine in my life came back yesterday afternoon."

The other boarders were settling down in their places when Doctor Maynard and Jerry came in. "Look who comes here!" said the dentist cheerfully. "The Grave Digger and the Sassy One."

Mrs. McCloud, in an organdie dress as gray and soft as her hair, beamed on the late arrivals. "Here's the rest of my family," she said warmly. "Doctor Maynard, we wish you belonged with us, too."

"Perhaps I'd better break it gently," he answered; "if you'll have me, I'm staying."

Mrs. McCloud looked up quickly, eagerly. "Really? You mean permanently?"

The man gave one of his rare enigmatical smiles and looked at no one in particular. "Well . . . it may be for years," he said evenly, "and it may be forever."

And across the table three plates down, the cheeks of a girl flew vivid, scarlet-flaming flags, which in Youth's signal code is a variable sign, meaning almost anything.

What God Hath Joined

This is the only story Aldrich wrote in which a main character seriously contemplates divorce, although the character Nell Cutter also briefly considers such action in "Nell Cutter Lets Her Family Shift for Itself" when she thinks that she might have made a mistake in marrying rather than having a career. Aldrich admires women who work hard, as she herself did, and her main character in this story is unflagging in her efforts to keep the boarding-house going.

Here, as in *White Bird Flying,* Aldrich examines the possibilities of accepting an offer that would provide life-long comfort and ease but would mean denying one's home and responsibilities. "What God Hath Joined" (*The American Magazine,* September 1922) probably involves more Christian imagery than any of her short stories other than her Christmas ones.

Mrs. Dilley hung up the huge dishpan and with a few magic sweeps of her capable right arm washed the big sink. The dishes, those Goths and Vandals, invading hordes of every housekeeper's peace, were conquered once more.

"THE TIME" had come.

If there were but three hours in the week that you could call your own, you would be apt to think of them in capitals, too. From three to six, on Sunday afternoons only, was Mrs. Dilley captain of her soul. So precious were these few hours, strung like wondrous gems on a tarnished chain, that to have anything happen to upset them was a disappointment that bordered upon tragedy. A headache . . . a neighbor coming in at that time . . . and the one little lighted candle of the week went out for Mary Dilley.

Three hours in which to drink in God's sunshine or, snowbound, to close her bedroom door on sordid care. One hundred and eighty minutes in which to follow some little winding fern-scented path, or, the rain on the roof, to lose herself in the charm of an old book. For the rest of the week—work! Blinding torrents of work! Work like crashing waves, through which she seemed to battle until those Sunday hours when she rose to breathe and rest on an enchanted island.

Tennyson once gave first prize for constant activity to the brook. But even a brook may occasionally find itself ice-locked in wintry arms. No, for perpetual motion the work of a boarding-house keeper is raised to the *n*th degree. For men may come and men may go, but the eating goes on forever.

Mr. and Mrs. Ezra Dilley kept a boarding-house. The word "kept" needs explanation. Mrs. Dilley kept the range covered with cooking, the cellar stocked with canned fruit, the pantry filled with baking, the house swept, and the porches scrubbed. Mr. Dilley kept the books. It was pretty hard on Mr. Dilley.

Some people never find their proper niche in life. They speak of Success as though it were a flesh-and-blood creature, a distant cousin as it were, who has treated them rudely. Their attitude is that when they find her they will compel her to apologize. And when Success eludes them, Success, which is not a thing of three dimensions, but only the resultant condition of our own acts, they meekly accept the ways of Providence or curse Fate for being an accessory before the fact.

Ezra Dilley was never the cursing kind. He was mild-tempered, contented, full of his jokes. At one time he had been the recipient of some good farm land. This he had traded for town property, which in time was exchanged for a little jewelry stock. As his knowledge of jewelry consisted in being vaguely aware of the difference between a bracelet and a breastpin, it is not surprising that, as the neighbors put it, he soon "petered out."

There followed a few years of various attempts to put salt on the tail of the bird of Good Fortune. There was one period of peddling, via a converted milk-wagon, some marvelous remedies warranted to cure man, beast, fish, or fowl; a summer of canvassing for a book that had sheer bulk for its one best asset; an unforgetable winter in which he interpreted a dying conscience as a voice from above calling him to preach. After exhorting for several weeks in a country schoolhouse where he found, to his infinite disgust, that he was expected to be his own janitor, he gave up the ghost, buried Pride and

Ambition in twin graves and took Mary and six-year-old Alice to his mother and sister in Bluff City. The visit had lasted now for eight years, during which time Ezra, when undue pressure was brought to bear, had painted a little, papered some, occasionally clerked in a store, and helped around the boarding-house. So much for Ezra.

Mary was made of different dust.

Mary Dilley was once Mary Newton of Woodington. Orphaned, she made her home with Uncle Alec and Aunt Lucy Newton, a childless couple of means. The summer Mary was twenty, she went to visit another uncle at his farm home. At the neighborhood gatherings she met Ezra Dilley, twelve years her senior, a widower with a nine-months-old baby. His recent sorrow seemed not to have made an indelible impression upon him, for he could joke and sing with the ease of a comedian. In that subtle way nature has of attracting people of opposite types, the serious-eyed girl with her high ideals thought him a most likable man. How could Mary Newton, with her inexperience, foresee that Ezra Dilley would never be the brave, gallant man she pictured, never show a sign of the dauntless spirit with which she invested him? How could she, with her youth, know that the songs would grow flat and the jokes stale in the long, long years to come? Poor Mary!

When in the course of the family's various flittings the three arrived at the home of Ezra's mother, Mary found the old lady and her daughter cooking for two boarders in the careless, half-hearted, Dilley way. It was not long before she herself was managing the work, doing the cooking, directing the others, and taking on more boarders.

They were all there yet: Ezra and Mary and Alice, Granny Dilley and Aunt Daffy.

Alice was fourteen now, a bright, winsome girl. She had her father's amiable disposition, but something more—an energy, a vivacity that the dying mother must have bequeathed her. But it was Mary Dilley who had kept her in school; Mary who had jealously watched over the dimpled body and brushed the long, shining strands of hair; Mary, the mere step-mother, who had craftily laid away money for music lessons, and turned and twisted the patterns on the remnants of silk and muslin that the little girl might look as well as other children.

Granny Dilley had grown old neither gracefully nor graciously. She attended church regularly, and harped constantly on her family's faults. She read her Bible persistently, and was the first to cast a stone. She lived in an atmosphere of arnica and argument, flannel and fault-finding, camphor and criticism. Old Age can be either an extremely beautiful or a very unlovely thing.

Aunt Daffy was Ezra's only sister. Physically, she was a mound of quivering fat that seemed to have been slipped out of a corrugated gelatin mold. It was almost inconceivable that she had ever been little, but entirely true that at one time in the formative period of her life an adoring father had called her his "dear little Daffy-down-dilly." Through all the years of growing up—and growing in circumference—the name had stuck.

For eight years now, Mary Dilley had been the mainspring in the machinery of the family. Mainspring and lever and shaft! Pedal and pulley and wheel! To have taken Mary out would have been to witness the falling apart of the entire apparatus. Ezra, Alice, Granny, Aunt Daffy—not one of them could have so much as put back half the screws of the complicated mechanism that was the Dilley boarding-house.

Which brings us by a circuitous route back to Mary as she finished the dishes on a Sunday afternoon in late summer. Up the narrow built-in stairs she went quickly and into her homely, low-ceilinged bedroom. To-day the room did not have its usual disheartening effect upon her. It was rather that she looked compassionately upon it, as one feels a tender forbearance for an uncouth old neighbor.

Quickly she changed her dress, trembling as she fastened the last hook. A childish fear that something might detain her took possession of her. And this day of all days must she be by herself, away off somewhere, that she might think.

She put on her hat and slipped quietly down the stairway. Through the thin partition she could hear Daffy's wheezy breathing. Stealthily she passed Granny's door. The querulous voice might call out. But no one spoke. Ezra and Alice were sitting in the porch swing, their heads bent over the comic supplement of the paper.

"I'm going out to the bluffs beyond Greenwood Cemetery," Mary told them briefly.

"Guess I'll go along," Ezra announced cheerfully. But Mary, half way across the yard, made pretense of not hearing. Only for a moment was she obliged to wait for the Greenwood car. As she climbed aboard and took her seat, her mind kept up a continual pæan of pleasure. Not for years had she felt such clarity of mind, visioned such a straight path before her. With bright, alert eyes she watched the people, country-bound on this hot, sultry afternoon. How happy they all seemed! And how essential it was that people should be happy!

She got off the car at Locust Street and walked leisurely through the cemetery . . . Land's End for those who had sailed .

She skirted the edge of the new addition, where only a dozen mounds lay; walked through the scattering oaks and elms, pushed through sumac and elderberry and wild plum, and came to the edge of the high bluff. There they spread before her: the river and the rolling country beyond. Exquisite, Dresden-like the landscape seemed, so far below. Green, yellow, ocher, orange, scarlet, and russet—a smudge of vivid coloring was splashed over the picture. God's tubes had been neither twisted nor dried.

Now, for the first time alone, she let herself think it: *Divorce.* The word that in years gone by had seemed an ugly thing was no longer hideous. Though she had often writhed in anger and impatience in the midst of the fallen ideals of her life she had felt bound by a thousand strands. Cobwebs! After all, just silken cobwebs that could be brushed aside. It seemed so clear now. It had taken a letter from Uncle Alec Newton to sweep them all away. Divorce! That was the answer to a life that was full of work and care and responsibility. Not just divorce from Ezra, even though her love for him was a long-forgotten, vague emotion, a dead thing, drowned in a sea of boarding-house dishwater. It meant the dissolution of partnership with drudgery and a severing of all the Dilley ties: Ezra, the failure; ailing old Granny and her harping ways; fat, trivial-minded Daffy; the grave responsibility of Alice's approaching young womanhood.

For a few moments she gave herself up to a hasty résumé of the years of her married life. While other men of Ezra's age accomplished things in the business world, he had been content to dawdle away the time with his geraniums, to weed his pansy bed, to transplant verbenas. At least his devotion to flowers was sincere.

Coming back to the present, Mary took the letter from her waist and opened immediately to the second page: " . . . sort of look after your aunt Lucy and me the rest of our lives; the bulk of the property will be yours. You wouldn't be tied down. You can come and go as you please. But you can't bring Ezra here, nor his youngster. He's been a millstone around your neck. Divorce him and come home. I'd rise up in my grave if that lazy loafer ever touched a penny of mine. I earned mine, but he . . . " She did not go on. What could Uncle Alec say that would even so much as touch all she knew of Ezra's failure?

She put the letter in her belt and gave herself up to the ecstasy of the moment.

"*Come home. . . .*"

It was as though the knots of a thousand strands had been cut and, like a child's balloon, lighter than thistledown, lighter than air, she floated up, up in her dreams. To go back! Back to girlhood!

She saw herself going up the long walk to the dignified old house . . . up the walk to peace and quiet and the luxury of time to herself. They would be there on the stoop, Uncle Alec and Aunt Lucy. Uncle Alec would be more portly, probably less ruddy, but so capable-looking. Aunt Lucy would look older, of course, and more fragile, but as willowy as a cypress, as dainty as a jasmine.

They would welcome her with out-stretched hands. With them she would pass into the house with its atmosphere of refinement. She would sink down into a deep chair. Other hands would serve her. Once more she would move through the dim old rooms with their dull mahogany, their friendly books and tasteful pictures. There would follow long days in which to do interesting, worth-while things.

Through all these years gone by there had seemed to be someone walking at her side, a shadowy, half-vague personality that was her other self, the woman she might have been: In contrast to her own rushing self, managing the household, urging, pushing, her voice nervous-sounding and shrill, walked this woman beside her—quiet, low-voiced, poised. *She was going to be that woman.* It was like the sudden bursting of a chrysalis. Or the release of an imprisoned bird beating its wings in the hollow of cruel hands. Or prison doors swinging wide. It was as though all the kingdoms of the world were to be hers.

The words had a hauntingly familiar sound. Where had she heard them? "Kingdoms of the world?" Not all at once, but slowly, haltingly, something was creeping into her thoughts to annoy her. The bright edge of the new-born pleasure seemed dulled. She began a mental searching for the cause of the discomfiture. What was troubling her? Something about that "kingdoms of the world." She tried to shake it off, but the forbidden thing persisted.

Suddenly, like a physical blow, it came to her. Someone Else had been shown the kingdoms of the world. Someone Else had stood on an exceeding high mountain and looked out over the kingdoms that might have been His. *And been tempted.*

This was the thing that was extinguishing the warm glow of her spirits, chilling the fine fervor of her plans; Could it be—was *she* being tempted?

Involuntarily, she rose to her feet, palpitant, alert. It seemed that she was being called upon to defend herself. Scarcely knowing what she did, she turned her face up to the palpitating hot blue of the summer sky, up to the low smothering white of the summer clouds. It was as though she addressed a Person.

"No, no! My mind's made up. Don't put it that way. . . . don't say those things. . . . He's been a failure. . . . I know he's been kind—clean and kind; but he hasn't been successful. . . . And that drives love away. And Alice isn't my own. She just belongs to him—to him and a woman I never knew. Mothers are divorced and leave their families every day. Things change . . . divorce used to be wrong . . . but it isn't any more . . . not any more. The world's different. . . . People used to say, 'What God hath joined,' . . . now, they know it's just man . . . just a preacher . . . What man hath joined God hath forever put asunder."

She fell to sobbing, dry, choking, tearless sobs that were wrenched from the depths. Her calloused hands with their broken nails worked painfully together. Pleadingly she argued with the Unseen One: "I'm going; I've got a right to. Ten, twenty—maybe I've got thirty years of my own yet. And I've done right by Alice; I've worked my fingers to the bone for her; but I'm not her mother; you've got to bear a child to be a mother; . . . And now I want to go back. . . . I want to go home; . . . I was only twenty . . . I didn't know . . . I'd have done different. . . . I'm tired . . . I've got a right to start over . . . I've got a right . . . got . . . a . . . right . . . " Her voice died down to a low incoherent murmuring. Exhausted, she leaned against the gnarled branch of a crab-apple tree, her mind tumultuous, warring against itself. For a long, long time she stood in anguish before the swinging of the mental pendulum. Back and forth the torturing thing swayed, dragging her sensitive, quivering mind with its every oscillation, the two points of the arc definitely, uncompromisingly, worlds apart: Ease, or Duty. . . . Pleasure, or Responsibility. . . . Herself, or Ezra. . . . A life . . . for . . . a life.

Suddenly, fiercely, like the sharp snarl of a wild thing, a crash of thunder sounded. Startled from her mental struggle, she whirled to see the heavens boiling. Unseen through the growth of the thicket, the storm had slipped up stealthily behind her back, like a warring savage.

Nervous in storms from childhood, Mary Dilley ran out into an open space with vague thought of making for the car line. But under the first bombardment of huge splashes of rain, with bent head she shrank back to the trees. It was only a moment or two before the drops changed to hail, became great pelting things that thudded angrily. Cowering there under the tree Mary Dilley was stoned, even as Stephen was stoned. The lightning seemed setting both the heavens and the woods on fire. But, bad as were these—the mad dashes of rain, the bruising hail, the yellow-red glare of the lightning nor the shattering thunder—nothing was as terrible as that far-off roaring, that warning as of something more demon-like to follow. The hail had stopped, even the thunder ceased for a few moments, as though to let nothing interfere with the right of the monster that was coming. The Thing was crouching before it sprang. If it would only come . . . whatever It was!

Then it came. It was wind—tempestuous, angry, snarling wind. Sixty-five miles an hour it blew, like a wintry North Atlantic gale, lost, and tearing over the Mid-West, seeking for the ocean. The rain came with it, thrown down like great ponds. The two evil partners, the rain and the wind, beat Mary Dilley to the ground and, pommeling her so, these wild things from the caves of the nether world, they drove her mind to dwell on one thing only—the shelter of home. If she had only gone home! How worried they would be! How they would be wishing she could come home.

"*Come home!*"

She saw herself, warm and dry, walking into the comfortable, homely sitting-room, the cheerful sun shining through the bay window where Ezra's fuchsias stood. Her body, numb with the stinging cold that the hail had brought, seemed driving her mind to greater activity. In her imagination she walked about the boarding-house, contented and happy. She clung to her mental pictures like a drowning seaman to wreckage. She reveled in the homely sights, smelling baked beans, great crocks of them, seeing pans of her light rolls rising on the long kitchen table, hearing the pleasant clatter of the dishes at meal time. Out into the back yard she went to hang up the freshly washed table linen, the grass fragrant with the sweetness of its recent mowing. She walked among Ezra's asters over which he was so boyish, with which he wasted so much time. The vision seemed like a haven—a heavenly haven.

The fury was doubling itself now so that she hid her eyes from the sight. If Ezra were only here with her! No one could say that Ezra was physically afraid. He had painted the steeple of the highest church in town, had been the first one to go into a house where there had been an insane killing. A tree crashed near, pulled up by the roots and hurled into the abyss of the river bed below, taking a great mass of earth along with it. Almost at the end of her nerves' control, she struggled to a sitting posture and moaned aloud. The rain, slackening for an instant, as though to get ready for its next onslaught, gave her the chance to see something moving slowly up the slope. Some animal, it must be, trying to get to its mate. No; it was a man . . . a man trying to get to his mate. It was Ezra. She sensed it rather than recognized him. With a great throb of relief she said to herself that it was like him to come for her. He loved her.

She called "Ezra!" But the wind carried the sound over the bluff as it had carried the tree. It reminded her that part of the bank was gone. Ezra wouldn't know that. He might go too near the edge. He had reached the open space now and, buffeted down, was crawling on hands and knees. Impulsively, she, too, started to crawl. At right angles their paths would cross if she could get to him in time. Her strength seemed leaving her. No; she was not going to make it. "Ezra!" she called again and again.

How kind he had always been to her, kind and clean and cheerful! Every atom of her strength she put into a call, the call of a primitive thing to its mate. Then he heard her. They found each other in the open space. Water-soaked, beaten, groping, their arms folded and clung. "Mary! Mary, dear! Was you afraid?" he whispered over and over.

Together they crawled to an oak. The storm was at the crest. The lightning hovered menacingly, constantly, over the hill top.

"It may strike us," she whispered.

"Yes, it may. But what matter if we go now or later? This way we could go together."

Suddenly she felt comfortable in Ezra's arms, every muscle relaxed. What matter, indeed? She was not afraid. Ezra had not made a financial success of his life. She had been disappointed in him. But what had disappointment to do with love? Love was everlasting . . . eternal, like the hills.

Another tree crashed. It was the elm where she had sat. A great ball of fire, dropped from the sky, rolled down the hill, bouncing gracefully, majestically, like a child's hoop.

"Mary, I want to tell you something now while we're here." Ezra had to speak very close to her ear to be heard. "I've kept it to myself for over a week. But I promised myself not to let this day go by without telling you. I've been ashamed and afraid to ask you. Jud Nelson wants to sell me his greenhouse. And, Mary, I want it! I've never wanted anything so much in my life." His voice was shaking. "But the only way I could get hold of it is to . . . to use the money you've laid by. It would be the first payment. It don't seem right that I should ask you. You worked hard with the boarders, and it ought to be your own. But I wondered . . . if you'd give me a chance, Mary!

We'd use it together for the greenhouse. I'd make good. I ain't amounted to much, I know. But this—*this* is different. Think of it, Mary, big beds of pansies like hundreds of little faces; rows and rows of sassy geraniums, English violets to intoxicate you, a whole room of gorgeous shaggy chrysanthemums; it'd be like play where there was never any work to do.

"I'd love the work so, I'd begrudge the night coming on. I'm serious, Mary. It ain't a passing notion—it comes from the soul of me. To work with flowers all the rest of my life! Raise 'em and sell 'em to folks who love 'em, too . . . and raise more." He was trembling. Yes, he was sincere. In all her years with him, Mary Dilley had never seen such evidence of energy.

Suddenly, it seemed very clear to her. Ezra's passion for flowers to be turned into his life work! Why, she had always *pulled him away from them.* Why had he not thought of this thing before? Why had not she?

"I ain't old, Mary," he went on pleadingly. "I'm only forty-six. I could make good yet. There's a little cottage with the greenhouse. You'd have work to do, but not so hard. Just help me with the office a little—the selling end; but let me work with my flowers. Anything will grow for me. I'll take good care of you all the rest of your days. I ain't done anything to merit your trust . . . but *trust* me!"

The woman slipped her roughened hand into the man's big one. "We'll do it, Ezra. You take the money. I know you'll succeed. Forty-six ain't old. We got ten, twenty, maybe thirty years together yet." The words came back faintly, dimly, like a vague echo from the earlier afternoon.

Ezra drew her close. "It seems too good to be true. I've dreamed it night and day since Jud told me he wanted to move and sell. And to know you're willing . . . and trust me. Promise me, Mary, . . . if the lightning . . . if we never get back home . . . say that we'll carry it out anyway . . . say we'll raise flowers together . . . you and me . . . Some place else."

"I promise!" Mary was sobbing a little. It was her second marriage vow to Ezra. She was only a plain woman, weary and drenched and toilworn. But hers was the spirit of Joan of Arc. And she was Mary the Mother.

The storm left, occasionally reeling back like a drunken man to laugh at the destruction his debauch had wrought. Stiff, soaked, chattering with cold, the two rose and started homeward. Hand in hand they picked their way through the woods. There had been havoc in the cemetery. There was no car, would be none until the debris was picked from the tracks. As they neared the little greenhouse, Ezra quickened his steps. "See, Mary, lots of panes of glass out! He'll have to fix that up first. But look, through the windows the carnations smiling out to me! Seems like they know me. Lord, Mary, I can't wait to get hold of 'em. Think of wasting twenty-five years."

The woman looked up into the face of the bedraggled man. "You know, Ezra, I think there's a certain work for every man and woman in the world. Lots of them don't find out what it is. But some place there's a work for everyone that's just like play, you love it so. Yours was flowers, and we neither of us sensed it."

He pressed her hand, his heart warm because of her sympathy. "I wouldn't change my work in that greenhouse, Mary, for—for the kingdoms of the world."

In the midst of a little group of anxious boarders the two went up the front steps, the shabby steps that swayed a little under their weight. Through the big dining-room with its long tables, set now for lunch, they passed into the kitchen. Fat old Daffy was sitting by the vegetable table crying big, easy tears, her wide face mottled and swollen. Granny stood swaying in the doorway of the pantry, one of her knotted brown-veined hands clinging to the door, the other clutched over her flat old breast. White-lipped, Alice rushed down the stairs and threw impetuous arms around her stepmother.

There are people to whom a soul victory means change—a moment of tender emotion, a softening of speech. Mary Dilley was not one of these. In the same half-scolding, half-joking tone with which she often met family crises, she laughed, "Well, keep your shirts on! We're here, ain't we?"

Then energetically, characteristically, she gathered together the loose, flapping ends of the Sunday-night lunch service: "Daffy, cut the bread. . . . Alice, fix two more lettuce salads. . . . Granny, steep Mr. Henderson's tea—be sure to get it out of his own box." And with a look that carried infinite love and trust, she turned to her husband, "Ezra, we both got to get into dry duds. Before you change, though, just step out and tell them lunch is ready."

For, in a boarding-house, drama may come and tragedy may go, but the eating goes on forever.

The Victory of Connie Lee

This story is unusual in that it has elements that will later appear in three Aldrich novels. "The Victory of Connie Lee" begins with an opening similar to that of *A Lantern in Her Hand,* has the outline of the plot that will become *The Rim of the Prairie,* and concludes the way that *A White Bird Flying* concludes. There also are elements that Aldrich uses in other stories: the grandparents, who rear protagonist Connie Lee (also seen in "Their House of Dreams" and "Through the Hawthorne Hedge"); the school superintendent, who will fall in love with her (from "Marcia Mason's Lucky Star"); and Fate, Aldrich's favorite term for coincidence, which turns a steering wheel to put the events in motion (from "A Long Distance Call from Jim," and "He Whom a Dream Hath Possest"). As Abbie Deal in *A Lantern in Her Hand,* this family "reads avidly" and takes—through books—trips to the Mediterranean and the Alps, much as, perhaps, Aldrich did.

"The Victory of Connie Lee" (*The American Magazine,* October 1923) has philosophical elements regarding the renewal of life that she attributes to her grandfather, Zimri Streeter, in sketches, short stories, and novels in which Zimri is the quintessential male heroic pioneer. Aldrich pioneers the name of "Ourtown," predating by fifteen years Thornton Wilder's 1938 play of that name.

This story also demonstrates facets of Aldrich's artistic and literary knowledge and does so with a tacit understanding with the reader that she or he has the same knowledge. Old Mrs. Lee's hands were like those painted by Gainsborough, patterns were as dainty as Alsatian lace, leaves were dancing Pierrots, the Mother Goose poem "Who Killed Cock Robin" is recalled, "Thanatopsis" is quoted, as is William Cullen Bryant's untitled poem that begins "To him who in the love of Nature holds," and a character from *Uncle Tom's Cabin* becomes a simile. Near the end of the story there are two lines from Joyce Kilmer's poem "Trees."

Ourtown sits complacently beside a great highway where once there were buffalo tracks. If you start on the highway—and travel far enough—it will bring you to the effete East. If you start in the opposite direction—and travel a few hundred miles farther—it will bring you to the effete West. Ourtown is neither effete nor distinctive, nor even particularly pleasing to the passing tourist. It is beautiful only in the eyes of the prairie-lover whose sojourn in the mountains or by the sea has left him homesick for the low rolling hills, the fields of sinuously moving corn, and the elusively fragrant odor of alfalfa. Sometimes the snow and sleet hold Ourtown in their deadly bitter grasp. Sometimes the south winds parch it with their hot, scorching breath. But between these onslaughts there are days and weeks so perfect, so filled with lilac odors and the rich pungent smell of newly turned loam, so sumac-laden and apple-burdened, so clean-swept with crystal rain, that to the prairie-born there is nothing like it on mountain or lake or sea.

To Ourtown, sixteen years ago, from an Eastern university, came Norman Harper, big, fine, clean-cut, with a life dedicated to teaching. And this is the story of Norman Harper and his love for Connie Lee.

For nine months Norman Harper had been superintendent of the schools in Ourtown. Unsettled as to whether he would remain for another year, he drove one night into the country, with the vague idea that the open spaces might help to clarify his vision. A little way out from town he stopped as the evening train passed by and, having stopped, pondered for a moment which of two roads to take. How could Norman Harper know that his whole future hung on that finely balanced decision? How indeed! We never do. Fate, that old woman who pushes her human checkers about, laid a bony hand on the steering wheel. To the north drove Norman Harper.

His way lay past orchards, where little pincushions of apples clung to sap-filled branches, past alfalfa fields ready for the first cutting, past corn fields in which green shoots were already ankle depth. Ahead of him an old man sat on a fallen log holding up his hand, a clumsy team beside him. Norman slowed down, stopped.

"I guess I'll have to have some help," the old man called. "This fool mare kicked me. I've fed her and watered her and curried her for eleven years. I'd 'a' said she was one of the best friends I got till she pulled off this trick. My name's Lee," he added.

Norman assisted the man to the car and, leading the team, they drove slowly into the farmyard with its heterogeneous collections of buildings. The house itself stood in a little picket-fenced yard away from omnivorous hens, where there were petunias and zinnias sending forth multitudinous blossoms. An old lady was shutting up a brood of tiny chickens for the night. She shaded her face with her hand and came forward with little birdlike movements.

The old man said curtly, "Ma, this is Mr. Harper, the professor in the schools." Ma shook hands with Norman. She was as brown as a gnome but sweet-faced and gracious.

"Topsy kicked me," her husband told her. "Darned fool! When I get around to it I'll take it out of her hide." Old Man Lee had never touched child or beast with a stick, but he enjoyed talking of the possibility.

Norman tied the temperamental Topsy and her phlegmatic mate to a post and assisted the man into the house. "Which doctor do you employ?" he asked.

"Great guns! You talk like they was grocerymen. The whole kit 'n' bilin' of 'em would starve to death if they depended on Ma and me. Got Ma some medicine a while back, but got it in a drug store. Paid a dollar for it too. You got some yet, ain't you, Ma?" Ma nodded, proud of her economy.

When the doctor arrived the old man greeted him with: "Seems a fellow can't stub his toe around here without callin' out the state militia." But by this time Norman had sensed the real nature of the kind heart that lay under the prickly armor. The old lady seemed to be of finer texture. She was gentle of speech, and her hands, in spite of their toilworn appearance, were as slender and pointed as a Gainsborough.

This, then, was the couple whose acquaintance Norman had made because Fate, that old woman of the roads, had intervened. Feeling a genuine interest in them, he went back for a second and third call. It was while on this last visit, in wandering around the little place that he discovered a wonderful view, where the orchard reached to the high bank of a bluff overlooking the far country. For an hour or more he sat there enjoying the scene. The wonder of the night filled and soothed him. The quiet was a living, brooding thing, caressing him like a soft hand on the forehead. The moon shone down into the orchard, making shimmering shadows of patterns as dainty as the lace made by old Alsatian women. The leaves on the Lombardy poplars stirred, twinkled, little dancing Pierrots in the moon. The scene seemed wasted, he thought . . . the beauty of it was so poignant. With a feeling of reluctance at leaving he turned to go to his car. It was then that the girl came up the path.

Up through the orchard came the girl, running as lightly as the swaying of the shadows. At the edge of the bluff she threw out her arms in a gesture of abandon. "Connie!" she called. "Connie Lee, come here!"

Norman stood silently in the black shadow of the trees. Again the girl called, "Connie Lee, are you here?" It was uncanny, weird.

Norman stepped from the shadow. "I beg your pardon. I was afraid I might startle you."

She stopped rigid with a short intake of breath, so that he quickly explained his presence, telling her of his visits to the old folks, and the discovery of the view from the bluff.

"You like it, too?" Relieved, she laughed a gay little crescendo laugh. "I always loved it when I used to play here. It has been seven years since I have seen it. I'm Connie Lee."

She, herself, was Connie Lee. She had called to herself to come. She might then be insane? Hardly. She was cool, laughing. She had poise.

"Connie Lee has been dead for seven years," she announced. "And I killed her. With my little bow and arrow I killed Connie Lee."

Falling in with the figure, Norman asked lightly, "Who saw her die?"

The answer came quickly, " 'I,' said Ambition, 'with my little eye, I saw her die.' " She stood looking over the bluff, apparently accepting Norman as part of the landscape. "Well,"—she threw her arms out in their characteristic gesture—"it has worked . . . the incantation . . . the fetish for the gods . . . the sacrifice to the idols. Connie Lee's alive again."

"You will be here for some time?" With something of a shock Norman realized that he was eagerly awaiting her answer.

She frowned, evidently disturbed. "That depends. I've run away." It seemed to give her a great deal of laughing satisfaction. "It has been a dream of mine to come back and stay a year with Grappy and Granny. Until a year from to-day . . . and then I vanish into the clouds like mist and the all-beholding sun shall see me no more. That's 'Thanatopsis.' Granny made me learn it once for throwing my patchwork into an old well in the pasture. But if I stay, I have to get some work to do. I thought maybe I could get a position in the schools. I planned to see the superintendent to-morrow."

"I am the superintendent." Norman was immediately on his guard. To have tapped the shell of a mud-turtle would have had the same withdrawing consequences.

"You? How terribly awesome!" But that was mere persiflage. He knew it had not awed her in the least.

"What are your qualifications?" Norman was all seriousness, wholly superintendent. No piece of femininity with a great deal of laughing through curved lips above a V-shaped cleft in its chin could pull the wool over his eyes.

She held up her ten fingers, dropping them one by one as she named: "I can read, write, sing, play the piano, and dance. I have sympathy, pride, loyalty, a sense of humor, and know first aid to the injured."

"A few of them are essential," he admitted; "but our teachers have special training. Have you?"

"Oh, I've been to school," she said vaguely. "Well,"—she made a little shrugging motion of her shoulders—"if I can't get it, the vanishing begins in a few days. Connie Lee will go again to be a brother to the insensible rock and to the sluggish clod which the rude swain turns with his share and treads upon."

"I'll talk to the board," he said hastily—too hastily.

"Perhaps it could be arranged if you would take some intensive work in the summer school."

"School? Oh, goodness, that means more money. But maybe Grappy would help me a little. You see before you the beggar maid. She has three dollars and nineteen cents to her name, besides a ticket back"—she waved her hand indefinitely—"back to the sluggish clod."

"Tell me about yourself," Norman said. "Where have you been living in the seven years?"

It was the girl's turn to run to cover. "Let's not talk about that." She was serious enough now. Then suddenly she fell into that care-free mischievous mood in which Norman was so often to see her. "If Connie Lee has been dead for seven years, why, she's been to heaven, hasn't she?"

There was a little more conversation relative to the view, and then she left. Norman watched her go lightly down through the trees, humming a gay little tune. For some time he stood by the bluff looking across the river, where the lights of the little town gleamed like a thousand eyes. A star fell, an ember from the camp fires of heaven. It might have dropped into the little gray farmhouse, for simultaneously a light shone from a gable window. The girl wanted to be here for a year. And, knowing nothing about her, he had promised to use his influence in getting her into the schools. Like Topsy, had his common sense that he had fed and watered and curried for years turned and kicked him?

But in the year which followed, Connie Lee did not embarrass her intercessor. What she may have lacked in technique she made up for in being a natural-born teacher, one of those rare souls who know intuitively how to explain. Norman began taking her out home in his car, although the distance could not have been his excuse, for a middle-aged teacher for whom he showed no such thoughtfulness lived three miles farther away. Together they discussed a hundred subjects, but of the past seven years Connie was always laughingly vague. By the time that Norman grew conscious of criticism from the other teachers whenever he visited Connie's room, and equally self-conscious when he neglected to do so, he sensed what was happening to him.

And then—it seemed almost unbelievable—the year had flown past. When the end came swinging into view, and Norman was sick with the thought of losing Connie, he put his love into words. For once the girl's merry way was sunk in an agony of appeal. "Oh, no, no!" she said in genuine distress, "not that—you mustn't," and sped precipitately into the little gray house. Nor did she report for duty the next day. She only sent Norman a note which said she had gone. But in it, somewhere between the lines, there was just enough of the shadow of wretchedness to make him feel that it had not been all easy for her to go. So, being nothing but the embodiment of simplicity and straight-forwardness, he set about to see her again.

Granny gave him her address, but, it seemed to him reluctantly, even intimating timidly that she did not want Grappy to know she had done it. So, half fearful, half exultant, Norman set out on the highway which had been buffalo tracks, and drove very far to a city of the East.

When he had cleansed and refreshed himself he started out to the number which Granny had given him. He found it, a huge pile of masonry looking as much like a public library as a home. If he was awed he gave no sign of it, for the trip was not to be fruitless. A butler admitted him to a hall through whose iridescent marble walls shone soft lights. A group of young people came down the wide stairway. One of them, in a blue dinner gown, a bandeau of pearls in her hair, was Connie Lee.

Seeing Norman, Connie went white to the lips and stopped, bewildered. Then she came forward. Yes, Connie Lee had ample use for her seven years of social training. With poise she shook hands with Norman and with poise she introduced him to the two girls standing nearest. While she was speaking, a young man who had come up slipped his hand familiarly, affectionately, into Connie's arm.

"Mr. McCune, Mr. Harper," Connie named them. Then adroitly she took the situation into her hands. "Mr. Harper has come from my other grandparents," she said to the young people; "if you will excuse us for a little while, I want to ask him about them."

While the God of Tact looked on approvingly, Connie led the way into the library. The door closed, she faced Norman. "I should have told you all about everything while I was there." She spoke hurriedly as though she would crowd a lifetime into the interview. "I blame myself terribly. This is my Grandfather Winters's home. My name is really Constance Winters, although Grappy always called me Connie Lee, just as my mother was named. Grandfather Winters's youngest son was my father. He came out to Ourtown years ago with two other college boys to work on farms during their vacation. He met my mother . . . they were both so young . . . and they were married secretly after a brief summer courtship. He came back East to finish college, and died with diphtheria. His letters to my mother stopped suddenly. She must have been wild when she could get no word. Then in her distress she confessed her marriage to Grappy and Granny. Grappy wrote the Winterses, and the answer came briefly that their son was dead. Then my mother in her grief died when I was born. I have never known what made Grappy dislike my other grandparents so, but at the slightest question on my part Grappy would fall into anger or silence. Grappy and Granny were the only parents I ever knew, of course. I had such a happy childhood. The first thing I can ever remember is Grappy catching me up when he came in from work, and saying 'Heigh-ho, your chin's startin' to split in two.' We three were so happy until I was sixteen. Oh, I tell you"—she broke off suddenly—"happiness is a queer thing. I've lived the life of a poor girl and a rich one, and I've learned a few things. You can laugh just as wholeheartedly in a steaming hot kitchen as you can in a ballroom, and you can shed just as bitter tears on a satin pillow as you can on a bundle of hay." A little ashamed of her emotion she hurried back to her story:

"Then, when I was sixteen, like a fairy tale out of my most cherished books, my other grandparents came to the farm. Grandfather Winters had become very wealthy in oil, and I know now, what I didn't know then, that Grandmother Winters found herself possessed of everything but social position. I think she must have argued that a young granddaughter, if she were passable, could assist her in getting a foothold. I know the first thing she said when she saw me was, 'Oh, Jim, I *do* want her.'

"But Grappy and Granny wouldn't let me go. Grappy was frightful . . . how he talked! And then the Winterses began to tell me what they would do for me. All at once Grappy's anger seemed to collapse, as though he were beaten. I think he must have suddenly seen that he and Granny had so very little to offer beside the advantages the others could give me. It was a pitiful moment as I see it now. He said he'd leave it to me. I can shut my eyes now and see Grappy's and Granny's drawn, stricken faces when I said I wanted to come. I told them I'd come back to see them. . . . I'd spend a whole year with them sometime; but Grappy told me never to darken the door of his house again if I went. That hurt me of course and it was a long time before I sensed that he himself was too hurt to know what he was saying.

"Well, I came. I had everything. . . . You see." She threw out her hand in a little impersonal gesture which took in the exquisite fittings of the room. "But I always wanted to go back. So I risked it. I hadn't an idea how they would treat me. I saw Granny first, and then went down to the barn where Grappy was. I stood in the stable door and said, 'Grappy, you never mentioned not darkening the *barn* door,' Grappy looked up startled, and then crumpled down on the milk stool and shed the first tears I ever saw from him. Of course Grandfather Winters didn't like it at all because I went. He threatened me; but it ended in his only stopping my allowance for the time I was away."

All this that Connie had been saying was merely a collection of words to Norman. In the first pause he went straight to the heart of the thing: "Who is Mr. McCune?"

Constance Winters dropped her eyes. "My fiancé," she said. And Norman's love for Connie loomed beside them like a colossal, accusing, third person.

"Let me explain that, too," Connie went on quickly. Which was the beginning of her confession, for one does not ordinarily need to explain a fiancé. "For several years there has been an understanding between the families that I was to marry Hal. Grandfather and Hal's father are interested in a great many things together. The two are very much pleased with it . . . it has seemed the best thing to do." Connie was floundering, when Norman interrupted, "Do you love him?"

Connie evaded, with miserable eyes. "I'm quite fond of him."

Norman was making it very hard for her, standing there, tall and silent and honest. "When I was out there," she faltered, "I began to feel . . . to know . . . but I thought if I came away quickly—Oh!" she said suddenly, "I thought it would be a lark living there like I used to with Grappy and Granny. But I should never have gone. I am terribly sorry now I went."

"Why?" Yes, Norman was exacting his pound of flesh. But even though Connie would not say why she was so sorry, a fourth person seemed to have slipped in to join the group—Connie's love for Norman.

For a few moments they stood silent, the man, the girl, and the two shadowy but vital personalities. Then the girl looked up and said earnestly: "Who am I? Connie Lee, or Constance Winters? You have everything I haven't—strength of character, decision. I feel like a dual personality. Sometimes I think I have two souls in one body. I'm weak, soft, my environment shapes me. Here, I countenance things I wouldn't in Ourtown. I actually had the feeling out there that I had gone back to my own self. I'm prairie-born and I love it. I was so happy all last year; but wasn't part of it due to the fact that it *was* a lark, and I knew I was coming back where everything was lazy and pleasurable and easy? If I'd go back out there . . . with you to stay . . . give them up here, Grandfather Winters would cut me off from him entirely. He told me so in no chosen words before I left last year. Help me; tell me—all our future depends on it: *Who am I?*"

Though his face was tense Norman held himself steadily. It was Life's big moment and Life had chosen to scourge him. He felt cold, shivering, even afraid, but he made himself go on.

"You're Constance Winters," he said evenly. "This is where you belong. Even if you hadn't promised to marry him—and a promise is an inviolable thing—you wouldn't be happy with me now. You'd remember all the things that you had cut yourself away from, and want them. You would need them to make you happy, and your unhappiness would be mine. My life is going to be largely a life of service. I'll not fool myself into believing otherwise. My income—good lord—after all this how could you live on twenty-eight hundred dollars a year in a six-roomed bungalow, with only my love for you to keep you from remembering what you might have had? No; you belong here."

Yes, Connie had been right in saying that Norman had strength of character.

She went white to her lips. "I expect that's true." She, too, spoke steadily.

"Good-by," Norman took her hand.

Constance Winters held her head very erect. "Good-by!"

So Norman Harper came back to Ourtown. No one knows what the outcome would have been if Grappy Lee's time had not then come to die. On a mellow Indian summer afternoon he stood on the steps of the back porch and looked across the field for which he had fought nature a half-century before. For a long time he watched the lazy waving of the elms and Lombardy poplars that he had planted, pondered on their drawing their substance from the earth, thought of the wonder of sap and bud, blossom and leaf; how the leaves fell to the ground, became mold, sank into the earth, were drawn up, and again there were sap and bud, blossom and leaf. Quite suddenly Grappy felt cold, stricken, crumbling like a shriveling leaf. For a time he was frightened, feeling the icy fingers, and then quietly, renunciatingly, as though he too acquiesced in the Great Plan, he turned and walked feebly into the house.

In the days that followed he wanted Connie to come. It was Norman who telegraphed for her and Norman who met her at the station. When the train came out of the east he steeled himself for the meeting. Well, life was like that. We fought off the cold, icy hands of death and the hot throbbing ones of love. Connie got off. "Is he living?"

"Yes. These sturdy old people . . . it is hard for them to pass out."

They drove out the familiar way in the soft haze of the Indian summer. But when they got there the old man was back down Memory's road. And he did not stop at the most important events. Little trivial things were the ones he talked about, resetting strawberries, the county fair, clearing out the underbrush. Was all of life, thought Connie, composed of little things, thousands of them to make a whole? Suddenly Grappy raised himself and spoke clearly: "She's my little girl . . . they can't have her. They didn't want anything to do with her then . . . defamed her dead mother's character. . . . She was a nuisance then . . . said to put her in a foundling home . . . orphan asylum . . . give her away . . . anything . . . but not to bother them. We took care of her . . . Ma and me. . . . Ma made her little dresses and I cut her Christmas trees. . . . "

When the cows were coming up the sumac-bordered lane Grappy passed out, an old man whose life had been circumscribed, but who left behind him an infinite number of kind and neighborly acts. After the manner of country communities people began coming to pay their respects. The president of the bank and the janitor of the Whittier School came. The division superintendent of the railroad sent hot-house roses and a man and woman whom Grappy had befriended in their covered wagon down the highway brought wild Bouncing Bets as ragged and unkempt and full of wanderlust as they.

Norman went out to the farm every day of the week that Connie stayed with Granny. He told himself it was the decent thing to do. On Thursday he made a request of her: "You wouldn't feel like taking your old room, would you, just for to-morrow while Miss Jones is away?"

"Yes," Connie assented; "I'd like to."

In the middle of that Friday forenoon Norman, very businesslike, wholly superintendent, stopped in Connie's room to ask her if she would hand in a report, as all the teachers were doing, recommending any changes in the geography outline. And Connie, very businesslike, wholly teacher, said that she would.

In the late afternoon Norman stood at his office window looking out at a fog settling down over the radiance of the day, truly typical of himself. Who was it had said that life was bright with its illusions, aspirations, dreams? It was not true. Life was raw. Illusions were mere fallacies of vision. Aspirations became aversions. Dreams were leaden vagaries. Wearily he turned from the window and picked up the reports of geography which had just come in. From the group he took Connie's paper and held it a moment . . . the last thing she would do for him. It gave some recommendations formally numbered. There was another sheet underneath. It said:

> I further recommend that these boys and girls be taught the difference between things worth while and those that are passing, so that when they are grown they will understand:
>
> 1. That a six-roomed bungalow may be a realm.
>
> 2. That twenty-eight hundred dollars will buy red firelight, a steaming kettle, a candle in the window.
>
> 3. That love, which is without fear, has nothing to do with *things.*

Dazed, Norman stood in wide-eyed fascination, looking at the swaying words. Then he stuffed the paper in his pocket, ran down-stairs to his car, and drove to the Whittier School.

Although he banged the door and strode noisily down the length of the room, Connie, who was at the blackboard, did not look up but kept on energetically filling in an autumn leaf with red chalk. When Norman was close to her she said, "Oh, how do you do?" She was frightened now. It was as though, having thrown a match in the dry prairie grass, the flame had turned on her. "I'm making an October calendar," she explained volubly.

Norman took the piece of gaudy chalk from her hand and threw it into the waste basket. "Connie, you're going to stay in Ourtown."

"Oh, am I?" she asked politely.

"You're not going back at all. I'm going East myself to-night and see this McCune and your grandfather. There's no power on earth which gives them any jurisdiction over you. You can't push and shove love around like that. It's not a commodity to trade or barter. A promise is big, but love is bigger. You belong to me just as I belong to you. There's no appeal from Nature's decision. We're through to-day—*now*—with this compromising for money and position."

She began no argument, made no resistance. She only said, "Oh, Norman, there never could have been anybody but you."

It has been fifteen years since Connie wrote Hal McCune and Grandfather Winters that she was sorry to disappoint them, but how could she do other than marry the man she loved? The Harpers still live in Ourtown. Norman has had his salary increased to thirty-six hundred dollars, which is almost two dollars and a quarter per year for each character which he helps to mold. No, Norman Harper will never set the world on fire; but in Ourtown he is like the Rock of Gibraltar for all that is strong and enduring. Connie is pretty and contented. The eldest boy, Edward, is fourteen. He looks like his father, but in the middle of his chin there is a V-shaped cleft like Connie's. Maybe Grappy in heaven pressed it in the baby flesh with "Heigh-ho, your chin's startin' to split in two." Ruth is eleven, a feminized Norman, grave and sensible. Marian is eight, and is Connie all over again. Then there is Norman, Junior, five.

In the fifteen years since Norman and Connie were married they have built on a bedroom, put in a furnace, and bought a five-passenger car. Sometime, when they get money enough ahead, they are going to take a trip, although Connie tells the children not to count too much on it. In the meantime they read avidly, and in imagination climb the Alps and sail the Mediterranean. "So that when you do have a chance to go," their father tells them, "you will have something to take with you to the mountains and the sea."

Two years ago Grandfather Winters died. In a few days Connie got an imposing letter from a firm of attorneys. She was trembling so she could scarcely open it. Just a few thousand dollars from Grandfather Winters, relenting at her disobedience, and she could do so much for Norman and the children. She opened it. Her hope was as ashes in her mouth. Grandfather Winters had kept his word: "To my granddaughter, Constance Lee Winters Harper . . . one dollar."

Still later the dollar check itself came. Norman cashed it and brought it home to her. For a few minutes Connie held it in her hand, looking soberly at it. Then she threw back her head and laughed, that merry laugh which was like water bubbling upward. That afternoon she put some sandwiches in the picnic pail and she and the children went down the alley to the pasture where the children played. The pasture had been planted to alfalfa and the purple and lavender blossoms were thick in the lazy afternoon sunshine. A half-block away the children began to sniff the air, like coast folks do when coming home they first smell the salt wash of the sea. When they arrived Connie told them: "I have a new game for you. All turn your backs and shut your eyes."

When they had done so, she took Grandfather Winters's silver dollar out of her apron pocket and, standing on tiptoe, silently threw it far out into the alfalfa field. "Open your eyes," she said. "Now, this is the game: Out in the pasture is one of the most valuable things in the world. The game is to find it. Whatever seems most valuable to you, bring it in to me."

All the rest of the afternoon Connie put deft patches on the under side of a tablecloth. The children roamed about in the field that was like a lavender sea, their happy voices shrill with laughter. When the sun was slipping behind the Lombardy poplars she called them, "Time's up. Come in to base."

They came scurrying in, all wanting to talk at once, but Connie stopped them. "Edward is to tell first."

And Edward said: "I couldn't bring in the thing I thought was the most valuable. It's the elm in the middle of the pasture. It stands there so pretty, bowing and waving. It made me think of the verses Father read to us:

> Poems are made by fools like me,
> But only God can make a tree.

"Think of never having a nodding tree, Mother!"

"I couldn't bring mine, either," Ruth admitted. "Oh, I *could* have, but I didn't want to scare it. It's a little meadow lark in a nest on the ground. Think of never hearing a meadow lark sing, Mother!"

Marian threw back her head and let out a rippling crescendo of laughter.

"*I* could bring *mine,*" she chuckled. "It's *Baby.* It's fair too, isn't it, Mother; because he *was* out there and I think he's the most valuable thing in the world."

They all laughed with her, but there were tears in Connie's eyes. "Well, well!" she said to them. "Trees! Birds! Babies! What lovely, lovely things you found."

Then they ate their sandwiches. After that they trailed home, where Father was sitting on the porch, and saying, "I began to think you'd moved away."

After a time the alfalfa was cut and dried and hauled to the barn. The field was plowed, and Grandfather Winters's legacy was turned under the sod. But even though the rain fell and the sun shone on it, nothing ever came from it! *Not a green thing—nor a singing thing—nor a human soul.*

The Weakling

Some of the same characters who appear in "The Victory of Connie Lee" surfaced two years later in "The Weakling" (*The American Magazine,* February 1925). It is possible that Aldrich was testing the idea of Norman and Connie Harper as another series, going beyond the small children in the Mason stories and the older children in the Cutters to the logical next step of having a young adult family marriage series. She considered other series at various times.

The verbose judge whose character appeared in "The Light o' Day" (1916) and who later was one of the individuals in *Rim of the Prairie* (1925) appears here. The theme of this story emerged as a subplot in *Miss Bishop* (1933).

It was an early fall evening with a hint of frost in the air. Norman Harper had closed the outer door and remarked to Connie that perhaps he could get some reading done, now that the summer was leaving.

Someone knocked, timidly at first and then impatiently. Norman felt irritated that he was to be disturbed. That was the trouble with having close friends and neighbors, he was thinking, as he opened the door to find Sam Pendle there. Sam's thin, bony face looked white and drawn. He was breathing hard, partly from hurrying but more evidently from agitation.

"Can you come over to our house, Mr. Harper?" he wanted to know. "I'm in trouble, and I've got to have somebody to talk to."

Hatless, Norman stepped out on the porch and closed the door. "Is it your father, Sam?"

"No. Father's well. He's gone to Kenwood to look after a little place there and collect some rent. He won't be back until the morning train."

"What is it, then?" Norman felt impatience with this mild little man, who could keep him in suspense over a mere trifle.

"Just a minute, Mr. Harper. Wait until we get over home. I wouldn't want anybody to hear."

Together they crossed the street to the old house. As they stepped up on the porch it occurred to Norman that in all the time he had lived in Ourtown he had never been inside the Pendles' home before. All the talking they had done had been in the yard. In the house, everything was neat, but old. Norman had the feeling that the blue-flowered vase on the table and the silk afghan on the couch were in the same places the mother had left them, years before.

At the bay-window end of the room Sam turned, and whispered: "I've got a sick man here in Father's bedroom. He's very low. He's been here since yesterday." He crossed nervously to the doorway and held back a faded brown chenille portiere. Norman could hear labored breathing even before he saw the humped bulky form under the patchwork quilt.

Sam dropped the old curtain and came back on tiptoe. He raised miserable eyes to Norman. "It's my brother," he said simply; "it's Eugene." Norman, startled beyond coherent thought, could only stare at Sam.

"He wasn't burned to death," Sam said quietly. "He came back last night."

Involuntarily Norman's mind flashed back to the time of his arrival in Ourtown, years before, when he had married Connie. Judge Pendle and his son Sam lived across the street in a big frame house with wavy gingerbread scrollwork on the porches and a church-like cupola on one corner, like a stiff hat over one eye.

When the Harpers first came to Ourtown, old Judge Pendle and his son Sam lived there alone. To be sure, the judge presided over a mere justice court, but no Supreme Court judge of the United States ever looked the part so perfectly as he. Tall and stately, with graying side-whiskers and thick eyeglasses held with a long, flat black cord, the judge seemed clothed in pride, wrapped in formality. Connie Harper used to tell Myra Lawler, her next-door neighbor, that to see the judge leave the house and go stepping down Locust Street swinging his gold-headed cane was like seeing an ocean liner leave port.

To talk with Judge Pendle was to be overwhelmed with formal phrases. If he wanted to say that the weather was mild, he preferred to tell his hearers that there was a noticeable lack of inclemency in the activity of the elements. And he talked a great deal about the weather, seeming to have inside information, as though he and the weather man were in cahoots.

After the manner of small towns, the judge and Sam had called on Norman and Connie when the Harpers were first married. A half-hour of the visit was consumed by the judge in a long-winded summary of the year's weather.

"It was much this same type of autumn when my son met his untimely death," he finished ponderously.

Connie, who had lived in the community during her girlhood, knew the circumstances; but it was news to Norman, who inquired solicitously about it.

"My son Eugene," the judge explained. "Death claimed him in the hotel fire at Mount Milton, twenty-four years ago. Five lives were snuffed out at the same hour, Mr. Harper. Five lives went out to eternity, and my son was one of them. Just a young lad in his freshman college year. A bright, scholarly lad, he was, sir. I may even say brilliant. He was to have taken up study of the law. Quick, alert, and brainy, as he was, he would have gone very far in his profession. I think, Mr. Harper, he would have made of the law a thing of truth and beauty and justice." The old judge's bombastry was as apparent as ever, but less obnoxious now that he was revealing the sorrow of his life.

"Eugene and Sam were very different," he stated openly, with no apparent loathness to admit it before the living. "Eugene had none of Sam's backwardness and timidity."

Norman felt so embarrassed at the bald description that he could not meet Sam's eye. But Sam seemed to accept the statement as a matter of fact. He even added to it: "Yes, Gene would have been a big man. Even when he was a kid he was as smart as a whip."

In the year that followed, Norman Harper was to become very familiar with the story, for the judge scarcely ever failed to speak of his sorrow and disappointment.

Mrs. Pendle had died several years before Norman Harper knew the Pendles. She had slipped out as quietly and modestly as she had lived, a humble personality like a little pale moon which could reflect but dimly the bright rays of her husband's light. Sam was like his mother, and a great disappointment to the judge. He was forty-three, and still clerked in Hammond's Combined Grocery and Meat Market. Sometimes in a pinch he even drove the delivery cart. The candling of eggs, the fluctuating price of sugar, the arrival of the first muskmelons were the big things of life to him. The greatest event he had ever known was the leaving of the store in his charge one week while Mr. Hammond went away.

All this ran through Norman's mind in the brief space while Sam was dropping the curtain. He could think of no remark appropriate to this astounding circumstance.

"It was late in the evening when he came," Sam began again, nervously. "Father was over to Maxwells', playing chess with Joe. Someone came up to the side door and tapped. I went to the door, and this man"—Sam was still having hard work to believe the incredible—"stood there, and laughed kind of foolish. My first thought was that he had escaped from somewhere. . . . There was such a leer on his face. Then he said, with that same foolish grin: 'I guess you don't know me. I know you, though, Sam. I'm Gene.'

"It was horrible. I was terribly frightened. It was like the nightmare. I wanted to call somebody, and couldn't speak. I wanted to go and get somebody, and I couldn't move." He looked up apologetically at Norman, and then took up the thread of his story.

"We both stood there a minute, and then he said: 'I guess you thought that night of the hotel fire I got my everlasting. Well, I never. I just slipped out to see the world a bit!' Then he stopped, and that foolish grin—like he wasn't right, you know—left him, and a sober look came over his face, sane, but bitter and terrible, and he said: 'Well, I've seen it, all right.' My God, Mr. Harper!" Sam burst forth, "he *has* seen it—the *under* side of the worst side."

For a moment the muscles of Sam's thin throat worked convulsively, and then he spoke quietly: "Gene stood still there outside the door, and I not moving, either. Then he went on: 'I hated school and the thought of a law course, but Father was so set on it and was so domineering. . . . I knew that that fire gave me the only chance I'd ever have to get away, and I just slipped out in the excitement.' Think of it, Mr. Harper,"—Sam raised an agonized face—"think of the selfishness of doing that to my father and mother!"

Norman, too deeply moved to answer, merely waited for Sam to go on: "Then Gene said: 'I meant to come back in just a few months and surprise them, after I'd had a little trip. I got passage for Hong Kong on a freighter and then, when I got there—' He just mumbled something about a Chinese girl, and some more that I didn't catch. I hadn't said a word yet. All I could do was to stand and stare. And then he asked: 'Are my father and mother—?'

"Then he sort of put both hands out on the door jamb and crumpled down. It was terrible getting him in. He's huge . . . a big, bloated, unhealthy hugeness. I pulled him into the sitting-room and tried and tried to get him up on the couch. I could see he wasn't dead—just unconscious. And all the time I kept thinking how Father would come home in a few minutes. Over and over in my mind kept going the thought of Father's pride in Gene.

"There wasn't any time left to hesitate. And quick—like that—" Sam gave his thin fingers a snap, "I decided to lie to Father. Lies don't come easy if you aren't used to them, Mr. Harper." He said it as naïvely as a child. "But now I knew I'd have to lie or else kill Father. And I owed it to Father. He—Gene—looked pretty near gone. I figured that if he came to and talked, I'd just pretend it was news to me, too. But he hasn't been conscious once. He talks sometimes, but it's disconnected ravings . . . just rambling things. Sometimes he thinks he's in Shanghai. Oh, you wouldn't want to hear him, Mr. Harper . . . awful stuff. But sometimes"—Sam's voice broke throatily—"sometimes he thinks he's a boy, coasting down Anderson's hill!"

For a minute Sam fumbled with the old blue vase on the table, and then he spoke again: "I couldn't think of getting him up-stairs, so I had to put him in Father's bedroom. I got Doc Sutherland, but I didn't tell him. You're the one I thought of to talk to. There's something about you that made me feel it would be safe with you.

"Father came home," the low voice went on. "He was annoyed by it. Scolded some for putting a tramp in his bedroom. Said I'd have him dead on my hands, and that if I'd had any backbone I'd have called the authorities the first thing. I've always been honest with Father, and it took all my strength of will to carry the lie through. When he said this morning that he'd have gone to Kenwood to-day if it hadn't been for this sick man here, I told him to go ahead. I felt so relieved and thankful. When he wavered about going, I could hardly stand it. But he went. I've prayed that Gene won't ever regain consciousness. To have him come to, and tell! Think how it would kill Father's dream of him . . . all his old pride in him."

When Norman nodded in affirmation, Sam said: "Gene won't last till morning. Doc's coming back. When he passes away I've got to carry the thing through. He can't be buried in our lot. Mother would want him over next to her. But then, there's Father?" He put it as a question, but his decision was his own: "No, I've thought it all out. He's got to stay just a stray bum that asked for his supper . . . name unknown . . . until after Father passes away. Then, if I out-live Father, I'll have him taken up and put in our lot, and tell folks."

Norman found his voice: "You're doing a big thing, Sam, a mighty big thing. Your father hasn't always—" Then he stopped, annoyed that he had said it.

Keen, sensitive, Sam looked up. "Yes, I know. He hasn't thought I've amounted to anything. Well, I haven't. You'll have to admit that yourself, Mr. Harper. Gene would have been—" He stopped. The old familiar phrase died away on his lips, and he changed it apologetically: "If he'd gone straight, Gene would have been a great man."

Now that the long-silent Sam had made a confidant of Norman, the floodgates of his heart seemed opened: "I know I've been a disappointment to Father. I've never amounted to much, but he's expected *that* all his life. It's no great shock to him, but *this*—" he motioned toward the old portière—"this would kill him!"

To Norman came a sudden illuminating idea. It flashed through his mind simultaneously with Sam's remark: "He's expected *that* all his life." It opened up a long train of thought. To what extent had this parent made of his son the thing he was? He gave words to the thought: "Sam, I believe all this backwardness and timidity and disbelief in yourself is your own father's fault. He should have had more faith in you."

"Do you think so?" Sam asked, half doubtfully. "I can't put in language what I feel, but if somebody long ago had helped me, I believe I'd have been like other boys. I was born that way—afraid to do things—like Mother. She always seemed helpless. All through my boyhood Father didn't seem to expect much of me. When I was in my twenties—nobody knows this, Mr. Harper—but I—I admired Myra Lawler very much. I said something to Father about it, and he said, 'Sam, she wouldn't look at you.' "

The doctor came. Norman telephoned Connie that he wouldn't be home. He felt very tender toward Sam.

It was just past midnight when the man died.

The judge came in on the morning train. Sam, pale but steady, met his father at the door. Only his lips trembled a little: "Father . . . the man . . . the man is dead."

The old judge was pompous and fussy: "Well, well! We all come to it. The stream of humanity flows even onward to eternity. Poor wayfarer. Somebody thought a great deal of him once."

His verbosity was very hard on Sam. And it was when the judge went into the bedroom that Sam prayed he would not recognize his son. If it had been the mother she would have seen traces of the boyish features looking out of the bloated, disease-marked face; but the old judge, nearsighted at best and wrapped in his cloak of memories, saw nothing.

There were formalities to attend to. Norman, in his sympathy, helped all that he could. Sam wanted one of the church quartets to sing at the grave, but the tenor was busy and the soprano had a cold. Only a few people stood through the short service, which was held on the side of the barbed-wire fence where the sleepers have left no fund for the upkeep of their homes. The tall dry grass rubbed brittle stems together in the wind. Grasshoppers thumped heavily on the plain black box. The minister prayed for the soul of the dead. But Norman prayed for the heart of the living.

By pressing his lips tightly together, Sam got through the ordeal bravely enough. He held himself erect, a thin little person in an ill-fitting suit. It was only when they were leaving that he broke down for just a moment. When Norman held the barbed-wire apart for him, "My God, Mr. Harper," he whispered, "we used to go fishing together down in Elderberry Creek . . . and we had a menagerie rigged up in the old carriage house."

In the days that followed, Norman often saw Sam with his father walking about the old yard or caring for the flowers. Once Norman went over to talk with them. After the weather had been disposed of, the judge said:

"Sam seems not to be in the highest degree of spirits. His appetite is not hearty. That stranger passing away here at our home had its influence. That's one thing we will have to admit about Sam. He is tender-hearted. Eugene, now, was not exactly tender-hearted. Harder, perhaps, but brilliant. If he had been spared he would to-day have been a famous man, Mr. Harper; a famous man well on in a brilliant career."

Sam raised understanding eyes to Norman. They glowed with light. They gleamed with unspoken pleasure. They said, "See! Because of me he has kept his dream." After all, why feel sorry for Sam? It had been the big adventure of his life.

And then the old judge died. Suddenly, pompously, spectacularly, in front of the courthouse. Sam grieved for him. "Not many boys had a fine father like mine," he told everyone. The Sunday after his burial Sam went out to the cemetery with flowers. He put some on his father's and mother's graves, and then slipped through the rusty barbed-wire into the tangled woodbine patch and put the rest there. For a long time he stood there and pondered what to do. Responsibility sat heavily upon Sam.

"I can't bring myself to decide," he told Norman. "Mother would want

Gene over close to her. But Father—you know how proud he was of Gene, and his pride seems still to live. Seems like it would hurt Father yet to have folks know."

"I'd let things be just as they are, Sam," Norman advised. "In the last analysis it doesn't make much difference *where* one sleeps, does it?"

There was a small insurance and the sale of the little house in Kenwood brought some money. It was then that Mr. Hammond, the grocer, surprised Sam by asking him if he would put the money into the business. Sam was excited beyond measure. "Only, he wants to retain the old name just as it is," he told Norman that noon. "That's all right too, you know, Mr. Harper. I wouldn't need my name up on the sign."

A sudden illuminating purpose struck Norman. He put it into action: "Sam, the time has come for a showdown with yourself. Hammond needs money and you have some. You know just as much about the grocery business as he does, don't you? All right. You go back to Hammond now, *this noon,* and you say: "We'll go into this right, Jim, or we won't go at all. Hammond and Pendle is the new firm name—equal shares—equal responsibilities—equal dividends—or I'll start a store across the street. You know what trade I'll get—Harpers, Lawlers, all my old neighbors from my part of town.'

"Assert yourself, Sam. You're only forty-three. That's not old. You've got years before you. I could name a dozen men who have tackled new problems at your age. If you fight this out with Hammond it will be the turning-point of your life. If you win, come back and tell me, and I'll advise you in your next move. If you don't, you needn't come to me. I'll know you are whipped. It's up to you, Sam."

Sam Pendle looked for a moment at his neighbor, then turned without a word and walked swiftly to the store. There was elasticity in his step, fire in his mild eyes, purpose in his heart. So surprised was Jim Hammond at the onslaught that almost before he realized it he had a full-fledged partner on his hands.

"And what was the other thing you spoke about?" Sam wanted to know, when he had returned to Norman.

"Now go over to Myra Lawler and ask her to marry you."

Sam flushed painfully, "I had intended to do that," he said quietly.

To the casual observer he was but an uninteresting little figure, this young-old boy of forty-three. Only to those who can see with the eyes of their hearts would Sam have appeared heroic, marching courageously over to Myra Lawler's on a late Monday afternoon.

Myra was sprinkling clothes when Sam walked in. He beat around no bushes. He went straight to the soul of the thing. "Myra," he said simply, "I've loved you for a long, long time. I came over to ask you to marry me."

Myra Lawler neither answered him nor evinced surprise. She dropped her head down among the clothes, which rattled starchily on the old kitchen table. Sam was alarmed. She was angry then! He might have known. His father had been right. Myra would not look at him. Sam's new-found strength was oozing. He walked over to her and laid a tender, clumsy hand on her soft brown hair.

"I've frightened you, Myra." He was very gentle. "I'm more sorry than I can tell."

Myra Lawler raised her head from the stiff banks of snow whiteness. "Oh, Sam," she said . . . "the *years* we've wasted!"

When Sam, shining-eyed and self-confident, stopped in to tell Norman about it, Norman asked him to stay to supper. That, too, was quite an event—eating in a neighbor's house. When he had gone, Connie said: "Norman, I'm willing to cream potatoes and make chicken sandwiches for Sam Pendle whenever you say so, but he's such a nonentity. What*ever* do you *see* in him?"

Norman put his hand under Connie's chin and tilted it upward. "Sometimes," he said gently, "I used to see a man who had failed. But lately," he added, "I see Saint Stephen, who was stoned."

And Myra and Sam in their belated romance went to live in the big frame house with its foolish scrollwork. Only they do not think it is foolish. They think it is quite artistic. And Sam Pendle has made himself one of the substantial men of Ourtown.

The Woman Who Was Forgotten

Shortly after this story was published in *The American Magazine* (June 1926), the National Education Association wrote Aldrich requesting permission, which she granted, to publish it in their journal. The story was also made into a movie of the same name; in the contract for the movie, Aldrich required that a portion of the proceeds go to fund homes for retired teachers in Washington DC. Still later, as a warning about the dangers of not planning for retirement years, the story was purchased by an insurance company as an advertising vehicle.

There are strong similarities between this story and *Miss Bishop*, although Aldrich claimed they were two distinct stories as this teacher was less hopeful than Miss Bishop. However, the similarities are pervasive: the building to be torn down, the finances, the conclusion.

The ceremony at the end of the story was reenacted for Aldrich's cousin in 1932, six years after publication of "The Woman Who Was Forgotten." The cousin, Miss Louise Barrett, was being honored for teaching for fifty-two years at Whittier School in Brainerd, Minnesota. While Aldrich claimed she never used one specific person but an amalgam of many individuals in her stories, Miss Barrett is probably the closest single model for *Miss Bishop*, for the two cousins, though a generation apart, corresponded and knew each other well.

The occasional use of "Whittier School" in this and other stories is a kind of private greeting from Aldrich to Miss Barrett.

Miss Miller sat on the porch of her little cottage in the soft June dusk. Miss Miller had a given name, but no one ever used it. In spite of the fact that there were a half-dozen others entitled to the same cognomen, she alone was "Miss Miller" to the entire town. Miss Miller, who had come from the East to this Midwest state in her young womanhood, had been principal of the high school for years upon years. And now she was old, with not much to show for those years of service to the community. Service is not a substance. It is immaterial, a disembodied thing. You cannot see it, nor show it to your friends, nor put it in the bank. Because this is true, Miss Miller, sitting in the lush warmth of the new-summer evening, faced The Visitor. Naturally cheerful and optimistic, she had avoided it hitherto. If it had been just Old Age she could have gone out to meet it with cheery greeting. But it was harsher—*Dependent* Old Age. It is a cruel guest.

A year had gone by since Miss Miller resigned her position. Voluntarily she had given up her work, to forestall any possible action of the school board. Like a surgeon she had operated. Never must anyone say that she had stayed too long, outgrown her usefulness. The phase of the affair which hurt was the agility with which the board had accepted the resignation. They must have been waiting for it. With hurt pride she had packed her household things, rented her cottage, and gone back East to live for a time with a married niece. Because she had helped the niece through college, she carried in the secret place of her heart, like an unborn hope, the thought that the niece would want her to remain for the rest of her life.

By a system of arithmetic as old as the science itself she had worked her problem. It was very simple: a fourth-grade child could have done it. The sum of money in the bank, plus that which would come from the sale of the cottage, made the dividend. The possible number of years which she might live became the rather pathetic divisor. The quotient resulted in a yearly sum which, with good judgment, would cover all her expenses, independent of the niece.

But inherent caution and good sense had caused her to rent her cottage until she could try out the visit. It was well that she had done so, for although the relative's roof was fully forty feet by fifty-eight, it had not seemed quite large enough for her.

The niece had been kind—but the husband, and the children! Miss Miller's sensitive soul shrank from the intrusion which she felt she made. So she had come back to the Midwest town which had seen the work of her life. After all, it was home.

To-day she had finished settling. The old furnishings seemed cordial and friendly. She had a foolish notion that they were glad to see her. Well, she would not leave them again. All day she had been settling them in their accustomed places. It had taken a long time to put the books on the shelves, for she had visited for a few moments with each one. The Shakespeare set, a geometry textbook, the orations of Cicero. The Latin grammar had fallen open at "*amo, amas, amat, amamus, amatis, amant.*" She smiled at the thought of the yearly struggle she had had with the freshmen to keep them from sing-songing it.

And now to-night everything was in order, and Miss Miller sat and faced The Thing. It seemed to have developed horns and cloven hoofs, to have taken on a demonlike leer. For the first time she felt genuine panic. If only she might have her old position back. She was not ill, not even so tired, since the year away. Not a faculty was impaired. To slip back into the old groove would not be at all hard. But to start in another town under new conditions seemed to her almost impossible.

Hitherto she had brushed away all cobwebby troubles with a broom of sane philosophy. But all her keen intelligence, all her humor and brave spirit, could not hide The Thing which stood before her to-night. As she faced the future, she told herself that there was one final sanctuary open to her when the time came—the old people's home which her church supported. She had visited it once.

A cold hand seemed closing around her heart as she recalled the visit. The home had been pleasant and comfortable; but the old ladies sitting on the porch aimlessly watching the world go by were alien souls, women from whom the glow of living had departed. Two of them had been having a long and tiresome argument over their knitting. Miss Miller laughed a little to herself. At least, if she had to go there eventually she would find plenty of things to amuse her. Pathetic rôles were not meant for her.

Over and over in the deepening dusk she worked on the problem of her life. If she sold her house, she would have nowhere to go. If she retained it, she would not have money enough to keep her many years. She might do private tutoring, take a roomer or two. Again and again, with sweet courage, she tried to work her problem—so much harder than algebra. "Let x equal the unknown quantity," she said bravely to herself. But there was no answer in the back of the book or anywhere. Not until God closed the book would she find what x equaled.

A little boy came running around the corner of the porch with the evening paper. Breathlessly he explained his tardiness: how the cow got out and they had to catch her before he could start with his papers. Miss Miller made a sympathetic comment. She had always been fair with children. She took the paper, went inside, and turned on the light. In a big chair beside her library table she settled herself and looked at the front page. In big black headlines it called to her:

Old High School to be Razed
Work Begins June Tenth

And then, because the editor was an alumnus, the third line said quite simply:

"Old School, Hail and Farewell!"

It affected her unaccountably, this coincidence of the building and her own life. They were both through, she and the old school, both to be torn down. If Miss Miller sat idly for a long time, let no one enter into the hushed aisle of her thoughts.

After a time she rose with that energetic birdlike movement which characterized her motions, got her knitted white shawl from the closet, and went out of the back door.

Down the walk she passed through a little gate in the rear of the yard and turned down the alley to Mr. Larson's home. That is what she had called him, in dignified courtesy, for all the years that he had been janitor of the high school: Mr. Larson, instead of Chris.

Old Chris was sitting near the back steps with his feet in the cool, dewy grass. He was tipped back in a kitchen chair against the side of the house, a sooty old pipe in his mouth. Seeing Miss Miller, he dropped his chair down on its natural legs, surreptitiously slipped the pipe into the grass, and curled his blue and white socks under his chair. That was the way Miss Miller had affected him for several decades. Jim Larson was there too, with his father. Jim had been one of Miss Miller's high-school boys, one of the few that she never seemed able to get hold of. A taciturn, gloomy-acting boy he had been, with no kindling response to her overtures of friendship. She had done her best to draw him out, but he had graduated with apparently no attachment for her. He had a wife now and two babies, and a harness shop.

"Mr. Larson, I saw by the paper to-night that the old building is to be torn down." Miss Miller had to make an effort to keep her voice steady. She had not realized that it was meaning so much to her.

"Yes; they'll begin the tenth, I see." Old Chris made signs to Jim to bring out another chair for the caller. Even if he retained his own seat, Old Chris knew enough to provide another.

"You still have the key, I suppose, Mr. Larson?"

Old Chris nodded. "Yes, ma'am," he added.

"I wonder if you would let me take it the evening of the ninth . . . that last night before they begin to demolish the building. I'd just like to go over the old place for the last time with a sort of—'We who are about to die, salute you!'" Old Chris had never heard of the *Morituri Salutamus,* but he recognized the emotion in Miss Miller's voice.

"You two men will laugh at me for being so sentimental?" Miss Miller questioned apologetically.

"I won't laugh at you." Old Chris, at the risk of a conflagration in his thick woolen sock, pushed his pipe farther under the chair. "It's got me a-feelin' blue a'ready."

Before the two had finished talking Jim Larson left. "He doesn't want to visit with me," Miss Miller thought; "I never got hold of Jim."

There was a little more conversation relative to the school board's plans, and then Miss Miller left with, "Good-night, Mr. Larson, and thank you. I'll come for the key, so if you see someone prowling around the old building don't shoot or call out the constable."

All week the old teacher went about her simple household tasks with something hanging over her. It was as though she had a meeting with a friend or a tryst with a lover, a little like a rendezvous with death.

The evening of the ninth was beautiful. As she stopped for the key, old Chris said, "Well, to-morrow is the day they begin. Sort o' sad, ain't it, Miss Miller?"

There was a moon and the heavy scent of syringa, a warm breeze, and crimson ramblers. It had the smell and feel of old commencements.

At the school grounds Miss Miller went up the broad front walk, worn with the steps of a thousand youthful feet. In the moonlight all discrepancies in the old building were hidden. One could not see the cracks in the brick nor the settling window frames nor the sagging steps. It looked sturdy, unyielding. It seemed to be holding up its head proudly. Like Miss Miller!

She turned the key and pushed the huge iron latch which had clicked to three generations. Softly she stepped into the shadows of the lower hall. It was warm and friendly, as though it welcomed her home. She crossed the room and mounted the stairs, her hand slipping along the banister, as smooth as old ivory from the polishing of countless human palms.

Straight to the main study hall she passed—a huge room with row upon row of seats half in the moonlight and half in the shadow. Her eyes took in the familiar bookcases along one side, the dictionary stand in the corner, and the big desk on a raised platform in front, with the straight-backed chair behind it. Toward the front of the room Miss Miller walked softly, as people do in the presence of the dead.

A composite picture of all the schools seemed before her. Personalities looked at her from every seat, but Miss Miller did not realize that in point of time they were sometimes twenty-five years apart. There sat Mart Richardson, mischievous, indolent, even stupid in the things he did not like. Mart Richardson was a banker now, heavy-set and opulent . . . *her* banker, who knew her small bank account to its last cent. There was Annie Grayson's seat; Annie was a missionary in China now. Over there had sat "Red" Hamilton; "Red" was a member of the legislature, slated for Congress by his party. Here sat laughing Nan Buskirk, a happy wife and mother. Their old teacher summoned them back, not grown nor successful, but young and needing her.

Slowly she circled the room, recalling a hundred events, funny, exciting, or serious. Then she turned toward an inner room, opened the door and stepped into her own office. Once it had been her Gethsemane: One day she had gone in there full of happiness and the joy of living, engaged to be married. The superintendent had come in to her with drawn face, and told her the heart-tearing contents of the telegram he was bringing. When she came out, some of her had died. The part that lived she had dedicated to her boys and girls, warming her heart at the fire of their youth, putting into her work all the love and interest she would have given to a husband and home.

Miss Miller crossed the little room, opened the one window and sat down by it. The June breeze, sweet with the smell of flowering things, came in and lifted the tendrils of her gray hair.

Memory went over the road of the years.

After a time she summed them up—the results of the journey. Foolishly she had thought the love and admiration of her boys and girls would compensate for all her devotion. But one could not eat past love nor clothe her declining years in ancient admiration. For the first time bitterness assailed her. It was not right, not just, to give all and receive nothing. She had been a fool to think that if she gave her best, the knowledge of service rendered would be its own reward.

Across the street and a block down, some evening social affair was in progress. A dozen cars were gathered at the curbing, and the sound of high gay voices came from across the way. She was left out of even those events now. She had returned from the East, and only a neighbor or two had noticed. She had not been in a pupil's home for a long time. They had forgotten her. Slow tears came, the more painful, because she had hitherto met life with high hope, deep courage, broad faith.

Miss Miller raised her face to the June sky as though to hold intimate converse with someone. How foolish she had been to think that by binding herself to Youth she could hold her own light spirits. That early dedication of hers to the lives of her pupils was all Quixotic. That old idea of carrying a torch ahead to show them the way to unrevealed truths was all wasted effort.

Not only had she dedicated her life to high-school boys and girls, but also specifically to the ones of this community. Several times when she had thought to go to a larger city the junior class had prevailed upon her to stay. "Just to see us graduate," they had pleaded, and she had been weak, soft, yielding like a mother who could not forsake a younger child. Every waking thought she had given to her pupils. There were teachers who heard lessons, and then left their responsibility, like a raincoat, hanging in the hall. She had not been able to do that.

It had told on her, too. One cannot expend such energy and not age. Service, like sorrow, may beautify only the heart not the face of a woman. She had given the best that was in her, not only that their minds should unfold, but for those other sides of their lives—the physical and moral. Strained eyes in a pupil—and she had not rested until the matter was rectified. Recurring headaches—and she had not known peace until the source was traced. And then that other thing, that elusive thing which was neither all physical nor all moral, the attachment of one for another. How she had pondered over it, questioned and advised. Many a mother, less motherly than herself, had either not sensed the danger or, having seen, had lifted no hand to guide. All this she had done for her boys and girls. And what was her reward? Poverty and loneliness. Tears came once more. Some were for her own lost youth and some were for shattered faith in humanity.

Suddenly, in a great whirl of beating wings, a mass of pigeons flew from the bell tower, their bodies almost brushing the window. And then, quite plainly, the bell tapped. Miss Miller heard it, distinctly, a long, low, resonant sound.

Startled, she jumped and looked furtively behind her. She had that queer suffocating feeling that one has when he is conscious of a presence near. For the first time she felt a creepy, frightened sensation. Her heart was pounding madly. All at once the building was cold and forbidding. It was as though there were soft footfalls, phantom whisperings. The ghosts of all her yesterdays seemed haunting the place. Was her brain addled? Had she played too long with her memories? All her poise was gone. She wanted to fly as from a tomb.

It seemed now almost a physical impossibility for her to return through that huge shadow-laden study hall. But there was no other way of egress. She must gather herself together.

With sheer will-power she made herself cross the office to the door. They came again—those eerie rustlings, low murmurs, faint, mocking laughter. There even seemed a far-away uncanny chant of "*amo, amas, amat, amamus, amatis, amant.*" The bell tapped again, low, reverberating. The pigeons swirled past the window. With an effort Miss Miller swung open the door.

If the room was full of memories they were substantial ones. If it harbored only dreams, they were materialized. In the moonlight she could see that the seats were full of people. The tops of the desks supported some. Others crowded the aisles. Several layers were banking themselves around the walls.

"*Amo, amas, amat,*" they chanted; "*amamus, amatis, amant.*" Then there was laughter, high and excited. Someone said, "Oh, don't *frighten* her." And someone else said, "Turn on the lights, Mart."

Blinding lights flashed on. Miss Miller blinked a moment before she could distinguish the countenances. And then—they were as familiar as the faces of children to a mother.

Miss Miller gasped, "Why, boys and girls, what *is* it?" She reached out for something to steady herself and caught at the chair behind the desk. Wide-eyed, she slipped into it and gazed questioningly at the sea of faces.

The laughing, buzzing crowd ceased its noise, for someone was raising his hand. It was "Red" Hamilton, sitting in his old seat and snapping his fingers. "Miss Miller, please may I speak?"

Everyone giggled nervously. But it was the Hon. A. J. Hamilton who arose and stood by the side of the seat:

"Years ago to many of us, more recently to others," his smooth, pleasant voice began, "we had a loved teacher who gave the very best that was in her that we might become good men and women. Many times after leaving her we said, 'Some day we will send her a box of flowers.' . . . 'To-morrow we will write her a letter.' . . . 'Soon we will go to see her.' But Time sped by on silver wings, and all the to-morrows became the yesterdays.

"So to-night we have put those promises to ourselves into action. All that is dross in us has melted away. All that is weak has been left behind. Only that which is best in us has come back to pay her homage. My mind is crowded with a hundred things she did for us, things that came to us forcibly only in years after, when lighted by the experiences of our own parenthood: the way she looked after our bodies as well as our minds, the manner in which she helped us and advised us in our small troubles, the way she increased our capacity for the enjoyment of good reading, her Shakespeare class, which inculcated in us an undying love for the greatest of bards. I have heard the lovely throaty voice of Ethel Barrymore, and the liquid, melting tones of Julia Marlowe, but never have I heard them read with more depth of feeling that her own:

"Good night, good night! As sweet repose and rest
Come to thy heart as that within my breast."

He dropped the third person and turned to the little lady on the platform:

"Miss Miller, all the things that you did for us will never be known. They cannot be counted, nor measured, nor weighed. And because this is so, we have come back to-night to tell you that many times in the midst of the world's work we think of you, that we appreciate you, that as long as life lasts we will love you."

When he sat down, Miss Miller half started from the chair. But there was no opening for her to speak: another hand was swinging in midair. It was Mart Richardson, president of the First National Bank. With a great creaking of the desk he succeeded in pulling his bulk from it and rose.

"I'm no speechmaker like Red here," he began jerkily. "But down at my place of business we handle something that speaks louder than words, something that really talks. Now, Miss Miller, years ago you used to make out our report cards, and have us take them home to our folks to sign. I'm not mentioning the time you mailed mine to my father all year instead of giving it to me, having a sort of foolish notion that Uncle Sam would deliver it more safely than I would."

There was a general laugh, and the banker resumed: "What I'm trying to say is that turn about is fair play. Each class you graduated has a report card ready for you to sign. Each class has given you a grade and, just like our old cards, they have to be signed on the back and returned. You sign these on the back, Miss Miller, and return them to my bank to-morrow morning. . . . All right, now. Roll call. Class of '88."

A middle-aged farmer squeezed out from the crowd around the wall, came forward and dropped the "report card" into Miss Miller's lap. It was an oblong piece of paper, thin and white. In the upper right-hand corner a number in three figures kept close company to a dollar sign.

"Class of '89!"

A pleasant-faced woman rose from a front seat and laid another piece of paper in her old teacher's lap.

"Class of '90!"

A. J. Hamilton went forward with the gift of his class. And each class, on to the last one Miss Miller had graduated, continued the little ceremony. Thirty-six checks lay in Miss Miller's lap—three dozen white messengers of love.

"Now, Miss Miller,"— Mart Richardson had more to say—"we wanted to give you something, tried to think what you would like best. You know people have to let out their feelings in presents. The boys wanted to buy up all the flowers in town, and the girls wanted to get all the candy. But we finally decided we'd just give you the money and let you make your own choice. You know, even the wise men brought gifts of gold. And I say that's where they were wise." There was a general laugh, and then the banker continued: "But don't think for a minute that mere dollars and cents can ever—can ever—"

Something was going wrong with the fat speaker. His voice broke, but he rallied his forces: "Why, when I think of all you've done for this community—I—I—" He ran his fingers through his hair in an impatient gesture, and then finished lamely, "Oh, pshaw! I might have known better than to try to make a speech. Let's open the baskets now and eat."

There was another laugh. But someone else had risen and was calling out, "Just a minute. Before we eat let's give a vote of thanks to Jim Larson for getting us stirred up. There isn't one of us but was anxious to do something for you, Miss Miller; but it took Jim to have enough gumption to get us started. I know that he took several days from his business to go to every member of the alumni in town, talk over the 'phone to those in the country, and write a lot of letters."

Jim! A great warmth flooded Miss Miller. Jim Larson, whom she had never been able to get hold of!

They did not ask Miss Miller to speak. For that she was very grateful. The baskets were opened and the picnic feast spread in the gymnasium. There were a great many foolish pranks. Someone drew cartoons of all his classmates, and someone else got out the old physiology skeleton. Eternal Age, pretending that there is no age! And Old Chris rang the bell for the last time . . . the tolling of the death of the building.

But it was when they were ready to go that the last drop was poured into Miss Miller's overrunning chalice. It was A. J. Hamilton who broached it:

"A few of us have just been wondering if you couldn't come back into high school next year, not for the principalship but just for the English work. You see, I'd rather you'd teach my girl what good literature is than anybody else I know. We thought maybe you'd consider it, seeing you seem so much better than when you went away."

"Why, yes, Red,"—Miss Miller flushed with the joy of it—"I could. I feel fine. I feel as well as I *ever* did."

Then they left, group by group. Miss Miller had a dozen dinner dates. Not that old indefinite, "Come to see me some time, Miss Miller," but "Tomorrow night at six" and "Next Friday, on the baby's birthday."

Every group put the same question, "Are you ready now? We'll take you home?" And as many times she answered, "Thank you. I'm not just ready."

Even when the last group asked her, the answer was the same. It was a woman who intuitively sensed it. "Come on," she whispered. "Can't you see? She *wants* to be left behind."

Down in the lower hall Miss Miller waited. Erect and smiling, she bade them all good night. Like a mother she stood, watching the last child break the tie which held it to home. Then she stepped back and climbed the stairs to the study hall.

Through the moonlit room she walked quickly, definitely, like one with a duty before her. Behind the desk she stepped as though having a sacred rite to perform. She picked up a piece of chalk, and on the blackboard, which tomorrow and other morrows would no longer be there, she wrote:

For life is the mirror of king and slave,
'Tis just what we are and do;
Then give to the world the best you have
And the best will come back to you.

Then Miss Miller walked firmly down to the lower hall, passed out of the big worn door and turned the key under the latch that had clicked to a thousand youthful hands.

I Remember

In 1949 Aldrich expanded "I Remember" into a chapter for the 1949 *Journey into Christmas.* It is the closest she comes to writing a biography, although snippets of her life appear in such articles as "How I Mixed Stories with Doughnuts" and "Why I Live in a Small Town." However, in this *McCall's* article of November 1926, Aldrich does not go beyond vignettes of her childhood memories.

This is not a story. It is a journey into the past. . . . a trip across the smiling meadow which leads to the childhood of a little girl in the late eighties. It is a group of simple childish memories in no way related to each other. I shall pick them up as one picks eggs out of a basket . . . this one . . . and this one . . . and this . . .

It has only one object: to make you, too, remember, and with that remembrance perhaps again deepen your sympathy for childhood's vagaries and renew your understanding of childhood's queer mental processes.

The mind of a child is a curious country. It has not the landscape gardening in it of our mature years, laid out with parallel walks of acquired truths which lead between symmetrical beds of right and wrong. Parts of it are unexplored. Wild things grow there. It has wandering by-paths of queer mental processes and curious caves where the heart of the child sometimes hides, lonely and frightened. I do not claim that I can quite clearly solve the problems of my children by these little experiences of mine. But I do know, that because I can look back and remember strange thoughts and peculiar fancies that my offspring too, must encounter strange thoughts and peculiar fancies even if these are not identical with my own.

In many of these little incidents I can remember the beginning and the end. In some I can not do so. The beginning is lost out of memory or the ending has faded from mind, and only a remnant of the happening stands out in colors. Why has the beginning faded or the ending grown dim? I do not know.

The most striking half-memory that I retain is the picture of a house at the end of a long green path or grassy lane with bushes on each side. By the side of the house I can see a great many flowers and vines over a lattice work. I seem to have been hunting for the place and in the picture I am running up the path, half afraid and rather tired. My mother, who has been stooping over the flowers, rises and turns to me, saying in a tone which savors both of relief and expectancy. "Oh, here you are. I've been looking for you." This memory is so plain and yet so disconnected with definite time or place that often during my mother's life I asked her if she could not help decipher the puzzle. I wanted to associate it with an actual locality. It almost worried me that I could never remember where it had been. Occasionally we discussed it as gravely as though it were of vital importance. Was it at Grandmother Anderson's? No, because the path at Grandmother's curved around the house, and this was a straight lane. Was it up at Aunt Sarah's? No, because she had an open stretch of lawn, and this had lilacs and snowballs beside the path. Was it at Uncle Tom's? No, because he had no porch, only a stoop. Perhaps it was a dream. No, the dreams of my life are but shadows beside this definite memory. So it remains . . . little half-memory with no beginning and no end!

I was the child of mature parents. My father was fifty-four and my mother forty-five when I was born. Because my parents were of such mature age and had grown and growing children I had a great many bosses. Certain rare advantages attend such an administration. One can always with impunity tell some of the members of the family that various other members have given their permission to do certain things. So I grew up among older people, reading, dreaming, fancifying, singularly free from care or responsibility.

Our home was plain and comfortable. Three times additions had been built on to it like so many post-scripts to a letter. Its design was not catalogued in any architectural book. It had stoves and lamps. The furniture was substantial and unmatched, a chair being a thing to sit upon and not a Louis-something *objet d'art.* On the floors were sale carpets which had to be taken up every spring and fall, beaten almost thread-bare, and put down again over a layer of newspapers and a load of fresh straw. Half the family crawled along one side of the room and pulled and stretched and tacked while the other half smoothed straw down so that the result would not be so Rocky Mountain–like as the year before. There was a high-topped buggy in the barn and a cutter with a soap-stone in it, and a fat lazy horse that my father thought too rampageous for any of the women folks to drive. There were a great many relatives always coming and going. There was a great deal of talk and laughter and fun. And that for which I am most grateful . . . there were a great many books there. The characters in those books were as close and friendly and well known to me as the neighbors. Once my mother took a half-read book away from me. It was one of the few things she ever did which I think was not sensible. It was Oliver Wendell Holmes' *Elsie Venner.* So active was my imagination that I mentally constructed the rest of the story for myself with far more disastrous results through this change of authors than if I could have read the original. I might keep a book from a child but never would I take away a half-finished one.

My parents had come into Iowa as pioneers before their marriage, Mother at eighteen with her family, and Father two years before that. Mother drove a team all the way out from Illinois, crossing the Mississippi on the ferry. She used to tell me how her wagon tipped over as she was driving up the bank of a steep creek bed, how the goose feather pillows all went floating down stream, about her consternation when the precious sacks of flour tumbled into the water and the subsequent relief at finding the water had made a thin-walled casing of paste and left the flour unharmed. Father and Mother were married in the largest log cabin in the settlement, but the furniture had to be set out in the yard to make room for the guests. When the time for the ceremony arrived Mother came down a ladder, backward, from the loft, but to offset this discrepancy she had a white dress which had been brought out from the village of Chicago, another dress of plaid silk and a white silk shawl—a most elaborate trousseau.

My people have told me about Indian scares, river floods, storms, drouth, snow sifting through the house onto the beds, and many hardships. Once in later years I remarked to my mother how sorry I was that she had endured such a hard life when she was young. She looked at me with an odd little expression of pity. "Sorry?" she said. "Why, we had the *best* time in the world." Her answer held food for thought.

There is one memory that seems to me the very acme of embarrassment and discomfort. One of the numerous long-distance cousins had come to pay a visit and immediately upon the removal of her hat and coat her eagle eye lighted upon me modestly effacing myself under the dining-room table. Dragging me from my lair with a sprightly: "So this is the little cousin I've never seen." She sat down in an ample rocking-chair, pressed me to her ample bosom and apparently forgot my presence. To this day I can feel her smothering arms, see her fat hands clasped in front of my supine person, hear her voice going on and on above my head as she verbally married off or buried all the relatives. There was no Child Welfare Association to aid me, merely a mother and three big sisters upon whom the misery in my eyes was lost as they cheerfully assisted in the marrying and burying. Just why I didn't have gumption enough to get myself out of the human trap is not the question. No modern child would stand it. The fact remains that I sat on. My legs went to sleep. My spine and brain atrophied. I used to think I sat there a month. I know now of course that it could not possibly have been more than a week.

For a time one of my younger brothers drove a milk-wagon for my oldest brother who ran a dairy farm. Sometimes I went with him on the route. The wagon held the damp, sweetish smell of warm milk. My brother had filled the inside with drawings and caricatures as good as Briggs ever made. I divided the women who took milk into two classes: the come-outs and the stuck-ups. The come-outs explain themselves. Shawls over their heads or aprons twisted about their shoulders they brought out their bowls and pitchers in response to my brother's ringing a high-voiced brass bell. Sometimes, the wind blowing hard and the dust swirling, big germs came up out of the road and perched evilly on the rims of the dishes, but as no one had ever heard of them they gave no alarm. My childish idea of the stuck-ups is not so clear. No doubt my brother growled about having to get out and take the milk up to the house. But I was a big girl before I could disassociate the words *aristocrat* and *plebeian* from my early division of stuck-ups and come-outs.

I remember how my first Sunday School teacher always had an Easter egg hunt in the yard of her home. But on a stormy day she staged the little party in her house which seemed very spacious and lovely to me. During the hunt I accidentally broke a blue-flowered vase and shed frightened embarrassed tears. To this day I do not know whether or not that was a valuable vase. But I do know that as she picked up the shattered remains my hostess drew me to her, comforting me and telling me that life was too short to waste sad tears over a vase. Dear old Auntie Sawyer . . . to understand that a little girl's feelings were so much more important than an inanimate object!

There was a house in my old home town which seemed to me the personification of elegance. I could not conceive of any home being grander. It had a conservatory on one side. I had never seen so much glass in one region before. The peculiar thing is that as the years have passed that glass has shown properties not usually credited to such material: plasticity, flexibility and contractibility. For I saw that big conservatory a few years ago and it looked very much like a large double bay window. Time, the laundry-man, is careless. He shrinks many of the things which looked huge to us in our childhood.

Then there is a memory about being misunderstood. We were to have a debate in one of the grades. . . . a little childish debate . . . Resolved: That winter is better than summer. Which is almost as inane as the one about fire being more destructive than water. But I was as much in earnest over my assigned affirmative task as though I were about to address the National Educational Association. I arose and to the other boys and girls said briskly: "Ladies and gentlemen. . . ." which caused a universal snicker, proving conclusively that my appellation had been unwisely chosen. "Ladies and gentlemen," I insisted firmly, "winter is cold and summer is hot but you can always get yourself warm on a cold winter's day but you can't never get yourself cool on a hot summer day." Due to my earnestness the audience tittered again and my teacher, a young and humorless one, said to me: "Sit down. This wasn't intended to be anything funny. If you can't give sensible reasons, don't give any." Dumbfounded I sat down. To be funny had been as far from my intentions as were Douglas's when he debated with Lincoln. Sensible reasons? Why, if I live to be one hundred and four I shall still believe that you can always get yourself warm on a cold winter day but you can never get yourself cool on a hot summer day.

Little fragrant, elusive half-memories! We try but we cannot place them. Some day we may surprisingly be able to remember. For shall I not. . . . on a day. . . . go up a grassy path, having been lost for a time, half-afraid and rather tired? May not my mother rise from bending over the flowers and say, half in relief and half in expectancy: "Oh, *here* you are. I've been looking for you?" And quite suddenly I shall know the end of the story.

He Whom a Dream Hath Possest

"He Whom a Dream Hath Possest" (*The American Magazine,* June 1927) shares with "Welcome Home, Hal!" (1934) the theme of two orphaned young men who are reared by their grandmothers and who are both artists. This story, however, is much more the tale of one of the grandmothers and her counterpart; it is another of Aldrich's richly drawn portraits of older people. Others are found in her short stories "Low Lies His Bed" (1934), "The Home-Coming" (1923), and "Bid the Tapers Twinkle" (1935), and in Aldrich's novels *Rim of the Prairie* and *A Lantern in Her Hand.*

When Aldrich describes John David's predilection for drawing on every available and permitted wall, she is also describing the activities of her own son James, who would become an artist and illustrator, eventually creating book covers and illustrations for some of his mother's works as well as for many other writers.

The title of the story comes from the poem "He Whom a Dream Hath Possest Knoweth No More of Doubting," by Shaemas O'Sheel (1886–1954), a contemporary of Aldrich's.

With that same paradoxical combination of courage and trepidation which Columbus must have entertained when the world was younger and slower, Grandma Burnham was getting ready to make a journey to Lake City.

Grandma Burnham lived alone in an old-time wing-and-ell house in an old-fashioned lilac-and-syringa-grown yard on the last street in the insignificant town of Edgeville. Which settles Grandma once and for all to any claim on a paragraph in "Who's Who." But if Grandma herself had no place in the pages of that dictionary of the well-known, the direct results of her handiwork might readily be found there, for John David Burnham was listed quite bravely among the B's.

John David was Grandma's sole claim to her honorary title. Early orphaned, he had been housed, fed, loved, and paddled by Grandma. The housing had been comfortable, if inartistically so; the loving as generous as the feeding; and as for the paddling, one of the main reasons for that occasional activity on the part of Grandma was John David's predilection for drawing charcoal pictures on anything and everything indoors and out.

He had filled the walls of the woodshed, the inside doors of the cupboards, the entry to the cellarway, and the white bottoms of Grandma's pine bureau drawers with caricatures of gaunt old whiskered men and fat old women, and a cow that was always making waggish remarks in an elliptical breath from a grinning mouth. And, after many years, so Puck-like is Fate, John David's gaunt old men and fat old ladies, and even the wag of a cow had landed him in "Who's Who," via the funny pages of half the newspapers in a nation which gives both money and prestige to one who succeeds in making it laugh.

It was to John David Burnham's wedding in Lake City that Grandma had just been giving a half-hour of thought. Miss Marjorie Jeffers—that was the name of the girl whom David out of the world of girls was to honor. Grandma was hoping she was good enough for him; but was having her doubts. She picked up a letter from her ample, gingham-covered lap and read part of it over again.

" . . . While I shall send you a regulation invitation in September, I am writing this note to you now, urging you to plan to come. David says you must come, and so do I. My own grandmother will be here. She is coming from the East to attend the big doings. I am her only grandchild, just as David is your only one, and we want you two grandmothers to know each other. . . . " There was more, and, then, "Cordially yours, Marjorie Jeffers."

In the days that followed Grandma consulted her bank book, which, by reason of the chickens, the garden, the cow, and several plump checks which David had given her for presents, presented material prosperity. In a wild orgy of buying she got goods for two new dresses, a gray crêpe for second best, and for the wedding itself a shimmering silk of changeable lavender and silver. Miss Rocky, the town seamstress, made them both, with much reading of directions from the paper patterns and much spicy conversation from between the pins in her mouth.

In every spare moment Grandma worked on the wedding present—a quilt with a creamy background for a crimson rambler rose design of blocks. Into it she wove ten thousand stitches and ten thousand thoughts of love. With all these elaborate preparations, the summer fairly flew. The dresses were finished and folded in tissue paper. The final tiny stitching had been put on the smallest petal of the last red rose of the quilt. The first Wednesday in September arrived in a halo of serenity and sunshine. No doubt, somewhere other people in the world were welcoming that particular day, but to Grandma Burnham it seemed her exclusive property.

It was thrilling to be the center of interest for the whole neighborhood. No spotlight on a stage favorite or focus on a movie star had ever made them more the center of things than was Grandma to the west end of Edgeville. All that morning there was a great deal of running back and forth to assist her in getting off, Edgeville belonging to that inferior type of town whose people render homely service to one another when it is needed.

Jennie Wing hurried up-town at the last minute to get Grandma some face powder. "Just a little," Grandma explained; "ten cents' worth if they sell it in bulk. All my life I've said plain clean was good enough for me; but I want to look good for David's sake."

Several others were there to speed the parting wayfarer. Fat Sue Maybrick and her daughter Mamie, from the house on the north; wiry little Mrs. Jensen from the cottage on the south; old lady Wing from across the street. Grandma was out on the porch with her suit case.

"You look as stylish as a picture, Grandma," Sue Maybrick told her. She had on the dress which had been her best one before the extensive purchase of the two new ones, a black silk with freshly laundered white collar and cuffs. Miss Rocky had helped her pick out her hat. It had a feathery pompon on the side, which the milliner had assured her was "chic." Grandma had it on now, and above her plump, placid face it looked about as chic as it would have looked atop one of Raphael's cherubs.

"Now I'm going to tell you all something, folks," Grandma addressed them *en masse.* "I've kept this from you, sort of in the back of my head all summer. I'm going to bring Grandmother Jeffers home with me, if she'll come, and ain't too feeble to travel. She's come clear from New York State to Davie's and Margie's wedding, and may be all tired out and not able to go farther; but if she can, I want to bring her home to visit me for two or three weeks. It would be awful nice to have another old lady around for a while to wait on. I've thought of just a lot of nice things to do for her. I'm afraid I'm counting more on it than I should, without knowing for sure if she can come."

"My goodness, Grandma!" It was little Mrs. Jensen. "I don't believe you're ever happier than when you're doing something for someone."

Grandma studied a moment, thoughtfully. "Come to think about it," she said soberly, "I don't know as I *am!*"

Mr. Jensen drove up for her in his feather-weight auto. Jennie Wing returned with the powder. Grandma went out to the car. She delivered the house key to Mrs. Jensen, with some of the gusto which the Lord Mayor of London might use when turning over the city's key to his successor.

"Now, let's see"—this leaving was a complicated procedure—"I'll sort of call the roll: The cow's at Magee's. Jimmie is to deliver the milk and have the money. Sue, you're to tend the chickens and have the eggs, and, Sue, you kill an old hen for a stew for next Sunday. I'd like to think of you eating it. I'll save those few fryers that are left, to feed Grandma Jeffers if I can bring her home. Mis' Jensen, you're coming in to water the plants. I've got some slips of my best Martha Washington geraniums done up in a wet rag and strapped to my lunch box for Grandma Jeffers. The rainspout's turned into the barrel. If there comes up a big rain, Mr. Jensen, and it goes to slopping over, I wish you'd come and turn the spout out to the ditch. Mamie's to have the sweet peas and pansies. Cut 'em every day, except the day before we come, a week from next Thursday. I'm going to visit a week with Margie's family—and then we'll come home. Listen to me say 'we,' will you! I declare, I'm that set on bringing that old lady here. I better not get my hopes up too much. Well, good-by, everybody!"

"Good-by! Have a good time, Grandma!"

Grandma leaned out of the car, her plump, kind old face beaming, the more-or-less-stylish pompon nobly erect.

There was a half-hour wait at the station because of Grandma's cautious early arrival. And then finally the train was coming in, and Grandma was settling herself. She put her feet on the suit case which contained the crimson rambler quilt, as though it might, from sheer naturalness of the roses, ramble out of the car window. "Now, I'll not say a single word to a person on the train," she told herself. "I guess I know what's what."

She kept her word so religiously that no one but the conductor, the brakeman, two school-teachers, and an automobile salesman knew that she was John David Burnham's grandmother traveling to his wedding.

And then after many hours she was in Lake City, sucked down in a whirlpool of noise and confusion, and trying to swim bravely out behind a red-coated porter with the suit cases. At last there was David, big, and fine, and clean-looking, saying, "Gee, Grandma, you look good to me! If you couldn't have come, I'd have kidnapped Marge and carted her out to Edgeville and married her in your old parlor!"

And this was Margie! The dear, dear, girl. So slender and pretty and fragrant! And Margie was saying, "I'm glad to have David's grandmother here. And, Grandmother Burnham, this is my own Grandmother Jeffers."

Her plump old face wreathed in smiles, Grandma Burnham turned. The smiles left as though snatched from her face. Grandma's head swam giddily. Before her stood a little lady as dainty as Marjorie, and as slim and fragrant. A very short and very fetching ensemble suit clothed her girlish little body. From the top of the close-fitting, bright green satin hat over brown bobbed hair, to the toe of the buckled pump over a silken-clad foot, she was the personification of arrested youth. She looked at Grandma out of young-old, restless eyes, and gave her a limp, daintily gloved hand. At once Grandma took an intuitive and unreasoning dislike to her.

And then they were all in a pearl-gray upholstered limousine, with a liveried chauffeur, riding to the Jeffers home. With Grandma's body tense from constant fear of the congested traffic, they sped over the paved streets, turning at last through iron gates and up a curving drive. They all got out, and with David's arm through Grandma's they went up a stairway.

Grandmother Jeffers, her silken skirts swishing about trim silken legs, mounted the stairs like a girl and was waiting at the top for heavy old Grandma. From there they went into a room more gorgeous than Grandma had ever seen. Marjorie's father and mother were presented and a cousin or two, with some house guests, all pleasant people and as sophisticated as gracious. "High-toned," was what Grandma called it to herself.

Suddenly she knew that the best black silk she had on was not right, neither was the new gray in the suit case, nor even the shining lavender and silver one. And her hair in its neat bun at the back of her head was not right, nor the stiff black hat with the pompon. And, for that matter, neither were red, needle-pricked hands, nor face and neck whose skin had been burned caring for the garden. Davie should have told her. In his letters he had written only about Marjorie—nothing at all about her family or surroundings. Grandma felt frightened, out of place, ill at ease.

And then she was alone in a bedroom. When the door closed she sat down heavily on the edge of an ivory chair upholstered in flower-covered English chintz, and looked about her. There was an ivory-enameled fireplace and there was more ivory furniture. Soft, gaudily-colored draperies were at the windows, and there were three silken-shaded lamps, one right on top of the bed. Old-fashioned Grandma in this room looked as out of place as one of her fat old hens would have looked.

All her plans and anticipations seemed to have tumbled about her head, and she was left sitting in the midst of their ruins. To think she had expected to stay a week and visit with the family after Davie and Marjorie had gone! She would go back—why, she would go back on the very first train after the ceremony. She only wished now that she had not come at all.

She must keep a stiff upper lip, and get through the wedding creditably for Davie's sake. But nothing was as she had expected. She felt as hurt as a child. Why, she had even brought a starched kitchen dress to help a little with the dishes! Her mind ran back over all those preparations she had made for the week's stay. Even the quilt, with its thousands of stitches and its thousand thoughts of love, would seem cheap and queer and out of place here with the other gifts.

But no destroyed dream, no blighted anticipation was so keenly regretted as the dissipation of that pleasant picture of taking the other grandmother home to visit. Imagine it! That old woman running around in kiddish clothes! All daubed up like a girl! But her hair was dyed and her neck was wrinkled, Grandma told herself jealously, and there were telltale creases at the sides of her hard old eyes. You could tell she was old, even if she had tried to cover it up. Old, and wearing a bright green, little-girl dress! And those silly slippers. . . .

There was a tap at the door. Grandma answered it shyly to find a trim uniformed maid, who said, "Mrs. Jeffers sent me to help you dress for dinner."

Grandma's head was high. "Why, thank you, dearie. But I don't need you a mite. I had my dresses made easy for that reason. But would you mind doing something for me, please? . . . Just throw these geranium slips out somewhere in the back yard or on the junk pile?"

Grandma got through the dinner. The silver worried her a little, and she felt timid. She knew she was not herself, cheery and talkative; but there seemed nothing for her to say. The conversation was trivial enough, but as though from another language. And the other grandmother sat next to her in a low-necked, silky dress. Against the linen, her slim, sparkling fingers appeared in sharp contrast to Grandma's plump old needle-pricked ones with the thin wedding ring.

The members of the family were all courteous to Grandma, hospitable in their way—but it was not Grandma's kind of hospitality. To her sensitive mind it seemed only a surface sort of effusiveness.

And then the time had come to get ready for the wedding. Grandma arranged her soft white hair in its usual neat bun, but crowned it with a high, fan-shaped comb with lavender stones, which Davie had given her once for her birthday. And then she put on the new silver and lavender silk dress. She gingerly touched her nose and chin with the newly acquired powder, as though Jennie Wing in her excitement might have purchased an explosive.

The ceremony was in the party room on the third floor. A long aisle was roped off with wide satin ribbons festooned from palms. Just inside the ribbons, near the improvised flower-bedecked altar, was a carved high-backed chair. It had been placed there for Grandma. Because they told her to do so, and led her to it, she sat in it. But it hurt her to think she could not stand up as everyone else did. Just as if she were an invalid. She guessed they did not know how she tended the cow and chickens, and how the neighbors were always saying, "Grandma, you're so spry and young for your age!"

Grandma Jeffers, adding supreme insult to injury, came and stood beside the chair. She was gowned in extremely short turquoise velvet, and waved a gorgeous golden feather fan. She wore pearls with the blue velvet, rings of them, bracelets of them, and a dog-collar. "Well," thought Grandma jealously, "all the strands of pearls in the world could not conceal the wrinkles in that old neck!"

And then Grandma forgot her grievances in the beauty of the service. Almost everyone was looking at the bride; but Grandma looked only at David. And that was Davie, was it, standing there so big and fine and smart? It just couldn't be! Why, it was only yesterday that Davie and Micky Miller had gone down to the creek with willow poles, and she had fried for their supper the three diminutive sunfish of their combined catch. And the day before yesterday, when old Mr. Wing had come over to see her because Davie had drawn his picture on the side of Tucker's store and everybody was laughing at it?

And then, all at once, the service was over. And soon the satin ropes were removed, and the orchestra changed from a throbbingly sweet melody to a crashing dance tune. With that little superior air which Grandma detested, Grandmother Jeffers took her by the arm and piloted her the length of the ballroom floor toward chairs at the edge of the palm-filled alcove, from which vantage point they might watch the dancers.

The journey over the slipperiness of the dark polished floor would have been fraught with as much peril to Grandma as that of Eliza crossing the ice, if Grandmother Jeffers had not guided her. The high-heeled, golden satin pumps of Grandmother Jeffers seemed to tow Grandma Burnham's flat and altogether sensible black kids over to the alcove like gay little yachts towing broad barges into the backwater of a harbor.

Grandma Burnham sank heavily into the waiting chair, with a breath of relief.

"My, that makes me feel old, the slippery floor and the bright lights and that awful loud, queer music!"

Grandma Jeffers settled in the other chair with birdlike lightness, and crossed silken ankles. "How odd! It makes me feel young." The voice was superior, condescending. "Young enough to enter into it, and get all there is out of life to get!"

Grandma did not answer. She was uneasy here alone with this woman. Evidently, she was to be with her all evening. It had been arranged, of course; Margie's family had assigned this painted old butterfly to the task of looking after her. For a long time Grandma said nothing. There seemed nothing to say. They had not a single interest in common—sophisticated, modern old Grandmother Jeffers and provincial, out-of-date old Grandmother Burnham. Their lives touched each other's no more than the Poles touch.

Well, Grandma thought to herself, to-morrow it would be over. She would go back home, and leave this silly old woman free to cavort around as she wished. She would tell the neighbors she just got homesick and took the first train for Edgeville. She looked timidly across at the other grandmother, sitting upright, poised on the edge of her chair, waving her feather fan with that little detached air of superiority.

Suddenly Grandma grew reckless. *She would just be herself and say what she pleased.* She wasn't going to be shy, or afraid of that kittenish old woman's opinion any more. And because she could not be long with anyone without expressing herself freely, she began talking, half to herself, half to the unwilling listener:

"This wasn't much like my wedding, I'm telling you. It makes me laugh to think of the difference. John and I were married in my folks' log cabin. We set all the chairs out to make room for the guests. There was two fiddlers for the music. My folks' present to us was two pigs and six chickens. My, my, how things have changed! But I was happy—just as happy as Margie. It *was* a happy time for us, too, in those days, wa'n't it?" Grandma's eyes were moist with memory.

"Yes . . . oh, yes," the other agreed without enthusiasm.

Shrewd old Grandma detected something. Grandmother Jeffers's wedding time *had not been happy.* Any woman, no matter how old or sophisticated, would recall it with some show of emotion here to-night in the midst of the flowers and the music.

"We stayed with our folks a while, and then we moved on a farm in Poplar County. My John, David's father, was born there. We hadn't much to do with. Nobody did. Times was awful hard; but such a happy time as we had, too, with all the hard work. I wouldn't change the memory of it for anything." Grandma's pleasant old voice flowed on reminiscently, monotonously: "Oh, of course, there are always some things you'd change. In those years there's one thing stands out more than any other, that I'd change if I could. I'll tell you what it was!"

Her placid voice swept by uninterested ears, as though water lapped against the stolidity of a rock. "It was a sin of omission I guess you'd call it, instead of commission. We'd just got through living in the old sod house and built the new one. It seemed awful big and fine to me to have three rooms. My mother was coming to visit me for the first time, and I'd washed and scrubbed and cooked all day getting ready for her visit."

Grandmother Jeffers's restless, indifferent eyes were turned toward the gay throng, and she was tapping her foot irritably. But it did not faze Grandma. She was intending to finish the story and her memories more for her own pleasure than the listener's.

"Well, there come a covered wagon along, and in it was a man and his wife and their two little girls and her young sister. The man was driving some cattle, and he stayed out and asked Pa if he could put them in our corral. But the women and the children come up to the door. The woman had a baby in her arms, and the sister was leading a little girl by the hand. The woman did the talking. She said they wanted to stay all night if they could. She said they had their own bedding and they'd bring it in and make up their beds on the floor. But I said 'No.' "

Grandma's plump cheeks crinkled in the effort to keep her tearful emotion from showing. "I guess I've 'most never had a day that I haven't remembered that sinful thing . . . with the weather getting colder and the night coming on . . . and turning them away in their covered wagon. I was tired, and my mother was coming to visit, and I wanted everything spick and span. . . . But there ain't any of those things an excuse. It's been a blot on my life ever since I did it. Some day I believe I'm going to have to answer for that. Some day I'm going to hear, 'Inasmuch as ye did it not unto the least of these, ye did it not unto me.' "

Grandma was preaching a sermon by this time—preaching to a sophisticated, disinterested audience. But she had chosen her text and she was going to see it developed.

"Think of turning folks away like that in an early day when houses were so far apart and everyone had to be hospitable! I heard they stayed at the next house; but that ain't going to excuse me a mite. Seems like that's the worst thing I ever did in all the time we lived between Deer Trail and Edmond, back there in Poplar County."

Grandmother Jeffers suddenly stopped tapping her foot nervously and stared at Grandma.

"Where did you say that was?"

Grandmother repeated it mechanically. "Between Deer Trail and Edmond, out in Poplar County. I've thought of that thing—"

"What year was it?" Grandmother Jeffers leaned toward Grandma. "Do you remember?"

"Do I remember? I guess I do. It was the night before the Fourth of July, 1888. I know, because that was the year—"

Grandmother Jeffers put a slender, jeweled old hand on one of Grandma Burnham's pudgy red ones. Her young-old eyes were not restless, nor hard, nor uninterested. They had gone soft and shining and concerned. "Don't worry about it any more, Grandma." Her voice was trembling. "*I was the sister!*"

"*You!*" Grandma said it incredulously and then definitely, "Oh, no, not *you!*"

"Between Deer Trail and Edmond, in Poplar County, on the evening before the Fourth of July, 1888." Grandmother Jeffers went over it slowly. "Yes," she said definitely, "I was the sister. We stopped at a house, my sister and my sister's husband and their two little girls and I. A woman said she couldn't keep us because she was going to have company. I remember it as though it were last week. And we went on to the next house.

"It was because of what happened there that I remember it all. There was a young man stopping there at the next house. He had been studying law . . . he had some law books in his saddle bags . . . and he rode on away with us when we went. His name was Benjamin Erwin. Did you ever . . . ?" Grandmother Jeffers's white hand clutched a little at Grandma Burnham's red one. "Did you know anything about him . . . where he is . . . what ever became of him?"

"Benjamin Erwin? Why, he died . . . a long time ago. . . . I guess he never married."

"No, he wouldn't have. He said he wouldn't ever. . . . He was—" old Mrs. Jeffers tugged at her pearl dog-collar as though it choked her—"he was . . . the only man I ever loved!"

Grandma's mind was still on her own part in this astounding coincidence, and she was clucking surprised little exclamations of "Dear, dear! And it was you I turned away!"

"No, no; don't you see?" Grandmother Jeffers was almost impatient. "If you hadn't turned us away we would not have gone on to the next house, and I'd have missed him. It was to be that way. I'll tell you about it. . . . " She pulled her chair close to Grandma's knee, like a child at confession. "I never told anyone . . . not a soul in my life. There isn't a friend I have . . . not one . . . I would tell this to now; but I can tell you. There's something about you that makes me know it is safe with you. We carry dreams around with us, you know . . . and Ben Erwin was my dream. But I never knew he died—I couldn't find out. He was the only man I ever loved. All my life I've thought maybe I'd run across him again. I wanted to stay young for him. He was going on West. He traveled with us several days. We camped on the prairie at night. He was going to start his law office farther West. I can shut my eyes and see it all yet . . . the wide sweep of the prairie . . . and the stars . . . and the wind . . . and Ben Erwin.

"It's nothing but a dream, of course. Anybody with sense knows that. But I've carried it about with me all these years. I was going to wait for him; but something happened. It isn't necessary to go into that. And we parted . . . and I never knew what became of him. I married Henry Jeffers and had a child. But Ben Erwin was the man I loved. I thought we'd meet again some day. I told myself it just had to be. But we never did. And now he's dead!"

Grandma's eyes were moist with sympathy. "Well, well, and if I hadn't turned you away, it would have saved you a lot of sorrow in your life."

"No. Oh, no! I wouldn't have it different, even now. Isn't it queer, Grandma? It was I and it was you! Well, I never could forget him. Forty-eight years ago, and it's still a part of me. You'd think a person would get over a thing like that, wouldn't you? With a thousand interests in life? I've traveled around a good deal. And it seems as though he has been with me. He's stood beside me at times . . . on a Scotch brae . . . and in St. Peter's . . . and once at Naples. At unusual times, you know. Then he's come. Forty-eight years ago, and the dream never left me.

"And I married Mr. Jeffers, many years older than I . . . and I had a child. Sometimes the dream seems wicked, and sometimes it seems beautiful. But, wicked or beautiful . . . it has stayed!"

There were tears in her young-old eyes. They welled over the touched-up lids, hard little tears, as though they came painfully, and slipped down the elaborate make-up. That little air of superiority, of condescension, was gone.

"Life wasn't what I meant it to be—roaming, restless . . . and trying to keep young, so if I should meet him. I suppose I ought to have accepted age sensibly . . . philosophically . . . like you have, Grandma. But I've thought life just couldn't go by without my seeing him again. And I wanted to be young for him. It's been my dream. A dream's a silly thing to carry around with you, isn't it? But there's no age or time limit to it. And even a dream is worth suffering for . . . if it just *possesses* you!"

A week from Thursday, Mr. Jensen's little featherweight car drew up in front of Grandma Burnham's, and Mrs. Jensen flew over with the key. Simultaneously, Sue Maybrick came from her yard, rolling down her sleeves over enormous arms. Children, coming home from school, stopped at the yard, and Jennie Wing hurried over from across the street. As they came up, Grandma stepped heavily out of the car.

She had on her best black with the white cuffs and collar. The erstwhile chic hat with the noble pompon was slightly awry. With uniform interest the neighbors all stared at the car. For behind Grandma a trim silken leg in a silver-buckled pump lightly touched the running-board, to be followed by a slender little bob-haired lady in a very gay and very youthful rose-colored coat and hat.

"Hello, everybody!" Grandma was beaming. Then she turned to the supple figure springing nimbly to the ground.

"This," she said, and chuckled wickedly, "is Grandmother Jeffers! I'll admit she ain't just what you'd call *feeble;* but we've grown to be mighty good friends, and she's come home with me to stay a few weeks!"

The Man Who Caught the Weather

The "germ" of this story, as Aldrich described the most basic of her plot ideas, began with the actions of one of the Streeters' neighbors in Cedar Falls, Iowa, well over twenty years before the story was written. Coincidentally, Aldrich also had a neighbor in Elmwood who studied the weather and shared his garden produce; he was thought by some to be the person about whom she wrote this story and may, in fact, have recalled to Aldrich the man she knew in her early years in Cedar Falls. Aldrich, too, was a keen observer of the weather and in her daily journal entries almost invariably mentioned the weather of the day.

"The Man Who Caught the Weather" made nearly thirty trips to various editors before the *Century* purchased it; it was published in the July 1928 issue of the magazine and went on to become an O. Henry Award winner of 1928. It also became the title and first story of Aldrich's 1936 volume of short stories, *The Man Who Caught the Weather.*

He lived next door to us when I was a girl—old Mr. Parline. To be sure, his wife lived there too, but we never saw very much of her. She was one of the immaculate housewives of that day, whose life was bounded by the hundred small tasks of a home into which the modern, button-pushing conveniences had not come. A shy, effacing woman she was—"mousy" describes her too well to abandon the term for its mere triteness. Mr. Parline was the one who did the talking, who neighbored with the rest of us, who came to the back door bringing us gifts from his garden.

The Parline house sat in the midst of trees and flowers like Ceres among her fruits. We were just then emerging from the dark age of fences into the enlightened era of open lawns. By your fenced or fenceless condition you were known as old-fashioned or up-to-date. One by one, the picket and the fancy iron and the rough board fences on our street had gone down before the god of Fashion. Mr. Parline, alone, retained his—a neat picket, painted as white as the snowballs that hung over it, Juliet-like, from their green foliage balconies.

The shrubbery was not so artistically placed as that of to-day. We had not learned to group it against houses and walls, leaving wide stretches of lawn. Single bushes dotted Mr. Parline's lawn, a hydrangea here, a peony there, a tiger-lily beyond, in spaded spots of brown, mulch-filled earth, like so many chickens squatting in their round nests.

The Parlines were of English extraction although both had been born in Vermont. There was a faintly whispered tale that they were cousins, but there was no one so intimate as to verify the gossip, and no one so prying as to ask.

Mr. Parline was a half head shorter than his tall, slender wife. He was stocky of body, a little ruddy as to complexion, like the color of his apples, a little fuzzy as to face, like the down on his peaches. There was a quiet dignity about him that fell just short of pompousness. "Mr. Parline" his wife called him, in contrast to the "John" and "Silas" and "Fred" with which the other women spoke of their liege lords. Where other women in the block ran in to our home with the freedom of close acquaintances, Mrs. Parline alone occasionally came sedately in at the front gate in a neat brown dress covered with a large snowy apron starched to cardboard stiffness.

It was Mr. Parline who came often. With that manner which was paradoxically gentle and pompous, he would bring us edibles from his garden all summer long on a home-made flat wooden tray. That garden, as neat as constant care could make it, was the delight and despair of every one who attempted to emulate it. Not a pigweed showed its stubborn head. Not a mullen-stock lifted its thick velvety self. The bricklaid paths, without sign of leaf, might have been swept, even scrubbed. As for the growing contents of the garden, they made a varicolored and delightful picture. In its perfection every cabbage might have been a rose, every beet an exotic tropical plant, the parsley dainty window-box ferns. To Mr. Parline there was no dividing line between the beauty of flowers and the beauty of vegetables. With impartiality he planted marigolds near the carrots and zinnias next to the beans.

"Just a little of the fruits of my labor," was his dignified greeting on those occasions when he tapped at the back door. In the center of the wooden tray might repose a cabbage, the dew still trembling upon the silver sheen of its leaves, around it a lovely mass of the delicate shell-pink of sweet-peas. One felt it as much of a sacrilege to plunge the cabbage into hot water as it would have been to cook the sweet-peas. Or he might have several bunches of grapes in merging shades of wine-red and purple, their colors melting into the wine-red and purple colors of shaggy asters. Old Mr. Parline had the heart of a poet and the eye of an interior decorator.

We never saw Mrs. Parline pulling a vegetable or cutting a flower. Occasionally, at evening, she walked in the paths with all the interest and curiosity of a stranger, evidently considering the garden as sacred ground as did the rest of us. Indeed, Mother was at their back door one day when Mr. Parline came up the path with the inevitable wooden tray. There were beets on the tray, their tops cut, their bodies like blood-red hearts, around them white sweet-williams and crimson phlox. "I was just bringing my wife some of the fruits of my labor," he said in his courteous, half-pompous way.

We laughed about the phrase at home. Ours was a noisy, hilarious, fun-loving family. One member might bring in a mess of dirty potatoes in a battered old pail. "A little of the fruits of my labor," he would imitate Mr. Parline's pompous dignity. Or another, coming in with the first scrawny radishes, might have placed a few limpsy dandelions around them as a floral satire on the contents of Mr. Parline's wooden tray.

If the garden was the old man's hobby, the weather was his very life. It was inconceivable that any one should be so wrapped up in the constant change of the elements. To other busy people the weather was incidental to their labors, the setting in which they performed their tasks. It might be pleasant or inconvenient, but it remained a side issue. To old Mr. Parline it was the important event of the day. He scanned the heavens, read the almanac, watched for signs of changes. Of the last he had a thousand at his command. If the sun went down in clouds on Friday night, if it rained the first Sunday in the month, if a dog ate grass, if the snow stuck to the north sides of the trees—he knew to a nicety what the results would be. To old Mr. Parline the weather was not the background. It was the picture itself. It was not the mere setting for daily living. It was life itself. No government official connected with the Weather Bureau made it more his life's thought. In the kitchen he kept a large calendar upon which he made notations for the day. Every vagrant shifting of the wind, every cloud that raced across the blue was recorded. For what purpose no one knew. *Another slight dash of snow at noon. Temperature 34. Sun came out at 3 P.M.* It seemed so small, so trivial, that a man should give so much time and thought to that which he could not change. He had thermometers by the house, on the north side to show the coldest registration, on the south to get the hottest, in the garden, by the barn. They were like traps everywhere—baited with mercury—little traps to catch the weather.

From Mr. Parline's conversation one gathered that an overseeing Providence had given him exclusive charge of the elements. If his words did not utter it, his manner implied it. "Well, how do you like my June day?" his attitude seemed to be. If the day was bad, he was half apologetic. If it was pleasant, he glowed with satisfaction. The summer afternoon on which we were to have a little social gathering, he came to the back door and, with genuine feeling, told us how sorry he was that the day was dull and rainy. His manner showed humiliation, as though from the standpoint of neighborliness he had failed us in a crisis. "I am very sorry," he said in his gentle, half-pompous way. "I had thought—had every reason to believe—that it would be sunshiny." We assured him that we bore him no grudge, and he went home relieved, returning with the wooden tray on which lay a heap of ruby cherries, a delicate mass of baby's-breath around them.

Was there a great national event, his talk turned immediately to the weather in which it was consummated. When he read the newspapers he seemed to ignore the main issue of the news. The weather, lurking in the background, was apparently of greater importance to him than the magnitude of the event. On the day of Dewey's triumph, he spoke immediately of the weather, wondering whether it had been dull or sunny in the harbor. At an inauguration there was no comment from him concerning the great issue of the day, the change in the policy of the administration. He gave forth no acclaim nor condemnation of the new head of the government. His mind dwelt only on the fact that the new President was having to ride up Pennsylvania Avenue in a mist.

Vegetables, flowers and the weather—they were Mr. Parline's whole existence. Such little things they were, we said. Whether his wife was bored by the triviality of his life, we could not know. She was too reserved for any one to sense her reactions to her husband's small interests. We could see her working about the house all day. Sometimes she brought out quilts and hung them on the line for cleaning. They were of intricate patterns, beautifully pieced and quilted—the Rose of Sharon, the Log Cabin, the Flower Basket and the Rising Sun. "I'll bet the old man sleeps under the Rising Sun," one of the family remarked and we laughed uproariously at the joke. In the evening Mrs. Parline often came out and strolled through the paths, stepping gingerly about like a stranger, listening to the old man's courteous, half-pompous talk. She was deeply afraid of storms, he had told us years before. And when one saw the first dark clouds looming up from the southwest in summer, or the first gray ones rolling in from the north in winter, one also saw old Mr. Parline hurrying home, his square, heavy body swinging along out of its accustomed slower movements. To get home to Mrs. Parline when there was rain or hail or snow, was his first duty. It was the only time when he ever seemed thrown out of his pompous calm. You saw them later through the windows looking out at the storm together.

The Parlines attended a little ivy-grown church where the old gentleman passed the collection-box. When his own part of the service was over he would take a seat near the door, one eye on the sky. It was as though he must have everything as auspicious as possible when the congregation should return home. One wondered if he heard the sermon at all. A queer old man.

But the queerest thing of all was his strange prophecy that the day would come when the weather could be regulated. We young folks guffawed at that. "He was eccentric before he sprung that one," we said, "but now he's a nut."

In his half-pompous, half-gentle way, he argued it. "In the centuries to come, who knows but that humanity will have progressed to such an extent that men can catch the weather and retain it—hold it for a time to their own choice? You smile at that." He was sensitive to our thoughts. "But strange things have happened. Who would have thought you could catch the human voice in a little box and listen to it through a tube to the ear?" This was all some twenty years ago. "Who would have thought a machine would rise up in the air under its own power? Who would have thought carriages without horses would go about the streets?"

"The whole trouble would be," we joked with him, "you would want rain the day we wanted sunshine, and living next door to us, there would be complications."

"I don't pretend to know how it could be accomplished," he said in his gentle, dignified way. "I merely suggest that in the years to come it may be so."

So the Parlines went on living their quiet lives. Refined, gentle folk, but different—and a little queer.

And then on a spring day, old Mrs. Parline died, as quietly and unostentatiously as she had lived. There was no fuss about it. A hard cold, the doctor coming and going, a neighbor slipping in and out of the back door, a cousin coming out from Chicago to care for her—death.

The various members of our family went over to the house. Other neighbors came, as they do in small towns. A man's sorrow is the town's sorrow. In a neighborly community, sympathy takes concrete form. It becomes buns and flowers and apple jelly and sitting up.

Old Mr. Parline greeted us kindly, courteously. Outwardly he showed no manifestations of his grief, except that his face was gray and drawn. He was solicitous of our comfort. He brought in fuel for the kitchen stove and oil for the lamps. He went to the cellar and came back with apples, polishing them scrupulously. He asked us if we were too cold or too hot. He went up and down his tulip beds pulling a few tiny weeds from the soil. Such little things in the face of death! He looked at the thermometer, at the almanac, at the sky, and predicted a pleasant sunshiny afternoon for the services. A queer old man, we all said. Not even death itself could take his mind away from the habits of a lifetime.

Mrs. Parline was buried in Riverside Cemetery. "It seemed very mild out there this afternoon," he said to us a day or two after the services. "There was a light breeze from the northeast." We knew where "out there" was.

By Memorial Day there was a stone at the grave and a mass of scarlet geraniums which he had transplanted, and some parsley. "How odd," we said, "parsley from the vegetable garden." But he was always odd. We walked around the stone to read the inscription. Propped up against it, in the lush grass, was a thermometer. We laughed a little—but only a little. Some laughter is half tears.

During that summer he seemed lost, a boat without a rudder. It was pathetic the way he went about his housework. He hung the quilts out on the line to clean them—the Flower Basket and the Log Cabin, the Rose of Sharon and the Rising Sun. We would see him walking about the yard in the evening with a lantern, reading the thermometers.

"Look at that," we young folks said, "he's batty."

"Oh, no," Mother said, "he's lonely."

And then, quite suddenly, we realized that he was going out to the cemetery at the sign of every storm. At the first glimpse of a thunderhead looming up over the trees, we would see him slipping out of the white picket gate and hurrying down the street. In some indefinable way he must have felt that he wanted to carry out that old habit of protecting her.

"It's ridiculous," we said.

"It's beautiful," Mother said.

If we expected his garden to deteriorate, we were mistaken. He took more pains with it than ever. More often he came to the back door with its products for us. Once, someone spoke tactfully about paying him, that he ought to have some compensation for his work. He looked pained. "Oh, no," he said, with gentle dignity. "Please do not speak of it again."

He found out the neighbors' various likes and dislikes. "I put out some turnips for you," he said to Mother. "I do not care for them myself, but I want you to have some." Yes, a kind old man.

And he continued to manage the weather. "I do not want to intrude." He came to the back door. "But I see your family is making preparations to go to a picnic."

"Yes, Mr. Parline. Wouldn't you like to go with us?"

"Oh, no, thank you. You are very kind. But I have work in my garden. I went to a picnic once in my youth. It was a very enjoyable occasion. I wanted to tell you that I think it will rain before night. The wind has switched to the east and the temperature is five degrees higher." The queer old codger.

And then, as the years went by, he began to include others than the immediate neighborhood in his gifts—people he had not known before and with whom he became acquainted in the cemetery.

A cemetery is a friendly place. You talk with people there whom you have not known in town. "The grass ought to be mowed," you may say to the wealthy widow by her husband's mausoleum, or "Do you think the peonies will be out by Memorial Day?" to the Italian fruit vender by his baby's grave. So people who talked to the old man "out there," even though they lived across town, became the recipients of his garden products.

For three years he lived his queer busy life there alone with his garden and his thermometers.

It was in December of the third winter after his wife's death that the gray clouds of the big snow began rolling up from the northwest. Someone saw him slip out of his gate, lantern in hand, and hurry down the street.

"You don't suppose that poor old man is going out there to the cemetery?" Mother was solicitous. She put a shawl over her head and hurried out a side door. We could hear her calling, "Oh, Mr. Parline!" When she came in she had deep sympathy in her eyes. "I told him I thought he ought not to go out when it looked so snowy. He said in his dignified old way, 'That's why I want to go. I must get out for a few minutes before the storm breaks.' I suppose he feels that he protects her just as he used to. Isn't it pathetic?"

We had supper. Company came. It began to snow—soft, damp, heavy flakes. It was late when it came to us that there was no light in the Parline cottage. Father went over. When he found no one, he went after two other neighbors and together they went "out there." I think from the first they expected to find—what they found. He was huddled up against the stone where he had crumpled while stooping down to look at the thermometer. The doctor said death had been instantaneous, that he had evidently taxed himself hurrying to make the trip before the storm broke.

They brought him home. Neighbors went into the little house, not so immaculate as in the old days, but in order. In the kitchen they talked in low tones about the old man, as though from the front room where he lay he might hear their comments.

A queer old man, they all agreed, but kind, unusually kind. Mother went into the cellar and brought up scarlet-cheeked apples and mellow pears. "He would have wanted to pass them around," she said, with that understanding of humanity which she always seemed to possess. Scrupulously she polished them before she served them.

The cousin and a young married daughter came. The cousin cried a little, tears that were not especially sad. "I didn't feel that I knew him very well," she told us. "When I took care of Cousin Sarah he was always very kind to me. He brought me everything from the garden and kept me supplied with fuel. But I never really got acquainted with him. When we did talk it seemed to be only about the weather. But he was a good old man."

They took him "out there" where his wife was, and the dead geraniums under their thick covering of snow, and the parsley from the vegetable garden and the thermometer.

In the evening Mother and I went over and sat a while with the cousin and her daughter. They replenished the fire in the kitchen stove with some of the wood Mr. Parline had brought in. They brought apples and elderberry wine from the cellar. The house had that lonely feeling which hangs over one from which a soul has just gone.

Drawn by thoughts of the old man's hobby, Mother walked over to the huge bank calendar hanging there on the kitchen wall. The last day of the year it was, and so the last of the calendar with its one vacant page. Mother thumbed over the closing pages, each one filled with the old man's wavering writing. *Indications of snow. Wind in the east. Temperature 20 at the north side of the house. 19 at the barn. 18 out there.* Underneath was a home-made set of shelves, all the old calendars of the bygone years in neat piles, the dates printed on the backs.

Through the clean, small-paned window, we could see low clouds breaking and slipping into the east. We were no doubt thinking the same thought—of the old man lying "out there" in the dignity of death, with the scudding clouds and the wind in the west, the old man who had lived close to the wind and the rain, the hail and the snow. Death would not seem so significant to him tonight as the importance of the setting—the rift in the clouds and the end of the storm.

There was the last vacant page on the calendar. He would have wanted it filled. Mother looked at it for a moment, then picked up the short, stubby pencil hanging limply on its long string, and wrote the weather for the day—the gentle old man's long Day: *Shadows gone from the valley—no night—and the need of no candle—sunshine—eternal sunshine—and the Seven Stars.*

For I have realized how the ogre contradicts himself. One day he says one thing and denies it the next. He doesn't know what he likes. Hi-lee! Hi-low! The proof follows.

These are some of the things the critic has uttered. And, always, in the comparative statements, they are concerning the *same* book or story:

Concerning one book the New York *Times* says: "That there is in ordinary life much interesting, amusing and appealing material for the novelist, Mrs. Aldrich proves anew in this book"; but the *Saturday Review of Literature* says: "Anyone who has lived for any length of time in the woods knows that it is peopled with just such yokels as these, but why write about them?" The Boston *Transcript* tells us: "Mrs. Aldrich's crowning achievement in this book is her humor. In a dashing way, touched with gay humor, her lines are very funny"; but the El Paso *Times* remarks: "There is some attempt at humor here, but it is of a formal, cumbersome and trite type." The Glasgow, Scotland, *Evening News* writes: "These characters live and move across the pages like flesh and blood people. They are international in type, for despite their American nationality, they might as well reside here in Glasgow"; after which the Memphis *Commercial Appeal* rises to say: "The book is well written but it is out of joint with the times. Such families existed a generation ago but are as extinct now as the dodo." The New York *World* puts in a good word: "Mrs. Aldrich tells the story of these people with such humor, such spirit, such understanding of human nature, and such unobtrusive recognition of the essentials of happiness and of the dependability of average humanity, that she makes of each chapter a charming sketch, vivid and gay as a water-color painting." But the Parkersburg (West Virginia) *News* thinks: "She writes these stories with a marvellously uninspired pen. One can truthfully say of them that they are wholesome, for they could not possibly inspire to any more criminal activity than yawning." New York *Evening Post:* "We have seldom met more charming, refreshing people." Beaumont (Texas) *Enterprise:* "The book contains the same old stereotyped characters we always have with us." A headline from the Boston *Herald:* "CHARMING ROMANCE BEAUTIFULLY TOLD." A headline on the same book from the El Paso *Times:* "Author tries to prove cabbages are beautiful." Minneapolis *Tribune:* "One of the most pleasing characteristics of this book is the satisfactory way in which the author has rounded out the final chapter, giving a résumé of the characters' lives." But the Philadelphia *Ledger* disagrees: "The book is most artistically handled up to the last chapter, when the author indulges in one of those old-time methods of rounding up her characters and placing them for life." Concerning a short story which made the O. Henry volume, the Atlanta

Journal says: "Bess Streeter Aldrich in her presentation of 'The Man Who Caught the Weather' contributes the most appealing story in the entire collection. It is done with artistic shadings." But, alas, the New York *Evening Post:* " 'The Man Who Caught the Weather' is a slight story related with sticky charm—but it is only fair to state that not all of the collection sink to this level."

How can I longer fear that nightmare of my dreams, The Critic, when in his composite form he makes ponderous statements one day and contradicts them the next? I congratulate myself upon my freedom from his tyranny.

Less flippantly—what is the effect of these contrary criticisms upon the writer? After weeks of conscientious labor upon a short story—months or years upon a book—what are his reactions to these diversified reports? Bewildering. Has he or has he not done a fairly pleasing piece of work? He does not know. There is only one way for the writer to view the whole bewildering report. Caustic criticisms are acids. Flowery commendations are alkalis. Acids and alkalis neutralize each other. One's sense of humor and his poise can keep the barbed shafts from stinging too hard. One's philosophy of life—his sense of his own limitations, his realization that what is being read today will be shelved tomorrow—can keep the laudations from seeming too important. If the writer has done the best he could—interpreted life as he has seen it, lived up to his own ideals, refused to barter his self-respect for thirty pieces of silver, then neither the criticism nor the commendation seems very significant. What is written, is written. And the next task lies before him.

Romance in G Minor

"Romance in G Minor" (*Delineator,* February 1929) is a rather unusual story for Aldrich, for although it uses the omniscient narrator, her preferred mode, it is told from the point of view of a somewhat scruffy hired hand, G. (George) Minor. His long tenure on the Benner farm makes him almost a member of the family, and, having watched Rus Benner grow up, gives him almost paternal concerns for Rus. Aldrich rarely wrote from a male perspective, and only "The Lions in the Way," which appeared in the *People's Home Journal* in February 1919, approximates this form. *Delineator*'s purchase price for "Romance in G Minor," which was $750, was the most she had received for any story up to that time.

"Romance in G Minor" was one of the stories considered for Aldrich's 1936 *The Man Who Caught the Weather* collection, but eventually it was not included in the book.

The title is misleading, as most up-to-date titles are apt to be. G. Minor was no melody of love. One's wildest fancy could not picture him as a dreamer of dreams.

Old George Minor was the Benners' hired man. Some fourteen years before, old George had arrived in the Miner back-yard from the steel bound highway of the railroad track. He was dirty and his whiskers were like tangled Spanish moss. He had come up to the house intending to ask for his supper. For a few moments he stood in the yard looking at Mrs. Benner's delphinium and hollyhocks, sea-blue and blood-red against the dazzlingly white picket fence. Then he asked for work instead.

All three members of the family had come out of the house to see him—Mr. Benner, Mrs. Benner and young Russell. Rus had been only fourteen then, too big for his clothes and too small for the arrogance with which he surveyed his small world.

"What's your name?" Rus had asked.

And the tramp had said vaguely, as tho one appellation were as good as another: "George—George Minor."

Mr. Benner, in need of hay hands, had hired the wanderer. Immediately old George had drawn water at the pump and washed his face and hands with much splashing. From the confines of a bundle he produced a faded shirt of good material and put it on in the lee of the harness shed. Then he borrowed scissors from the house and, in front of a Texas-shaped piece of mirror, cut off the wildest sprays of the whiskers. With evident satisfaction at results, as tho man could not do more for fellow man, he sat down in the doorway and drew from his pocket a mouth-organ upon which he played a combination of ornate chords as mournful as they were lusty.

Gentle Mrs. Benner, cooking an appetizingly odorous supper, said: "Dear, dear! That makes me want to cry. I haven't heard 'Sweet Belle Mahone' since I was a girl."

"If that's *sweet* Belle," said young Rus cockily, "I'd hate to have him give us something about a *sad* sister."

That first summer the three members of the family often wondered about George Minor. But at any reference to his past the old man was silent. Once he referred vaguely to England and once, more definitely, to Middletown, Connecticut.

"Mother thinks he's a duke in disguise," Rus would say.

"No, I don't," gentle Mrs. Benner would retort, "but just the same he's seen better days."

In the late summer he said: "I'll be goin' on now."

"Oh, you'd better stay, George," his employer suggested. "You can help with the husking."

And old George stayed. George and his depressing mouth-organ! All winter he stayed, choring around, his Bolshevik-looking beard wrapping his throat like a muffler. And then a bluebird sang, and old George trimmed his beard.

In the years that followed, the trimming of George's rough beard grew to be as definite a sign of spring as the greening meadow.

He became as permanent on that prairie farm as the silo. Ten times, since his arrival, the crocuses had come up for the cows to snatch off their lavender heads. Those ten years had brought grave changes to the family. Rus grew up and went away to college. Mr. Benner met death under his own tractor. Mrs. Benner died as quietly and gently as she had lived. Rus came home to run the farm, and old George said again, "I'll move on, now, Rus?" It was more of a question than a statement.

And Rus, grave, worried over life's new problems, all his youthful arrogance gone, said: "Don't go, George. Stay on and help me."

Old George went down to the railroad track and looked wistfully up and down the steel highway. Then he shambled back. He tended the bulbs and pruned the bushes and he kept the picket fence and the garden gate immaculately white. It was a memorial service to Mrs. Benner. Rus sensed it. "Much obliged, George. I appreciate it."

And George in his emotional distress sat by the harness shed and played mournfully:

"*In the hazel dell my Nellie's sleeping,*
Sleeping there so long—"

And other years went by. Rus, running the farm, grew more grave and quiet, more aloof from the young people of the neighborhood. He went about his business, reserved, altogether lonely. He spent his long winter evenings at home with books, a radio, an atrocious pipe and old George. Some evenings he would take no interest in any of them, but would sit in a deep chair staring into the fire.

It worried old George. It was not right—that a fellow no older than Rus should sit and brood—a good-looking fellow with a farm. Out of the chaos of his simple thoughts old George evolved an idea. It was about a girl that Rus was thinking. It was over some old flame that Rus was brooding.

"*Snappin' crocodiles!*" old George ejaculated when it dawned on him. "If I knew who she was, it wouldn't take me long to get hold of her and fix it up . . . Wish there was a woman some'eres I could talk to about it."

All that winter Rus worked, read, listened half-heartedly to the big radio, smoked his atrocious pipe, stared into the fire. Then a teal flew out of the pasture. The daffodil bulbs peeped thru a thin coating of dirty snow. Old George trimmed his beard.

And then old George's woman confidante appeared. She was in the person of Mary Allen, age twenty-two, who arrived on the next farm for her annual visit to her grandparents. Old George did not admire Mary Allen. Too sassy, was his verdict. And scrawny. No meat on her. A little smarty, too, with her tipped-up nose and her city ways. Rus had gone down to see her quite a bit the summer before, but all at once he had stopped going. That was where Rus had shown he was wise. Sensible boy—that Rus!

And old George, brooding over Rus's apparent sorrow, made up his mind to go down and ask Mary Allen's opinion. Even if he and Rus didn't like her, he would give her credit for knowing a lot. So old George washed himself at the pump, put on a clean shirt and plodded down to the Allens'.

Mary was sitting in the hammock. Old George cleared his throat and with one crashing sentence broke the ice.

"Rus ain't happy."

"So?" said Mary Allen, coolly.

"And he ought not to be so unhappy."

Mary Allen looked up toward the Benner home. "No," she said thoughtfully, "he ought not."

George leaned forward confidentially and whispered the suspicion: "I believe it's about a girl."

"It always *is*, isn't it?"

Old George rubbed the back of his hand across his beard. This Mary Allen was too deep for him.

"Rus has loved a girl some time," he ventured. "Never said nothin' about it, but *I know.*"

Mary Allen looked at old George with steady blue eyes. "Yes, I think he did," she said softly. Then she added definitely: "I'm quite *sure* he did."

"If I knew who she was," old George threatened, "I'd go get her and haul her right to the house to talk to Rus."

"A man," said Mary Allen emphatically, "a *real* man goes after a girl himself."

If Old George had expected any help from Mary Allen, he was fooled. Apparently she was not so smart after all.

And then, Old George's sympathetic interest received a sudden strengthening. Rus, taking an unusual notion to go into town to a picture show, asked George if he didn't want to go along. George was as pleased as a seven-year-old. The dim lights, the music, the people on the screen all fascinated him. The feature picture ran its nine melodramatic reels with old George completely absorbed in the intricate troubles of a dark-eyed heroine, and a dashing hero upon whose trail camped an oily villain. In the ninth inning, as it were, the misunderstood damsel, with a flower-basket on her arm, took her melancholy way into an old-fashioned garden with a neat white gate.

Old George suddenly sat bolt upright and nudged Rus with an excited elbow.

"Looks just like our gate," he whispered thru the Spanish moss of his beard.

Rus nodded. Then the gate opened and the hero strode into the garden. Old George liked the stylish way he looked in white pants and a dark coat. With superb disregard for all the previous eight reels of misery, the man took the girl's basket from her, crushed her hands in his and (if the caption told the truth) remarked with cave-man authority: "This has gone on long enough!"—apparently meaning the eight reels of agony and not the flower-picking. Then he took the girl in his arms and presented her with a rather long and effective kiss.

Old George was emotionally disturbed. He reached in his pocket for his mouth-organ, suddenly remembered where he was and surreptitiously slipped it back. Over his shaggy beard he stole a hasty glance at Rus. Rus sat with folded arms, looking intently at the picture.

"*Snappin' crocodiles!*" Old George jumped to his conclusion. "That's the girl Rus likes or else it's one just like her." As far as old George was concerned, girls might have come by the dozens in paper cartons.

For several days he pondered the fact that Rus had sat looking hungrily at the girl in the picture. And then—events following each other with lightning-like rapidity—a friend of Mary Allen's came to join her for a few days at the next farm. Old George, driving a lumber wagon to town for fence posts, saw her and was quite upset at the sight. *She was the girl in the picture.*

At home he made subtle approaches to Rus. "Rus, there's a girl visiting Mary Allen."

"That'll be all right with me, George."

"She's got dark eyes and—" old George searched his mind for another fetching characteristic, but finished lamely—"and a mouth."

"Fine, George. Quite convenient, both for eating and speaking."

"Why don't you go down and see her?"

"For that matter, why don't you go down yourself?"

It irritated old George, that Rus should brood and gloom around and not do anything about it. "Leaves the whole thing to me," he muttered crossly.

It caused him to make another trip down to Mary Allen's. He found her among the few plants which the Allens courteously called their flower garden. Old George eyed it with ill-concealed contempt. Then he went immediately to the point. "I know now who that girl is that Rus likes."

A smile lighted, butterfly-like, on Mary Allen's lips. "So? And how did you find this out, George?"

Old George leaned forward and whispered confidentially: "It's the girl that's visiting you."

The smile, butterfly-like, flitted away. Mary Allen's hand flew to her throat. "Oh, no," she said hastily, "not Elaine—not Elaine Forbes?"

Old George nodded knowingly.

Mary Allen continued to stare at the old man. "They *were* in school together," she admitted. Then she added: "Well, so *that's* it, is it?"

George brightened. For the first time he was receiving encouragement. For the first time his ideas seemed important. He warmed up to his subject. "Now, he's got to see her some way and fix this up, and he won't come down here." Mary Allen winced a little at that but old George did not notice. "I've got an idee all thought out to have her come up to the garden for some flowers. I'll have Rus there and if me and you can get her to come thru the white picket gate tonight for some flowers—" old George cocked a watery eye, "—it's goin' to come out all right. Can you think of a way to get her to come up?"

"Why, yes—if you really know Rus is unhappy about her. I think I'd even do that—for Rus."

"And I don't want you along." Old George was brutally frank.

"No—" said Mary Allen wistfully, "I suppose not."

For a few moments she stood looking at nothing in particular across the apple-green of the cornfields, then she threw up her head and said briskly: "We're having a little party for Elaine, a tea tomorrow afternoon, and I'd certainly like some of your roses and delphinium." She motioned apologetically toward the limited collection of flowers at her feet. "George—" she turned suddenly to him, "do you honestly know that this is true?"

Old George grunted. "Don't I *live* with him?" Mystery and finality were both embodied in the crisp question.

By supper time old George was having a nice case of nerves. But no stage manager was ever more careful of his settings. The Forbes woman must come thru the white gate just as the girl in the picture did. Old George pondered all this with attention to details. She might appear at the other gate—the one at the foot of the lawn. That would never do. Some submerged dramatic instinct told George that it must be the white gate behind the roses. After some scheming, quite casually he walked past the little lower gate and left a heavy hand-plow leaning against it.

"What are you doing, George?" Rus called. "Get that out of there. Don't you see, no one could get thru, with all that in the way?"

Old George sulkily pulled the hand-plow away, but when Rus went into the house he slipped a small padlock over the latch of the disqualified gate.

After supper, to his alarm, Rus ran his roadster out of the garage, but his fears subsided when he realized Rus was going back into the house to change his clothes. With studied nonchalance he suggested: "Rus, why don't you put on them white flannel pants of your'n?"

"Why all the dog, George?"

Old George rubbed the back of a nervous hand across the swamp-grass beard. "Somebody might be droppin' in."

The chores done, old George had scarcely settled himself in a chair tilted back against the side of the house when he saw the girl coming. Suddenly he felt scared. He was glad Rus was in the house. As he had predicted, she went straight to the wrong gate.

"Ssst! Go around," old George called to her, jerking a stubby thumb toward the white picket gate. "Rus," he then called, "here's a girl to see you."

The girl opened the gate and stepped in. She put one hand up on the white post just as the girl in the picture had done. Her lovely face glowed. She looked like a flower herself. Old George was so emotionally disturbed that he reached for his mouth-organ, but hastily put it back—for Rus had come to the door. Why in tarnation hadn't Rus put on his white pants?

And now that the great dramatic climax was about to be reached, it seemed that nothing was going right. Rus should have sprung to the girl's side, taken her basket, her hands, then the girl herself. Instead he stood inside the doorway and ejaculated under his breath: "Good lord, what does *she* want?"

"This old gentleman that works for you said we could have some roses," the girl appealed to Rus. Her eyes were as big and brown as the girl's in the picture. Old George could have slain Rus cheerfully for standing there like a numbskull.

"Sure," said Rus pleasantly. "George, go get the scissors and cut some roses for Miss Forbes." Then he turned and walked briskly out to the roadster and drove away.

Old George swore softly under his breath and cut the flowers sulkily. Miss Forbes went home. It was all over. The scheme old George had planned and worked on for Rus's sake had gone into nothing. He was disgusted beyond measure. Nothing could keep him hanging around these diggings longer. All foolish for a man to waste his one life hanging around a farm—jogging back and forth with a load of grain—tending silly flowers like a woman.

Old George heard the creaking of the gate and paused to look back. Mary Allen stuck her head around the white post, her saucy nose uptilted.

"What you want?" old George called gruffly.

"Rus isn't here, is he?" she called. "I saw him drive away or I wouldn't have come. Elaine got the roses but she forgot the delphinium."

"Help yourself," said old George crossly "and don't trample on them new aster shoots."

He was still muttering to himself, when he heard Rus's car purr into the driveway. He was just irritable enough to be pleased at Mary Allen's discomfiture.

"Mary, what are you doing here?" Rus was saying to her in a stern voice. Old George could hear every word. It was going to be as good as a show to hear Rus call her down.

Mary Allen's tip-tilted nose went up a little higher. "Getting delphinium," she said shortly.

Rus stood still and scowled at Mary Allen. Going to tell her to get out and be quick about it, old George suspected. Lord, how Rus hated her.

And then—quite suddenly—Rus was striding over to Mary Allen, stepping on all the new aster shoots. The grin on old George's face froze. His mouth dropped open. For Rus had taken Mary Allen's basket and tossed it into the barberry. "Mary," he was saying, "this has gone on long enough!" Then he took Mary Allen's hands in his—and then Mary Allen herself. Then he kissed her, long and effectively. Old George stood tense, his eyes glued to the scene. Then he slipped behind the hedge, and tiptoed across the driveway to the harness shed, where he dropped down weakly on a pile of gunny-sacks. He took off his hat and wiped his moist forehead.

"*Snappin' crocodiles!*" he swore gently under his breath. Then he reached in his pocket for his mouth-organ. The notes were weird and mournful, with long-drawn ornate chords of his own invention:

> "*Down in the cornfield, hear that mournful song*
> *All the darkies am a-weeping, Massa's in the cold, cold ground.*"

"Hey, George! This isn't a sad occasion Rus called across the hedge. "Cut it for something more cheerful."

"Sure, Rus!"

> "*Forsaken, forsaken, forsaken am I.*
> *Like a grave in the churchyard,*
> *My buried hopes lie.*"

When he finished the dirge, he could hear voices across the hedge—Mary Allen's light hearted like a linnet's, Rus's, low, tender, contented. Old George got up and plodded across the barnyard, thru the pasture, to the railroad land.

"Now I'm goin' for sure," he said decisively. "Looks like they'd be a wedding. Don't want no little sassy upstart with city ways around here bossin' Rus 'n me, a-spoilin' things." He looked wistfully up the railroad track.

Suddenly he slapped his knee. "*Snappin' crocodiles!*" He said it out loud. "Just happened to think. Might some day be a *little* Rus! Why, he'd run around with me—have a little spade 'n dig in the flower-beds with me—ride in the grain wagon alongside o' me—I could get him a little mouth-organ—learn him to play—"

Old George turned away from the railroad track and shambled up to the farmhouse.

Pie

An assistant supervisor of the primary training school was one who had already received a degree in teaching and was working toward the advanced Primary Training Certificate. Aldrich seems to have enjoyed recalling her year spent in this training at Iowa State Normal School (she enrolled in the fall of 1906 and received her certificate in the spring of 1907), for she created three short stories in which the protagonist holds such a position. This story was published in June of 1930 in the *Country Gentleman*. Always there is humor in Aldrich's pieces. The other stories with a similar character are "The Two Who Were Incompatible" and "Miss Livingston's Nephew."

Aldrich also enjoyed writing of mistaken identities, as in "The Patient House" and "Marcia Mason's Lucky Star."

It was ten minutes past two on an October afternoon in Room Twenty-one of the primary training department of Midwest Teachers' College. To be sure it was also ten minutes past two in other departments of the large and well-organized factory of learning; but in Room Twenty-one of the training school it seemed most specifically ten minutes past two—that lazy, languorous time of day.

Summer, having once departed from the place, had rushed back that week, quite like a woman who had forgotten something important, and having found it, with the changeableness of femininity, decided to stay. The windows were open to the warm breeze. An unsanitary-looking fly buzzed in and out by the tennis courts. Multitudinous leaves spiraled down from the huge elms, like so many elfin airplanes using the green campus for a landing field.

Thirty-four girls, who were taking the course, lined the walls of Room Twenty-one, notebooks in hand. Some of them were majoring in primary training and minoring in other subjects. Some of them were minoring in primary work and majoring in getting engaged. But on this Wednesday afternoon at ten minutes past two, there was no way of dividing the gayly frivolous from the deadly earnest by their appearance. Due to the Indian-summer weather, all alike looked sleepy, dull, uninterested. A pudgy girl with thick glasses over protruding eyes made objectless marks on her notebook. A homely blonde, whom the discriminating gentleman would have preferred, was frankly nodding.

Across the room, near one of the open windows, sat Miriam Foster, the assistant supervisor. The title bears an important sound, as one representing both age and dignity.

But it would have taken thirty-five guesses to have picked out the owner of the title, for she had not as yet achieved a greater age than twenty-five, and she looked as dignified as a wood sprite. Warm brown hair swirled about her forehead in a fetching cut, and her brown eyes held the same little red-gold glints in them. She was dressed in russet brown with just enough scarlet about it to give her the appearance of a gay autumn leaf.

If one could not have picked her out of the group from point of age or appearance, neither could one have recognized her through any manifestation of unusual interest in the work going on in the center of the room, for she looked as uninterested and bored as any of the takers of the course.

The children in the circle were playing games under the direction of a short, olive-skinned student; and no one could have accused the children, themselves, of being bored. With that wide-eyed interest in life in which the mere matter of weather has no part, they were entering into the oft-repeated plays with as much ardor as though participating in them for the first time.

At that particular moment, a very immaculate little girl, whom one knew at a glance to be a specimen of the perfect female child, spoke: "William is not standing correctly." She said it definitely, didactically and critically.

William immediately straightened his spindling, overall-clad legs, and the perfect child looked about her for further opportunity of correction.

"In years to come," said the assistant supervisor—of course, to herself—"she will be president of a woman's club or chairman of some reform league."

A health game was now well under way. William, of the temporary slouchy attitude and the permanent overall legs, took the center of the circle.

"Will you have a dish of oatmeal and cream?" he asked and pointed to one of the expectant group.

"Yes, thank you," said the honored one.

"Will you have some fried potatoes?" He pointed to another.

"No, thank you."

"Will you have a dish of stewed prunes?"

"Yes, please."

Any rank outsider could have sensed the point. It was as apparent as the pointer, himself, or the pointee. All the edibles which did not contain vitamins and health were scorned. All the dainty morsels which were overrich received the "thumbs down" of these modern little Romans. Their attitude was that if you ate fried potatoes you would be relegated to some region of the lost. If you ate oatmeal you would enter some Valhalla of bliss.

"Will you have a piece of pie?" William's active if soiled index finger veered to the perfect female child.

The p.f.c. shook her yellow curls and assumed a horror-stricken air of dramatic proportions.

"Oh, no, thank you." She threw into the answer a world of repugnance. And then, further realizing her own nobility of soul, she turned to the student teacher: "Miss Anderson . . . my mamma had pie this noon . . . raspberry pie . . . a big piece sat right by my plate . . . and I never touched it."

"Why, you little halfwit!" said the assistant supervisor. (Oh, certainly to herself.) From which unuttered exclamation you will gather how very far afield had gone the assistant supervisor's regard for her own teachings this warm afternoon.

Sitting there in the midst of her chosen life work, Miriam Foster was admitting to herself a waning interest in it. And simultaneously with her digression she was mentally flaying herself with a bludgeon of self-criticism. As mystified as chagrined at the way her attention was slipping, she realized that for some unknown reason she felt at odds with her profession.

Too often recently she had been picturing herself down a vista of years in a future of training schools and lectures, dividing the fried potatoes from the oatmeal, the pie from the prunes—and the perspective was not so satisfying as she had once thought.

So far as men were concerned, she assured herself they were out of her life forever. There had been one serious affair for her, resulting in a broken engagement, with the man marrying soon afterward. As a consequence she had consecrated herself, nunlike, to her work. And now only the mild-mannered, safely-married men of the training school constituted her one connection with a masculine world that was false.

In the midst of Miriam Foster's self-chastisement, and near the close of the children's health game, the door opened and the Head appeared. Not a head, but the Head. Miss Evaline Jones, the head of the department. If one wanted to be facetious, he might say that there was a hat upon the Head, for Miss Jones was hatted and gloved in the correct tailored way that one would expect Miss Jones to be. She was large and imposing. She carried about her person all the dignity and age which the assistant failed to possess.

Quite suddenly the atmosphere in Room Twenty-one changed. It was as though, upon opening the door, Miss Jones had inserted the cord of an imaginary electrical charger into an invisible socket. The occupants of the room came to life. The blonde leaned forward with a deep and vital interest in the health game. The fat girl with the thick glasses began writing unimportant words vigorously in her notebook. The fly disappeared into an outer sun-flooded world, as though there were no use trying to fool with a personality like Miss Jones'. Miriam Foster, the good lieutenant that she was, almost saluted her superior.

The Head crossed to that young lady now, said a few low words of explanation to her, looked complacently at the keenly interested girls flanking the walls, stopped to say good-by to the participants of the game circle, and vanished into the sun-flooded world herself, although not by way of the window.

The figurative electric cord having been withdrawn from the socket, the occupants of the room slumped into their former lethargy. The homely blonde closed her eyes. The fat girl tucked her pencil into her blouse pocket. Miss Miriam Foster returned to her own analytical soliloquy.

The circle game was changing now. They were about to perpetrate the classic known as "Chicken Little."

"Heavens!" said the assistant (oh, most assuredly to herself). "If I'm ever in a large brick building with bars at the windows it will be from an overdose of Chicken Little."

"The sky is falling," said Chicken Little, in the person of William the conquered. "I will run and tell Henny-Penny." The orgy of gossiping was on.

In the midst of the wild rumors which seemed to obsess Chicken Little there was a knock on the door of Twenty-one—a loud and vigorous knock, almost immodestly so, for one usually approached the model training school with something of timidity, silence and veneration.

"I heard it with my ears, I saw it with my eyes. A piece of it fell on my tail," declared the newsmonger of the circle.

The girls all straightened up, cheered with the pleasant anticipation of having the monotony relieved, although it would probably prove to be nothing more exciting than a student or a parent. Miriam Foster rose, crossed the room, and opened the door, preparatory to slipping out. But she did not slip. It was not a student. One had grave doubts about its being a parent. A very tall, very well-groomed young man stood on the threshold.

"I beg your pardon," his voice, with cut-out open, boomed hollowly from the empty hall.

"You'd better," thought the assistant, critically, if not grammatically.

"May I speak to you for a moment?" His voice was still far from weak.

"I will run and tell Turkey-Lurkey," said the tattletale in the circle.

The assistant had time to say acridly (yes, indeed, to herself) "All right . . . go on and tell," as she stepped out and closed the door.

The man looked at Miriam Foster, standing there, cool and aloof and questioning. "I'm sorry to bother you." He had a most engaging smile. "My name is Jones, Barton Jones . . . of the law firm of Bartholomew, Baker, Mead and Jones of Chicago. And while I'm here between trains, I'm trying to form a rather belated acquaintance with a cousin of mine."

"Oh!" Miriam Foster smiled then also. And that made two engaging smiles turned loose in the hall. "You're Miss Jones' cousin." She became gracious and friendly.

"Miss Jones is the head of our department. But she's not here. She has just gone . . . starting over to Leeds College to give her lecture. She's been gone such a little while—she was here just a few minutes ago—that I'm sure you could catch her. She takes the yellow bus at the northeast corner of the campus."

"Yes?" Miss Evaline Jones' cousin looked at the cleft in Miriam Foster's chin, and repeated with certain slight variations, "I see . . . the northeast bus at the corner of the yellow campus."

"You can take a short-cut," the owner of the chin declivity suggested.

"Yes?" said Mr. Jones vaguely, and added more definitely, "Oh, yes."

"You go down these first steps and turn to the left. Then you follow the walk past the Domestic Science building. . . . Do you know where the Domestic Science building is?"

"No," said Mr. Jones, almost in despair. "Oh, no."

"It's the first building to the north. Then you take the curved walk and you will find the busses at the end of it."

And while the consensus of opinion among the other members of the Bartholomew, Baker, Mead and Jones firm was that Mr. Barton Jones was far from dull, he seemed to have acquired a sudden impenetrable density.

In the intensity of her desire to do the gracious thing for the head of the department, the assistant further volunteered: "I'll walk out to the steps and point it out to you." Which all goes to prove that stupidity occasionally has its place in the scheme of things.

They went out on the training-school steps, where the elm leaves spiraled down and the October sunshine lay in little golden pools.

"The campus is gorgeous, now, isn't it?" the man said affably.

"Lovely," the girl agreed. "Now, there . . . around that walk . . . over there."

"It's a perfect day, isn't it?"

"Quite perfect. You've only a few minutes."

"Thank you so much. I hope taking you away from your class like this hasn't queered you in any way with your teacher."

"I," said Miriam Foster, a little coldly, "am the teacher."

"You? Do you mean to stand there and say . . . Well, can you beat . . . ?"

"You'll have to hurry," said the teacher with finality. "Good day." And she went into the building and closed the huge door impressively.

As she stepped back into Twenty-one, her head very high, thirty-four girls watched her keenly, sixty-eight adult eyes looked at her curiously.

"They ran into Foxy-Loxy's den and they never came out," accused the gossiper of the circle.

Several girls grinned openly, not to say suspiciously. The homely blonde tittered and nudged the owl-eyed fat girl in her well-cushioned ribs.

"Just for that," said Miriam Foster (oh, absolutely to herself), "you will pay . . . and pay . . . and pay. . . ." Aloud and quite distinctly, she said: "Observation class dismissed. You will each hand in on Thursday a well-written fifteen hundred-word paper on "The Relation of Games to a Child's Health." And knew, with an unholy glee, that she had nipped in the bud more than one joy ride and dance date.

At four o'clock, preparing to leave her office, she pushed back the calendar on her desk, weighted down a bunch of lesson plans with a plaster cast of The Laughing Child, straightened the sepia copy of The Gleaners, and closed the desk. When she turned, Mr. Barton Jones of Bartholomew, Baker, Mead and Jones stood in the doorway.

"I missed her," he grinned cheerfully.

"I'm so sorry," said Miriam Foster, and added (oh, exclusively to Miriam Foster), "Oh, no, you're not so grieved."

"And now I'm stranded here until ten o'clock, and you're the only one in town I know."

Know! The nerve!

"Well," she suggested pleasantly, "the college library doesn't close until nine."

He was thoughtful. "And I never *have* read Fox's Book of Martyrs or Saints' Rest," he admitted.

At that, Miriam Foster laughed aloud. And Barton Jones laughed too. And the plaster cast laughed hardest of all—diabolically—but behind their backs.

All of which is the long and circuitous sequence of events which led Miriam Foster to dine at six-thirty at the New Van Deere with a man whose existence she had not known at two o'clock in the afternoon, to dine with him solely from duty and out of courtesy to the absent Head.

And then, along came Thursday . . . and Miss Evaline Jones. It seemed nothing short of dishonest not to speak about Mr. Barton Jones immediately to the Head, but he had asked her not to do so, for the reason that he wanted to surprise her by dropping in at the college again in a few days.

On Monday of the next week, whenever she heard a noisy approach in the hall, she grew slightly chilly and showed a tendency toward flushing at the cheek bones. But two days of the week went by, and he had not come.

On Wednesday afternoon, as she went down the steps of the training school and rounded the building to the north, she nearly collided with him—the returning relative of the Head.

"Oh . . . !" She was genuinely distressed. "Didn't I tell you? I *thought* I did. Miss Jones goes over there *every* Wednesday afternoon," she explained earnestly.

"Does she?" Mr. Barton Jones was apparently torn between the intensity of his surprise and the depths of his mental pain.

"Every Wednesday," repeated Miriam Foster.

"I see . . . persistency . . . perseverance . . . stick-to-itiveness. It's in the blood."

To mitigate Mr. Jones' disappointment over the unintentional misunderstanding, Miriam Foster dined with him again at the New Van Deere; and after that they walked up to the house where she lived with an old retired professor and his wife. One of them could not see well and the other could not hear well. So the half-deaf old lady spied upon the two young people and the half-blind old man listened intently, and after the caller had gone they put their respective findings together and decided it was a budding romance. And still, Miriam Foster, feeling like a traitor, said nothing to the Head because the cousin wished to surprise her.

October flung one last gorgeous flaming week to the world. On Wednesday afternoon the assistant supervisor stood before her desk calendar and absent-mindedly drew two distinct circles around the two previous Wednesday dates. Then, with sudden alarm, she rubbed them out so vigorously that there were only smudgy holes left where the figures had been. When she looked up from the calendar, she saw Mr. Barton Jones standing in the doorway.

"My cousin . . . ?" He was beaming cheerfully. "Is she here?"

"You know she isn't," said Miriam Foster coldly.

"But you told me she went Wednesdays."

"*This* is Wednesday." There were icicles on that statement. "You know it."

"Is it?" He walked over to the calendar and ran an investigating finger up the columns. "Why, so it is," he admitted amiably, and then asked curiously, "What made those two holes in your calendar?"

"Days that were wasted," said Miriam Foster evenly, "so wasted that I cut them out."

Quite suddenly, Barton Jones was not flippant. "They were not wasted." He was all seriousness. "They were delightful . . . so lovely that I came back to have one more of them before we have to take my cousin with us." And then, as quickly, he returned to his former lightness. "The year's at the fall . . . the car's at the curb . . . my face is all clean . . . your hair is all curled . . . God's in heaven . . . all's right with the world."

There is not a particle of use in trying to trace the various processes by which Miriam Foster's mental equipment finally assured her that it was her duty to entertain Mr. Jones again for the sake of the Head, in spite of his flagrant fabrications. Eliminating all psychological analyses, and looking only at results, one might have seen the two, fifteen minutes later, driving through a woodsy road where the sun flecked the tire tracks through dancing shadows. The drive ended at the Mellow Moon, popular with faculty and students, alike, for its dinners.

It was while they were eating that they heard a shrilly triumphant, "Miss Foster . . . oh, Miss Foster!"

"Somewhere a voice is calling," said Barton Jones, "tender and true."

The voice was the voice of the perfect female child, and with its insistent decision and two forceful hands, she was dragging her parents to the table nearest the beloved teacher.

Miriam Foster spoke to the obedient parents, made a pedagogical sounding remark to her adoring pupil, and then turned to discuss the critical question of dessert with Barton Jones.

"I'd love a piece of pie," she said wistfully, "but I can't have it."

"Can't? Why the 'can't'?"

"Because this energetic creature across from me"—she spoke very low—"watching my every movement, is the personification of all my work. She is the symbol of my career. I teach her to scorn fried potatoes and laud oatmeal . . . to eschew pie and chew prunes. I know that's an awfully low type of humor, but I couldn't help it. I ask you then, could I sit here, under her eagle eye, and order pie . . . and let her see all my theories come tumbling down?"

Barton Jones grinned his interest.

"But if I ever leave. . . ." she threatened.

Mr. Jones sat forward. "Yes? When you leave? You mean when you marry?"

"Every woman teacher who marries must leave the faculty," said Miriam Foster definitely. "There is a ruling to that effect. But it does not necessarily follow that, inversely, everyone who leaves, has married. As I was saying. . . . " She was a little confused. "Oh, yes . . . if I ever leave, I shall do just that . . . recklessly, before them all . . . the student teachers . . . your cousin, the Head . . . The perfect female child . . . all of them. I shall order the richest pie I can get . . . and eat it in their presence. It would be a gesture of freedom. It would be signing the emancipation proclamation. It would be snapping my fingers in the faces of the gods."

The light-footed colored boy came up for the order.

"Prunes," said Miriam Foster to him, resignedly, "stewed prunes."

It was when Barton Jones was leaving in the evening that he quite brazenly came out with the declaration that he wanted to dine with her again the following Wednesday. And Miriam Foster, with one fleeting assurance to herself that there was no more comforting bit of philosophy than that one might as well be hung for a sheep as a lamb, said she would expect him.

On Monday, October took summer by the hand, and the two fled precipitately, leaving behind them cold, rainy, disagreeable weather.

And then on Tuesday, the Head, a letter in her hand, came into the assistant supervisor's office. "This terrible rain!" she began in her ponderous way. "I'm glad I'm all through with the Leeds lectures."

Miriam Foster's heart missed a beat and then hippity-hopped to catch up. So Miss Jones was through with her Wednesday trips. The perfect tête-à-têtes would cease.

But the Head was speaking: "I've just had a letter I wanted to tell you about. It's from the girl my cousin is engaged to. She's coming through here tomorrow and I want you to meet her."

Miriam Foster's heart apparently crashed head-on against the stone wall of the news. But her mind was saying stanchly: "People have more than one cousin. No doubt she has a dozen. The woods are full of Joneses."

"Her name is Daphne Dunham . . . rather euphonious, isn't it?" The Head went placidly on. "He is the only unmarried cousin I have, and I do hope he is getting a lovely girl. I haven't seen him for some years. He's a dear boy . . . but something of a philanderer, they tell me. Now that he's to be married, though, I'm sure he'll settle down."

Miriam Foster's heart seemed scarcely able to move in the midst of its wreckage.

All unaware of the disastrous emotional catastrophe which had just occurred, the Head went calmly on: "I thought we three could have dinner together tomorrow evening . . . perhaps at that new Green Candlestick place. They say it's good."

TOMORROW! Why tomorrow was Wednesday—the DAY—the day that Barton Jones was to come.

"Have you an engagement for tomorrow night's dinner?" Miriam Foster could hear Miss Jones asking it as naturally as though the question were any ordinary one.

"Yes," said the assistant, dully. "I *did* have . . . but. . . . "

"I'm sorry. Some other time, then, she may be going through." And the Head was moving away in her ship-leaving-the-dock manner.

Miriam Foster's mind began to take charge of the situation. "Snap out of it," it whispered to the prostrate heart. "Get up out of there. 'Something of a philanderer' his cousin says." It was amazing how completely resuscitated her mind was. It even took pains to sneer cruelly at the bruised heart still unable to function with regularity. It assured that fluttering organ that it, at least, could keep its wits in order. With nimbleness it came to a decision. Why not bring this cheerful philanderer face to face with his fiancée under embarrassing circumstances? Evidently Miss Daphne Dunham would never expect to see her Barton at the college. Most assuredly Mr. Jones would not be looking for his Daphne. The opportunity to teach the young man a lesson was too good to pass lightly by.

"But, Miss Jones," Miriam Foster called to that rather slow-moving dignitary, "why couldn't all of us—you and your friend . . . and I and mi—mine—have a table together tomorrow night?"

All the rest of the day and Wednesday morning it rained, a soggy, dripping rain.

All Wednesday the assistant supervisor went doggedly about her work.

In the late afternoon, swathed in a brown slicker, with the swirling bob of her redbrown hair tucked under a cap, she splashed through the damp, dripping campus toward her room. To bolster her courage she kept assuring herself that what she had planned for Barton Jones was just what he deserved.

With the swishing sound of a water-soaked raincoat, someone was coming rapidly behind her. She stepped aside, but a masculine hand closed over her own hand that held the umbrella.

"My cousin . . . ?" He had the nerve to laugh at that—this modern Claudius who could smile and smile and be the villain still.

"Your cousin. . . . " She forced herself to laugh too. Her every act must seem natural until the dénouement. "Your cousin has gone to the county commissioners to report your weakening mentality."

There was a blazing fire in the grate of the old professor's living room when they arrived. Miriam Foster left the villain standing in front of it, looking after her, when she mounted the stairs to dress. She wished he hadn't looked like that—clean-cut and attractive—standing there so easily in front of the fire.

In her room she put on a little one-piece brown dress, decided she looked ghastly, and changed it for a crimson jersey. When she came down, the two made their way under the dripping elms, over the slippery walks to the Green Candlestick. Two students, the homely blonde and the fat girl with glasses, smelling romance, left their seats in the far end of the room and came to take places at the next table.

"Miss Foster . . . oh, Miss Foster," broke forth an adoring sound.

"Ha!" said Barton Jones. "There's the voice that breathed o'er Eden."

"Why don't they ever eat at home?" commented the object of the adoration, irritably, as the perfect female child pulled her pliant parents to the other adjoining table.

The two vacant chairs, turned against their own table seemed to eye Miriam Foster like silent accusers. Evidently the train was late. Miss Jones had said not to wait if they had not arrived at six-thirty. So the two ordered, ate, and conversed—the last activity being somewhat handicapped by the close proximity of many ears. Miriam Foster was more nervous than she had ever been in her life.

And then—the waiting ceased. She saw Miss Jones come in. And the girl was with her. So that was the girl whom Barton Jones loved! She was not over nineteen or twenty—lovely, lithe, radiant.

Quite suddenly Miriam Foster felt that she could not do this thing. Something within her rebelled at embarrassing this fine, clean-cut man. After all, he had a perfect right to be engaged. She had been with him all these past weeks of her own free will.

"Look, Mr. Jones," she said in a small voice that sounded flat and unnatural.

"At the what?"

"Don't you see them?"

"Which 'them'?"

"Your cousin . . . and your . . . Miss Dunham . . . over there by the door."

"Oh, is my cousin over there? I thought you said she went every Wednesday."

"She did . . . but she's finished."

"Then so am I. Listen, Miriam Foster. There's something I want to explain to you before they come."

"Oh, don't try to explain." She was looking at the heavy figure of the Head, who had stopped to introduce the girl to an English instructor. "I know all about it. I fancied I was hurt because you didn't tell me yourself. It made me want to . . . to bring this embarrassing situation upon you. I had a childish idea it would be clever. I'm wretched about it now. I wish I hadn't done it."

"I should have told you." He was all seriousness. "I've just let things drift carelessly along . . . and happily . . . from week to week. But you won't let it make any difference with us, will you?"

Any difference! Miriam Foster smiled. She was thinking that Napoleon might have asked it of Josephine when he divorced her.

When Barton Jones saw the tremulous smile that was meant to be cheerful, he said quite savagely: "I'm all kinds of a cad to let you hear it from someone else. Who told you?"

"Miss Jones . . . your cousin. She said Miss Dunham was a lovely girl. I can see that . . . lovely and charming." Miss Jones and her protégée were now talking to the football coach and his wife, halfway down the room. "And I congratulate you."

"What for? Who's charming?"

"Miss Daphne Dunham . . . your fiancée."

"My what?"

"Fiancée." And then, quite didactically, she explained: "The girl you're engaged to."

"Good lord." He was gazing in deep amazement toward the chatting group. "I'm not engaged to anybody . . . Daffy-down-dilly, or anyone else . . . not for a few minutes yet anyway. I don't know where you got that, but it's immaterial just now. Listen, Miriam, listen closely." He leaned nearer to her across the college café table. "I'm not the Head's cousin . . . nor her uncle . . . nor her grandfather. I never saw her before and I don't care a tinker's dam if I ever see her again. I never heard of her before the day you first talked to me. I'm terribly sorry to tell you this here . . . and now. Can you hear me? These two human dictaphones over here are taking it all in."

The blond girl and the fat one with glasses scarcely moved a spoon, so anxious were they to catch the conversation.

"You mean you haven't been her cousin?"

"Not any of the time . . . not even Wednesdays." He grinned.

"But you said you were."

"Oh, no, I didn't. You came out in the hall looking as sweet as a peach and as cold as a peach ice. *I* said: 'I'm looking up my cousin.' And *you* said, 'Oh, you're Miss Jones' cousin'; and thawed out and acted cordial. My cousin is a little freshman. Her name is Bartholomew—Mary Bartholomew. But when you insisted that Miss Jones was my cousin . . . and looked at me like that. . . ."

"Don't be talking about it. They're coming this way."

"Yes . . . I'm going to talk about it. I'm going to be talking about it after they get here, if you won't listen now. Would you have gone out to dinner with me if you had known I wasn't the Head's cousin?"

"Most certainly not."

"Don't you see . . . I had to? There was nothing else to do. The minute I saw you I knew you were the girl for me."

The girl-for-him gasped.

"I love you . . . and I want you to marry me and leave school. You'd have to. You said there was a ruling."

Miss Jones and her young friend came up. They formed the four corners of the cross-word puzzle: the assistant, the Head, the erstwhile fiancée and the villain. There were introductions and explanations for being late.

The little student waitress came up. "Go right on and order," said the Head in her supervising way, "while we look over the dinner card."

"Prunes and cream as usual, Miss Foster?" asked the little waitress familiarly.

Like needles to two magnets, Miriam Foster's eyes turned to the eyes of Barton Jones. The eyes of Barton Jones were twinkling . . . and then the twinkling changed to something less mischievous.

"Or pie, Miriam?" He asked it gently—so gently that, instead of a prosaic item on the menu, it sounded like the first few bars of an old love song.

Miriam Foster looked across the table china at the impostor. Over at the next table the homely blonde and the owl-eyed fat girl strained their aural organs to catch every word. Across the other aisle the perfect female child bent worshiping eyes upon her adored teacher.

Then—quite deliberately the assistant supervisor made the gesture. Quite definitely she signed the proclamation. Quite distinctly she snapped her fingers in the faces of the gods. For even as she spoke to the little waitress she was smiling across the china toward the junior member of Bartholomew, Baker, Mead and Jones.

"Pie . . . " she ordered recklessly, "*the chocolate pie with the whipped cream and marshmallow icing.*" And, instead of a prosaic item on the menu, it sounded like the rest of the melody of the old love song.

The Faith that Rode with the Covered Wagon

Aldrich was commissioned by the editor of the *Christian Herald* in 1930 to provide this article, which they printed in two parts (9 and 16 August). That year was recognized as the one hundredth anniversary of the first wagon train to venture northwest across the continent from St. Louis on what would later be called the Oregon Trail. Because of her love of history and her understanding of the pioneer as an individual, writing this piece probably was a pleasant respite from Aldrich's frustrating efforts to start her next novel, *A White Bird Flying.* While this article for the *Christian Herald,* for whom Aldrich was also a book reviewer, stresses the religious faith of the majority of the pioneers, it also underscores her great love for the Midwest.

This is the year of an important celebration—the occasion for commemorating the one hundreth anniversary of the first wagon train leaving St. Louis for Oregon. On February twenty-second, President Hoover issued a proclamation calling upon the nation to pause and give heed to the memory of the pioneer. His message calls attention to the fact that Ezra Meeker, the grand old man of the trail, was born in that year of 1830, and that the Oregon Trail Memorial Association, which he later founded, has sponsored the movement to observe this summer and fall as the Covered Wagon Centennial. The words of the nation's head are: "Therefore I, Herbert Hoover, President of the United States, do call upon our people to employ this fitting occasion to commemorate the lives and deeds of the heroic pioneers who won and held the West."

It is my privilege to pay, briefly, a tribute to the pioneer through the pages of *Christian Herald.* Viewed from the standpoint of my regard for the pioneer and admiration for his achievements, the task is far from hard; but from the standpoint of doing justice to that tribute, it is a difficult one.

As the mind turns naturally to the specific rather than the general, my thoughts go back to the groups of pioneers who were my own forebears. The clan of my father's people, of sound Revolutionary stock, came into Blackhawk County, Iowa, from Illinois in 1852, their means of locomotion the slow-moving, stolid ox teams. Mother's side of the house, from Scotch ancestry, came two years later, her widowed mother and brother driving the ox teams, mother, herself, driving the team of horses, with three weeks of time consumed in making the trip out from Chicago. To the time of her death in her eighty-first year, she was fond of recalling scenes on that memorable journey, the camps on the edge of the woods, the odor of the night winds, the ferrying across the Mississippi, the teams plunging up and down the bridgeless creek beds, the tipping over of a wagon once, with the eight precious sacks of flour slipping into the water and the feather pillows floating gaily down stream while the children chased after them with hilarious shouting. She had the faculty of describing the scenes so merrily and with such fascination that, as a child, I used to wish that I had been born in an earlier and, what seemed to me, a far more enchanting time of the world. Her set of dishes carved out of acorns, and her doll, which was only a stone with a round formation for its head, grew, through her telling, as familiar to me as my own china dishes and doll.

Father and mother were married, on New Year's Day in 1855, in a log cabin from which the furniture had been removed in order to make room for the guests. When the time for the ceremony came, mother descended the loft ladder backwards in view of the guests, this seemingly peculiar maneuver being somewhat compensated for by the fact that she had an unusually elaborate trousseau consisting of a white wedding dress and another silk one, the cloth for which had been sent out from Chicago by ox team.

Father hauled freight by ox team from Dubuque to Waterloo and Cedar Falls several years before the Dubuque and Sioux City Railroad (later the Illinois Central) came into Blackhawk County. This was before the Civil War; in fact the Dubuque and Sioux City road terminated its line not two miles from the farm homes of my people when halted by the war. One of father's favorite stories concerning this freighting was that on an election day he was on his way back from Dubuque with merchandise for the general store, when a man on horseback came down the trail and told him that, as he was the only man in the community who had not voted, the polls were being held open for him, and that he was to get on the horse and ride to the settlement, while the messenger was to take charge of the slow-moving oxen. Father always told with ill-concealed pride that the votes would have tied without his deciding ballot.

My grandfather, Zimri Streeter, represented Blackhawk County in the first Republican legislature, and was known as "Old Blackhawk" by his colleagues, and, inveterate joker that he was, bore the reputation of being the wag of the house. The Democrats had been responsible for getting Iowa separated from Wisconsin and admitted as a state, but by 1857 the Republicans came in power, including my grandfather, who had made the painless transition from Whig to Republican. I have in my possession a letter written from him to my father, when in Des Moines attending the legislature seventy years ago. In it he says that he hopes my father can comfortably till the soil, that a friend has just left for Springfield by stage coach, that the Pikes Peakers are beginning to run, that he looks for quite a rush to the gold regions, and (proving that human experiences remain very much the same) protests about the high cost of living by saying that they are skinning the legislators alive with their exorbitant charges for board—three dollars per week. Later when the Civil War had sent most of the young men of the community into the South, grandfather was delegated by Governor Kirkwood to go down to the first division of General Logan's Fifteenth Army Corps to bring the vote of the Iowa contingent back to the state. All communication to the South was soon severed. Atlanta had fallen, and grandfather was not heard of for weeks. For, with his old carpet-bag to hold the votes, he was marching with Sherman to the sea.

Besides our own family, the two branches of pioneer relatives were made up of sixteen sets of uncles and aunts and countless cousins, so that even though my own tardy arrival in this clan took place after most of my brothers and sisters were grown, and even though I personally missed all the early pioneer experiences, coming as I did at the tag end of a big family after that family had moved into town, my childish ears were constantly hearing stories, anecdotes, and experiences of those early days.

This clan of pioneer ancestors which made such a lasting impression upon me and to which I refer—for the members seem composite pictures of all pioneers—were sturdy, courageous, energetic, fun-loving, God-fearing, working always with their hands and planning with their minds. They are mistaken who think of the early days of the settling of the trans-Mississippi country as a time when men were stupid and women brow-beaten. The men were not dull and deficient because of their contact with the soil and their fight with the elements. There were storms and winds, drouths and blizzards, and the worry of a thousand fears. But there was fun and there was laughter. There was living and there was loving. There were hopes and plans and dreams for the children. Human characteristics remain much the same, generation after generation, with only the settings of life different, the extraneous problems of the social state varying. Once when my mother at eighty years was relating some of her early experiences about the snow drifting through the chinks of the logs onto the patched quilts of the beds, I remarked to her in sympathy that it was too bad she had endured such a hard life in her younger days while those of her daughters had been lived in a more modern and convenient time. She looked at me with an odd little expression and said: "Oh, save your pity. We had the best time in the world." Yes, in the pioneer days there was the same living and the same loving, the same providential meting-out of joy and sorrow, the same wise limitations put upon laughter and tears.

And so I feel a deep and righteous indignation when I read the conception of those who feel that all people who have had contact with the soil are pitiful specimens of warped humanity, struggling souls who never find deliverance from sordid surroundings. For my pioneer farmer forebears were not such. Sturdy, courageous, playing their parts in the scheme of things, they were builders and not destroyers, creators and not parasites.

Last summer I visited the cemetery where the whole clan lies sleeping a few miles from the homesteads where they felled the first trees and turned the virgin sod. They lie there together, old Grandfather Zimri Streeter, who put aside the plough to ride horseback down through the timber and across the prairie to the legislature of seventy years ago; old Grandmother Lucinda Streeter, who molded tallow candles, and spun and wove; all the uncles and aunts—a host of pioneers. It seemed fitting that they should lie there together with only the green grassy aisles of God's cathedral between the various branches of the family. I thought of all that had been told me as a wondering child, the clannishness of the group, of the countless times the different families had come together in the early days.

Danger had thrown them together—the alarm that the Indians were coming, when they had put a few cherished possessions in the wagons and gone down through the damp dark river road and over the wild prairie to grandfather's larger and stronger log house. *Joy* had thrown them together—on the nights that the furniture had been set out of some cabin when there was a festive occasion, with the home-made candles flickering on the shelves and the fiddles being tuned up for the singing games. *Hope* had thrown them together—the expectation of better advantages for their children than they themselves had experienced, resulting in the building by all hands of the log schoolhouse with its mud-chinked walls and rough benches. *Faith* had thrown them together—trust in a God who held the elements in the hollow of his hand—finding expression in the class meetings and preaching services held in the school house. And now *death* had thrown them all together again where they slept on the sunny side of a sloping hill.

I have been writing of my own Iowa forebears, but, after all, the story of my native Iowa is the story of the other Western States in all its essentials, the spirit of my ancestors was the spirit of all the pioneers.

And so this year, the one hundredth year after the first wagon train creaked its way out of St. Louis toward the far West, we are asked to pause a moment in the midst of the rush of modern living and give heed to the courage and the foresight and the hardihood of those brave men and women who settled the trans-Mississippi states.

It is an impossible task to give a history of that migration in a few short paragraphs, for there were a thousand interesting stories connected with it, countless fascinating incidents in all their wealth of detail. For in all the great migrations of history none has been more picturesque than this westward trek of our own immediate ancestors. No one of our present day civilization can visualize the fight, the weariness, the obstacles, unless perchance it be those who have made a definite and complete study of the trails. No two men in the mid-West are better versed in these details connected with the migration than are Mr. A. E. Sheldon of the Nebraska State Historical Society and Mr. J. G. Masters, principal of Central High School in Omaha. It was my pleasure to listen to Mr. Masters at the recent semi-annual meeting of the Nebraska State Writers' Guild. With a huge map stretched across the front of the luncheon room in the hotel he gave a swift but comprehensive review of the whole migration that made one listen in amazement to the data he had at his command. Each summer Mr. and Mrs. Masters and their four children travel by auto to seek out old pioneer landmarks that are still visible and to locate places of historical significance where every trace of former activity is obliterated.

Briefly, the migration began in 1830 with the wagon train of Captain William Sublette setting out from St. Louis with Wyoming as its destination. Prior to that there had been only the fur trappers and traders making the journey. William Sublette at the head of the caravan of ten wagons and two carriages followed the general routing of that which had been taken by those earlier adventurers. Later came the men who pushed out on the same trail with Oregon as the destination, there to start settlements in the great Northwest. It is worth one's thought to remember that none paid any heed to the settlement of the intervening land at that time, for it seemed only a trackless wilderness lying under scorching suns or choked in the grip of terrific blizzards, a land which was good only for the Indian, the buffalo and the coyote. One can not recall this impression held by all those adventurers in that century-ago period without calling attention to the beautiful and richly productive section that arid land has now grown to be with its acres of corn and wheat lands, its towns and cities, its homes and schools and churches, its cattle upon a thousand hills.

We are told that the old Oregon and Santa Fe trails were one and the same for forty miles out of Independence, Missouri, and that at a point west of what is now Gardner, Kansas, was a sign post pointing to the northwest with the words "Road To Oregon" on it. The trail entered Nebraska at the southeast corner of Jefferson County, not far from Inscription Rock in which the names of Kit Carson and John C. Fremont, with the date 1842, are cut, and which will be legible for other centuries to come.

The trail in its Nebraska wanderings follows the Little Blue north of Hebron past the spot where occurred the terrible Indian raid of 1864, during which the members of a family of settlers by the name of Eubanks were killed, and Mrs. Eubanks and a young sixteen-year-old neighbor girl, Laura Roper, were taken captive by the Indians. A year ago when attending the annual meeting of the Nebraska State Historical Society, I sat next to the "young sixteen-year-old Laura Roper," then eighty-one years old. A plump little old woman she was, with a dimpled face like a round rosy apple, giving every evidence that she had once been unmistakably pretty. I was never to see her again, for the news of her passing was published a few months ago. She told me that she had come from Oklahoma, and that she was expecting to go out to the old homestead near Nelson, Nebraska, to retrace her steps about the hills and ravine where she had been captured sixty-five years before. The details of that day stood out in her memory with far more clarity than most intervening ones, she said. And how could it be otherwise? She had gone over to the neighboring home of the Eubanks family on that hot, dry August day, to spend the afternoon, Mrs. Eubanks "going a piece home" with her. When the two were rounding a hill, they heard the Indians and slipped down a ravine to hide. They were sighted by one of the young bucks, however, placed on the ponies and taken to the camp, where they were held three months before they were set free. One can read of Indian raids, and the scenes seem far-off and vague, descriptions which do not quite savor of reality; but when a little old lady of eighty-one describes in marvelously clear detail the crackling of the sticks under her feet as she tried to slip noiselessly into the ravine, the dry heat of the day, the sounds of the Indian ponies' hoofs beating over the prairie, the fear that clutched her heart and throat, one's imagination is no longer dormant. The thing is real, and the listener's heart beats fast to visualize the long-ago scene.

The old trail runs on to a point near Kenesaw where it crossed the Platte, joined farther on by the Nebraska City trail, where the two made a common one running on to Fort Kearney, the ruins of which may be seen. On past the old station for stages near Gothenburg, Ft. McPherson, just past Sioux Lookout, from which vantage point came many a speeding arrow sent by Indian hands as the settlers' wagons passed; Brule, Ash Hollow, the best of the camping places, with its springs and trees, Scott's Bluff, and then the long hard trek into Wyoming where old Fort Laramie offered shelter and protection. How quickly the historical spots can be written in review, when all the time these points were long, heart-breaking miles apart, for ten and twelve miles a day constituted the maximum speed at which wagons could travel. And one hundred years later Colonel Lindbergh and his wife spanned the entire continent in the time of a twelve-mile trek of the wagons! *God moves in a mysterious way His wonders to perform.*

The creak of the dozen wagons which set out from St. Louis on that memorable day soon changed to a swelling sound as the stream of migration grew. By 1860, three thousand wagons were passing along the grass-grown ruts worn by the tires of those that had gone before. By the late fifties there was a regular stage-coach line and freighting lines were established between the Missouri river and the west coast. Thirty-eight days were required for transporting freight or passengers. By 1860 the Pony Express took over the mail, cutting it to a ten-day service.

But this is not an historic article of definite dates and statistics. It is rather a memorial to pioneer men and women, a tribute to the courage and foresightedness of the forebears of many of those who may chance to read it, for from the men who swung the blacksnake by the side of their oxen, and the women who jolted along under the dingy canvasses of the prairie schooners, came countless numbers of our present-day population. A plea it is to the present generation to pause for a brief period of recalling that where a wagon stopped to emit its occupants, wherever dishes and bedding and household treasures were taken out to set up a new home, there also was brought out a Bible. For after the first trappers and hunters, the men and women who sought homes for themselves and children had always in their minds, in addition to the thought of those homes, the plans for schools and churches. The idea of seeking knowledge was ever with them, and the God of the old sheltered Eastern home was also the God of the Prairie. Like a yeast leavening the whole loaf of existence in the settling of the West was the religion of the Christian fathers and mothers.

As I write, I recall my mother's placid face upon which, to the eightieth year of her life, was that light which comes from faith and hope and love, and as always, the greatest of these was love. And I recall her at an earlier period, recounting to my childish wonderment the story of her trip into Iowa from Illinois in 1854, of the fear of the Indian, the howl of the wolf, the loneliness of the trail. "And weren't you afraid?" I would ask. "No, God was with us," she would say simply. And so, wherever a little family climbed out of a covered wagon, there to build a log cabin or pine shack or a soddie, wherever one experienced all the hardships of storm and blizzard and drought, there also grew the faith and the hope of the humble heart. For all through the tales of the pioneer, runs like a silver thread, the faith that was the foundation for the building of the church in the new country. Coincident with these stories runs the sacrifice of the early missionary and the circuit rider, beginning with Narcissa Whitman and Eliza Spaulding, who were the first women to cross the great Rocky divide, when alighting from their horses, and "kneeling on the other half of the continent with the Bible in one hand and the American flag in the other, they took possession of it as the home of American mothers and of the church of Christ."

The history of the founding of all communities on the old trail carries with it, from the first, the history of the beginnings and growth of the church. For no sooner had a few homes been established than the early circuit rider assembled the people in one of them, or perhaps in the shade of a grove for song and prayer. No sooner had a little schoolhouse been built on the bleak prairie or in the deep woods than there was organized something in the way of community worship. A concrete example of these new beginnings lies close at hand. In the small-town community in which I reside, twenty-three miles east of Lincoln, Nebraska, the first Methodist class was organized nearly sixty years ago, at Stove Creek schoolhouse, the heads of the Bailey, Clements, and Hylton families constituting the entire class. A short time afterward these three men went over to another school several miles away and organized a second class, both of these being for some time on the circuit of an itinerant minister.

Six years later the two classes met in a little frame G.A.R. hall, half-way between schools, united into one class, and planned immediately for the erection of a church in the tiny village which was then under the process of being incorporated. The church was built by all hands donating lumber, money, and labor. Small and insignificant Methodist history? No, important and significant Methodist history, for it has been duplicated a thousand times in the Western States. God-fearing men and women stepping from the covered wagons to make homes in the trackless wilderness of the raw prairie, building a log or rough lumber or soddie school in which there met a class on Sunday, with the circuit rider facing storm and blizzard and hot winds to speak the word. From such simple beginnings have risen the spires and domes of the St. Pauls, the Wesleys, and the Trinitys.

One old pioneer grandmother, describing to me her first church associations in the new country, said: "Meetings were held in the schoolhouse—a poor enough structure at best, where we sat squeezed in the seats between the rude desks. Sometimes the wind shook the little building so hard that we thought it would go over under the onslaughts. Sometimes the snow sifted through the cracks and the old stove would be red to the danger point. Those near it almost cooked; those far away froze. We went in wagon-boxes placed on home-made sleds, sometimes a single sled taking more than one family. There was straw in the bottom of the wagon-box and we had heated stones at our feet, with old quilts and buffalo robes to keep us warm. One family had a reed organ that it took to church each time and then back home after each service. Our first preacher worked at his trade of blacksmith through the week and thought out his Sunday sermons over the anvil. And," she added with a twinkle in her eyes, "he used the same force in his sermons that he put on the anvil."

Dozens of old settlers have told me of their early-day hardships and varying as they do in details, they are all similar in the main. Only a few weeks ago I asked one of these pioneer grandmothers what time in her early life stood out as the hardest. "I think the worst time I can remember," she said, "the time when just everything seemed the most discouraging, was the winter before my Frank was born. My husband had typhoid. I had four little children and was expecting the fifth. The snows had come before the corn was shucked and there it was under the snow all winter, what there was of it. I had just a twenty-five-cent piece in the little soddie . . . had had it ever since summer, and was holding onto it like grim death . . . for it seemed that if I let it go for anything I was letting go my last hold of things.

"A man rode into the yard and when I went out to see who it was, I found out it was the sheriff. He showed me the papers which said the farm had been sold for taxes and that was the notification that we were to leave March first. I told him we didn't know anything about the place being sold for taxes and he said it had been printed in the Weeping Water paper the required number of times. But as no one had any money in the community not one of us had taken the paper. Well, I hitched the horses, and leaving Pa in the care of the children with directions just what to do for him, I drove eighteen miles to see an old friend of the family that I thought could maybe help us out. I had to take a shovel along to scoop my way through some of the snow banks. Our old friend loaned us the money with just my promise that the corn lying under the snow would be his in the spring. In some way, because we hadn't seen the paper, the law let us redeem the place. I've seen lots of hard times, no money, little to eat, and all, but I guess the day the sheriff drove up to the soddie and served notice that we were sold out, with Pa in bed with typhoid, four little children to be fed, the fifth one expected, and a twenty-five-cent piece for our bank account, things were at their lowest ebb. But. . . . " and this is the predominating note underlying all the old pioneer tales as I have heard them, "the Lord took care of us. In some fashion we managed to hold body and soul together. Times began to get a little brighter. Pa got up. Frank was born, a husky, healthy baby. The next crop was a little better. Somehow, I managed to dress and feed the children, and hold the household together by selling butter and eggs and chickens. Pa paid off the indebtedness with the crops a little at a time. And we came out, with the Lord's help." A deeply religious current underlies all the talk of the old settlers. I happened to know a few days later that this old pioneer woman's granddaughter paid ten dollars to replace a single broken plate in her dinner service. Surely, a far cry from that grandmother's experiences to those of her granddaughter in her faucet-turning, heat-regulated, button-pressing, radio-equipped home. And yet, all the problems were not of that former day. The granddaughters have their own, perhaps more intricate, maybe less simple than the basic ones of food and shelter and clothing.

Last fall my adopted State of Nebraska celebrated its seventy-fifth anniversary as a State. A diamond jubilee committee in Omaha sponsored a pioneer-story contest of which I was asked to be chairman of the judging. Over two hundred manuscripts were submitted. The rules were simple. Each story, anonymously submitted, must be true, and must show some service to the State. Such a wealth of material as was sent in! There were stories of early settlers who had planted crop after crop with infinite care and patience, only to see them eaten by the grasshoppers or killed by the hot winds. There were stories of pioneer mothers who faced all the privations of those days with courage and faith. There were stories of circuit-riders facing storms and dangers to carry the Word to some isolated community. There were stories of school-teachers tying their pupils together as they faced the blizzards of the prairie. There was the story of Major North and his service to the State in connection with the Indian uprisings. Of William Hill, the pathfinder, who set out from Nebraska City to blaze a new trail. Of Cozad, who built the bridge across the Platte, only to see it torn away again and again. Of early physicians who rode through untold dangers to aid the sick. No harder task ever confronted one than choosing those who had rendered the most distinctive service, inasmuch as all did their share, circuit-rider and school-teacher, settler and cowboy, army man and pathfinder, in helping build one of the States in the great West.

Various ceremonies are taking place this year along the old Oregon route in accordance with the president's expressed wish. One of the most elaborate will have been the covered wagon centennial and national Boy Scout rendezvous at Independence Rock. Another, the dedication of the red granite boulder placed at the foot of the Scotts Bluff national monument, and dedicated to the memory of the pioneers whom the bluff served as a beacon and guide, when in that century-ago day they traversed the Oregon trail.

It is fitting that we pay tribute to these old pioneers on this centennial year of the migration of the first wagons. It is fitting that these sentiments find their full fruition in various forms of creative art. Each State has awakened to the realization that much is due its builders. Trails are being marked. Historic sites are being preserved. Oklahoma's majestic monument to the pioneer mother is outstanding. Mere familiarity with Nebraska's part in preserving the past, causes me to comment at greater length on its plans, as all States are equally cognizant of their obligations. Before his untimely death, Bertram Goodhue, the architect, had caught the vision of the dreams of the Nebraska settlers in a new design, and the people have built it in a marble and stone capitol especially planned for a prairie setting, in which appears a distinctive native decoration of corn and wheat, goldenrod and buffalo, and whose murals are representative of the early days of settling the State. Various historians have been collecting all the available material they could while there is still contact between the old generation and the new. John G. Neihardt, poet laureate, has been at work for many years on a heroic poem of the early history of the country, fitting together the episodes like the pieces of a mosaic, which in their completeness will be an epic of the West.

Several writers have attempted to catch bits of the spirit of the times between covers in novel form, that the young people of coming years may know that not all contact with the soil brings forth only despair and stupidity. Butzon Borglum, internationally known Nebraskan, has put his regard for the pioneers into a group which is to stand over-looking the Missouri. I had the pleasure of sitting by the famous sculptor at a dinner of the Pioneer Memorial Association in Omaha when the model for this group was unveiled. In speaking of his work, Mr. Borglum said that it had been his purpose to bring out the spirit of courageous high adventure, which was the dominant characteristic of those men who were builders of the West. Coming generations in looking up to the bronze faces of the group may see there something of the strength of character of the men and women they represent.

And now there are at least two other forms of creative art which should pay tribute also to the pioneer. There should come native American artists to paint a series of canvases which would depict the pioneer in his prairie settings, and which, in their perfect artistry, eventually would be to the West what *The Gleaners, The Sower,* and *The Angelus* are to France. There should arise some native American composer who would put his artistic soul into a symphony—another *New World Symphony,* if you will—through which would be heard the endless sound of wagons rolling to the West, of the wild unhampered winds that blew across the open spaces, of the low-voiced prayers of the prairie mothers, and through which would be woven the liquid song of the meadow lark, which was the song of hope. So that building and painting, book and monument, school and church, poem and symphony, alike, could speak to the world in the words of the verse by Jessie Wellborn Smith:

"... . I hold the key;
The prairie secret abides in me.
I know the ache of the prairie sod;
I know the prayers that ascend to God. . . .
A lighthouse sent in an upland sea,
With frontier strength built into me."

It's Never Too Late to Live

"Rose Leaves in a Jar" was Aldrich's original title for this work, but the editors of the *Delineator,* who published the story in January 1931, felt that "It's Never Too Late to Live" was a more appropriate title. Aldrich had sent an earlier, somewhat similar story, "The Cashier and the Little Old Lady," to *McClintock's Magazine,* who published it in their January–February 1923 issue. The theme seems to have been one that disturbed Aldrich, and she would return to it in a similar vein in "The Heirs" in 1949. Because she and her husband were half owners of a bank and because of the closeness of the small community in which Aldrich lived, she undoubtedly knew of an individual such as Ella Burke.

Old Ella Burke climbed laboriously down from the ramshackle buggy, walked gingerly around to the heads of the heavy horses standing stolidly in the muddy gutter, and tied them to one of the two hitching-posts left in town. Bird having surprisingly acquired the notion to stamp one shaggy leg, Ella held her long dress carefully away from the flying particles of mud.

She tied the last knot in the leather hitch straps and stepped up on the sidewalk. There she took off a big, clumsy pair of men's gloves and tucked a wisp of gray hair up under the back of her hat. The hat was symbolic—the very epitome of old Ella Burke's life. It was drooping, forlorn, rusty, on one side a wilted little bunch of violets which had once been jauntily purple, even as Ella had once been jauntily colorful.

From some mysterious region of the petticoats Ella extracted a man's wallet and opened it. The pocketbook had belonged to Jake Burke, her husband, and the only reason that old Ella dared carry it today was the simple one that Jake had died the week before and almost unbelievedly had not taken the familiar wallet with him on this last journey. The fact was that he had not planned to take the trip at all.

He had always scouted the idea of death. People died occasionally, to be sure, but not Jake Burke. No sir, not by a jugful did Jake Burke ever die. He had given his neighbors to understand that he thought it all tommy-rot to succumb. He had never made a will, either—boasted that he could look after his property, he guessed, without having any shyster telling him where to get off. But death had played a mean joke by slipping up on him with no more advance notice than a cold, which proved in the end as stubborn as old Jake himself. At Ella's timid and frightened suggestion that the doctor come out to the farm, old Jake had gone into a rage. No sir, not by a damsight would any doctor have a chance to get hands on him, charging him for the visit and for mileage into the country. And so when old Jake, breathing raspingly through the night, at last gasped, "Mebbe—he'd better—come," old Ella had run across the frosty meadow to a neighbor's house to phone. When she returned, death, who charged neither for the visit nor for mileage, had been there and gone.

And now, with Jake strangely non-committal out there in the Prairie Hill cemetery, Ella cautiously opened the big brown leather pouch. Almost unconsciously she looked over the heads of Bird and Belle as though expecting to see an impatient, irritable old man step around the buggy and snatch the battered pocketbook from her hands.

Standing there in the lee of the buggy, out of the crisp fall wind, Ella carefully extracted an envelop from the wallet. It was directed to her, and up in the corner there was printing—*Prairie Hill State Bank.* She pulled out the letter inside and read it for perhaps the ninth or tenth time. "At your earliest convenience, will you call at the bank?" was the principal sentence—and it was signed with Mr. Thomas R. Howard's name—the president of the bank.

Old Ella had taken butter to town and delivered it at Mr. Thomas Howard's back door many times. A woman in a white apron and white cap always took it, but once or twice Mrs. Thomas Howard had come by and said pleasantly, "Won't you step in and get warm?" or "Won't you step inside and cool off a little?" Old Ella had never done so, for Jake had always been waiting, but she loved the glimpse of the shining kitchen through the open door.

"At your earliest convenience, will you call—?" She had received the letter last Saturday. It had not been convenient to come to town on Monday or

Tuesday. Habit, the tyrant, had held her captive to Monday's washing and Tuesday's ironing.

Old Ella walked down the side street and turned into the paved Main Street, passing the Prairie Hill Drygoods Emporium with its windows filled with gay-gowned wax ladies. She had always wanted to stop and linger by the windows, but with Jake waiting impatiently by his team, she had never been able to do so. She passed the Bon Ton Shoe Shop, the Easy-Payment Hardware, and Jackson's Music Store. She walked by the narrow yellow front of the Sunset Café where she took eggs every Friday, and came then to the Prairie Hill State Bank on the corner.

It was the first time she had passed between the pillars and into the vestibule of the bank without Jake leading the way. There was a seat near the door, and always before, Jake had said: "Set there." And she had sat, waiting until he was through with his business. So now, hesitant, she paused and looked about her.

And then a strange thing happened. Mr. Thomas R. Howard himself came hurriedly through an iron gate and spoke: "Come right in, Mrs. Burke."

He opened a heavy door, and Ella, sensing that he meant for her to go in first, slipped past him, like the fleeting shadow of a woman, into a small room. Mr. Thomas R. Howard stepped to another door and spoke to a small, slim man with close-cropped gray mustache, who came in immediately; Mr. Victor P. Mapes that was, the cashier of the bank.

It was Mr. Mapes who had been appointed administrator by the court, a foolish procedure in old Ella's mind, when all there was to look after was the animals. And it was Mr. Mapes who spoke now, crisply, in nervous phrases: "We have a rather distasteful piece of news for you, Mrs. Burke. We have communicated with the townspeople in Mr. Burke's old home and find that there is another heir; and so, according to the laws of our state, your husband having left no will, you will only get one-half of the property, the other half reverting to his heirs, which in this case is a nephew."

Old Ella did not quite understand it. She turned bewildered eyes toward Mr. Thomas R. Howard. There was something about Mr. Howard that seemed more sympathetic.

"Yes," Mr. Howard said kindly, "it is just as Mr. Mapes says—one-half of the property must go to your husband's heir. We are sorry—you deserve it all."

"Well," said Ella, her gnarled fingers working nervously with the wallet, "I can get along. The chickens and the two cows will pay the taxes—and I don't take much. I'll have to have some help with the planting, but I can cultivate—and husk."

Mr. Howard looked at her, a little queerly, old Ella thought. "I guess that will hardly be necessary. You know, of course, that your husband held two mortgages—on the Rasmussen and Talbot farms."

Ella was frightened. *Mortgage*—the word had an evil sound. All his life Jake had held it over her head. There came to her a swift, horrible picture of being turned out of the little weather-beaten house.

"They hold some mortgages over me?" she queried.

"No, oh, *no.*" Mr. Howard was smiling, his fat face looking boyish. "*You* hold mortgages on them. Eight thousand on the Rasmussen farm, eleven thousand on the Talbot farm. You own now—or will when the estate is settled—one half of all Jake's property; and these two mortgages total nineteen thousand dollars. Then you know, of course, there are about twenty-seven thousand dollars' worth of bonds, and a little over four thousand dollars on a time certificate here in the bank—in addition to the home place."

No, old Ella did not know it.

She was dazed. It seemed that she could not think clearly. "Will you explain it all to me again?" she said.

"In addition to the farm in which you hold your homestead rights, half of your husband's estate of approximately fifty thousand dollars will be yours."

Surprise, incredulity, took possession of old Ella's mind—and then, as the knowledge fastened itself in her mentality—bitter resentment. She had slaved all her life *and it had not been necessary.*

More swiftly than her timid sluggish brain had worked for years, pictures slipped through it—a picture of herself dressing chickens in the cold lean-to kitchen, her hands tortured between the iciness of the temperature and the heat of the water—a picture of herself emptying the sudsy wash water to get the one tub ready for the rinsing water—of herself ironing with two old flat-irons next to a cob fire—turning her rusty black dress until it was falling to pieces. *And it had not been necessary.* Money in the bank, money on interest, bonds, mortgages on other folks' farms. And Jake had made her think there was barely enough to scrape together to pay the taxes!

She was brought to the present suddenly by Mr. Mapes' quick, nervous voice: "One thing we want to find out today is what you want to do about this time certificate. This four thousand dollars is due now and we wondered whether you wanted it renewed or put in your checking account."

Old Ella did not know a time certificate from a centipede, and checking accounts were as foreign to her as Greek philosophy.

So Mr. Howard took a hand again. "If the time certificate is renewed—that is, if we put it back the way it has been—you can't draw the money out until the time is up—at least not without losing your interest; but if it's in your checking account, you can use it just as long as you wish. Do you have any special need for ready money now?"

Old Ella raised faded eyes to Mr. Howard—eyes that were like an old shepherd dog's.

"Yes," said Ella, "I've always wanted another washtub and have some company visit me."

Mr. Thomas R. Howard dropped his own eyes, and took off his horn-rimmed glasses, intently occupied for a moment in working their bows. Then he said briskly: "All right—we'll convert that certificate into cash, and part of it, at least, can go into the checking account. How much do you want in there, Mrs. Burke?"

Old Ella did not know. Beyond the limits of a few dollars, all amounts of money seemed lost in a meaningless haze.

"About—" it was her very own, she assured herself, "about—fifty dollars." It seemed a fortune, limitless in its possibilities.

Mr. Howard gave her a little narrow book. He explained its use, showed her the way to write a check, patiently waited for her to write a model one for him so that she would be sure of herself, told her how he always wrote the object of his purchase down in the left corner for his own benefit.

The business call was over. And it was well for old Ella that she did not hear Mr. Victor P. Mapes' comments when she had gone.

"Administrator!" he was saying acridly to the older president. "*Guardian*—that's what *that* estate needs, and it's what there will have to be in a few months. She's no more competent to handle money than a child."

"Oh, I don't know." Mr. Howard was more optimistic. "I think she's all right. She'll be competent."

Up the street, old Ella untied Bird and Belle, their shaggy legs pulling up a few flies which the first frost had not killed. Into the west rode Ella Burke, her tanned, seamed face turned toward the sun.

She was strangely exultant. A thrilling sensation enveloped her whole body. It made her hands and feet tingle. She felt that she was floating up and away from the ancient, odorous leather of the buggy seat. She kept feeling for the little black book. It was the symbol of things to come.

Cars swept by her, their dust lost in the distance while Bird and Belle were covering a few scant yards. When she passed the country cemetery with its abandoned church standing back in a cluster of cottonwoods, she did not look that way. Her heart thumped strangely at its acknowledged lack of sorrow and reverence. All the little meannesses, all the larger trials of her life were accentuated now. She recalled those first few years of tears—and then when there had been no more tears—nothing but a dull acquiescence to life. All the way home she felt hard and triumphant.

Arrived there, she unhitched and turned the old team into the pasture for the night. Released from their heavy harnesses, the stolid old mares broke into clumsy and kittenish gallops and then stopped suddenly as though realizing their age.

Ella unlocked the back door and went through the low lean-to kitchen into her bedroom. She put the little black book carefully in a bureau drawer, then took off her dark dress and substituted a calico of colorless material and ancient cut. She went outdoors, fed and watered the chickens, and gathered the eggs. The coops were scattered through the grove; makeshift affairs, laboriously botched together out of weather-stained boards. She milked the two cows with strong, knotty hands. When she had strained the milk in her dark pantry, she prepared some supper for herself.

She went early to bed. But she did not sleep. For a long time she lay staring into the night—tense—excited—planning—planning——

All the next day Ella scrubbed and cleaned the old house to soap-and-suds neatness. By four o'clock in the afternoon she was at the back door of the Reeder Memorial Home. She had taken butter there the summer before.

There was no hitching-post at the Home, and one of the little girls had always run out and stood by old Bird and Belle when Ella took in the butter. Anna May Peters, her name was. Ella smiled now to remember the time she had asked it, and the youngster had said, "*Miss* Anna May Peters."

It did not take long for the matron to come to a decision. She saw no reason why Anna May could not spend a few days with Mrs. Burke, the respectable old butter woman. In fact, she thought it would be a nice experience. "Poor child," she said to Ella, "we do get to depending on her to look after the smaller ones." And she helped Miss Anna May Peters put a forlorn little wardrobe into an equally forlorn little bag.

Anna May, a bit of the flotsam of life, was nine years old. Her canary-colored hair was stringy, and her face sloped thinly to the acute angle of her chin. But she was happy to the point of exultation over three days on a farm.

Conversation on the way back to the farm was limited, the hostess apparently as diffident as the guest. Once Ella asked with sedate politeness: "What did your ma die of?"

And Anna May, with equally sedate politeness, answered: "Tombstones."

Ella turned her head. My, my, didn't children say funny things!

"Now, play around," old Ella said, when they had alighted from the ramshackle buggy. "Make some noise if you want to. Make a *lot* of noise," she added recklessly.

But Anna May did not make a great deal of noise. She walked quietly among the patched chicken coops and gnarled apple trees.

There was not a great deal of conversation over the supper table, and when the dishes were washed and the kerosene lamp was lighted, Ella tried to think of some way to entertain her guest. Once she went into her bedroom and came back with a little jar.

"Smell!" she said.

Anna May pushed a diminutive, freckled nose down into the jar.

"Can you smell?" Ella waited.

"Yes," said Anna May, "just faint—somethin' sweet."

"Roses . . . " old Ella said. "Roses I picked thirty-nine years ago."

"My gracious!" Anna May clucked her astonishment. "Rose leaves in a jar—thirty-nine years!"

" 'Tis *so*," said old Ella, "and when I think about the day I picked 'em, it seems like it's *me* that's been in that little jar thirty-nine years. I guess you couldn't understand that."

"No," said Anna May, frankly, "*you* couldn't a-been packed in a jar—I guess you're jokin'."

It was the next day that Ella put into execution the great plan that had formed itself in her mind. It was Friday—the day she always took her eggs to the Sunset Café. To see old Ella and Anna May start to town in the afternoon, one would never have suspected that the journey was of the same import as that taken by one Ponce de Leon, some few centuries before.

Arrived in town, they drove through the alley back of the restaurant and left the eggs. And then—the moment had come. Old Ella began to pluck the fruits of desire. With Anna May—the one no more experienced than the other—Old Ella went into the Drygoods Emporium. There the child who was like an old woman, and the old woman who was like a child, each picked out a dress for herself. It was so simple—just to write one's name, and the name of the merchant, and the amount of the purchase. Then, as Mr. Howard had shown her, she wrote the name of the article in the left hand corner of the check.

They went into the Bon Ton Shoe Shop and both bought pairs of shoes. Next door the Easy-Payment Hardware Store beckoned the adventurers, and Ella bought a large galvanized wash-tub.

She did her shopping in orderly fashion, not missing a store. The Jackson Music Store looming next on the shopping horizon, Ella went in and bought a banjo. When asked by the mystified clerk whether she wanted a teacher, old Ella said no, he needn't bother about her, that she thanked him very kindly just the same, but she merely wanted to strum on it a little.

In each place up and down Main Street, old Ella and Anna May made purchases. Even the Sunset Café did not faze her. She and Anna May went in and sat down in one of the little stalls that looked so much like church pews. And when the red-lipped, sloe-eyed waitress asked her what she would have, Ella was courtesy itself: "Oh, most anything that won't put you to too much trouble." At which the girl, suppressing a mint flavored giggle, suggested Sunset Special sandwiches. Ella was a little disappointed when the sandwiches came, for they seemed to have only lettuce and hard boiled eggs in them.

When the orgy of buying was over, Ella and Anna May rode home behind the fat old mares. Ella was happier than she had ever been in all her dwarfed, cramped life—Anna May by her side, and all the things she had ever wanted there in the wagon.

When they passed the cemetery, old Ella looked straight ahead, her eyes on the sun slipping down behind the elms and cottonwoods along Plum Creek. But Anna May called attention to the very thing Ella did not want discussed. "Mr. Burke would-a liked to know you was havin' all these grand things, wouldn't he?" And when Ella made no reply, she continued politely: "He must a-been a kind old man."

"He was a hard worker," Ella parried. "Nobody could ever beat Jake up or into the field."

"I wished he'd lived so I could know him. I'd a-liked him, wouldn't I?"

Ella, who knew that Anna May would never have visited at the farm had Jake lived, swept a lean arm around the little girl and drew her up in a spasm of awkward devotion. "Couldn't anybody help but likin' *you,* Anna May," she countered.

At the weather-beaten back door they unloaded the purchases. They took out the banjo and a set of dishes, the bright new wash-tub and the dresses and shoes. They carried in an oak rocking-chair with a blue plush bottom, a yellow and purple hammock, and a fat lamp with a frosted globe shade. They unpacked a dozen green glass tumblers, a checked table-cloth of a vivid redness, and a half dollar's worth of peppermints.

All night long old Ella Burke dreamed of the things—a chaotic mass of color and form and odor, that tumbled and turned and twisted before her eyes, and would not let her rest.

On Saturday morning the work of the Prairie Hill State Bank was well under way, the six employees speeding up their labors in preparation for the usual busy farmer trade of the afternoon. Towards noon Mr. Victor P. Mapes came up to the president's desk, snapping a bunch of checks nervously against his hand.

"Look here, Tom. What did I tell you? That old Mrs. Burke's checks. . . ." His voice held deep disgust as he uttered the one word: "*Overdrawn.* Way overdrawn. As far as I can see, there's a big check here from practically every store in town."

Mr. Howard took the checks in his hand and ran through them, reading the cramped notation in each lower left-hand corner: *Dishes, shoes, dresses, wash-tub, lamp, banjo. . . .*

"Well—what do you think about her now?" Mr. Mapes urged.

Thomas R. Howard grinned. "Just what I thought at first—that she's not incompetent. She'll be careful later. But I would say right now she's on a spree. When she sobers up, I bet she'll be as stingy as the old man himself."

At that very moment, out at the old unpainted farmhouse, Ella was saying to Anna May: "My! My! Anna May. I spent an awful lot of money yesterday, didn't I?"

"I should say!" Anna May clucked her sympathy. "Most a million dollars, I guess." And with precocious instinct she added: "You ain't worryin' about it, be you, Mis' Burke?"

"I should say I am, Anna May—worryin' a lot about it this morning. I haven't thought of nothin' else but me doin' that tomfool thing of spending all that money. I'll have to look out or I'll land in the poorhouse. Do I want I should have a mortgage over my head? I reckon I was plumb crazy to get all them things."

Then her eye fell on the bright new wash-tub standing jauntily in the middle of the lean-to kitchen. She threw up her head. "No, I ain't, Anna May. I ain't *one mite* sorry. I'd do it all over again—I'd get every single thing I got, unless—" her voice trailed off, a little dubious—"unless it was them sandwiches. I can't say I think them sandwiches was a good buy. Anna May, did you ever stop to think we sold our eggs at the back door of the Sunset Caf-fee for thirty-eight cents a dozen, and then went right around to the front door and bought two of 'em back in sandwiches for forty cents? And that," said old Ella with amazing sagacity, "*that ain't good business judgment.*"

Will the Romance Be the Same?

In the days that Cap Aldrich was cashier in his bank, there were usually only two officers, the president and the cashier, and Aldrich almost invariably has any main character banker be the cashier. Her brother-in-law was the president of their bank, and she would not have employed his title.

This story is an excellent example of Aldrich's persistence and demonstrates why she never wrote a story she didn't sell. She first sent this story to *The American Magazine,* who rejected it; she then sent it to the *Country Gentleman, Ladies' Home Journal, Christian Herald, Farmer's Wife,* and, finally, to *Physical Culture Magazine,* who accepted it, publishing it in September of 1931. The story had been going out and returning for almost two years. The Aldrich name was well known, but that was no guarantee that every story would sell easily, even though many magazines, including those named above, wrote her often, asking for more of her work. This story would later appear in her short story collection *The Man Who Caught the Weather* (1936) and in *The Bess Streeter Aldrich Reader* (1950).

The character of Hettie Hess is similar to Tillie of the *Mother Mason* stories (1924), who filled a household position similar to that of Aldrich's Gussie Rosenkoetter.

One afternoon in the merry month of May, Mrs. Mary Wakely, forty-seven, clothed in a kitchen dress with a towel bound round her graying hair, sat on the floor of the attic in her home, sorting pieces of cloth from an old scrap-bag, and was not so merry.

There are those who will scent at once the battle of spring house-cleaning in the air.

Mary Wakely was the capable wife of Sam Wakely, the active mother of six hilarious Wakelys, the energetic overseer of a big house, and consequently the holder of that undistinguished position which the world at large in jocular vein lists as "no occupation."

The Wakely house sat in the middle of a grassy yard in the middle of a small town in the middle of one of the middle western states. And as the United States is the most important nation in the world (save in the prejudiced eyes of the inhabitants of a few other countries) it follows without controversy that the Wakely home was quite the center of the universe. And so it was, just as all the homes of the Browns and the Smiths and the Joneses are the center of the universe, to the Browns and the Smiths and the Joneses.

The whole place had a lived-in look, which is a polite way of saying that it was not quite as neat as it ought to be. Because the Wakely family was large, and expenditures waxed equally large in that bold proportion which bills bear to the size of families, not everything was in repair at one and the same time. When the lattice under the porch was in perfect condition, the screens would begin to have a faded, peeled look. When the screens were finally repainted, the porch boards would show signs of warping.

Every spring the dandelions slipped up brazenly in the clover and bluegrass. And every spring, with exasperated repetition, Mary Wakely made a noble gesture toward eradicating the pests, but with indifferent success. Always in the middle of the task, neighbor boys came for Tod or Ken or Bo to go fishing, and neighbor girls dropped in to hold giggling converse with Gwen or Louise. When Mary Wakely saw her family melt away, one by one, she invariably remarked apologetically to the butcher knives and bushel-baskets: "Oh, well, let them go. It's the very happiest time of their lives." Which was quite the key to Mary Wakely's character, a little too lenient maybe, a bit too sentimental perhaps.

To give the roster of the Wakely family sounds like calling the roll in a classroom. Mary Wakely (née Bohanan) had been the town belle twenty-five years before when she married Sam Wakely. Sam was a bookkeeper then in the Oakville State Bank, but a kindly providence removing one man above him, and a wrathy board of directors removing another, he had been cashier now for many years. The husky and noisy results of the Wakely-Bohanan nuptials were: Hal Wakely, aged twenty-four, Louise, aged twenty-one, Gwen and Ken, who arrived together seventeen years before, Thaddeus, who had almost forgotten that dignified appellation in the "Tod" under which he had moved and had his very lively being for fifteen years, and Paul Bohanan Wakely, called "Bo" by Oakville friends and enemies, who trailed along seven years behind Tod.

It seems almost a matter for abject apology that, added to this number, there were also Aunt Dell Wakely and Hettie Hess, both of whom the family had inherited along with the old Wakely estate. Aunt Dell was Sam's aunt, a fleshy, florid, fatuous woman who believed that she had been marked for apoplexy for years. But the stubbornness with which she met all minor issues bidding fair to thwart her, had so far refused to yield to the various "rushes of blood" so frequently and eloquently described in detail to the family. Hettie Hess, of problematical age, who often remarked acridly that she wished to the land she had some meat on her bones, might have passed in more sophisticated circles for a maid, but not in Oakville. To be sure she worked for her bed, board, and a stipend; but on days when her "rheumatic" sent her to lie on a bony, twinging shoulder, or days when she felt an additional grievance toward life in general and the Wakely youngsters in particular, she simply sent word that she was not coming downstairs. No, one could scarcely insist that Hettie Hess was the typical modern maid.

On this specific day in merry spring, Mary Wakely and Hettie Hess were cleaning house. And Mary Wakely, in a kitchen dress with a towel bound round her graying hair, sat on the attic floor sorting an old scrap-bag contents, and was not so merry. For there were so many things stored away on the third floor that the task looked stupendous. All of the old Wakely things left from another generation were there, and some of the Bohanan ones which Mary had brought over home when her mother died, old Wakely and Bohanan dresses, bonnets, cushions, pictures, curtains, quilt scraps, patterns. Every year Mary Wakely put forth strenuous, if subtle, efforts to get rid of them, but Aunt Dell would puffingly climb the narrow built-in attic stairs, settle herself in an old arm chair, and watch the sorting process with an ancient but alert eye.

Surreptitiously, Mary would attempt to throw out some of the flotsam left upon the shore of time, impersonated by the floor of the attic, but the covert act could never be consummated without Aunt Dell seeing it. A few moments before this, Mary had attempted to rid the figurative beach of some of its wreckage in the form of an old bird-cage, to be met with Aunt Dell's, "Dear, dear, that's Dicky's little house. I can remember so well how he always chirped when we put seeds in this very same little dish. I couldn't bear to see that thrown out, Mary. I believe I'd hear his little chirp in my sleep." So Mary, with superb resignation, had replaced the battered home of the departed Dicky, lest such dire consequences as a phantom cheep cross Aunt Dell's heavy slumber.

And now, as Aunt Dell appeared to be engrossed in an old photograph album, Mary slipped away from the piece-bag and casually edged a wire dress-form toward the top of the stairs. But Aunt Dell was on the job instantly.

"You ar'n't intending to throw *that* away, are you, Mary?" Her voice held volumes of reproach.

"Yes, yes, I was, Aunt Dell. What good will it ever be to us?"

"Oh, I wouldn't think of it, Mary. Why, you might want to fit something on it some day for one of the girls when they are away at school."

To be sure the form was as foreign to present-day maidenly figures as though it were of some prehistoric female. Wide-shouldered, padded, wasp-waisted, it looked like a wire skeleton of Queen Elizabeth. But back to the cluttered shore of time Mary Wakely rolled it, with a fleeting wicked thought to the language the fastidious Louise and the artistic-minded Gwen would use when she told them.

Hettie Hess was dusting a pile of old things in another corner. "A mess, I call it," she was grumbling. But that was scarcely an innovation. She always grumbled. The family thought no more of Hettie's constant mumbling than of a continuously leaky faucet. It might be annoying if one stopped to think about it, but if it could not be repaired, why stop to think about it? She mumbled and grumbled her way through the day's work, her mind a little at loose ends, going off on tangents, her sentences never finished, trailing off into nothing.

Just now she brought a pile of dog-eared books and dumped them aggrievedly down by Mary Wakeley. "Them old scrap-books . . . that there corner . . . I declare, Mis' Wakely . . . leaves tore out . . . I suz . . . every year . . . pick up 'n pick up. . . ."

Mary Wakely opened the top scrap-book. Originally it had been a book of her father's, recording the uprisings and the downsittings of the members of a lodge known as "The Knights and Ladies of King Arthur's Round Table," although just how the ladies happened to be sitting in at that particular round table she had never known.

Over the erstwhile memoranda of the lodge knights and their ladies, verses were pasted. Mary herself had pasted them in when all the world was young and joyous and romantic, when Sam Wakely and Matt Dorring and George Hines had all wanted to go with her. How had she ever found time to paste poems in the old secretary book? Her days were so rushed, now, so filled with countless necessary activities, that it did not seem possible she had ever had leisure to cut out poetry, to say nothing of pasting it back in a book. She turned the pages of the long-forgotten record of flamboyant ceremonies.

Where had they gone, those old thrills, that old romantic feeling she and Sam had felt for each other? How golden and dream-filled and illusioned life had been! Mary Wakely, forty-seven, maturely heavy, in a kitchen dress, with a towel bound round her graying hair, sat and turned Time's pages.

Was his love then, the love of the river? And she—
Had she taken that love for the love of the sea?

She could hear Sam's deep mellow voice as he read the smooth, singing verses aloud. She could see him, too, in his white flannels, sitting in the hammock on the old Bohanan lawn. How much in love they had been! How romantically, deeply, terribly so! Not all the masculine movie stars were more ardent in their love-making than Sam had been. Where had they gone, those old romantic moments they had planned to keep alive? Where were they now, those old thrills which they had said could never die? They had not kept them alive any more than all the other long-married, staid old couples. Their conversation now consisted for the most part of the annoying fact that Bo's teeth needed straightening, of the big expenses incurred by Hal and Louise away at school, of gravel taxes and a leaky kitchen roof. Oh, *why* did romance fly out of the window when children came?

She turned the stiff, mucilage-crusted page. Alone on the page and in a bracket of purple ink, as though set aside for special honor, was a little poem, evidently cut from a magazine. There were several verses, but they all ended with:

After years I'll come to meet you
Will the romance be the same?

Above the purple-inked framework a bunch of little dried violets was crushed into the soft pulpy paper. Under the violets, in Sam's writing, were the words: "To be read together on our silver anniversary."

It might have been written the day before, so clearly did the picture come to her, the resurrections of a little dormant memory which had been lying away under a shroud of crumbling violets. They had read the verses together, pressed the flowers together, and then Sam had taken her fountain pen and written the words. They had laughed at the mere thought of any change, at the absurdity that romance would ever die. It had been one of those certainties of life not even debatable. As for the thought of a silver wedding, that had been too far in the future to contemplate, a huge joke, that in the then glamourous present, they should have spoken of a date so far removed. It had seemed centuries away. And now their silver anniversary was one week from the next Saturday.

Mary Wakely sat on the attic floor and thought of Sam, young, ardent, lithesome, wooing her under the trees of the old Bohanan home; and Sam, now, heavy, wide-girthed, bespectacled, gray patches above his ears, talking of gravel taxes and dental bills and a leaky kitchen roof. That, then, would be the answer. Romance was never the same. But this was the queer part, when she stopped to analyze it, she herself was still romantic. She still cared for sentiment. That seemed always the way—one kept the romance and one ceased to remember. Suddenly she realized that the idea was almost identical with one of the Ella Wheeler Wilcox poems she had just passed in the book, and over which she had thrilled and wept in her youth. She searched until she found it and read it avidly:

This is the way of it the wide world over
One is beloved and one is the lover

Yes, that was for all the world the way it had turned out. And the humbling thing about it, the pride-eating thing, was that Sam, whose soul had once been aflame with a god-like passion, was soon the beloved, and that she who had been so ardently wooed, proved in the long run to be the lover.

She turned back to the pages of the violets. "To be read together at our silver anniversary." Neither one had remembered the verses. Only by chance had she run across them. Already preparations were under way to celebrate the occasion. Very well, they *would* read the poem together. The evening of the anniversary, after the guests had gone, she and Sam would read the verses. And perhaps, no, certainly, Sam would tell her that he had never forgotten those moments of exquisite romance. Possibly, no, assuredly, it would take only the sight of the verses and the violets to have Sam reveal the fact that he had never ceased to remember those glamourous hours of young love.

All that week they worked hard at the cleaning of the big rambling house, Mary and Hettie Hess.

On Friday, Louise arrived home from the University, gay and lovely and full of sorority gossip. Something always seemed to happen to the household when Louise blew in. It took on a foolish gaiety which it had not previously possessed. Louise had on a fetching new green and white sport suit. "I hope you don't mind, Mother. I got it at Garwin's and charged it. We hadn't planned it, but when I found they were wearing sports to the Beta party instead of the printed chiffons we first thought, there wasn't time to write."

More bills! How they crowded always in a sort of unending nightmare. But how fresh and glowing and deliciously pretty Louise looked in the gay outfit. Only one more year and she would be through.

Louise did not appear to be what one could call vitally interested in the house-cleaning. She seemed to have something vaguely important on her mind. At the first moment in which she could catch her mother alone it came out with geyser-like burst. "Mother, I've been dying to tell you . . . but with everyone around . . . the kids all under foot . . . Hettie all ears . . . and Aunt Dell calling from the far end of the house: 'What's that you're sayin'. Louise-y?' I haven't had a chance. Mother, next week I'm having company . . . here at home. Listen—Rod Robinson, himself. Can you feature it?" Hands on her mother's plump shoulders, she gazed into her mother's blue eyes with rapt expectancy.

"And who," said Mary Wakely, "is Rod Robinson—himself?"

"Oh, Mother," Louise's voice held deepest reproach, "please don't show such ignorance—such abysmal ignorance. Rod Robinson," she lowered her voice to a reverent whisper, "made the winning touchdown in the game with the Aggies."

Mary dropped her eyes that they might not show their tell-tale twinkle. When she looked up her heart missed a beat, for she saw somethings in her daughter's own brown eyes that she would not ignore.

"Why, Louise," there was a little catch in her throat. "You—you like him?"

Louise's head dropped to her mother's shoulder. "I'm just nuts about him. I think of him in the daytime—" Louise's muffled voice went on, "and dream of him at night. The very glimpse of him gives me high blood pressure."

"And he—?" Mary asked. "Is he—" she dropped into Louise's vernacular, "nuts about you?"

"I don't know," Louise said forlornly. "Sometimes I think he is—but more times I think he isn't. It just keeps me palpitating between subnormal and high fever."

Dear, dear! How different girls were than they used to be. How frank!

Why she herself had not even acknowledged to her mother that she loved Sam until after his proposal.

Louise was speaking again huskily. "That's why I'm so crazy about his stopping here. A week from tomorrow he's going through Oakville, and he asked me if he could stop off. I just went *deeleerious.* I want everything just ideal, Mother. His family is a regular Rolls-Royce, up-to-the-minute family. Things just have to be nice here. You and Dad will be all right—but the kids—I wish they'd be *half* civilized for once. And I want Hettie to keep her place, and her mouth shut—and it wouldn't make me sore if Aunt Dell would have that stroke she's always talking about."

"*Louise!*" There were limits to which Mary would allow her modern children's talk to go.

"I didn't mean that, but you'll see that she fades gently somewhere into the scenery, won't you?"

Mary was reassuring. "Don't worry. We'll have everything nice, dear. The house will be all clean, and the children, models. When did you say he was coming?"

"A week from Saturday night."

"Why, Louise, the anniversary night!"

"Oh, no, Mother." Louise was the embodiment of despair. "It's the only night he can stop. We wouldn't want the whole town coming."

"But the invitations are all out."

"Imagine—that gang being here—if he has to meet all the natives. You know yourself, Mother, that a big bunch of Oakville people look like the villagers in *Faust* or *Carmen.*"

"They are our friends, Louise," Mary was a little stiff. "And though they may not be as sophisticated, they are assuredly as fine people as the young man's friends."

"And there's no way out?"

"Absolutely, there's no way out. You'll just have to entertain him someway at the party." Mary's voice held the last expression in finality.

On Monday morning Louise went back to school. All that day and the following days, Mary and Hettie Hess worked under extreme pressure in order to get through before Saturday.

But to Mary Wakely, all through the rug-beating and varnishing and turning of curtains, shone a little gleam ahead like a light in the forest. She had kept the incense burning before the shrine of romance, and perhaps Sam had kept it also. Steeped in business, hustling day after day to make a living for the big family, no doubt Sam, too, still cherished the memory of those glamorous days, would recall them with fervor on their anniversary night.

Saturday, itself, dawned bright and lovely with the scent of peonies and syringa on the sweet May air. The household was early astir, Mary and Hettie Hess beginning the baking of cakes and nut wafers immediately after a sketchy breakfast.

Louise blew in just before noon when preparations for the event were well under way. But all the activity for the party was to Louise but an accompanying chorus to herald the approach of the star performer, Mr. Robinson, himself. "You're positive everybody will be up on his toes for a good impression, Mother?" she repeatedly asked.

By six, the House of Wakely was as near perfection as it could ever hope to attain. Only once in a blue moon did it ever have that highly polished, finished appearance, Sundays, perhaps, for a few fleeting moments, the late afternoon before a holiday, an hour or so before an expected guest would arrive, was everything in place and everyone well-groomed.

When Mary Wakely was dressing in the soft new silk, a little rose-colored thread of fancy wove its gay way through her heart as definitely as the rose-colored thread shimmered in the white of the new gown. When the guests would have gone, she was to meet Sam, and they would read the verses together, not as Mary Wakely, the mother of six, and Sam Wakely, the middle-aged, bespectacled bank cashier, but as young Mary Bohanan with stars for eyes, and young Sam Wakely, lithe and handsome. Sam could not have forgotten that moment of high rapture when they had read the verses in the old Bohanan hammock, could not have forgotten that pledge to romance any more than she.

To be sure there were some moments before the guests arrived which one could scarcely call of a romantic nature. Sam's waist-line having added a cubit to his latitudinal stature since last it had been encased in the suit he was to wear, necessitated setting over the buttons. He stood and waited impatiently while Mary made the change. There was one mad search by half the family for little Bo's best necktie, in which drawers were whisked out and the contents madly turned over, until someone happily remembered that Bo had taken it off Sunday afternoon and stretched it around a young plum tree. Gwen and Louise, possessing a velvet jacket in common, each chose this particular occasion upon which to claim individual ownership. They argued pleasantly, but definitely and continuously, with a certain stiff politeness.

"Pardon me, Louise, but you certainly heard me say that I was wearing it with the blue silk crepe."

"Pardon *me,* Gwen, but with Rod Robinson coming, most assuredly I ought to have first choice."

Aunt Dell, dressed in an ancient magenta-colored watered silk, which made her anticipated stroke seem imminent and her entire cameo set—brooch, earrings, bracelet and watch chain—ornamenting her person, sat heavily in the biggest chair and waited for the guests.

When Mary was dressed, she took a fleeting survey of herself in the glass. She saw there a blue-eyed woman in her late forties with too much weight, her blonde hair sprinkled with gray, small lines about her eyes, deeper ones in her forehead and a duplex chin. What she failed to see was that the lines bespoke character, the plump pleasing face radiated kindness, that from the blue eyes shone faith, hope and love, and, as always, the greatest of these was love.

Turning away from the glass, she took the old scrap-book under her arm and started down stairs. To an onlooker it was only a dog-eared scrap-book. To Mary Wakely it was the altar to Romance—the odor of dead violets—the incense—the rhythm of the verses a prayer.

They all made comments about her: "Gee, Mom, you look ritzy," and "Gloria Swanson has nothing on you."

When for a moment there was no one around, she slipped the scrap-book back of a reading lamp on a table in the big hall. It was open at the verses, and the words in their purple framing and violets pressing their little blue faces against the poem gazed back at her with assurance. Across the border of Time they called to her:

After years I'll come to meet you—
Will the romance be the same?

And then the first of the guests arrived. Incongruously, they were Dick Edwards and his wife, and Sue McIntyre and her husband. Dick had been Sam's best man, and Sue had been Mary's bridesmaid twenty-five years before. Also they had been engaged. They both mentioned it, even laughed about it. To Mary Wakely, obsessed with her idea of resurrecting Romance, it seemed almost sacrilegious. How could they mention it? How could they laugh? After years they had come to meet, and the romance was not the same.

The rooms were soon filled with the gay, friendly folks of the small-town crowd who knew each other so well. Their voices floated high with talk and laughter. Sometime during the early evening, the hero of many a football war arrived and was introduced, after which Mary Wakely was vaguely conscious of the fact that he and Louise had slipped out to the swing on the side porch.

And then there was a little program. Grace Ivorson sang just as she had sung at the wedding. Perhaps not "just as she had sung," for Grace's voice at fifty was not what it had been at twenty-five. The minister made a talk, and Dick Edwards of the Oakville Bon Ton Grocers, on behalf of the guests, presented Sam and Mary with some very nice silver. Sam made a neat little speech in which he confided the fact that they had had the six children for the express purpose of being able to use the eight-piece set.

And all through the happy, informal, small-town party there sang a little silver song in the heart of Mary Wakely.

And then the affair was over. The last of the guests were going down the steps into the moon-filled, sweet-scented night. The last gay words floated back: "Good-night, Sam—good-night, Mary. Lovely time—coming again to the golden wedding."

Sam and Mary turned into the big hall.

Sam was standing there only a few feet away from the table where the book stood open at the verses, where Romance waited to be recognized and welcomed. In their little purple bracketing the verses waited for Mary's lover.

"Nice party, Mother." Sam was not noticing the scrap-book. But one could not expect him to do so with it standing against the wall, surrounded by a half dozen other things, a vase of flowers, a reading lamp, two or three magazines, a framed photo of Louise, a dish of nut wafers.

"Sam," Mary's voice quivered in its earnestness. "There's something over there on the table I've been saving for you."

Sam sauntered over to the table. The years turned back for Mary Wakely. What was a quarter of a century to a gay, gallant knight who had picked violets and promised that after years the romance would be the same? Starry-eyed, she watched her lover approach the little altar which together they had once erected to Romance.

The moment in its deep importance, fraught with the sincerity of its meaning, should have been very quiet. It was scarcely that. The radio, tuned to a highpowered station, was emitting " 'Tain't no treat on the rumble seat, sittin' by yourself in the moonlight." Hal was clogging to it on the newly varnished floor. Ken was adding to the gaiety of the nations by accompanying the ensemble with his banjo and shouting the words. That both his voice and his banjo were off-key seemed not to worry him to any extent.

With one part of her brain, Mary Wakely heard all the turbulent family noises. The other was turned toward the Great Moment, as Joan of Arc may have paid no attention to annoying trivialities, but kept her eyes turned to the Light. Sam was looking in the direction of the verses, now, the verses with their fragrance of by-gone Junes. His hand was on the book, now. He picked it up—looked at in a puzzled way. And then he spoke, "I'm glad you saved me some. They're cracking good." *And he set the book aside and reached for the wafers.*

The light in Mary Wakeley's eyes slowly flickered out. It gave place to a baffled expression, half chagrin, half incredulity. She looked at Sam Wakely, heavy, wide-girthed, bespectacled, with gray patches above his ears. Under his very nose the faint old fragrance of the violets pled with him, and he thought she had meant the wafers. Before his very eyes the rapture of the little poem called to him, and he thought she had saved him something to eat.

He took a handful of the brittle cakes and began munching them. He swung his jaw vigorously, the crisp wafers crackling a little.

Hettie Hess came through the hall, her best brown silk crackling with the wafers. Over on the table the sweet fragrance of the dead little violets and the sweet rhythm of the forgotten little verses looked out from the old scrap-book. Hettie's ferret eyes landed on them. "Looky there, Mis' Wakely . . . good suz . . . one of them old scrap-books . . . my land . . . got down from the attic . . . such a mess . . . beats all . . . shall I take it back up?"

"No, leave it there," said Mary Wakely. She used the same tone that one might use in saying "No, leave the flowers on the grave."

Hettie trudged out of the room, mumbling mild execrations.

Sam Wakely, big, substantial, wide-girthed, stood and munched the nut cookies with keen enjoyment. "Well, Mother?" He was slipping his arm through Mary's and starting with her toward the dining room. "They tell me the first twenty-five years are the hardest," he said blithely, "but think of the next twenty-five—with our slippers and the radio and books and magazines and a lot of grandchildren—won't they be comfortable though?"

Psychologists say that two emotions can not occupy the mind at the same time. The king, Romance, has no humor. And the king's fool, Humor, knows no romance. Quite suddenly, in the throne-room of Mary Wakely's mind, Humor, the fool, slipped up behind Romance, the king, sent him sprawling and threw him out. At the sight she let forth a laugh, a chuckling, rippling, body-shaking laugh.

Hal was still tap-tapping on the bare varnished floor. Ken was adding to the general confusion with the sixteenth verse of " 'Tain't no treat on the rumble seat, sittin' by yourself in the moonlight." The backfiring of Tod's motorcycle came from the rear of the house.

Mary Wakely laughed as she looked up at Sam Wakely, heavy, wide-girthed, unlithesome, munching nut wafers in the midst of all this familiar hilarity. "Comfortable?" she repeated, her too, too solid flesh shaking with vigorous laughter. "I'll say they will."

And then, suddenly, simultaneously, they stopped by the double windows. Outside in the cool, dark porch stood slim young figures in such close proximity that, while it was only surmise that their two minds held but a single thought, there was direct evidence that their two hearts beat as one. For the arms that had so effectively enfolded the wet, slippery pigskin on the field of honor, now appeared to be repeating the process with a daintier, lovelier burden.

Overwhelmed at the import of the words they heard, the parents seemed too nearly in a state of partial paralysis to move on out of range of the low, earnest voices:

"And you'll love me all your life, Louise?"

"Oh, Rod—all my life—and forever."

Sam and Mary Wakely turned to each other, gropingly, clingingly, in the surprise of those bewildered emotions which parents inevitably experience at the first startling realization of such news. Sam's arms went around Mary and he drew her close. "Golly, Mother," he whispered, cheek to hers "romance is always the same, isn't it?"

"Always!" Mary whispered back.

And they tiptoed away, stealthily, guiltily.

The Day of Retaliation

The Nebraska area in which Aldrich lived was heavily populated with German-American citizens, and in this story she demonstrates how finely attuned she was to the speech patterns and variances they occasionally used. When she needed to know a specific German term such as the *gans närrisch* of this story, she often asked Gussie Rosenkoetter, her household helper, for correct pronunciation and spelling.

In "The Day of Retaliation" Aldrich provides not only correct spellings and use of a language but also a glimpse of the social mores of the times. She writes of the protagonist, Anna, that when she went out to fetch the cows from their pasture, "she took a shawl down from a nail and drew it around her, not for need of warmth in the moist spring air, but because there were times when a woman should wear a wrap." Anna was on a farm with no close neighbors to see her, yet she put on a shawl: she was pregnant. Even by the early 1930s a woman did not appear in public without trying to conceal that "condition."

"The Day of Retaliation" is one of the few stories Aldrich wrote that demonstrated anger or a desire for revenge; her own positive outlook required that there be redemption.

This piece, which was published in the *Ladies' Home Journal* in February of 1932, would appear later in *The Man Who Caught the Weather* and in *The Bess Streeter Aldrich Reader.*

Anna Brunemeier dressed a chicken at the sink of the farmhouse kitchen. The strong raw odor of the scalded feathers made her head ache. The unpleasant sight of the entrails sickened her. Her feet pained. She felt unusually tired. But then, she was always tired these days. She arose mornings unrefreshed, dragged through long working hours, and fell into bed heavily soon after supper. She felt burdened, oppressed and clumsy. It is the price of coming motherhood.

It was April, and raining. Not the usual soft bud-unfolding, misty rain of April, but a fierce, pommeling downpour. Just outside the screened porch door the water rushed out of a tin spout into the rain barrel, filled it, and dropped sloppily over the sides.

Gus, her husband, came to that door now, stepped inside the porch, shook himself like a spaniel and slipped out of his boots. As he came on into the kitchen there was an odor about Gus, too, that sickened Anna—his wet, steaming clothes and the rubber of his yellow slicker.

"Pretty damp," he remarked amiably.

Anna acknowledged it with a dull "Yes."

Gus hunted around on the clock shelf for his jackknife and, finding it, started back to the porch. As he passed the sink he paused.

"Elsa didn't ever cut the leg off the thigh joint," he volunteered, and pointed a wet, stubby forefinger at the designated piece. "She left the second joint on the leg bone. It made a bigger helping."

He was not cross. He was not dictatorial. His mild voice held no definite disapproval. He had merely given forth a simple statement, casual and informative.

But a hot wave of anger flooded Anna's body, a tingling, uprolling tide of resentment that swept over her and settled in dull red puddles of blood on her cheek bones.

Elsa! Elsa! Always Elsa!

Having deposited his unpremeditated information, Gus got into his muddy boots and went out again into the rain.

Elsa! All the dislike that Anna possessed for the dead Elsa wrapped her now like a garment. All the jealousy that she felt for Gus' first wife concentrated in a dull pain of hatred. If only she could remove the memory of the girl that Gus had loved—still loved—she could be happy. If only the dead Elsa would let her alone, allow her to be Gus' wife with no interference. But she seemed to come to Anna—Elsa did—and stand beside her. Soft-eyed and dark haired and gentle she came. It was as if she said, "Just a year ago these things were mine. At this time last year I went about these rooms. Just so I did my housework. But Gus came and took my hand and spoke tender words. *I* was loved, Anna."

It was an unbearable thought—that Elsa had been the loved one.

The chicken finished, Anna went about other tasks, paring potatoes, chopping cabbage, cooking beans. All the rest of the day at her work she was bothered by the unseen presence of the dead Elsa.

All that day, and the other days of that week, Gus himself brought Elsa many times into the house. Once it was with, "Elsa she culled out her chickens about now and sold the irregulars." Again it was with, "Elsa she baked her bread on Fridays." And one day it was, "Elsa she made *Kaffeeküchen* every little while."

Not cross, not unkind, just casually informative, it wore on Anna's mind like the dripping of water from the eaves. For it rained all week. The creek was high. The world seemed a soggy thing over which there would never again be sunlight.

Anna was never idle. She sewed and baked and swept. She cleaned the cupboards and the downstairs closet, brushing Elsa's coat and sweater which were now rightfully hers, but which nothing could have persuaded her to wear. She hated every one of the garments. And looking at Gus, sitting smoking by the stove on rainy evenings, she half hated him too.

It did not seem possible that one person could be both so loved and so hated. Every fiber of her being loved him—his big strength and his good looks—and yet it seemed, at times, that every fiber of her being also hated him, loathed him for still loving Elsa. For she felt it was of Elsa he was thinking, sitting so quietly by the range on the rainy evenings. She wished that she could shake him out of his silence, bring him back to her, have him for her very own.

On Saturday it stopped raining and the sun came out in a blaze of warmth that fairly pulled the green from the trees, turning the farmyard into a place of steaming humidity. Gus came to the door in the late afternoon and tossed his heavy raincoat into the porch.

"Anna, I got to help Emil Schlappe with a sick horse," he called. "You feel like you could go after the cows?"

"I can go." There was something stolid in Anna, a trace of blood in her that had not changed with two generations of living in a country where women are not stolid.

She finished cleaning a window and washed her hands. Then she took a shawl down from a nail and drew it around her, not for need of warmth in the moist spring air, but because there were times when a woman should wear a wrap. She put on heavy rubbers and started out, picking her way between pools in the lane road. As she walked she was thinking that it was just such a late afternoon and on just such an errand that Elsa had been drowned.

There had been hard rains earlier in the season the year before and the creek had been on this same sort of rampage, rolling sluggishly over the rye land. Elsa had gone for the cows, just as she herself was going now. No one ever knew how the accident happened. There might have been a cow at the edge of the creek and Elsa might have waded into the water to drive her out. She might have tried to get a switch off an overhanging willow tree. Or she might have fainted on the high bank at the far end of the pasture. The whole countryside had discussed the possible cause and had come to no conclusion. The body had been found floating gruesomely against the wire fence down on the Emil Schlappe place. The entire community had sorrowed.

Anna herself had been contentedly at home with her parents five miles away when the word came over the phone that Elsa Brunemeier was drowned. It had meant nothing to her then but the excitement of the news, the loss of a none-too-well-known church acquaintance, a general sort of sympathy for Gus.

And then, so strange is fate, last fall she herself had taken Elsa's place.

She had reached the end of the land now, and stopped to pick up a cottonwood stick with which to whack old Spotty if she proved lazy. The sun shone warm across the spongy pasture. The ground was sticky, the new wild herbage steaming. The cows were at the far end of the pasture still nibbling the juicy grass. Anna picked her way across to them, her feet denting the soft ground. She could see the high creek now. It flowed darkly through the willows like a pleasant old friend turned sullenly unrecognizable. And Elsa had in some way been a victim of that treachery, a sacrifice to that unfaithfulness.

It made Anna stop and look at the picture, fascinated by the ugly danger concealed there under the willows. She paused to imagine the unpleasant details—finding Elsa, bringing her home, Gus' grief. She, herself, had sat in the Lutheran church through the two long sermons of the service. Brother Roerheimer and Brother Schulte had reviewed the beautiful life of the dead woman. Gus had kept his head bowed in his pew. Had hung over the casket when they were leaving the church. Had called "Elsa, come back," so that everyone heard him. Had almost fainted as they finally pulled him away. Even then, she had wondered vaguely how it would seem to be so deeply loved by a nice fellow like Gus.

And then a few months later, as unbelievable as it seemed, Gus had come over to her father's house in his car to call on her. On his third trip he had asked her to marry him. There was no time to make any special preparation for the marriage. Husking was on and Gus needed her immediately. He had said there was plenty of bedding and linen in the house—all of Elsa's things—no use to wait. So she had come. There had been nothing romantic about it. Just a ceremony at the minister's—and then cooking dinner for corn huskers.

No, she was not particularly loved. She sensed it. She was a housekeeper, a drudge, a convenient helper. Gus was not unkind. Nor especially kind. Just matter-of-fact and very quiet. And he still loved Elsa. That was what hurt. She would not have minded the work, or the quiet, unsmiling way of the man, or the ill feelings with which her body was now racked. But to live with—and work for—and bear a child for a man who did not love you. . . . It did not seem right.

She was leaning now against a wet post of the pasture fence whose rotting bark sloughed off on her dress. It was not like Anna to be idle, but her thoughts seemed of more importance today than her duties. She clung to the distasteful idea: Bearing Gus a child and he loving Elsa all the time. She wondered if she, too, were to drown in the little stream like Elsa, whether he would care a great deal.

Standing by the fence, idly whacking her cottonwood stick at the bushes, she let her mind dwell on the picture of her own death, imagined the people gathering in the church and sitting solemnly waiting for the mourners to come. She visioned Gus hanging over her dead body—heard him call her as he had called Elsa. "Anna, come back"—saw them pull Gus away from her coffin. It gave her an abnormal desire to hurt him by her own death, to drown herself in the dark waters in order to shake him out of his moody quiet, and make him give his mind wholly to her.

The cows had come slowly and lumberingly across the pasture now, snatching greedily at a few last choice morsels of lush grass. Reminded of duty, Anna relinquished her dark thoughts of drowning, turned and plodded behind the cattle.

Gus was not at home when she arrived at the house. She put potatoes in the oven, sliced ham in readiness for frying, and set the table for supper. Then she climbed the narrow stairs to her bedroom.

As one throwing fuel on the fire of her jealousy, she opened the top drawer of the shining pine dresser where Elsa's things still lay. In orderly precision they stared back at her—the collars and cuffs and the folded aprons. They affected her strangely, these intimate things of the woman she hated. For half a year she had seen them there in the drawer just as Elsa had left them, and not once had she ever touched them. All her own things were across the room in a highboy she had brought with her from home.

Now she reached forth a cautious hand and picked up a lace collar. The thought of Elsa's white neck rising from it maddened her even as it fascinated her. She laid the collar down and picked up other things one by one. She wanted to crush them, to tear them, in a symbolic crushing and tearing of the love Gus held for their owner. One fragile undergarment she wrung between her strong hands until it lay crumpled and torn in her lap. The act gave her an unholy pleasure. Replacing the rumpled garment, she reached for a green plush handkerchief box at the back of the drawer and drew it out. The lid lifted to her trembling, jealous fingers and disclosed a tumbled array of handkerchiefs.

Vaguely she wondered then at the confusion of the contents, in marked contrast to the neatness of the rest of the drawer.

With an inborn sense of orderliness she began straightening the squares of cotton and linen. Her hand, slipping under them, touched paper.

For only a moment Anna hesitated, and then she drew the paper out.

"April nineteenth. My dearest Fred," said the letter.

Anna stared. *My dearest Fred!* Some intuitive thing deep within her consciousness knew the contents even then. Fred was the name of the young fellow with whom Elsa had kept company before marrying Gus. Her heart stopped with chilliness for a moment, and then raced hotly on. One long ink-stained blur across the page blotted out the words so that part of the closely written letter was illegible. A corresponding long ink stain ran across the soft whiteness of a handkerchief.

April nineteenth! The date on which Elsa had met her tragic death in the high waters of the treacherous creek. Wide-eyed, Anna was taking in the words that remained unblotted, the broken sentences left to carry their startling revelation.

"—can't go on longer with Gus . . . loving you all the time . . . living a lie . . . stand it longer . . . when we were students in the Lutheran college . . .

awful mistake . . . always wanted to marry me . . . crazy this way . . . stand it longer . . . that I've been with you again . . . about out of my head . . . since you were here . . . couldn't sleep . . . come to my decision . . . write you definite plans . . . must burn this . . . no one ever find it . . . always your own Elsa."

Again and again she read the shocking message beginning with "My dearest Fred," and ending with "must burn this . . . no one ever find it. . . . "

And no one *had* found it—not then. And no one at all but the very one who most needed to find it. As though the sky had opened and dropped its message of peace to Anna! As though Fate had taken care of the secret for a year, saving it in the cheap plush handkerchief box until Anna should come for it!

Anna lifted her eyes from the amazing thing in her hand and looked out of the window toward the sullen creek. Elsa, the good, had sinned. Elsa, the worshiped, had deceived. Elsa, the loved, had not loved. Why, she, Anna, was the good one of the two. *She* was the true one. *She* would be the loved one when Gus found this out. *When Gus found this out.* The words poured into her heart like a softly flowing ointment, miraculously soothing and healing the raw, smarting sound that had hurt her so long.

She heard a sound downstairs—the closing of a screen door—so that she hastily shut the drawer and placed the paper in the bosom of her dress. She walked hurriedly down the narrow stairs, her hand at her breast where the letter lay like a weapon ready for use.

Gus was coming in the door with a little pail of cookies from Mrs. Schlappe. With a soothing calm flooding her whole body, Anna greeted him cheerfully. Instinct told her that the time for the amazing revelation was not ripe. After supper, when Gus would sit smoking and silent, thinking of Elsa, she would tell.

In that new tranquil manner she prepared supper. After the meal she washed the dishes, set her bread, and took up some sewing by the kitchen table. With the rise and fall of her breathing, the letter against her breast rose and fell too. She felt a security in its faintly crackling presence, a sense of holding the upper hand over Gus. For a long time they sat so—Anna, sewing, feeling the fluttering nearness of her child and the fluttering nearness of the letter; Gus, idly smoking, staring at the shining blackness of the range.

After a time Gus rose to wind the clock and lock the doors. And Anna had not told. When she went up the narrow, built-in stairway to bed she hurriedly took out the amazing letter, opened the green plush handkerchief box and slipped the paper into it. Then she locked it and placed the tiny key in another drawer. Tomorrow, if even once he mentioned the name of Elsa, she would turn on him and tell.

It was toward noon the next day that Gus, coming up to the house, said to her: "Elsa she used a different broom for the porches." It was not cross, not dictatorial, just casually informative. And surprisingly, it did not seem to hurt Anna today. She smiled to herself as he said it. Yesterday at this time it would have been almost unbearable. To-day it had lost its sting. She would wait until he said something more biting, something that she could not stand, something that cried out for an answer. And the answer would be waiting upstairs in the green plush handkerchief box.

A week slipped away. Several times Gus brought unknowingly the presence of Elsa, the loved, into the house with him. Once it was with "Elsa she churned oftener," so that Anna, tired from much pushing up and down of the old-fashioned dasher, almost turned on him with the weapon of her news. But she held herself, and waited for something more crucial.

The week slipped into a month and the month into August. And Anna had not yet told. Always she was waiting for that more bitter thing—that critical thing which she could not endure.

By September, with the corn safely maturing, there was no rain. So dry was the grass that it made a rustling, crackling sound when the chickens walked in it. Anna canned grapes. The heat from the sun and the heat from the range seemed to burn her like fire from two giant caldrons. Gus, coming into the kitchen, passed the range. Then he paused and turned back. "Elsa she dipped out some of the juice first and made jelly of it before she canned the rest," he volunteered.

A fly buzzed aggravatingly around Anna's perspiring forehead. A bit of hot juice splashed across her hand. Suddenly the thread in her brain snapped—the slender, cautious thread that held her secret. At last Gus had cut the fragile thing with the knife of his criticism.

Anna whirled to him, her face livid with the heat and something else. Her gray eyes flashed wild. She flung out her hand.

"Oh, Elsa! Elsa! Elsa!" Her voice rose in a crescendo of madness. All day it had been coming and now it had come. "Elsa!" she shrieked. "Always Elsa. Some day I'll tell you. . . . " She threw back her head and laughed, high, mirthless laughter. "When I tell you . . . one of these days about Elsa. . . . "

She looked at Gus, standing there speechless, his mouth dropped open in amazement. She wanted to hurt him, shame him out of his calm, compel him to love her. "I'll tell you *now,*" she shrilled suddenly. Anger and jealousy were boiling up in her like the thick, purple sauce in the kettle. "Right *now.* I'll go get it . . . " She dropped the long-handled dipper on the table, and the sweet grape juice dripped stickily onto the floor.

She ran clumsily from the room to the foot of the built-in stairway. "Now . . . right now," she called back, her voice high, strident. "Then you'll talk some more again of your nice Elsa!"

Up the stairs she ran, lifting the cumbersome weight of herself violently. At the head of the stairs she flung herself across the hall into her bedroom and ran to the dresser. With hands fumbling madly for the key to the handkerchief box, she suddenly sank to the floor.

"Gus!" she called. "Send for help, quick!"

In a daze she could hear disconnected sentences from Gus at the phone: "No . . . don't wait . . . right away. Get off the line, you curious coyotes!" He was calling the Schlappes. "Tell Emil to bring your mother, quick!" Gus' voice was no longer mild.

People came. They moved about Anna strangely—sometimes dimly and far away, sometimes coming close like huge, distorted giants with false faces. She was conscious that she was saying foolish, meaningless things, but they were quite beyond her volition. Gus' face came and went with the others, white and staring. Once she made an effort to speak to him: "The grapes, Gus! I got to get up and finish the grapes. Elsa she always finished. . . . " But she was swept away on a black wave which her struggling senses thought was the swollen water of a sullen creek.

A long time later—whether a day or a year or an eternity she did not know—she floated back to rest on the shore.

Vaguely she sensed a rustling, pecking noise over in the basket near her bed. And quite suddenly her mind cleared and she knew. It was her baby. A deep feeling of peace enveloped her.

Out in the hall on the couch she could see old Mrs. Schlappe nodding sleepily. Anna called her weakly. Mrs. Schlappe jumped and sat up straight.

"My baby—which is it?"

"Oh, ya. . . . " The old woman got up laboriously and hobbled over to the bed. "A fine girl."

"Where's Gus?"

"Gus?" The old woman could scarcely get herself awake. "Gus . . . oh, him? Vy, Gus has vent up to Omaha to get a nurse . . . a *trained* nurse. Between you 'n me 'n de gate post, you don't need a *trained* nurse any more'n I do. But you couldn't stop Gus, I tell you."

The old woman's voice went querulously on: "I say to him, 'All right, if you vant to pay forty-two dollar a veek . . . it's all right mit *me.*' 'N he say . . . de *softy* . . . 'I'll pay forty-two dollar a *day* if it'll save my Anna.' So doc televoned. He say a goot one is shust registered. Ain't dat folderol? Like a hotel. So Gus has vent. It's a vonder he t'ought I was goot enough to lay here by you. He acted *gans närrisch* over you. Valked de floor 'n talked about you till doc make him go outdoor. . . . I guess you got him scare talkin' about a note you hide."

Anna was fully roused now, all her faculties clear.

"What did I say? Tell me quick. What did I say?"

"You say foolishness a-plenty all right, about a note dat you hid avay and locked under de vater of de creek bed already yet. You say Gus couldn't find it for de key is in de kettle of grape sauce. But most of 'em do like dat. I know a voman vonce who say ven she get up she is goin' to poison de neighbor takin' care of her . . . and dem goot friends."

The old woman brought the sleeping baby and placed it in the crook of Anna's arm. Fascinated, Anna watched it stretch its arms in little sleepy, objectless motions and then open its eyes. Gus' eyes large and blue. Gus' hair—dark and wavy. Gus' mouth—full-lipped and generous. For a long time Anna lay without taking her rapt eyes from the face of the child.

Subdued noises downstairs roused from her long reverie and then, clumsily tiptoeing, his hat in his hand, Gus came into the room and up to the bed.

Anna looked up to the man hanging wonderingly over her. "Gus, you're disappointed?"

"Not on your life. I'm glad it's a girl."

"Ain't she nice . . . her round little head and her funny little hands?"

Anna's plain face was glorified.

"Gus. . . . " Anna looked up at the man bent protectingly over the bed. "I been thinking . . . poor Elsa . . . she never knew what I know now . . . the feel of a baby in the crook of your arm. It made me sorry for her . . . and I been thinking it would be kind of nice . . . if we call the baby Elsa."

Gus' face turned a red, a brick red that ran below the tan of his skin. "I got no wish to quarrel with you Anna." He twisted his hat on nervous fingers. "But I told quite a few folks already yet about the baby . . .

and when I was drivin' past the newspaper office . . . the editor was standin' out in front . . . 'n I guess I felt kind of important about it . . . Anyway, I drove up by the curb and told him, too, and the paper was just goin' to press. Maybe you'll give me Hail Columbia for this . . . but already yet I told the editor to put in the paper that her name was little *Anna.*

"Gee, Anna—" He broke off suddenly and dropped on his knees by the side of the bed. "I'm glad I got you safe. You had me crazy. I thought I was goin' to lose you. Anna, if I'd lost you I'd a-gone too. You was out o' your head from the start, I guess. Anna, do you remember runnin' up the stairs talkin' about Elsa—how you had something you was goin' to tell me about her? You must have been out o' your head, wasn't you?"

Anna nodded. She slipped cool fingers through Gus' hair. "Sure I was, Gus. Don't pay any attention to it. I must have been plumb daffy!"

And then Gus rose hastily, edging away with a lingering look at Anna, because the new nurse was coming in. The nurse was tall, cool-looking, calm-eyed. She came over to the bed and took Anna's hand in her own capable one. Anna clutched at the hand in her eagerness.

"Listen," she said quickly, very low. "Before any more time goes by I want you to do something for me." Her voice shook in the intensity of her earnestness. "There's a blurred-looking letter in a—my handkerchief box, over there in the right drawer of the dresser. The box is locked and the key is in the left drawer behind some aprons. I want you to get the letter out and take it downstairs to the cook stove. Don't let Gus—my husband—see what you're doing, and don't let that old Mrs. Schlappe even catch glimpse of what you've got. You burn it in the range. Stay there right by it till there ain't a scrap left. Promise me that, and then I'll rest or do anything you say."

"You're not asking me to do something you'll be sorry for when you get up?"

"No—oh, no! I'll never be sorry. I can't rest with it there!"

With taut nerves Anna waited until the white-uniformed woman came back. Then she raised herself a little so that her hot, searching eyes could read the calm ones of the other. "Did you burn it?"

"Yes."

"All to ashes?"

The nurse nodded and smiled. "*All to ashes!*"

Anna Brunemeier dropped contentedly back on her pillow, and lifted the baby's little pink, clutching hands to her cheek.

Trust the Irish for That

Aldrich sold "The Ring of the Piper's Tune" to *The American Magazine* in December 1924 for $450; for an unknown reason, *The American* did not publish it, and Aldrich repurchased it for $500 seven years later. She may have revised it some as she usually did, retitled it "Trust the Irish for That," and sent it off to *Cosmopolitan,* who purchased it in November of that year for $2,500 and published it in January of 1932. In 1936 the story would be included in Aldrich's collection, *The Man Who Caught the Weather.*

Aldrich had great affection for both the Scots and the Irish. In the earlier "The Two Who Were Incompatible," the Scotsman gives the baby girl hair "like the mists around Glenco," and the Irish Teresa O'Conor gives her eyes "the color of the blue-black waters at Kilkee." The Scotsman then passes on to the baby a "stable, thrifty, Scotch mind, but the woman . . . [gave her] an Irish heart." Finally he "gave her the sturdiest of square Scotch chins, but [she] . . . pressed a roguish V-shaped cleft right in the center of it." Each had three chances to mold the life of this descendant. In her books and short stories Aldrich often quotes old Scottish sayings, undoubtedly picked up from her mother, who came from Scotland with her parents. In "Trust the Irish for That" she turns to the Irish brogue for Maggie O'Riley and demonstrates again her unique sense of language as spoken by first- or second-generation Americans.

Old Maggie O'Riley sat in a wheel chair by her kitchen window. She stared out at the garden, the cow shed and the chicken house, desolate-looking in the clearing against the great wall of dark pines. It was late September in the north country, and there was nothing left in the garden but a few frostbitten tomatoes. For the rest there were dead beet tops, dried bean vines and weeds.

It ought to be cleared off and spaded for spring, old Maggie was thinking. Last year at this time she had spaded it and worked the dirt over until it looked as square and flat as a huge stove top. And she would never do it again.

The cow shed out there by the pines was apparently no different from usual, but old Maggie knew that Daisy was not inside it. They had taken Daisy away and sold her because an old woman in a wheel chair cannot take care of a cow. The chicken house, too, was empty. The neighbor boys had loaded the boxes of Plymouth Rocks on their trucks and taken them to the dealer over at the Corners because she could never again go out to feed them.

"Never"! It is the most cruel word in any tongue.

The chair in which old Maggie O'Riley sat was new, of shining oak and rubber-tired. "A lovely chair," Mrs. Schulter, her nearest neighbor, had said when she helped unpack it. The big chair had come all the way up from Minneapolis by train and truck after Mrs. Schulter had written the letter and sent the money from the sale of Daisy.

Yes, it was a nice chair, Maggie had agreed grimly. But it held you with iron hands. Its wood drew you and absorbed you into itself. Its rubber-tired wheels sucked at your heavy old limbs and clutched them tightly in their grasp.

Maggie looked down now at those two limbs that a few weeks ago had so unexpectedly failed her, had so suddenly turned traitor to her. They had taken her back and forth between the house and the garden, the chicken yard and the cow shed, the woods and the lake shore—back and forth tirelessly for years. They had made her no trouble, given her no complaint. They were part of her. They were herself.

And then, as though they had been concealing something from her, concocting a joke behind her back, they had suddenly failed her. It had proved a cruel, malignant joke. For now they were no longer a part of her, no longer her own self. They were alien things, heavy, cumbersome, like knotted white birch logs. Dead timber!

Maggie looked sullenly down at their outlines under the gray calico dress. Dead timber! Useless! Maggie had always made use of everything around the little house in the woods where she lived alone. With a neatness that was proverbial with the few neighbors, she had kept up the place in the clearing. And if there was no use for a thing she either buried it or burned it. But this time it was different. There was no use in the world for two dead legs, and yet she could neither bury them nor burn them.

For all the rest of the afternoon Maggie sat looking out toward the cow shed, the chicken house and the garden with the dark wall of pines in the distance. She might have sewed. She might have read. But old Maggie O'Riley's hands, gnarled and rough from much spading and cow-tending, were clumsy with the needle. And as for reading—that was a secret of Maggie's.

Even the Schulters, who had lived close to her for two years now, were unaware of it. A few times when she had been cornered she had slipped out of it cunningly, had laid it to her glasses that were broken or mislaid. And even the Schulters had not guessed that old Maggie O'Riley could not read.

This afternoon, Maggie was more grieved than ever about her condition. There were people in the world, she was thinking, who did not like to work, lazy folks who shirked the burden of labor. And all she would ask of life would be to go about and work hard again. *How* she would work! Up and down the little place she would go tirelessly. Never would she stop except for sleep, if they would only come to life again—those dead legs.

Suddenly a wave of rebellion swept her. It seemed that it must not be true that she was this way. It could not be. She told herself that she would rise above it. She would not let it be so. She would get out of the hated chair and step on the floor.

With magnificent strength of will she threw herself forward. But only the trunk of her body moved. The dead, immovable weight held her fast. *Och! Mother of Christ!* It was true. Old Maggie broke into sobs, great wrenching noises that came from the depths of a racked soul. The dusk deepened. The old woman saw the Schulters' light appear like a star against the black pines. But she did not move. She knew it was time for her supper, that it was ready for her in the lower part of the cupboard within easy reaching distance, but she made no move to wheel herself over to it. Instead, she gave herself up to thinking of the thing that had come into her mind a week ago.

At that time she had put it aside as wicked, but from much brooding over it during the monotonous days, she had begun to ask herself why it was so bad. She went over it again in her mind, while the dusk settled thickly.

This was it: Up on the highest kitchen shelf was a little box of white powder. If she should put a little of that powder into her coffee some morning, and drink the coffee as though nothing were different, she would go to sleep in her chair. Very soon she would rise up and slip away from her body—leave her body sitting there in the hated new rubber-tired chair. She imagined herself looking down on it, looking back at old Maggie O'Riley sitting there asleep.

She believed it would make her laugh to look down and see old Maggie sitting there so helpless in the chair, while the soul of her swept up and away from Maggie—away from those dead old legs. Her imagination stopped at that picture. She could not quite conceive what incidents would follow. She only knew that it would be worth the doing—to have that fine exhilarating feeling, that buoyant sensation of getting away.

For a long time she toyed with the subject. The church forbade it, but it did not seem wrong. It was not really like killing one's self, she argued. People killed themselves with guns and ropes and in other terrible ways. But this—this was just a little white powder. All there was to it was to drink her coffee with a little cream and a little sugar—and a little white powder. She herself would not be harmed. She would go away free. Only those old dead legs would be left behind.

The church ought not to mind that. It seemed so fraught with ease, so filled with relief for such small effort. A little white powder! And then for reward—that great moment, that laughter-provoking moment of looking back and crowing over old Maggie O'Riley's dead legs.

Even the Schulters would never suspect. To find an old woman dead in her chair sometimes happened. They had found old Mrs. Mendenhall that way over at the Corners four or five years ago. If she sat close to the stove and threw the little box into the fire just as soon as she drank the coffee . . .

She mulled over the details in her mind. She would have everything ready. There was no one to care a great deal. Mrs. Schulter would probably throw her apron over her head and cry a little, for they had been close friends for these two years. But after all, she would be relieved. She would not have to come over any more and get old Maggie into the chair or help her back to bed. Ernie and Emil Schulter would not have to take their time to do her chores.

She ate no supper at all. When Mrs. Schulter came over to help her to bed she was still planning craftily. For a long time she lay thinking of the various catastrophes that might overtake her in her present wretched state. She might get so much worse that she would be bedridden. The Schulters might move away. Mrs. Schulter might get sick. Some other unforeseen thing might happen. Yes, it was best. She was quite calm about her decision.

The next morning when Mrs. Schulter came over, Maggie was ready for her. She assumed a forced cheerfulness as Mrs. Schulter helped her dress and get into the chair. At first, weeks before, when the thing had happened, Mrs. Schulter had brought over all of Maggie's meals and cared for the little three-roomed house. But with the arrival of the chair Maggie had insisted that such work cease. "No," she had said, "if it's got to be, it's got to be—and it's me that's goin' to do my own work."

They had all been good to her. Schulter had come in with his plane and hammer and chisel, and had pried off the old-fashioned threshold boards between the rooms and planed them smooth, so that the chair would slip easily from kitchen to sitting room to bedroom. Emil and Ernie took turns filling the wood box and bringing the water. "Anything else, Maggie?" they would call loudly, thinking that because she was old and helpless she was also deaf.

Emil had sawed off a broom handle for her and she had learned to sweep from her chair. It took her a long time, but Time was something Maggie did not begrudge. Time was something of which she possessed a great deal. And her shoulders were still strong and active. It was only those old leaden limbs that would not let her go. So this morning when Mrs. Schulter said, "Anything else, Maggie?" Maggie was ready for her.

"Yes," she said, " 'tis the medicines on the top shelf I'm wantin' down lower. There's a toothache one and the peppermint I might be needin'. Would ye be kind enough to clean off the top shelf and get 'em down close to me?"

So Mrs. Schulter, thinking, perhaps, of the canned blueberry pies that she must make, swept everything into a lower shelf.

Maggie eyed her as she handled the boxes and bottles. But Mrs. Schulter paid no attention to the labels. Maggie watched surreptitiously—peppermint and castor oil, the toothache medicine, liniment, sassafras, the little white powder . . .

All morning, at her slow, laborious tasks conducted from the chair, like a silver thread through her thoughts ran the idea of the release after sleeping. It was something to look forward to, like a meeting with a friend or a tryst with a lover. She would think it over a long time to be sure of her decision, but always it would lie there before her—the way of escape.

In the afternoon it rained, a slow, cold fall drizzle, with the pines dripping clammily. Maggie wheeled herself to the kitchen door and called to Collie to come into the sitting room. Collie, in his simple dog fashion, was thoroughly amazed. Such a thing had never happened in all his days.

"Come on, Collie," old Maggie called. "You might's well come on in here with me now."

But Collie whined and thumped his tail on the kitchen floor and would not come in. A long time Maggie coaxed, but Collie was bashful, as though pleased at the invitation but too wary to commit himself, so that she gave up trying to get him in.

For the two or three days following, old Maggie existed in an apathetic way. And then the unforeseen thing, that she had half predicted, happened. Trouble came to the Schulters.

It was an early October day with pine needles ankle-deep in the woods, bare branches on the pin cherries and birches, mallards at the lake edge, the sun pale in the clearing—and old Maggie tied to a chair. Just before noontime it was that she saw the men go past her house and made out from her window that they were carrying Emil Schulter into his house. Emil, who had been on a vacation from his work as a forest ranger, swinging along that very morning with his young, powerful strides, had been brought home injured.

Maggie at the window an hour later saw the doctor come from his long drive through the woods. He was in the house for several hours.

It was late evening before Mrs. Schulter could get in to Maggie. Mrs. Schulter told her more about it. Emil had been over to the Corners in the truck. Something had gone wrong with the steering gear and he had run into a tree.

"It'll be weeks before he's out again, months maybe," his mother said. She threw her apron over her head and broke out crying. "To see him there helpless, wantin' me right by him all the time . . . always so big and strong and full of life." Then she thought of Maggie and added apologetically: " 'Tain't so hard for you, Maggie. You're old and you're a woman. 'Tain't half so hard for you."

Maggie said nothing. Yes, she was old and she was a woman. But it was hard. She looked at Mrs. Schulter sitting there swaying back and forth in her misery and crying about her boy. Even before this happened, Mrs. Schulter had worked all day long, and now with this added burden of taking care of Emil . . .

"You can't come over to take care of me any more. 'Tis too much to ask. I ain't worth it. It's me that ought to 'a' died insteada hangin' on good for nothin'."

Mrs. Schulter wiped her eyes. "Don't you say that again, Maggie. I'll manage. I'm strong yet."

When Maggie was in bed she told herself that the little white powder was the answer to the problem. But she would not take it just yet. It would only add more to Mrs. Schulter's burdens. It ought rather to be when Emil was over the first danger. And it would be so simple—just her usual coffee with a little cream and a little sugar and a little white powder . . . Then sleep, and that wonderful moment of rising up and floating away from the cumbersome body; that great moment of looking back and laughing to see old Maggie O'Riley sitting heavily there in the chair.

In a few days they lifted Emil, too, into a big chair by the window. From across the clearing he waved his hand to Maggie. It seemed queer to look out and see the bulky outline of Emil Schulter sitting idly there. Even at that distance Maggie could sense his restlessness, the constant turning of his head from side to side.

Late in the afternoon of the second day that Emil sat by the window, Maggie saw all the other Schulters come out of the house together: Schulter and Mrs. Schulter and Ernie, who worked in the garage at the Corners. Ernie and Schulter fixed a wire up on their chimney. Then they got down off the house and ran it across to a pine tree. A clothesline! Why were they putting it up that high for? The Schulters were daffy.

Mrs. Schulter did not come over until time to put Maggie to bed. Then she was excited and in a great hurry. "It's the radio they've been puttin' up for Emil," she told Maggie. "It's goin' to be wonderful. We can get to hear the music from Minneapolis." She was anxious to get back.

It made Maggie feel sensitive. She thought it over in bed. There was some quirk to it. The Schulters were not so bright. It wasn't sensible that anyone in Minneapolis should sing a song that the Schulters could hear up in the pine country.

Most of the next afternoon through her window Maggie could see Emil sitting quietly enough. In the evening all the Schulters gathered in the living room.

When Mrs. Schulter came over at bedtime she began at once: "We got the singin' from Minneapolis all right. It was grand. You'd 'a' thought they was in the same room."

Old Maggie listened incredulously. It wasn't sensible—such talk.

The next few days Mrs. Schulter did not come over except in the early mornings and to put Maggie to bed. Every morning she asked cheerfully and hurriedly if there was anything more she wanted. But Maggie could see how anxious she was to get back to her injured boy.

"There's nothing more, thank ye," Maggie would say humbly.

All day now she could see Emil near the window working on something. He picked up some object and put it down again, over and over. His mother waited on him constantly. Of course she would wait on her boy and get things to amuse him. Maggie told herself that it was foolish to care, to think they had forgotten her. But she could not help but recall the days when Mrs. Schulter had brought little things over to her: a dish of custard, a glass of chokecherry jam, a bit of news from the Corners.

She brought nothing these days, told her no gossip. She was always hurried, breathless, almost impatient. Maggie brooded over it in her helplessness, nursed her sorrow. Once she wheeled herself to the cupboard and took out the little white box. So small it was, so harmless-looking and so powerful. She told herself she was cowardly. Why did she put it off? If she had any backbone she would set the very morning.

And then came the next Monday when Mrs. Schulter, with her washing and her waiting on Emil, did not get over until hours later than usual. All morning Maggie lay helpless. It was after ten when Mrs. Schulter came, tired and hot and apologetic.

"Everythin' was at once, Maggie. The dishes and the washin' with the clothes boilin' over and me havin' to stop in the very midst of it and get somethin' for Emil. I never saw a mornin' so rushed."

It hurt Maggie anew. She was put off until after ten. She quivered with the pain of it. Well, tomorrow it would not matter. Mrs. Schulter could come over at seven or eleven or not at all. When she came over in the evening, she would find Maggie asleep in her chair by the stove. Never to bother her again!

All day from her chair Maggie cleaned the house. She put everything in shape. Tuesday morning it was to happen. Coffee with a little cream and a little sugar, and a little white powder—and then that high buoyant sensation of getting away from her loathsome self, away from those dead limbs.

All afternoon she sat by the window. The slanting rays of the pale October sun hung over the lonely little house.

Suddenly something was happening over at the Schulters'. They were coming out of the house and over this way—all of them—Schulter and Ernie and Mrs. Schulter. Emil, too, sat leaning out of the opened window, watching. The men-folks were carrying a lot of contraptions: a black box and a big iron horn and wire—a great coil of wire.

They came in the back door. They filled the tiny kitchen. Maggie, frightened, wheeled her chair out toward them.

"Maggie, it's for you!" Mrs. Schulter's voice was high and excited. "Emil made you one, too, from a secondhand one with some parts missin'. The week and more he's put every minute on it. 'Twas for this I had to quit my washin'. 'Maggie must have one, too,' he tells us the minute we had his put up. 'Settin' there like she is all day. 'Twill put new life into her,' he says. And Ernie bringin' him the parts from another old one a summer tourist left at the Corners. And me bringin' the tack hammer and the bit and brace every minute of my time, till I thought I'd never get a thing done, let alone takin' care of you.

"I felt terrible neglectful, but Emil, he's that set on finishin' it quick. It made me torn betwixt the thought of my neglectin' and the anxiousness of you havin' the singin' and the speakin' too. It seemed for all the world like I was harmin' my own mother, Maggie, leavin' you go that way—me losin' her when I was little makes you seem like my own."

The men-folks were setting the contraptions together. They bored a little hole at the edge of the window and pulled a wire through. They strung a long wire from Maggie's chimney to the old cow shed. Collie ran excitedly before them.

"Jenkins said the old automobile battery was wore out," Ernie was telling his father; "told me to help myself to it, but it'll hold juice for Maggie for a spell yet."

Maggie could scarcely adjust herself to all this commotion after the quiet of the past days. And she worried about the wire running through that little hole at the side of the window, having a distrust of wires in general.

All at once they had finished. And Mrs. Schulter had thought of the bread in her oven, and was running back home. Schulter took his tools and went away. Ernie stood in front of the black box and the horn that craned its neck like a goose, and turned the little wheels. A band began playing on the inside of the black horn. It did not seem sensible. But with her own ears Maggie O'Riley heard the fife and the drums.

"Here, Maggie, I've only a minute to stay." Ernie shut off the music. "Listen while I explain. You'll have to do the best you can with it by yourself till Ma gets back over. See here! You'll get on to it pretty soon. You get your long wave lengths here and your short ones here."

Ernie might as well have been repeating the Iliad in the original.

"There ain't much I can tell you about it now for tonight, except just to turn the dials and get what you can. You turn *this* and when you get your station, to tune in better you turn *this.*"

"What if I'd turn wrong, Ernie? What would happen?" Maggie was fearful.

Ernie laughed. "Oh, 'tain't goin' to blow you up. You just wouldn't get anything. And before you go to bed you turn this around. There ain't a chance in a dozen there'll be lightnin' this late, nor a chance in a million it would strike if there was, but if it did, it would run down into the ground."

Maggie did not like anything running around loose in her house, mice or lightning. And she did not want Ernie to leave her alone with the machine.

"You're all right. You'll get onto it," he assured her. "Remember, first you turn *this* and then *this* and then *this.*"

And then Ernie went away. And Maggie sat in front of the little black box with the striped wheels. She would not have felt more helpless in front of the steering apparatus of an ocean liner.

"*This* and then *this* and then *this,*" Maggie said over her lesson. And then she took the plunge. She turned *this.* There was a long whistle-like sound. She was agitated, but she kept her head. And then she turned *this.* There were a few faint notes of singing. Then they died away. Almost immediately a man was saying something about signing off.

Maggie sat in front of the mysterious black box and waited. Nothing happened. The man had said he was signing something and she figured that he would come back after he had signed it. But there was nothing but a sound of squeaks and rushing air.

After a time Maggie decided upon another Columbus-like venture. Cautiously she turned the little black wheels. And right in the room a man started to sing:

"Oh, the days of the Kerry dancing!
Oh, the ring of the piper's tune!
Oh, for one of those hours of gladness . . ."

Old Maggie had not had one hour of gladness for months, but suddenly her heart was leaping to the piper's tune.

"When the boys began to gather
In the glen of a summer night . . ."

Old Maggie could see them as plain as day—Michael and Patrick and Terry. Ah, well! It was because there had been only one Terry in the world that Maggie had never married.

"And the Kerry piper's tuning
Made us long with wild delight."

It was all there before her. The work was done. The peat was gathered. The moon was shining through the trees. All the young folks had come into the glen. And Terry was coming toward her.

" 'Lads and lasses, to your places,
Up the middle and down again.' "

Terry touched her hands. She slipped her own into them. And then a strange thing happened. Old Maggie O'Riley seemed to leave her body. She rose out of it and joined the throng of young people dancing on the green. She was red-cheeked and lithe and spry. With Terry she was dancing. All the magic of youth she had in her feet. And she looked back at old Maggie O'Riley sitting there so helpless with the immovable limbs. Threw back her head, she did, and laughed at old Maggie, so old, so helpless, with two dead logs for legs. She made sport of her—old Maggie, tied to a chair. "Is it grindstones ye're havin' for feet?" she mocked. "Watch me!" she called and danced the faster.

"Ah! the merry-hearted laughter
Ringing through the happy glen!"

Faster and faster she danced. "Look at me," young Maggie O'Riley called to old Maggie O'Riley, "you wid yer dead legs! Is it the wings like the lark I have? Or maybe 'tis the thistledown I am!"

They had whirled to the trees at the edge of the glen. Terry held her close and kissed her, so that she half swooned at the sweetness of it.

"And the sound of the dear old music,
Soft and sweet as in days of yore."

The song died away on its last lovely melting note. A man's voice was saying briskly that this was Minneapolis.

Old Maggie sat back heavily. *Saint John the Kind!* It was so. From away down in Minneapolis a man had sung to her up in the pine country—sung the gayest and dearest old tune of them all.

And now Ernie Schulter was hurrying over again. All dressed up he was, to go after his girl at the Corners.

"How you comin', Maggie?" he called. "Did you like it?"

" 'Twas heaven itself," said Maggie. And then she was wanting to know: "Who did it, Ernie? Who got it up—was smart enough to know how to fix the little black boxes to catch the music?"

Ernie laughed. "You mean, discovered that sound could be transmitted? Oh, I guess you'll have to give a man by the name of Marconi the credit for that, Maggie."

Maggie repeated the name after him reverently.

And then Ernie was gone and Mrs. Schulter was back with a fresh loaf of bread. And together they listened to a sermon and dance music and a talk on tree culture. Praying and prancing and pruning—it was all the same to Maggie, so eagerly did she drink it in.

After it was over, she could not get to sleep for excitement. She was not forgotten. The Schulters had not neglected her. Emil had made her the magic box. Ernie and Schulter had put it up. Mrs. Schulter had said she was like a mother to her. All evening she had forgotten herself, forgotten the old legs that were like dead birch logs.

Now she would always know how to forget them. With a few turns of the little black wheels she knew how to rise up and away from old Maggie O'Riley sitting there so heavily in the chair.

On Tuesday morning she poured her coffee. She put in a little cream and a little sugar. And that was all. When she had finished her breakfast she wheeled over to the cupboard. From it she took a little white box. Then she wheeled herself over to the stove and put it in the fire.

All the morning she worked at her accustomed small tasks. She would not permit herself even to glance toward the enchanted black box. It was after eleven when she finished. She wheeled herself to the lighting switch and turned it cautiously. With fine bravado she turned the wheels of the box. A man's voice: "This completes the market quotations for the day. Signing off at eleven-thirty-nine, Central Standard time."

Signing off! You couldn't fool old Maggie a second time. Signing off meant *quitting*. She chuckled at her own smartness. Then she turned the wheels and heard a violin playing. But at that moment she saw Ernie Schulter drive into the clearing. She wheeled herself hurriedly to the window and raised it.

"Ernie," she shrilled, "sure, and I feel grateful to that Mar O'Conner you told me about. You could tell he was Irish, pulling music out of the air that way. Trust the Irish for that!"

The Runaway Judge

One type of individual who amused Aldrich was the efficient woman who had little sense of humor, a characteristic that Aldrich found so necessary. Aldrich portrays such a person in "The Runaway Judge." She depicted similar efficient women in her *A Lantern in Her Hand* (1928) and some of the Mason and Cutter short stories. Rarely does she indicate an approval of these kinds of women, but she does so in this particular piece; however, she gives the judge the last words.

Originally Aldrich titled this story "The Mountains Look on Marathon," a quote from Byron (*Don Juan*, Canto III, 1821), but when the *Ladies' Home Journal* published the story in July of 1932, they changed it to "The Runaway Judge." When Aldrich included it in her 1936 *The Man Who Caught the Weather*, she returned it to its original name.

Father you must take a nap this afternoon. If you're going to try to make a talk at the Knife and Fork dinner tomorrow night, you must conserve your strength."

The decisive voice of Mrs. Chester Cunningham bounced against old Judge Cunningham's ears from some point behind him. The crisp click of his daughter-in-law's thin heels on the tile of the sun-room floor seemed to put the command into italics. The definite odor of a penetrating perfume struck his nostrils as she passed him. Two of her bracelets tapped together distinctly.

There were no halfway characteristics about Rita Cunningham, no pastel shades in any of her personal traits. Where others might have made suggestions, Rita gave commands. When others lounged comfortably about, Rita sat upright, ready for action. Even her gowns were chosen from definite primary colors. Just now the old judge could see out of the tail of a belligerent eye that she was in red—the flamboyant turkey red of an Indian's blanket. Red! On this hot afternoon. It irritated him beyond measure.

She click-clicked now over to a window shade, lowered it with quick, efficient movements, turned with a swish of the barbaric gown and a snap of silver bracelets. "I'm playing contract this afternoon, father." She would be, he thought. The hotter the day the better her game, he'd bet. "Don't forget the afternoon soda water. And above all, *don't* neglect to take the nap."

The old judge emitted something unintelligible which might have been "huh" and "well"; but running in together as they did, the result was scarcely an example of refined speech.

After her departure he continued to sit unmoving in the huge chair of English chintz, his short stocky legs reposing on a stool of French needlework and his mind vaguely registering the sound of a Mexican orchestra broadcasting a German waltz. Sitting there in apparent relaxation in the midst of these international contributors to his comfort, he looked the picture of supreme contentment—which only goes to prove that one, Phædrus, was quite right when, many centuries ago, he gave forth: "Things are not always what they seem and first appearances deceive many." For old Judge Cunningham was not comfortable, wholly unrelaxed, and most decidedly not contented.

Rita! How she irritated him with her quick, efficient ways and her brisk commands from which there was never escape. Was it because she had once been a trained nurse that she now assumed he was a buck private and she the head of the War Department? No. For a few moments he pictured her in different settings—a teacher, a stenographer, a newspaper woman—and always she was the same brisk, dictatorial creature. If he had known what freedom he was giving up when he disposed of the substantial brick home over in Silver City and came here to live in the pretentious one of his son's, nothing could have induced him to make the change.

He recalled Chet's "You'll not have to do a thing any more, dad," and Rita's "Yes, father we're going to take care of you now." Well, they had kept their word all right; there was no discounting that. He had grown fatter and logy and definitely stupid. The first two weeks had been pleasurable, the next few passable, and the last few painful. He who had given freedom to many a tortured one was now himself a prisoner; bound by a thousand strands of repressions. He had sold his birthright for a mess of his son and daughter-in-law's pottage. He felt intensely sorry for himself.

"Eat some spinach, dad. You need the iron." "Don't go out now, father. It's raining." Even little Margaret was beginning. "Where are you going, grandpa? *Should* you?" All day it went on. At first it had seemed merely gracious and interested. Now, by heck, it was tyrannical. It was getting on his nerves. If he left his light on half an hour longer than usual, someone came to his door and asked if he was sick. If he turned it out half an hour sooner than usual, they tiptoed in to the bed, probably to see if he had gone into a state of coma. He was tired of it, by thunder!

Liberty! Freedom! They were the two most glorious words in the language. And they were no longer in his vocabulary. He tried to put his finger on the exact time he had lost them. It must have been during those few days of sickness. But that hadn't amounted to anything. Pshaw! Just because Chet was a doctor he didn't know everything. Made mountains of molehills. Doctors were all like that. Acted as though you were going to die. If you did they'd crow because they'd been right in their surmise. If you didn't they'd brag about the grand job of saving you they had done.

Well, he hadn't died, but he might as well have done so, as far as calling his soul his own. And he was as sound now as he ever was. Going to make a little talk tomorrow night at dinner. That proved he was all right again, didn't it? Why, in the name of all that was sensible, didn't the family drop this eternal bossing him around, then? If he could only shake off the sensation of their eternal supervision and feel like himself! He was no old man. Strong as an ox, quick and agile.

At that, he sat up suddenly, grabbed a plump knee and groaned aloud, looking around hastily to make sure no one was near. Then he pulled himself heavily from the depths of the big chair and went out to the hall to get his hat and cane.

He opened the side door softly and started down the long grassy slope toward a gate in the clipped hedge.

"Oh, grandpa—" The fresh young voice came from an upper window. He knew it. *He knew it.* It was not possible to leave that house without interference. "Mother said to watch and if you started away from the house to tell you not to be gone long—the sun is too hot."

He walked stubbornly on, unheeding. His ears were as sharp as a chipmunk's; but if they thought he was such a decrepit old man, he could be deaf too. He went past the pool where the goldfish nosed stupidly against the lily pads, past the hydrangeas clumped together near the side gate, and passed through the hedge out to the street. He stood for a moment looking up and down the avenue much like a little boy trying to decide what to play, and then started down toward the river, swinging his ebony cane—with "Presented by the Cedar County Bar Association" on its gold knob.

As he walked he was wishing he could take a trip by himself. But something told him it was no longer possible. They would make some excuse. He would wager his last dollar that if he should propose it, Rita would find some reason to tag along. Even if he succeeded in getting away, their influence over him would stretch out like long flexible fingers, following him wherever he went. "Tell us your exact route, father." "Where will you be on Sunday, dad?? I'll send you those tablets." No, he'd just give up. Genuine freedom—it would never be his.

He walked heavily along in the hot sun, the cane whacking maliciously at hedges, his thoughts as belligerent as a little boy's.

The river reflected back the sun with blinding brilliance, but the old judge walked stubbornly out to the end of the wharf and stood gazing across the water. Right up there—about where that strip of pines jutted out—was the place he and some of the old gang used to go when they were kids. Seemed a hundred years ago—and yesterday.

As he lingered, a dingy boat pulled up to the dock, a wizened-looking man at the oars. He watched the queer little fellow swing an agile leg over the boat's edge and clamber up the piling, a string of river cat in his hand, their bodies glistening in the strong light. From his appearance the judge could not tell whether he was an active old man or a weather-beaten young one. His face was tanned and seamed, the chin and lower cheeks covered with smoke-colored hair. His clothes were nondescript—soiled loose trousers and a shirt of black and white checkerboard squares pinned with a safety pin across his dark chest.

Coming up to the judge now he gave a wide, hairy, half-toothless grin, so that he presented the appearance of an animated baboon.

"Guess you don't know me?"

The judge was shaking his head slowly, and then—something in the little ice-blue eyes, the shape of the small head, an outstanding left ear, and so rapidly does the mind travel that in the flash of introspection Judge Cunningham was remembering a boy from "up the river" waiting for him in the dark dawn, lying outside in the lush grass. Together they had slipped away and together they had stayed in the woods for a day and a night. That day had stood out on his boyhood's calendar unbelievably red—a day of complete freedom. Only they two had lived in a world of their own. No one knew where they had gone. They had hunted and fished and penetrated deep into the timber. They seemed to belong to no civilization or time. It was as though they were nonexistent. All night, too, they stayed in the cool depths of the forest, lost to the wonder of the dark. In the dim early morning they returned home, he to distraught parents who had been up all night seeking him, the other boy to an indifferent family who had no worries concerning their offspring's lax ways. He remembered even now the nonchalance with which Jim Shaffer had left him and gone on home, whistling, while his own family gathered around with excited comments. Almost he could hear the gay, insolent tune:

Oh, come with me in my little canoe,
Where the sky is calm and the sea is blue.

And so old Judge Cunningham, standing there in his tailored clothes with his presented-by-the-bar-association cane, was saying to the dirty old river rat:

"Not . . . it isn't . . . Jim Shaffer?"

The grin widened in assent.

"Well . . . well. . . . " The judge presented a fat smooth hand to a bony soiled one. "Jim . . . I haven't heard anything about you for years. How are you? Where do you live?"

"Got a shack over by Lake Tanner."

"Tanner! Why, that's where you and I ran away to—that time. Remember? Golly, how scared my folks were!"

Jim was nodding. "Ya. Same place." His little ice-blue eyes twinkled above the leather of his cheeks.

"How did you know me, Jim?"

"Took fish up to your son's home. Saw you through the window. Didn't say nothin'. Too swell."

The judge ignored that. "Whatever came of some of the rest of the boys? That little devil of a Red Prescott? Where's he?"

Old Jim grimaced. "Methodist parson," he said dryly.

"Don't tell me," Judge Cunningham chuckled. "And Goody-goody Meeker—teacher's pet—where's he?"

Old Jim pursed his lips and aimed a dusky-hued stream at a dock post. "In the pen," he said laconically. And they both laughed at the irony of it.

"Well, well, Jim! What do you do with yourself?"

"Fish a lot. Pick blueberries 'n' chokecherries. Lay around. Hear the herons go slippin' 'cross the sky. Sleep under the pines. Come 'n' go when I please."

Old Judge Cunningham eyed the dirty little man with something which approached perilously near to envy. "Lord, Jim, that sounds pleasant."

" 'Tis. Wouldn't change places with nobody. First one to see the flash of a teal's wing in spring. Partridges feed on pin cherries right outside my cabin. Squirrels run over the roof. Mallards settle down in the rushes in front."

"How about winter, though? Do you stay there then?"

"Sure. Just as good. Stop up the cracks with putty. Big fire in the stove. Listen to the pitch sizzlin' out the pine. Melt maple sugar. Pop corn. Go huntin' rabbits. Lots o' wild things around. Little deer come nosin' around last winter. Fox tracks. Trap muskrats. Got four minks last year."

To old Judge Cunningham, bound to civilization and his son's family by a thousand strands of inhibitions, the pictures drawn by old Jim Shaffer seemed fascinating. There was something alluring in the vision. It was as if old Jim were playing upon some chord in the judge's make-up which responded with music. And the music was of poignant sweetness.

Quite as though he were putting words to the music, the old judge said throatily:

> "*The mountains look on Marathon,*
> *And Marathon looks on the sea;*
> *And musing there an hour alone,*
> *I dreamed that Greece might still be free.*"

"Huh?" said Jim Shaffer politely, his first-hand knowledge of Byron being somewhat limited.

"Just an old man's fancies, Jim. Say, Jim, you're two years older than I am. But, by George, you seem twenty years younger—agile, wiry, spry as a grasshopper. How does that happen?"

Old Jim shrugged a checkerboard shoulder. "No worries. Just livin' fer a day at a time. Lay in the sun. Splash in the lake. Smell the balsam."

Judge Cunningham gave a hasty glance backward down the years—studying cases . . . night work . . . speeches . . . the troubles of the community on his mind. . . .

He sighed, and then said, "So you never married." It was a statement rather than a question.

"Sure," old Jim said testily. "Sure I married. Three times."

"Three times. Why—what happened?"

"Well, one was drowned; the other two just walked off . . . vamoosed into thin air."

"That's hard luck, Jim. A death and two divorces."

"Never come up against no divorce."

"But how—you didn't remarry without one?"

"Well, she was gone, wan't she?" Old Jim shrugged an indifferent shoulder. "How'd I know where she'd went?"

Why, the old reprobate! He had remarried without benefit of court.

"And so you just come and go as you please."

Old Jim nodded silently. The tears came to his little ice-blue eyes. Freedom was too sacred a thing upon which to comment. He felt immeasurably sorry for the old man standing by him in the pressed suit and swell hat. "Tied down, Sam?"

Judge Cunningham's first inclination was to cover it largely. "Oh, no, no. I've a little money. I can go anywhere." But in his heart he knew well enough that it was not true.

So he leaned forward. "Terribly, Jim. I half envy you your freedom. Why, do you know, one of the happiest memories I have is the time I ran away with you. Remember catching bass in the early dawn . . . doing our own cooking over a fire . . . fish and bread and coffee . . . not seeing anybody all day and all night . . . not hearing anything but the noises of the woods?"

Old Jim nodded in wordless sympathy.

"Lord, I'd like to live that all over, Jim."

"Well"—Jim wiped a hairy brown paw across a stained mouth—"what's hurtin'?"

"What do you mean, Jim?"

"What's hurtin' you run away agin?"

"Nothin'." Unconsciously Judge Cunningham dropped into Jim's and his own boyhood vernacular. "Nothin's hurtin' that I know."

"Come on, then." He motioned airily to the dingy flat-bottomed boat.

"No, thanks, I couldn't today, Jim."

" 'Fraid of your son and swell daughter-in-law?" the old river rat jibed.

"Afraid of——" the old judge grew almost apoplectic. It was as though he were little Sammy Cunningham again, fearful of the opinion of the independent Jim Shaffer. "Say, what's eatin' you, Jim? 'Fraid of nobody. I'll go. Sure I'll go. But not now. How's early tomorrow morning?"

"Any time with me." That was the old Jim, ready to do anything, any time—free.

All evening the old judge harbored the guilty secret. Tomorrow morning at the ungodly hour of three o'clock, he was going on a fishing trip with Jim. It was true, he admitted, he did have a sort of lurking fear of the family. He could hear Chet's joking, "Father, I'm afraid you're getting into bad company in your old age." Could imagine Rita's chagrin and disgust at the sight of dirty old Jim. It was ridiculous that he had to slip out like a thief, but they watched over his every movement.

He made an excuse to go to bed early and, just as he expected, it caused comment. "You aren't sick are you father?" "Sure you feel all right, dad?"

Rita came click-clicking down the hall as he was getting out an old panama hat, so that he slipped hastily into bed.

He couldn't get to sleep. For a long time he twisted and turned. Then he slept fitfully and wakened at two. Fearful then that he would oversleep, he lay waiting for three. Strange how boyish and happy he felt!

He rose and dressed and, shoes in his hand, slipped stealthily down the back stairs. On the kitchen table he left a note for Rita: "Will be back in time to dress for the dinner." He chuckled to think how he was outwitting her. If she had known where he was going, she would have driven him to the dock and taken along a camp chair and pillows and a first-aid kit.

Down the street he went in the semi-dark, and the faint faraway smell of the river greeted his nostrils so that he quickened his pace.

There was the wharf, now, outlined against the gray water. There was Jim rowing along in the faint light, the swish of his oars soft and rhythmic.

And then old Jim had pulled up and was waiting for him to get in. He tried to drop down as easily as he knew Jim could have done, but it was a sorry attempt. With suppressed puffings and wheezing he finally crawled down backward, an entirely unsportsmanlike proceeding.

Then they were off, with a soft sound of oars. This was the life, the old judge thought. No little mill girl of Browning's Pippa Passes could have so enjoyed the freedom of her one great day, he was sure.

A light wind played along the top of the water. Old Jim sniffed and turned his face into it. "Bass morning," he said laconically. And the old judge nodded, wordless, too full of gratitude to his old playmate for speech.

Across the river old Jim docked, jumped out and pulled the flat-bottomed boat with the fat judge in it farther up on the sand. Evidently, the little wiry man had the strength of a burro.

Together they plunged into the undergrowth of the woods where light had not yet penetrated, only the white of the birches standing out from the dark shadows. The odors were fragrant—crushed ferns and little wild flowers and the pungent smell of the pines.

In time they came out to the lake set like a lovely stone in the green filigree of the woods. Old Jim led the way down the steep winding path to another shell of a boat in which there were rods and bait. There was a slight delay and then they were off, old Jim's brown sinewy arms rowing steadily, slowly, up the shore line just outside the rushes, while old Sam trolled. Far up the lake they changed to casting.

Old Jim was right. Jim had always been right about Nature's signs. Bass were biting. The fresh wind whipped the water in ruffles of waves along the fringe of rushes. Old Judge Cunningham, reeling in a big-mouth bass, was in a state of perfect contentment.

All day long that contentment grew. After a lunch of fish and bread the two sprawled on the needle-carpeted ground and drank in the pungent odor of the pines while old Jim talked about woodsy things. The years had swept back. They were boyhood pals.

In the afternoon they anchored for still fishing in a sheltered cove. Jim wound in and out of the rushes, sighting a spot opposite a fallen monster of a tree. They caught a crappie or two, their flat bodies flashing silver. Suddenly, it grew warmer and more sultry. The water took on a dark gray hue. The leaves of the birches drooped listlessly. Old Jim turned his face to the woods and sniffed. "Rain," he said laconically. "with wind."

"Rain?" Why, there hadn't been rain for quite a while. Today, of all days! "I must get right back, then. I have to attend a meeting, Jim."

"Have to get a move on you, then."

Even as old Jim pulled up anchor, the great billowing clouds began foaming up above the birches. Greenish-yellow they were like the cheeks of some sickly, jaundiced giant. It seemed an interminable time that it took to get to Jim's old weather-beaten dock.

Up the sloping bank to Jim's shack, and then the storm struck. The rain crashed on the roof like stones.

The judge held his watch in his hand. "Now," he snapped it shut. "Now, I've *got* to go, storm or no storm." But when he went to the door the wind and rain forced him back against Jim's old rusty stove. It was exasperating, ridiculous that he was held here in this old shack. At home a closed car would have taken him to the dinner without wetting a hair of his head. Chet and Rita—how worried they would be! What a monstrous thing to cause them one moment of anxiety!

At ten o'clock, sick with remorse, he gave up going. The rain was still pelting in great driving sheets, the wind roaring in its fury. Jim gave him his own bed. He shuddered as he looked at it.

All night long on the dirty bed the judge twisted and turned and called himself choice names. He was cold. One of the two covers over him was a dressed cow-hide. Toward morning he felt ill, as though he had eaten great hot balls of fire. Jim's greasy cooking, that was.

At the first suggestion of dawn he shook Jim from a snoring sleep. No, he couldn't wait for coffee. Every bone in his body cried aloud, his head was bursting.

Together they started through the woods that still dripped clammily. The soggy underbrush slapped the judge in his face. Every leaf was a miniature dipper to throw its contents on him. It was hard to walk. There were a dozen strong, disagreeable odors—crushed plantain leaf and decayed toadstools and rotting wood. His feet squashed in the oozy interior of his shoes. The boat contained so much water that they had to bail it. The judge's back hurt with every toss of the tin can he was using. That pain in his side—he believed it was pleurisy.

"Want I should go along up to the house with you?" Old Jim was playing the host to the bitter end.

The judge turned a mottled face to him. If that pain should turn out to be pneumonia— "Maybe you'd better, Jim."

All the way up the side streets in the ghostly dawn Jim Shaffer stepped along blithely. Wet to the skin, he was merely a little brown gnome—one with the woods, a child of the river.

The judge wished he could get rid of him before they came to the house. It wasn't quite square to feel that way after Jim's hospitality, but he would rather Chet and Rita needn't see him. At the end of the street where he was to turn he put out his hand. "Thanks, now, Jim."

They were no longer boyhood pals. One was a judge and the other a river rat.

"You don't need to go any farther, Jim. I'll be all right. Good luck to you." He must be cordial. It wasn't old Jim's fault that he had made one grand fool of himself. "Better look me up one of these days—maybe I could get you some better quarters here in town for winter." That is, *if he lived.* Someway, he wasn't sure he would ever recover.

"Good-by, Sam. See you later." Old Jim Shaffer turned and went jauntily down the street past the lovely suburban homes. The old judge could hear him whistling blithely:

Oh, come with me in my little canoe,
Where the sky is calm and the sea is blue.

Off and on all day the judge slept in his soft bed, warm food within him and hot water bottles without. Whenever he woke it was with a deep sense of well-being.

When Rita had taken away the supper tray with its delicious broth, she came back with the evening paper and his glasses, fitting pillows to his back. With a feeling of utter peace, he opened the sheet. His eyes took on a rigid stare.

"Federal officers," the item said, "raided the shack of Jim Shaffer on Lake Tanner this morning and arrested the owner. . . . " The old judge's pulse was throbbing wildly and there was a queer creeping sensation in the back of his neck. " . . . officers were planning to make the raid yesterday afternoon but the storm broke and they remained at a local hotel all night. . . . "

Rita was coming into the bedroom, her heels playing a staccato tune whenever she stepped off the soft rugs. She had an orange blouse. Little pendants in her earrings tinkled. The pronounced odor of her strong perfume preceded her.

"You are to take this, father," she spoke authoritatively. "Open your mouth."

The old judge shut his eyes and swallowed meekly.

"You're a good girl." He looked up at her with the humble eyes of an old dog. "I hope I appreciate you."

"I hope you do," she said briskly.

"And, Rita"—his old eyes twinkled a little—"do you know that Schiller once said a very true, a very beautiful thing. He said, 'Freedom is only in the land of dreams.' " He patted her hand. "Now, run along, Rita dear. I'm a tired old man and I want to sleep."

Why I Live in a Small Town

Writers insulting or sneering at her Midwest and its rural environment would call forth the Aldrich ire, and in "Why I Live in a Small Town" she takes issue with those writers. As early as 1925, she had given a talk at Iowa State Normal School expressing a similar defense of the small town, saying many writers have "almost hopelessly misrepresented" rural dwellers. Aldrich cut from a paper and placed in a file an article that took Sinclair Lewis to task for his *Main Street* (Harcourt, 1920); it expressed her sentiments as well. Small towns had few better defenders than Bess Streeter Aldrich.

This piece, published in the June 1933 issue of the *Ladies' Home Journal,* reflects her modesty; it is also one of the few times that she identifies her work as realism.

There are fiction writers who would have us believe that just three types of people inhabit small Midwestern towns. There are those who are discontented, wanting to get away; there are those who are too dumb to know enough to want to get away; and the rest are half-wits. Not qualifying for the first section, I must, perforce, belong somewhere down the line.

Our town is small. In fact, to speak of our "town" at all is rank hyperbole, for it is not even a town, but is incorporated as a village.

It is so small that, with the exception of Main, the streets are not called by their names and you have to look on a map or an abstract to find out what they are. We glibly say "over by Clement's" and "down by the high school," and in the last few years have been putting on airs by saying "across the park" instead of "the meadow."

It is so small that we have to go to the post office for our mail, where the postmaster knows everyone so well that a letter coming in one day addressed briefly to "Clara," minus any surname, immediately found its owner by the process of elimination.

It is so small that whether you choose to or not you are obliged to hear the band practice every Monday night in the old G. A. R. Hall. Not that it is such a hardship. To be sure, its repertoire may not be so extensive as the late Mr. Sousa's and it may be top-heavy with brass, but it's a good little band at that.

"Tell why you continue to live in a small town," wrote the editor. The question makes me stop and wonder. Perhaps it's inertia—just small-town stagnation. But I do not think so.

It is true I do not always stay here. Out of the twelve months of the last year, five of them were spent away—three on the West Coast and two in the pine-and-lake region of Northern Minnesota. But my home is. I live and do my work here where the streets go unnamed, and the one train and one bus each way per day slip through town with few passengers, and the band lustily executes Poet and Peasant and Under the Double Eagle March.

No one and no circumstances are compelling me to remain. In the eight years since my husband's death there has not been a day that I might not have packed the typewriter and moved to Lincoln or Omaha, my state's two largest cities, or to any big city east or west. Not that I depreciate the many advantages of living in one of them, but to me they are for visiting, and my little town for home.

It was just twenty-three years ago that as a young married woman with a two-month-old baby girl in my arms I arrived at the boxlike station and was met by my husband, who had preceded me by a few weeks. I had not wanted to come to Nebraska. My earliest recollection of hearing the name of the state was a picture of my mother sending me over to the church basement with some old clothes and dried apples which she explained were to be sent to the poor folks out in Nebraska. The impression persisted, so that when my husband and my sister's husband negotiated for the purchase of the bank here, I was not at all enthusiastic about the move. I did not want to wear old clothes and I did not want to eat dried apples.

On the day on which we arrived there was a typical Nebraska dust storm of no modest or refined proportions under way. But my loyalty to the state of my adoption insists that I digress here and explain that the old windstorms are becoming less and less frequent. No doubt it is the diversified farming as it is practiced today which has steadied weather conditions in the Midwest. In the days when the hot winds blew from an unbroken expanse of stubble fields and barren lands, serious damage was done. But under modern conditions the landscape is broken with such regularity by crops still unmatured that serious damage from winds is no longer likely.

Si Maris, whom the menfolks had hired to meet us, was at the station with a two-seated surrey and team to take the women of the party up to the cottage that my husband had rented. Because the wind was blowing so hard that I would not trust my baby out of my arms, my husband and my brother-in-law wheeled the empty cab up to the house, while my sister, mother, the baby and I rode in state with Si. Si was not sure which of three cottages at the end of the street was the one Mr. Aldrich had rented, but it did not take me long to pick it out, for through the blasts of dust I could see my best upholstered rocking-chair, a wedding present, sitting on a little porch with an arm hanging limply down at its side, evidently broken in shipping.

Through the gusts of dirt we hurried up to the little cottage, and it was then that I had my first taste of Nebraska small-town hospitality. Si's sister had come in to get the dinner, which was all ready for us. On my stove and with my own dishes she had prepared a delicious meal for the strangers, that they might feel welcome.

I have experienced it a thousand times since—that warm-hearted hospitality, loyal friendship and deep sympathy of the small town. And it is these characteristics and others of the better features of the small town and its people that I have tried to stress in my short stories and books.

Why quarrel with a writer over realism and idealism? After all, an author is a glass through which a picture of life is projected. The picture falls upon the pages of the writer's manuscript according to the mental and emotional contours of that writer. It is useless to try to change those patterns. If one writer does not see life in terms of grime and dirt, adulteries and debaucheries, it does not follow that those sordid things do not exist. If another does not see life in terms of faith and love, sympathy and good deeds, it does not follow that those characteristics do not exist. I grow weary of hearing the sordid spoken of as real life, the wholesome as Pollyanna stuff. I contend that a writer may portray some of the decent things of life around him and reserve the privilege to call that real life, too. And if this be literary treason, make the most of it.

Much water has trickled down Stove Creek since that long-gone day. The baby girl I clutched in my arms from the force of the prairie wind has been married several months now. The two boys who followed her into the family circle are of college age and studying away from home; while a third boy is here in the seventh grade.

Once a story of mine, syndicated in a newspaper, carried in brackets an indulgent explanation from an editor that the writer "goes right down into small towns and mingles among the people for her material." Could anything sound more smug? As if I had gone slumming with drawn skirts. I have not gone small-townish for material. I *am* small-townish.

Of course, to be honest, I admit I would not choose this little place if I were driving across country seeking a town into which to move. I may have expressed something of that in the introduction to A Lantern in Her Hand, for, while the Cedartown of the story is fictitious, it is frankly located in this section of the country.

"Cedartown sits beside a highway which was once a buffalo trail. If you start in one direction on the highway and travel far enough, you will come to the effete East. If you travel a few hundred miles farther in the opposite direction, you will come to the distinctive West. Cedartown is neither effete nor distinctive nor is it even particularly pleasing to passing tourists. It is beautiful only in the eyes of those who live here and in the memories of the Nebraska-born whose dwelling in far places has given them moments of home-sickness for the low rolling hills, the swell and dip of the ripening wheat, the fields of sinuously waving corn and the elusively fragrant odor of alfalfa."

After all, it is contact and familiarity that help endear people and places to us. I came here in a happy day, and perhaps I am trying to cling to old happiness.

As I write, I have only to glance outside my study window to see in the cement of the driveway the tracings of a fat hand with grotesque square fingers, a date of nine years ago, and the straggling initials C. S. A. I have one son who has always had a perfect obsession for leaving his footprints, not only on the sands of time but in every piece of new cement about the place. There are hands and feet of every size, width and length on sidewalks, driveways, steps and posts, all duly signed and dated.

It would be absurd to say that the sight of that traced hand outside my study window holds me here, but it may readily be a symbol of all that does. It would not be possible for me to follow four young people with widely diversified tastes and talents out into the world—and to keep the home with its old associations means more to me than any advantage gained by moving cityward.

Unbreakable Radii of Love

This is the home my sons and daughter knew in childhood, and I have a notion that in this rather hectic day of complicated life it is well for young people to have some substantial tie which still holds them to the anchor of unchanging things. You cannot break the radii which stretch out from the center of a good home. They are the most flexible things in the world. They reach out into every port where a child has strayed—these radii of love. They pull at the hearts of the children until sometime, somewhere, they draw the wanderers all back into the family circle.

Small-town people are popularly supposed to be narrow. And yet—are the realities of life narrowing? Birth? Marriage? Death? Small-town life is not artificial. It need not be superficial. Calvin Coolidge, in his autobiography, has expressed it in his simple, effective way: "Country life does not always have breadth, but it has depth."

Small-town people are no longer mere isolated villagers. Although the whiskered farmer gent with the straw in his mouth is still the joy of the cartoonists, there is no character which adequately represents the Main Street man. Small-town people move about now, go places.

When I was a little girl, we used to drive six miles out in the country to an uncle's—jog . . . jog . . . jog over the country roads. And, incidentally, it had one advantage. It gave us time to see things—pink bouncing Bets at the side of the road . . . a meadow lark's nest . . . all the little wild things that we so easily overlook now while the needle trembles toward sixty. From our small town, in far less time than those six miles used to consume, we drive on a paved road up to Lincoln, with its beautiful homes and parks, its wonderful capitol, its ninety-eight churches and its four universities. An hour in the opposite direction finds us in the still larger Omaha.

Our physician and his wife recently took a Cuban trip . . . a young chap has just gone down to see South America for a month . . . my daughter's girlhood chum across the street studied music in Paris last summer. Even Heinie Mollen, the cobbler, put down his hammer last fall and went out to take a look at Hollywood to see if the stars really looked like the pictures tacked up on the walls of his shop.

Keeping an Author Humble

A small town is a good place for a writer to live. Not only is he close to the people, and so close to life in the raw, but also it keeps him humble. For instance, if you are a professional writer, living in a small town, perhaps on the day on which you are coming home from the post office with a letter from the committee that a story of yours has been judged one of the best of the year and chosen for the O. Henry Memorial Award volume, you meet an old man who stops you and says:

"Say, I just been readin' one of your stories." Ah, you think, everyone reads them—the O. Henry committee, young people, middle-aged, old men; babies cry for them. "Yep," he says, "it was the one in the — Well, I forget the magazine, but it's one my daughter takes." You overlook a little thing like that and wait for him to go on. "Anyway, the name of the story was — Say," he apologizes, "that slips me too." Oh, well, that's a mere bagatelle. What's a title? "Anyway," he brightens, "the story was about —" He takes off his cap and scratches his head. "Don't that beat you? I clean forget what the darn thing was about."

And there you are. If a story was not clean-cut enough for a nice old man to remember overnight, it wasn't very good.

Then there was the time I had received the annual report showing that a book of mine had been third in sales for the entire country for the year. With that rather pleasant bit of news uppermost in my mind, I went to a little social affair in my small town. When I sat down among the ladies, I made a remark about just coming home from Lincoln—that I had been so busy at the desk, I had not been there in five weeks. A little woman looked up from her fancywork and said:

"Did you say you hadn't been there for five weeks? Well, isn't that queer! I was in Lincoln yesterday myself and stopped to buy some groceries. When I gave the groceryman a check he said, 'I see you're from the town where Bess Streeter Aldrich lives. I suppose you know her?' Now, will you tell me," she questioned earnestly, "if you hadn't been in Lincoln for five weeks, how that groceryman could have remembered your name all that length of time?"

Humble? I'll say they keep you humble. A prophet in her own village isn't a prophet at all, but just a woman who buys groceries. And isn't that as it should be?

Alma, Meaning "To Cherish"

After the stock market crash of November 1929 that signaled the beginning of "The Great Depression," there were those who could not face the realities of sudden financial reverses, as was true of the banker of this story, Mr. Withers. Small towns such as Aldrich's Elmwood, Nebraska, and bank owners such as Aldrich herself felt the economic calamity much as did those in the cities. The Depression was an important element of Aldrich's writing during the early 1930s. It is mentioned only briefly near the end of *A White Bird Flying* (1931), and is a major factor in the novel *Miss Bishop* (1933), in the short story, "The Silent Stars Go By" (1933), and here in "Alma, Meaning 'To Cherish.' "

This work, published by *Cosmopolitan* in June of 1934, returns to a plot line Aldrich used previously, that of the main character pretending to be the owner of a fine house, a scenario she used in 1921 for "The Man Who Dreaded to Go Home."

Aldrich used two specific personal touches in this story: first, naming the dog "Jack" would have pleased her family, for when they were children that was the name of their family pet; and second, describing the Withers house as "of dark-brown brick with gay striped awnings and stretch of sparkling glass windows clear across one side" would also have pleased her family and would have been fun for Aldrich because this is a description of their Elmwood home, which they all loved.

Alma was nine years old when she came to live with Grandpa and Grandma Drew, a nondescript little person with freckles like so many pale raisins across a tip-tilted nose, big blue eyes that made her thin face look top heavy, and ashy light hair tied tightly back in horsetail formation.

Because Alma's dead father had been an only child, Grandma Drew had never sewed for a little girl, so she made the child dresses rather like her own of the early eighties, with very full skirts gathered on to deep yokes. Alma knew they were not right but she didn't know just what she could do about it. Once when she had ventured to suggest something ready-made, Grandma explained patiently, tearfully, that they couldn't afford it, that there was some money in the bank for Alma, but that it must never, never be touched until after high school, for if they were economical and did not use a dollar of it, Alma could go away to college some day. If the little girl vaguely sensed that an occasional dress in hand would have been worth two in a bush on some potential campus, she would not hurt Grandma's feelings by saying so. And after all, it gave one a feeling of importance to realize that one had money in a big gray stone bank.

The big stone bank belonged to Mr. Withers—and Grandpa Drew (who was really old Peter Drew) took care of Mr. Withers' yard. The Drew house, a small one-story frame, stood on Eleventh Street next to the alley and at right angles to the garage end of the Withers home, which fronted on Sherman Avenue.

To the diminutive Alma the Withers place constituted the last word in grandeur. Paradise itself probably could contain nothing more lovely than that which lay beyond the privet hedge. The house was of dark-brown brick with gay striped awnings and a stretch of sparkling glass windows clear across one side. In spring the yard was a riot of snowy bridal wreath and blood-red tulips and blue irises. There were white garden seats, a winding brick path, and a pool where a green iron frog spouted water impudently at an iron bird that was either a heron or a stork.

Grandpa had other yards, too, which he sometimes scrupulously groomed, but for the most part he was busy at the Withers place where the bridal wreath and the crimson tulips and the blue irises took his attention until the roses came on.

When Grandpa mowed, Alma would sit on the steps and pretend she lived there at the great house with the sun parlor and the gay awnings. She would lose herself so deeply in the pretense that she fancied she could hear people driving past say enviously,

"Wouldn't it be grand to live there like that lovely little girl?"

It is quite possible, however, that she caused very little envy in the hearts of her observers, for there was no one in the whole community who did not know that S. T. Withers lived there, and that he and his wife had one son, Rexford, and not even a lovely little girl, to say nothing of one with freckles across a tip-tilted nose, a horsetail of ashy-light hair, and dresses with yokes.

To Alma, the three Witherses were all that storybook people could possibly be. Mr. Withers was tall and slender, with an iron-gray mustache, and he walked springily, not like Grandpa, who plodded heavily. Mrs. Withers was slight and sparkling. Her dark eyes laughed, and when she talked, her voice laughed, and when she served tea out on the brick terrace, her hands moved over the cups like white birds fluttering. Rexford was fifteen, and he had everything a prince could want, including a watch and a kodak and a bicycle. Alma did not know him. She merely knew all this by the simple process of peeking. Only once, just before he went away to a boys' school, did she come face to face with him near the pool where the green frog sat spouting all day.

He said, "Hey there . . . kid . . . how are you?"

And Alma said, "All right," and began humming with assumed nonchalance and hippity-hopped back home through the hedge.

He did not even know her name. But Alma was glad of that, for she had no deep admiration for it. It was too short and sounded too babyish. Just Alma. It had no meaning. If she could have renamed herself the way the teacher said the Chinese did, she would have been Rosamond Dorothy Drew. Always when she sat on the Withers steps waiting for Grandpa, she thought of herself as Rosamond Dorothy instead of the babyish Alma that had no meaning.

And then one day at school when she was browsing about idly in the back of the big dictionary, she found some pages titled "Common English Christian Names. I. Masculine. II. Feminine." Quite suddenly her research work in department two became feverishly intensive. It was scarcely possible, of course, that it would be there. *Abigail . . . Ada. . . . Alice . . .* It was there . . . *Alma. Alma,* meaning *to cherish.* As she was quite in the dark about what it meant to cherish, she laboriously looked that up, too. It seemed that it was *to hold dear, to treat or keep with tenderness or affection, to nurture with care, to protect and aid, to harbor in the mind, cling to.*

Just what it was that she was to hold dear, to harbor in the mind, cling to, she had not the remotest idea. In fact, she was fifteen before she knew.

But one does not jump from nine to fifteen as nimbly as it is written. One lives through long painful years if one doesn't like funny-looking dresses but loves the maker of them—if one is obliged to hear one's grandfather called "Old Peter" by children when one knows what a nice old man he is. But to offset the distressing experiences, Alma's freckles at fifteen were gradually and mysteriously disappearing into the soft pinkness of a lovely skin, her ashy-light roll of hair looked neat against the white column of her neck, and she was beginning to make her own clothes. Anent this last, she had figured out that if the material must always be cheap, dresses must be made cleverly, so she wore slim, plain brown ones with sheer white collars and cuffs, or blue batiste that matched exactly the shade of her eyes.

Not once did Grandpa or Grandma touch the money for any of these modest expenditures. It was safely there in Mr. Withers' gray stone bank gathering interest like some golden-fingered magician and waiting until the time when Alma would be ready for college.

No longer did she go over to the big yard with Grandpa. A sophomore in high school, she was too old now to hang about childishly. But she was still not above peeking through the hedge at times to watch the gay life over there. Rex was in Yale, but he always came back for the Christmas holidays and for a few weeks each summer before he and his mother went north to their lake cottage. For those few weeks of each year there were exciting doings beyond the hedge.

"Mr. Rexford Withers gave a dancing party . . . " or "Mr. Rexford Withers was host at a dinner . . . " would head the *Courier's* society column. These parties were always exclusively for The Crowd.

The Crowd was a group as inextricably set apart from the rest of the young people of the town as is the Supreme Court from its associates, as definitely limited by boundary lines as the Withers' yard by its hedge. For the most part the members were from the homes that faced the park or those farther up on Sherman Avenue—Irene Bently, who was Rex's girl, and the Barlow twins, Sallie and Nancy, and Ted and Marian VanScoy, and Bob Robertson, and a few others.

They fascinated Alma, peeking surreptitiously through the hedge to see them drive in, gay and noisy. She used to imagine how they would look later coming down the winding mahogany stairway that she had glimpsed through the door—the girls in their modish gowns and the young men in their evening clothes. It was the ideal—the way life ought to be lived. The background against which they moved was a standard of perfection, not one of the golden oak furniture and geraniums in paper-covered tomato cans, and Grandpa's pipes and papers lying about.

The Christmas vacation that Alma was fifteen was the gayest holiday time over at the Witherses' she had ever known. Lights blazed from the basement to the third floor. Rex was home from Yale, Bob Robertson from Amherst, Ted and Marian VanScoy from State University. The Crowd went in and out constantly. The paper announced Irene Bentley's and Rex's engagement. When the lights ceased to burn and the gay affairs were over, Alma felt that nothing would be worth while until the coming of the summer when she could again be an onlooker at a life that was ideal.

But when spring came on, with the tulips nosing up through the moist turf, events happened that changed everything. The Witherses' Christine told Grandma through the hedge that Mrs. Withers hadn't been well since Christmas, that they had taken her to the hospital now, and no one could tell how it was going to turn out. Then even before the outcome was certain, the astounding news came that Mr. Withers' bank had not opened that morning.

When Grandpa and Grandma heard it, they went white and stared at each other as though bereft of their reason. "The money," they said in unison. "The money for Alma's college education."

Alma had forgotten all about that phase of the catastrophe in thinking with horror that the Witherses could never live that lovely way any more, that all the gayety of The Crowd was a thing of the past, that life could never again go on over there as it had done. She wouldn't for the world have wanted Grandpa and Grandma to know, but she was more sorry about that than on account of her own loss.

The town was wild about the closing of the bank. Threatening talk flew about because Mr. Withers had lost people's money, but Grandpa said he could not associate the things they were saying with the kindness of the man for whom he worked, that there must have been great forces behind it for which Mr. Withers was not to blame.

Mrs. Withers did not get well. Christine, with red eyes, told Grandma across the hedge that she guessed the news had killed her, but Grandma said that if bad news alone could kill, lots of folks who were living would be dead.

Rex was home from Yale, but no longer was The Crowd over there. Just Rex and his father. Alma could see them walking up and down the brick walk where the bridal wreath was bursting into white froth. Sometimes she would hear Rex trying to coax his father to go into the house, but he would only walk up and down—up and down. Alma on her side of the high hedge ached with responsive anguish for the anguish of Rex and his father. Up and down—up and down—

It was one evening when Rex was in the house that Alma heard the weird staccato sound in the garden like something cracking and saw Grandpa rush faster through the hedge than she thought he could move. Alma, too, was rushing after him when Grandma called her sharply to come back and wouldn't let her go at all. It was true—Mr. Withers had killed himself on the seat by the pool where the green frog sat. All those things had happened to the Withers family between the gayety of the holidays and the blossoming of the bridal wreath. It seemed unbelievable that all this made no difference to the garden—that crimson tulips bloomed as lovely as ever, and the blue irises.

A few days later when Grandpa came home, he said he had a good piece of news to tell. Mr. Withers' insurance money which would have gone to Rex was to be turned over to the depositors. Grandpa said that he heard the place had been in Mrs. Withers' name, and Rex was going to keep it, that except for enough money to get to New York, he was turning over the insurance, and that Alma was to get seventy cents on the dollar now instead of the fifty or sixty she might have had. Alma knew she should have been pleased about it, but somehow she couldn't be.

Christine, who was moving her things away, told Grandma through the hedge that Irene Bentley wasn't going to marry Rex after all, and that, to Alma, seemed the hardest of all to understand. If Irene had loved Rex at holiday time, why did she not love him when the irises bloomed?

The next night just before time for the flyer, Rex and his dog came through the hedge. Rex had on a dark suit and a turned down hat pulled over his eyes, and he gave Grandpa a key to the house and said to keep the yard up a little and he would send money. He had not paid any attention to Alma standing near until he was turning to leave, when he said, "Hey . . . kid . . . would you mind feeding Jack for me?"

Alma took an impulsive step forward. "Oh, I'll do . . . *anything.*" It was a cry of human sympathy from the depths of a grieving fifteen-year-old-heart.

Rex said, "Thanks," and started back through the hedge with Jack trying to follow him so that he had to stamp his foot and tell him sharply to go back. Then suddenly he called Jack and put his arms around him and bowed his head and turned his face away.

And Alma ran into the house and cried for Rex and for all the lost loveliness of life. And from that day on she knew what it was that she was to cherish.

For the next day or two Alma could not bear to look over toward the big house, so forlorn now that it seemed a human being from which the living soul had fled. But Grandpa went over several times. He set out the gladioli bulbs as though nothing had happened, and trimmed the terrace.

On the third day he said to Grandma: "I think you better unlock the door and go in. I can see through the window, and, boylike, he's left food on the kitchen table, and there are ivy plants in the sun parlor."

So Grandma, walking slowly with rheumatism in her bad leg, and Alma went through the hedge and over to the big house, carrying the key to Paradise. When Grandma was unlocking the big hall door, Alma knew that never again in life would she experience that same, queer, suffocating feeling of expectancy. The house where she had glimpsed such lovely things was to be entered. And with no prying eyes to see. Just she and Grandma going in as though they owned it.

They opened the big door and stepped in. The great mahogany stairway curved down into the hallway—darkly gleaming against the white of the woodwork. The sun came through a window on the landing and caught and held all the soft lights of the rug. Alma stood and visualized The Crowd coming down the stairs, heard them laugh as they descended—Rex and Irene Bentley and the Barlow twins and Bob Robertson and the others. And they would never come laughing down the stairway again. She felt a sadness that was overwhelming in its intensity.

For a little while she and Grandma walked about, tiptoeing, peering into the various rooms, shy as trespassers. The drawing room was in dull green with mahogany furniture, and the walls were satin. The dining room was dark and paneled, and Grandma thought it was kind of gloomy, but Alma knew it was just right. There were fireplaces and books, rugs as thick as Grandpa's blue-grass lawn, and a grand piano from which a single silver-framed picture of Rex watched them with his dark smoldering eyes. It gave Alma an uncanny feeling of guilt.

They went upstairs, Grandma pulling herself up by the mahogany railing. One bedroom was all in rose color with stiff taffeta curtains tied back over china knobs. One looked as though the blue irises and the tulips from the garden had been scattered over all the fat chairs and the bedspread. And then there was Rex's room. They could tell by the college pennants and the pictures of The Crowd. The bed was tumbled and unmade. So Grandma took off the pillowcases and the sheets and tied them in a bundle to take home to wash. If Grandma hadn't been there, Alma knew she would have cried. But she didn't want even Grandma to know how she cherished the memory of Rex.

There was a stairway to the third floor, and Grandma told Alma she'd better run up and see if everything was all right there. She was gone so long that Grandma called to know what was the matter. There was nothing at all the matter except that Alma, in the great stillness, had fallen to dreaming of the young people who had come there to dance on the shining floor and who would never come again.

They took the perishable food home. Grandma wrote it down on a little pad in her kitchen: "Seven eggs, a loaf of bread, three strips of bacon, and a quarter pound of butter." She would keep it so she could pay Rex back if he came home that fall.

But Rex did not come home. Grandpa took up the bulbs and nailed boards across the basement windows. Leaves blew into the pool and covered the green frog and the iron legs of the heron-or-stork.

Then spring again. And Grandma and Alma went over to the big house because Grandma thought they ought to take out the quilts and look them over for moths. This time she took home the canned fruit in the basement and used it. But each summer thereafter she would can the exact number: eight quarts of cherries—ten quarts of strawberries—five quarts of peaches—to have them ready for Rex.

It came to be as the years went by that Alma had cleaned everything. She had even taken all the lovely dresses out of the closet, brushing them tenderly as though attending to some religious rite—the black lace over silk and the dark wine-colored velvet and the black velvet evening coat with the white satin lining. Sometimes Grandma said Alma was foolish to put all that work on it when she wasn't getting any pay, but Alma would never answer her.

For no one was getting any pay, not even Grandpa any more. The money had come from Rex for a while and then it ceased. But each year Grandpa trimmed the honeysuckles and the bridal wreath and the roses—cut back the blue irises and set out the gladioli bulbs. He never told anyone that he was no longer the gardener.

"You'll get old Peter Drew after you," people would say to anyone attempting to trespass. And everyone thought he was the hired caretaker.

Alma went away to college and very soon she was twenty-one.

But one does not jump from fifteen to twenty-one as nimbly as it is written. One lives through happy, important years. And if one has not had many dollars in the first place and must, perforce, get along with only seventy cents for each one of these, one must be very careful to dress cleverly, to see that one's good looks become genuinely lovely and one's happy disposition makes countless friends. If one can do this, the other thirty cents do not matter so much.

It was June with the crimson ramblers queening it over the old garden—and Alma, graduated from college the week before, was now making her first summer pilgrimage to the Mecca of her childish dreams. The place looked run down, she was thinking. Grandpa was getting older and slower, and six years is a long time for a home to be without a tenant. Grass was matted between the bricks of the path, the green frog had lost one of his bulging eyes, and the heron that might have been a stork was tipping a little giddily on his thin iron legs.

She was thinking that Grandpa had told her Rex's taxes were delinquent for the last legal time, and the place would be sold if he didn't come home and see about it. The news saddened her, but she quickly put it from her mind for a happier thought—that three of her sorority sisters were driving through town that afternoon on their way to Yellowstone and would stop for an hour or so. She was wishing that Grandma wasn't bedfast and nervously fussy just now about callers, and that the golden oak furniture by some wave of a magic wand could be . . .

That was as far as she went in her wishing, for inspirationally she knew she was entertaining the girls in the Withers home. Why not? Hadn't she and Grandma cleaned in every corner of it? Didn't she feel quite at home there now? Wasn't it a happy solution? Temptation, unlike vice, is not necessarily a creature of frightful mein.

With gay energy she set about making preparations. She aired the stuffy house and went over it with her dust cloth and floor mop. She set bowls of crimson ramblers about, and with only a slight stab of conscience took down some Spode tea things. She would bring over an alcohol burner for the tea, for, of course, there was no electric current now.

After all these energetic preparations, two o'clock found her sitting on the steps of the Withers porch watching for the car. The girls would be looking for the Eleventh Street address, and so she must not let them drive by.

It gave her a queer feeling to be sitting there on the steps just as she used to do when she was little. For her own amusement she repeated her childish formula, "I'm the lovely little girl who lives here." Which was fifty percent more true than in the old days, for had she but known it, two women driving by at that moment and seeing her there were saying,

"Didn't Alma Drew turn out to be the prettiest thing!"

She recalled her old feeling of awe for The Crowd. How queer the way life had treated some of them. Irene Bentley was assisting in her husband's store. The Barlows had been having a hard time. Marian VanScoy was working in a tea room. Rex's taxes were unpaid. The Crowd now represented a whole economic upheaval. It would have taken a treatise on world conditions to have written about them as they had been and as they were now.

There they came—the girls—driving slowly and looking for the house. Because the Witherses' number was hidden by ivy vines, they would not notice the discrepancy in the address. She waved at them, and the car slipped up the drive and came to a stop near her. There were gay greetings and noisy laughter, so that instinctively Alma gave a swift thought to the fact that they must have looked and acted quite as The Crowd had in years gone by. Jack lumbered around the corner of the house and wagged a friendly tail with feeble dignity.

The four went into the house, and the college reunion against the background of the mellow old furnishings became a very pleasant thing for Alma. She felt neither uncomfortable nor strange. If she had made any plan to explain to them that she was borrowing the house because of Grandma's illness, she did not do so at once, and when the first opportunity had gone by, she found she could not tell at all. She evaded false statements adroitly and made gay inconsequential answers to pertinent questions. As, who was the good-looking man in the silver frame on the concert grand? "Just a neighbor boy," she said—and *that* was over.

No one knows why these uncannily strange things happen—why, for instance, out of all the days of all the years that had gone by, this was the day on which Rex Withers came home.

Alma had been saying, "When I started to read it, I found it so interest . . . "

The words snapped off on a broken syllable. For a key was turning in the lock of the side door that had been closed for six years, and Rex Withers was opening it—was standing on the threshold of the room. His face was grave. Unsmiling he stood, looking with somber eyes at the group, apparently showing neither surprise nor annoyance, merely suspended thought concerning the situation.

Alma's mind seemed blank, her body paralyzed, as though neither mentally nor physically were her faculties or members able to function. Rex had come, and she was entertaining guests in his home. Obviously something must be done about it. For that long vibrant moment she stared across at him, and then quite suddenly her brain sprang into action like a soldier called to duty.

Immediately she became Alma Jekyll and Alma Hyde. Nerves taut to the finger tips. Alma, the college graduate, who in four years of training had learned to carry herself graciously through various social crises, was walking up to Rex with extended hand, was saying:

"Why, Rex, I didn't know you were in town. How are you?"

And Rex was saying gravely: "Very well. And how are you?"

"These are sorority sisters of mine who are on their way to Yellowstone and whom I want you to meet. Let me present Mr. Rex Withers, Adele—Miss Langdon."

"Ah, the neighbor boy," Adele said with bright pertness.

"Yes, the neighbor boy . . . " the girls took it up in jesting tone, so that the blue eyes of the other personality, the Alma Drew who was only the gardener's little granddaughter, darkened with embarrassment and fright, met the questioning eyes of Rex Withers, and said with all the force of her mentality:

"Don't give it away. Please play up to me."

And he did. If he was mystified, he did not show it, for in the next half hour he assisted materially in keeping the conversation on the general and remarkably safe topics of Yellowstone Park, the new books, aeronautics, modernistic paintings, daylight hold-ups, and the habits of owls. And when Alma went to the kitchen to get the tea things with a gay, "I'm both hostess and maid," Rex asked if he could help. Alma said no, that each one was to carry out her own things.

When they had gone out to the terrace in laughing single file, Jack came lumbering up, gave his bleary old-man look at Rex, and began pumping his tail wildly, so that Adele Langdon said pertly.

"Aha . . . I have it . . . you're the favorite caller."

For the next hour Alma Drew, with the one endeavor in life to keep the situation in hand, quite possibly proved she had missed her calling, for no actress ever put on a better performance. And all the time over her head the sword of Damocles was swinging . . . and swinging . . .

But all groups of sixty minutes do eventually pass, and Adele was saying:

"Time's up, girls. Signing off. We promised an aunt of mine we'd honor her with our presence this evening. Three down and two hundred miles to go. I wish you could go with us, Alma."

So did Alma. If only she could have put on her hat and crawled into that back seat, never to look back, never to come back—merely to have thrown herself comfortably and peacefully into Old Faithful geyser!

And now one of the girls was saying, "Alma, this is just the way I would have imagined you—all cool and unperturbed like this, with an old garden behind you." And to Rex Withers, "She fits in the picture, doesn't she?"

Rex Withers looked for a moment into the depths of his mother's old Spode teacup. "Perfectly," he said.

There were farewell quips and laughter. Rex moved his own car so that the girls could get out. They backed, turned by the garage, waved gayly, were gone. And Alma Drew and Rex Withers stood alone on the brick terrace.

Alma did not let a moment pass. "I know what you're thinking," she said courageously, "and the worst isn't terrible enough. I don't know why I did it." The relief of getting the horrible thing off her mind was immeasurable. "I want you to know I have never done it before. Grandma and I came in every year and cleaned . . . and kept things in good condition . . . you'll find them so, I am sure. But not until today did I ever take advantage of having the key. To ask the girls here . . . " She spared herself not at all. "It was cheap . . . chiseling . . . " She talked on and on with self-flagellation.

Rex was looking at her with the somber, smoldering eyes she remembered so well.

"Wait . . . do I understand you're apologizing for . . . " he motioned toward the old house there behind them in the mellow June sunlight, "for being here?"

"If it could be called by so mild a thing."

"Let's walk," he said suddenly, picked up one of Alma's hands and tucked it under his arm. Down the brick walk straight to the pool he went . . . by the white seat where . . . it had happened.

It did not seem strange to Alma to be walking down that brick path with Rex. It seemed very natural, as though she were living over something that had happened many times before in another world. Perhaps that was because it had happened in the world of dreams.

Still with Alma's hand tucked under his arm he was saying:

"It's my turn to talk now. To make it clear what I want to say to you, you must know that the first year away was—well, not so good. The world pretty well collapsed for me that spring here at home. When I went east, I tried to get into something . . . but couldn't seem to get going. I had always expected in a careless fashion to go in with Father here in the bank . . . so when I was thrown out on my own . . . Well, you know these little robins that can't seem to get to picking up their own worms? I couldn't find any worms. It appeared that there was no place for a bright young college man whose ideas of work had been mostly those revolving about his fraternity's social affairs. Once I got so low that I almost thought I, too . . . " He made a passing gesture toward the white seat, so that Alma said with a little cry,

"Oh, no."

He grinned and patted her hand. "Oh, I'm all right now. The world's a pretty decent old place. Banking being in the blood, I suppose, I finally landed a job in a bank; and two promotions in five years aren't so bad. I'm no moneyed plutocrat, but things are jogging along very well." He dropped his lighter tone and said gravely: "All those years I hung on to the place here like grim death. It seemed dumb not to sell . . . but I couldn't quite bring myself to it . . . with their things all here. Fate must have had a little something to do with it, though, for Robertson of Dad's old bank, reorganized, ran on to me when he was east awhile ago, and finding that I wasn't doing so badly, offered me the assistant cashiership here."

"Here?" said Alma, and caught back the excitement in her tone with, "That's very nice for you."

"The offer was tempting," he went on, "but whenever I thought of coming back, it seemed too dreadful to contemplate . . . unbearable. I decided to come and prove to myself that it couldn't be done . . . to live here. Perhaps you can sense how I had to steel myself to do it? I've lived this home-coming over a hundred times . . . and the experience was terrible. And now, after all that . . . when I get here . . . to find you. I don't understand. It isn't awesome nor unbearable . . . and I think I am staying. It isn't . . . not even very sad. It's merely peaceful and homelike . . . as though I'd found . . . "

Suddenly as though he realized he was rushing things a bit, he broke off and bent to look into Alma's lovely face.

"And so you're the little kid next door? Old Pete . . . Mr. Drew's granddaughter. And you've been away to college? Say, you're not engaged or anything, are you?" he asked in sudden alarm.

"Yes," she said blithely, "for a year—to the school board."

And they both laughed the gay untroubled laughter of youth.

"And your name is Alma," Rex went on. "I guess I never even knew your name. It's funny . . . I've known a lot of girls, but somehow I never happened to know one by the name of Alma. I'm glad I never have . . . for now it's just you."

Alma turned blue eyes to him—eyes that contained mirth and something infinitely more tender.

"It means," she said—not shyly nor sentimentally as femininity might once have done, but humorously and daringly, quite in the modern way—"it means *to cherish, to hold dear, to treat or keep with tenderness and affection, to harbor in the mind, cling to.*"

And the green frog leered impudently with his one good eye at the heron that probably *was* a stork.

How Far Is It to Hollywood?

Aldrich discussed writing on several occasions, once mentioning that when she created a character, she felt she must figuratively crawl into that character's skin and button it around herself. In "How Far Is It to Hollywood?" Aldrich does this with Emma-Jo, becoming both the little girl and the movie star from a little girl's point of view. Emma-Jo probably bears some resemblance to Aldrich's childhood friend, Grace Simpson [Bailey].

"Ginger Cookies" (1920), which appears earlier in this volume, has a boy who also tries to sell seeds and other items in a neighboring town; the fright that an adult puts into each youngster reveals how well Aldrich understood the world of children. "Ginger Cookies" and "How Far Is It to Hollywood?" (July 1934) are good examples of the pleasure Aldrich derived—and gave—when writing with the undercurrent of laughter.

Greta Garbo and Mae West sat on the back fence and swung their legs over the tops of the milkweeds and the boxes of empty tin cans.

Greta was small and dark, with black hair cut like a boy's, and restless, jack-in-the-box movements. Mae was fair and pleasantly plump with a wide-eyed and innocent complacency that, if one were very critical, could justifiably be termed stodginess.

Miss Garbo lived at the Brysons'. In fact, she was known to Mr. and Mrs. Bryson, her sister Louise, the neighbors, teachers, and most of her playmates as Angie Bryson. Miss West lived at the Thomases'. In fact, she was known to

Mr. and Mrs. Thomas, her brother Bob, the neighbors, teachers, and most of her playmates as Emma-Jo Thomas. To carry the statement still further, even to a truthful conclusion, it was *only* to Emma-Jo that Angie was Greta Garbo; and inversely and frankly it was *only* to Angie that Emma-Jo was Mae West.

A talented and wordy gentleman who once said "The play's the thing" might almost have foreseen the coming of Emma-Jo Thomas and Angie Bryson. The play was indeed the thing in life just now. The masquerading, personifying, emulating—whatever the game was, it had been going on now for three weeks, and so completely had the two sunk their little-girl personalities into character that once Angie, forgetting she was in school and so forced temporarily to abandon the pretending, had called Emma-Jo by her name of "Mae," to the mystification of her classmates and the red-faced mortification of Misses Garbo and West.

In truth, the aforementioned school had become a decided nuisance of late, interfering as it did constantly with the making of Greta's elaborate costumes and Mae's jewelry. All day they toiled at the disagreeable tasks inflicted with humiliating regularity upon them by the exigencies of a public-school system, until that magnificent release at four o'clock when they could throw off the debasing shackles that bound them to a world of which they were no longer an integral or interested part.

At that magic hour they simply ceased to be such mundane creatures. Chrysalis-like, from the drab cocoon of school life they would emerge and become the great Garbo and the popular Mae West—their minds, their hearts, their very souls sunk into character. And only those who understand a certain phase of imaginative childhood can comprehend how possible was this merging.

So on this Thursday afternoon the two actresses sat above the milkweeds and tomato cans and swung their legs.

Although it was only Thursday afternoon, quite surprisingly three whole days of freedom loomed before them. Almost unbelievably, there was to be no school the next day, for the pupils from near-by country schools were coming in to town to take the county examinations, and the room constantly if unwillingly occupied by the Misses Garbo and West was the one happily chosen for the giving of the tests.

Thursday afternoon, Friday, Saturday, Sunday—world without end! The lovely and strange interlude trailed on into infinity in the immensity of its length.

Gratefulness for this unexpected intermission on the part of her who was known as Mae West was pathetically immeasurable. And all on account of problems. Now it must be known that Mae was the craven possessor of that complex known as "dumbness in arithmetic." It was terrible. It was like unto a disease. The mere sight of a problem confused her. Anything beginning "If a man . . . " had the immediate effect of sending her into a mental lethargy.

Reading she loved; geography was interesting; language not so bad. But problems! "Find the area of a farm . . . " the teacher was forever writing on the board. It was so silly and so unnecessary to actual living. Men always knew the areas of their farms. Uncle Jasper had a farm and he knew it was one hundred and sixty acres without any figuring. Cousin Mel's was eighty acres. He could tell you the minute you asked him.

"If a train goes so-many miles an hour—how many miles is it to Denver?" Angie's father was a conductor and he could tell distances everywhere. You could hardly catch him on anything. When Emma-Jo asked him that time how far it was to Denver and put down his answer by the problem, the teacher had said it wasn't right. It had shaken Emma-Jo's faith in the teacher.

After reading a problem through two or three times, Emma-Jo's mind seemed to lapse into a form of coma. This was because she never had the slightest idea what to do first. Occasionally when someone started her off on one, told her the initial step to take, she had sudden and unexplainable inspirations by which she was able to continue to the bitter end. It was due to these lucid, if infrequent, moments that she received any grade whatsoever.

This time, the problems for Monday had been on the board. There were two of those impossible ones beginning, "If a man . . . "; one almost equally bad, "If a train leaves at . . . "; and the inevitable and silly "If a farm . . . " But the worst of all was the last. "If there are telegraph poles one hundred feet apart from here to Hollywood, and there are sixty-eight thousand, seven hundred and forty-two of them, in terms of miles how far is it to Hollywood?"

That one was perfectly dreadful. The teacher must have made them up, too, for she had held no book in her hand when she wrote. How *could* she have thought up that last horrible one? Emma-Jo could not know that the problem might have sprung from the same fountain as her own suppressed desires, for the teacher was very pretty. All she knew was that if you lived almost in the middle of the United States and the teacher made up a problem like that Hollywood one, the answer was sure to be composed of four or five figures.

Emma-Jo had brought the problems home. She always did. Even if the teacher said no one was to take them, Emma-Jo managed to smuggle them home with all the slyness and finesse given to transporting anything of contraband nature. It is safe to say Emma-Jo Thomas had bootlegged more problems than all the rest of the pupils put together.

Sometimes her father helped her, sometimes her mother; Bob, once in a great while when he was home. Strangely enough, Bob, of the same flesh and blood, was working with figures for his living, as he was a bookkeeper in the State Bank at Hawksbury. But whoever "helped," it always resulted in that person becoming almost wholly the author and finisher of results.

But now she put away the thought of the problems as the Maid of Orleans might have thrust aside the thought of her doom. For was there not before her all of Thursday afternoon, Friday, Saturday, Sunday? It seemed so very long until Monday morning; until one must know with awful finality in terms of miles how far it was to Hollywood.

"Well, let's get started." The restless and wholly imaginative Angie was desisting from her leg-swinging activities.

"All right, let's." The complacent and stodgy Emma-Jo was assenting.

They slipped across the tin-filled boxes and into the welcome vacancy of an unused yard. And it was as though they left their Thomas and Bryson skins hanging on the fence like two dull locusts—for suddenly they were the glamorous Garbo and the sumptuous West.

The people who had moved away from this particular neighboring house three weeks before were really responsible for the present state of affairs in the lives of the two little girls. For since they had been donated a vacant house and yard, it followed that something must be done about it.

Angie, with her natural Robinson-Crusoe mind, followed by her Friday in the pudgy form of Emma-Jo, had been exploring the premises by the time the departing moving van had turned the corner. Everything had been securely locked excepting the screen door to the back porch. In that haven, an almost unbelievable wealth had been found lying there before the naked eye and immediately available for use. *Just dozens of movie magazines!*

Because Emma-Jo's mother held a peculiar notion about supervising her offspring's reading, Emma-Jo had never seen enough of them in her life. Angie, whose mother had no foolish scruples about overseeing her daughter in much of anything, was familiar with every phase of the industry, including the plots of the plays marked "for adults only."

Until dusk descended and penetrating voices from the less interesting world of reality called shrilly through the gloom, Angie and Emma-Jo had pored over the fascinating contents. They had scarcely been able to wait until school was over the next day before getting back to the happy hunting ground.

In the week that followed, the mental and emotional processes by which the little girls became metamorphosed into two actresses of the screen were so intricate as to be beyond the understanding of the adult mind. From choosing the actresses they were to impersonate, on through constant conversation in the actual roles, and with the setting of the play in the silence of the vacant yard where no prying grown person came, it had become very easy to change their personalities. The thing is quite possible to that portion of humans unhampered as yet by such phases of life as jobs, taxes, politics and monthly bills.

"Hops on being Greta Garbo," Angie had taken her pick with superb nonchalance.

"Who had I better be?" the less grasping Emma-Jo had asked.

"Let's see." Angie had run the studio favorites over in her mind. "Mae West," she had suddenly dictated, "with just *loads* of jewelry."

It had appealed to Emma-Jo—especially the jewelry, which was so miraculously easy to obtain here in the vacant yard. There were white-clover diamonds, syringa pearls, nasturtium-leaf emeralds, violet amethysts, and large rubies from a vine whose name she did not know.

The new Mae had set so diligently to work making bracelets, necklaces and earrings that Greta, who had to supply much of the imagination for both, finally insisted there was more to the play than the mere manufacturing of jewelry.

But this afternoon the buxom Mae began her usual task of making fresh jewelry, her adornments being of such delicate nature that a daily renewal was necessary. Angie, however, was not so materialistic. She had a far-away expression in her eyes that would have done credit to the one for whom she had named herself. She seemed lost in contemplation of something far from mortal ken. Almost would one have said she was seeing visions and dreaming dreams. Perhaps it was the languid spring-like atmosphere that put the call of the road into her mind. Perhaps it was the intoxication of the free days before her. Mayhap she was descended from one of the Maidens of Odin and was only now sensing that she could conduct the worthy to Valhalla.

Whatever the motive, suddenly she pulled her pudgy fellow thespian into the cool cavern of the back porch and said in the low, intense tones of one laboring under great stress: "Mae, listen. Why don't we go to the *real* Hollywood?"

The eyes of Mae the Second widened in darkened alarm. "Oh, we couldn't—not really. We're too—too young." Emma-Jo's life was circumscribed by old-fashioned family law.

But to Angie, whose family life included the new freedom, the idea held possibilities. She even brought forth arguments to that effect. "Clara Bow went when she was young, didn't she? And—and others. Mitzi Green, for one. And look at Jackie Cooper. Look"—she threw out her hands in conclusive proof—"look at Baby LeRoy."

Emma-Jo looked. She had only to gaze at one of the fifty-seven varieties of pictures pinned to the inside of the porch to see the gentleman who was much, much younger than herself.

"But how?" Indeed, how? Aye, Angie, there's the rub.

But Angie was made of initiative as well as imagination. "We'll earn our way as we go. We'll start tomorrow. We'll take things to sell at each town; with some of the money we make, we'll buy more things to sell. Out there we'll get into the pictures. Then we'll write back and send money to our folks. Emma-Jo, wouldn't you like to send money to your folks? Remember"—her voice dropped to a dramatic pitch—"*your father is going to lose his job.*"

Emma-Jo wilted under the accusation. Didn't she know it? Why, for months, now, Father had been talking anxiously to Mother about what they were to do. To be able to send money home to him—it gave her a warm little feeling of gratitude toward Angie and a ready acquiescence to the plan.

There were other recent troubles in the clans of Bryson and Thomas. Emma-Jo's brother Bob was engaged to Angie's sister Louise, or rather he had been, but something had happened—the girls did not know what. All they knew was that there had been many tears on the part of Louise and much solemnity on the part of Bob.

So it came about, after some conversation concerning the troubles of the families, both financial and romantic, that the acquiring of picture jobs seemed a natural procedure on the part of the two most talented members of the same.

That evening, when Emma-Jo's mother kissed her good night just as a faint silvery new moon was caught in the top of the maple tree, nothing but altruistic thoughts of helping her father kept the counterfeit Mae West from breaking out into loud lamentations and thereby spilling both tears and the beans.

Came the dawn, and much secret preparation, including fresh jewelry for Miss West—a white-clover diamond necklace, a half-dozen syringa-pearl bracelets, a crescent ruby brooch effected by means of a pasteboard background, and lastly, the invention supreme, huge hoop-shaped earrings, looking faintly like fruit-jar rubbers in those spots where the diamonds were thin.

This Friday was Club Day for the feminine heads of the families of Bryson and Thomas. Mrs. Thomas, however, was not going. She said she had plenty to do at home and she thought a mother's place was right there, where she could oversee her child on a day when there was no school. But Mrs. Bryson was going. She had worked long on her paper, "Modern Child Training *versus* Old-Fashioned Methods," and no upsetting rearrangement of school hours would keep her from reading it.

It was easy for the two potential travelers to have picnic lunches put up, for both families knew what long hours the girls spent in the vacant yard. It was not so easy, however, to get things to sell en route. When they met and took an inventory of resources, Miss West had accumulated a small glass of jelly, some caps for toy guns and a package of radish seeds. Miss Garbo's plunder consisted of a pair of Louise's silk hose, a card of buttons and the current number of her father's railroad magazine.

From the alley back of the vacant yard, each carrying a basket, their faces turned toward the klieg lights, the two set out. Ah, well, older and wiser moths than Angie and Emma-Jo have fluttered their feeble wings in the direction of that fascinating radiation.

When they left the last of the scattering cottages behind and were really out on the paved highway, Emma-Jo had a sudden inspiration. *She could count the miles to Hollywood.* Then, as quickly, the idea died with the remembrance that she was leaving school and would not have to answer the problem at all.

Cars passed them. After some time, one drew up and a hearty voice called, "Want a lift, kids?" It was a man from back home. He wanted to know right away whither they were bound.

"Center Schoolhouse," the clever Angie informed him, while the less adroit Emma-Jo opened her eyes and mouth at the astounding statement.

They got out at the country schoolhouse, and when their temporary but inquisitive benefactor was out of sight, began trudging on toward the West.

At Robbinsdale the girls prepared to do business. The little town lay basking in the sleepy noon sunshine, apparently in a deep somnolence until it should be awakened to the privilege of buying buttons, jelly, hose, railroad magazines, gun caps and radish seeds.

Miss Garbo immediately chose the south side of the street as looking more prosperous; Miss West, perforce, took the north. But neither patricians nor proletarians were visibly affected by the bargains offered at their front doors.

To Miss West, especially, were the constant rebuffs trying, for she was made of more sensitive, less audacious stuff than Miss Garbo. It was very warm. Her jewelry was shriveling. The toe on her left foot hurt. Up and down the front walks to various houses she pursued her way without apparent results.

In front of an unpainted cottage an old man sat tipped back in a chair against a tree. He was deaf, and Emma-Jo had to shout about her wares. It embarrassed her exceedingly to be yelling about radish seeds, jelly and gun caps.

"Guns," he said; "wall, now, I ain't shot a gun sence the war." He dropped his chair down on its front legs, pointed a shaking old finger at her and shouted: "What year was the Civil War? Quick, now."

It was worse than problems. She said faintly: "I guess I'll be going now, thank you," and fled precipitously.

At the next house a woman with a long face like a horse's came to the door.

"Would you"—Emma-Jo gulped at her Dobbin-like appearance—"would you like to buy gun caps, jelly or radish-seeds?"

The woman glared. "Have you got a license?"

Emma-Jo was frightened. Bob and Louise had been going to get a license before they quarreled. "I wasn't going to get married," she said faintly.

"Well, I should hope not. Have you got a license to sell things in this town?"

"No," said Emma-Jo faintly.

"Then you ought to be reported to the town council—and maybe the NRA."

Emma-Jo almost ran. She had to wink fast to keep the tears from falling. Town council! The NRA! Her heart was beating violently. She looked behind her, half expecting to see the President or an NRA committee coming down the street. But there was no one but Angie, who was motioning to meet her over in the park.

It was a crushed little Emma-Jo who sought a shady seat to ease her hurting foot. Not so, Angie. Angie was mad through and through. She took it out on the town. She thought of a great many violent things to say about it and the inhabitants thereof. She said she would like to put the buttons in their food, plant radish seeds in their old park so radishes would grow up all over their old town and smother their flowers and grass. She was all for going right on out of the place as soon as they had eaten lunch. "I wouldn't—I wouldn't *lower* myself to sell them anything," she stated to her peddler partner.

They ate their lunch and were well on their way to Hawksbury by two o'clock. Hawksbury was larger; people would have more sense there, Angie said. But they must plan not to pass the bank where Bob worked. It was just possible Bob might not see eye to eye with them about this western trip.

It was getting warmer. Their baskets were bunglesome. Cars passed. They began to look wistfully after them. Some men in a big shining car must have noticed their longing looks, for the car slowed. There were two men in the front seat and one in the back.

"Want a lift, girls?" they called. Strangely enough, it was Angie who hung back, Emma-Jo who was ready to meet unknown people. It was such a nice-looking car, she thought, and the men were so well-dressed. She even climbed in ahead of Angie. Her feet hurt, and it seemed providential to have the problem of transportation settled.

There appeared to be some difference of opinion among the three whether or not it was a good idea to take them in; one man evidently did not like the plan. The one in the back seat was talkative. "Where you bound for, girls?"

It was Emma-Jo who volunteered: "Hollywood."

"That's just where we are, too." He liked his own joke, it seemed.

"All the way?" asked Emma-Jo.

"Sure. We've just signed for the pictures. We're to play Uncle Tom, Topsy and little Eva." And he laughed again.

One of the three was surly. He swore at the talkative one—words that no Bryson or Thomas ever used. Angie with her quick wits was worried. But Emma-Jo would have risked a great deal to ease her aching feet.

They were getting into Hawksbury now, and even the talkative one was sitting silent and tense. "Please don't drive past the bank," Emma-Jo said politely. "My brother works there—and he doesn't know I'm going away."

One of the men glared at her.

Angie said quickly: "We'll get out here, thanks."

"Oh, no, you won't."

The one in the back seat had changed, too. He wasn't laughing any more. He said in a low voice, "Yes, we're going by the bank. We're going *into* the bank." He uncovered a queer-looking gun and turned it toward them. "You're to do just as I say, sisters. When we come out, you're to be standing on the running board. Whichever one stirs off the running board, this guy at the wheel he'll blow out her brains. Get me?"

Angie, having attended more than one gangster picture, had "got" him long before his speech was ended. Emma-Jo had, too, now. She had found fault with her brains at problem time, but such as they were, she wished mightily to retain them.

The car stopped in front of the State Bank of Hawksbury, facing the long slope that led to the highway. The little girls stood on the running board, frightened and obedient, waiting for the thing to happen: the thing that Angie had long since sensed, that Emma-Jo had never dreamed.

The two men went into the bank, while the third kept the engine running, swearing under his breath. Soon they came tearing out, with their guns up, and threw some bags into the car. It started almost before they were in, down the hill toward the highway.

The two little girls, one on each side, hung on tightly. The highway stretched straight before them. A mile beyond, to the left and right, several roads turned into the thick woods along the river bank. The men were arguing excitedly about which turn was to be made on a woods road.

Emma-Jo thought she was in a nightmare. She would wake up soon and see the silver moon caught in the top of a maple. But no, she was on the running board of a car tearing madly down the highway. They would soon make a turn, too, and Bob and the Hawksbury men wouldn't know which way to come to find them. In "hare and hounds" they dropped little pieces of paper to leave a trail. Although in the grim reality of what was happening to her she was no longer Mae West, she remembered the former actress' jewels and dropped one of the wilted bracelets in the highway—then another—and another.

When they were gone, she surreptitiously yanked at the pasteboard crescent brooch. In a few minutes now they would turn into one of four roads. Her sharp little teeth bit through her white-clover-diamond necklace, and when the turn was being made almost on two wheels, she dropped that, too, where it lay like a long accusing finger, pointing out the way they had gone.

It was just at that moment that Mrs. Bryson, reading her club paper, was saying, "Children without complete freedom have no chance to develop their initiative," and wishing heartily her neighbor were there to hear.

The girls could see a car standing down the woods road, now. The driver of their own car suddenly turned into the edge of the woods, bumping along until he stopped back of a clump of trees. The men were out, tearing over to a car waiting at the side of the road.

The talkative one said: "So long, kids. Give my love to Janet Gaynor."

They were gone. The girls climbed down slowly from the running boards, looked at each other a moment with no words, peered out through the underbrush, and tiptoed out to the road. But soon other men were coming in cars from which guns bristled. So the two waited until all had gone by; then they started back toward Hawksbury. For reasons best known to themselves, neither mentioned going on to the Coast.

When they trudged into Hawksbury, a great many people were in the bank. They went in, too, with their market baskets, and pushed through the crowd over to the president.

"Mr. Winters," said Emma-Jo, "here's one sack of your money. I put it into my basket when they threw it in."

Bob was in a back room with a bandage tied around his head and, strangely enough, Louise was there, holding his hand right in front of everyone. When Bob and Louise saw Miss Garbo and Miss West, their eyes stared as though they would pop out of their heads. But because Miss Garbo was hot and tired, or, mayhap, because Miss West had no jewels, Bob and Louise thought they were merely their two little sisters.

The robbery was over. Club was over. The trip to Hollywood was over. The crime, intellectual and romantic waves had all receded into the sea of an exciting past.

Twilight was soon to settle down in the small midwestern town which numbered the Thomases and the Brysons among its citizenry. Many words had been spoken anent the various activities of an unusually active day.

Mrs. Bryson had said that it had all come out right—that the whole thing proved that if children were left to their own resources, were thrown on their own, so to speak, they could take care of themselves in any crisis; also, that the only punishment a child should ever have was the self-knowledge that it had bungled matters—and Angie now knew she had bungled. Mrs. Thomas said it proved that when a mother took her eyes off her brood, anything was liable to happen; also, that getting Emma-Jo safely back home did not minimize the fact that she had done wrong; that as a punishment, Emma-Jo was to stay in her room all day Saturday, getting her schoolwork in the meantime.

So it came about that Emma-Jo sat now by her open window with the problems in her lap. The sweet spring evening smelled like syringa pearls and a faint silvery moon rode in the sky like a crescent-shaped brooch.

Someone was hoo-hooing in the yard below. It was Angie. The statement is significant. It was not Greta Garbo—merely Angie. All the illusion was gone. Angie did not look like Garbo at all; she looked just like a little dark-haired girl of Emma-Jo's own age. All the glamour was gone, the romance dead.

Perhaps Angie felt the same way, for she was calling the old name: "Emma-Jo."

Emma-Jo called, "Here I am, up here."

Angie had a plan, it seemed. She was saying: "Come on down. Dad gave me money to go to the show. Can you get your folks to let you go, too?"

To Emma-Jo the possibility of getting her folks to let her go to a show was as remote as the silvery moon.

"No," she said, "I can't. I've got to stay in my room all day tomorrow for—for doing what we did." The sight of Angie, free as the wind, money on her palm, brought a sudden gush of tears to Emma-Jo. It was then that all unconsciously she fell back into character. "Angie," she said, between gulps, "come up and see me sometime."

Angie left on the wings of freedom, and Emma-Jo picked up her problems. Life can be very hard, for if Sunday comes, Monday is not far behind.

She tried the two problems beginning "If a man . . . "; then moved patiently on to "If a train . . . " Very soon, realizing there was no use in further endeavor, she tackled "If a farm . . . " She gave that up almost immediately and came then to the last. "If there are telegraph poles one hundred feet apart from here to Hollywood, and there are sixty-eight thousand seven hundred and forty-two of them, in terms of miles how far is it to Hollywood?"

She read it through three times, looking at it with a dulling lackluster eye. Miles—telegraph poles—feet. If someone would only tell her which one of them to start with. She experimented impartially with addition, subtraction, multiplication and division, and when not one seemed to give satisfactory results, she succumbed to the mental lethargy which was stealing upon her.

And under any circumstances, she comforted herself, the problem was not sensible. If you were going to Hollywood by train or airplane, the conductor or pilot could easily tell you how far it was. If you drove your own car, your speedometer would register it. And if you were not going at all, you didn't need to know. *And she was not going.*

Welcome Home, Hal!

One of Aldrich's tactics to free a character from the closeness of parental bonds is to skip a generation and have the character reared by a grandparent or grandparents, and that is the approach she takes with Hal in "Welcome Home, Hal!" Some other stories in which she uses this method are "Through the Hawthorne Hedge" (1919), "The Victory of Connie Lee" (1923), "He Whom a Dream Hath Possest" (1927), and "Alma, Meaning 'To Cherish'" (1934).

As with the young man in "He Whom a Dream Hath Possest," Hal Dening in this story is an artist, and Aldrich is again enjoying the memories of her own son, Jim, practicing his artistic talent around their home as he grew up.

Here also is Judith Marsh, teacher and resident of the small town of Mayville, who suddenly sees her town as it might appear to a city dweller, and she recognizes that it would not seem a special place to an outsider. After "Welcome Home, Hal!" appeared in the *Ladies' Home Journal* in September 1934, a woman who lived in a small Texas town wrote Aldrich saying this story was the best portrayal of small town people she had ever read. Aldrich, of course, knew her rural dwellers and their towns well, and she portrays them with insight and respect as well as affection.

The last school bell rang throatily, and Judith Marsh, leaving her desk, stepped to the hallway of Room 3 as quickly as though she were a robot connected by some mysterious wiring with the mechanism of the unseen clapper. This quick response to duty may have been very creditable to her as a teacher, but when that immediate reaction to the sound of a noisy brass summons has been going on steadily for eight years, it might, forsooth, also be termed monotonous.

Miss Marsh, of the third grade, was pretty and dainty, and a stranger would have said very young. But when one is teaching in the town of one's nativity—and a small town at that—one's age is neither a matter of mystery nor of speculation. So there was not an old woman in Mayville who did not remember the blizzard of the specific year and month in which Judith Marsh was born, not a parent of her pupils but could say glibly: "Judith Marsh is twenty-nine years old, for she was seventeen the year she graduated, and she graduated in the class of twenty-two." Verily, to abide permanently in the land of one's fathers has its pains and its penalties.

The children came trooping into the hall now for the afternoon session with the same characteristic entrance that all those other seven sets of pupils had affected since Judith started teaching—the first class of which was now of second-year high-school age and engaged at this particular moment in straggling up the long stairway to its study hall. If the third-grade teacher looked no different to them than she had when they were in her room, it was because of the truthfulness of the fact that her soft brown hair lay in just as attractive shining waves, her wide blue eyes looked as merry as ever, and the texture of her skin remained as delicately pink.

These present third-grade pupils, having hung up their wraps, were passing into the schoolroom now—the girls first, with that pious air of desiring to get right to work which is a wholly feminine one; the boys depositing their baseball bats noisily and dragging their heavy, thick-soled shoes in that quarry-slave-at-night-scourged-to-his-dungeon attitude which is wholly masculine.

Judith sent Red Murray back to the hall to brush his wildly upstanding carrot locks—this performance having become a ceremonial part of every school session, as one might always open services with a litany. Red returned almost immediately, his hair showing a faint suggestion of having made the hasty acquaintance of either a toothless comb or a garden rake and thus rendered obeisance to the god of appearances.

Near the front entrance, Emil, the janitor, who had been shoveling coal, stood ready to sound the tardy gong, like a grimy St. Peter about to close the pearly gates.

From the far end of the main hall, her face red with her exertions, a little girl came running breathlessly. She was Ruth Jean Edminston, the child of Judith's girlhood chum.

"Miss Marsh"—Ruth Jean was obliged to use the formal name at school, although her teacher was merely "Judith" to the family—"Miss Marsh . . . I was so scared I was going to be tardy. Daddy was late getting home and he had a letter he was reading to mother, and I waited a few minutes to hear it. Miss Marsh, you *never* could guess! We're going to have company Saturday and Sunday. *Important* company! *From New York!* Miss Marsh, he's a Mr. Hal Dening *from New York.* He's a cartoonist *from New York.* Daddy says *in New York*—"

Well, Ruth Jean could not have known it, of course. If she had brought one of the baseball bats from the end of the hall and struck Miss Marsh a smashing blow between the eyes, the results would have been both surprising and painful, but not more devastating.

Miss Marsh looked at the child with the same blank expression she might have used had the bat done its deadly work. Then a sibilant tidal wave of whispering behind her brought her out of the frozen stupor and she was all teacher, dismissing the child with "All right, Ruth Jean."

So Hal was coming home.

Ruth Jean could not know that Hal Dening was the romantic reason that Miss Marsh had not yet married, the reason that she could not quite bring herself to marry good, substantial Doctor McDonald, even though he was offering her one of the nicest homes in Mayville; that whenever she had almost persuaded herself to take the step, it was the memory of that wicked grin of Hal's intruding itself or the twinkle of his eyes—or any one of a dozen lovable characteristics—that kept her from it. Unfortunately, one may not happily mate with Æsculapius if she has known Pierrot.

It is no less than miraculous how the human mind can divide itself into two compartments. The teacher, Miss Marsh, living on the ground floor of her mental apartment house, so to speak, now conducted a very creditable reading class with no perceptible diminishing of her constant oversight of the lesson. "You may take the part of the peacock, Marian. The part of the duck, Joe." While the girl, Judith Marsh, inhabiting the upper apartment, simultaneously talked with Hal Dening, walked with him, rode with him, went up the river with him, saw him in his Grandmother Dening's house as a big gangling boy in Mayville, long before he had become nationally known.

"I do not see why you st-st-strut so," masculinity was floundering.

"Because I am proud of my fine feathers," the deadlier of the species read glibly.

"You may go on from there—Ruth Jean and Edgar."

And while the peacock swaggered and the duck threw the cold water of a stupid philosophy upon his gay happiness, Judith recalled many things.

She remembered little Grandmother Dening, whose one endeavor in life seemed to have been to bring up Hal so he would miss neither his mother nor the father who had been her only boy. And Grandma Dening's hands apparently had been full, for Hal was constantly dipping into all the small town's mischief-making. And incidentally, he had thoroughly decorated that town with chalk and pencil. High board fences, woodsheds and sidewalks bore his imprint. Schoolbooks introduced to snickering onlookers a rakish Columbus sailing unknown seas in a bathtub, a silly-looking Benjamin Franklin knocked into ludicrous insensibility by his lightning, foppish Indians calling out ridiculous questions to a pertly retorting bunch of Pilgrims. The bottom of Grandma Dening's dresser drawers, her cupboard doors, the whitewashed cellarway—from all of them those absurd figures of Hal's had looked at one with their foolish sayings billowing out from grotesque mouths in elliptical-shaped pencilings.

Grandma had endured them all until the day she found the caricature of a terrible tramplike person in those bold strokes embellishing the freshness of her newly pasted kitchen wall paper. Hal must have been larger than grandma by that time; but size or no size, in her indignation she had given him a sound thrashing—but admitted she had merely cried a little and laughed a little the next day when, across from the tramp, she found a companion piece of an abnormally diminutive person who was herself, and over her knees an exaggeratedly large boy whose long legs trailed out across the picture, with a "Wah! Wah!" in that balloon-shaped flourish of pencil coming from his cavernous mouth.

In the clarity of the recollection Judith smiled, and the children, thinking she was overcome by the antics of the duck and the peacock, all laughed immoderately.

"The last page—Edgar and May."

Well, to grandma's prideful relief and perhaps her ever-wondering surprise, Hal, instead of turning out to be a nitwit, had turned out to be a genius. And, at least in the eyes of Mayville, rather rich. For the great American public, liking nothing so much as to have its risibilities tickled, pays its clowns more than its statesmen. And as though in reparation for all his trouble to her, Hal had later given grandma everything her heart could wish—everything but her youth.

So all through the afternoon it went—like the sound of music through the monotonous reciting and writing and study periods. Hal was coming. Hal was to spend two days with his boyhood friends, Joe and Mabel, who in the old days had made up the foursome with Hal and herself.

He had been back only twice before in all the years. That last time; all the walks and talks—she had thought——But he had gone away with all that might have been said, unsaid.

Looking out through the window now, she could see the back yard behind Joe and Mabel's pretty brick house, the low white fence and the last of the season's garden chrysanthemums. A suit of Joe's on the line turned and whirled and flapped its sleeves in the autumn wind, as though Joe were inside and dancing about in an ecstasy of gladness that his old chum was coming home.

She wondered what Saturday and Sunday would be like; hoped that they would be lovely, so the four of them could turn back the clock and go picnicking up the river just as of old. Mabel's mother could look after Ruth Jean and the baby at her home. Everything would be just as it used to be—the scarlet oaks, the old log cabin for lunching, the river running its lazy way to the sea, Joe and Mabel and she and Hal. Nothing would be different. All afternoon her heart sang a little song of thanksgiving that was both solemn and merry.

It was dismissal time now, and the pupils were passing out with complete and ironic reversal of their entry, the boys enthusiastically, the girls half reluctant to leave.

Ruth Jean stepped out of line because of the weighty thing she wanted to tell Miss Marsh. "Miss Marsh, I have to hurry home and help mother." She had that little girl's importance of helping which becomes quite lost a few years later. "Mother's got a lot to do before our company comes *from New York.* Mother says coming from *New York* that way they will be used to everything nice."

"They?" said Judith weakly.

"Oh, yes, Miss Marsh; I forgot to tell you. He said in the letter there'd be a young lady with him. *From New York.* Her name is Grace." She came close to Judith, raised herself on her toes and whispered through her fat little hands, "*His girl,* mother says."

"I see."

"Good night, Miss Marsh."

"Good night, children. No, Mark. You don't need to stay. I'll erase the board myself this time, thank you."

Judith slipped back into her room and closed the door, tried with all her strength to close it on the sweetness of the memories in which she had reveled that afternoon—but it would not shut them out.

Oh, why was he coming? To have buried your heart and to have tried to forget where the grave was—and then at a piece of news to run right to the spot and begin frantically digging it up, only to find it all red and alive and palpitating. It wasn't fair. If he had stayed away—he and his Grace—where he belonged! Why, only recently she had begun to think that perhaps—after all—good, steady Doctor McDonald—

The wind blew around the school-house. Leaves whirled and spiraled, as foolishly active as her memories.

For a long time she sat idly at the desk until Emil, the janitor, still grimy from the coal, came in and deposited an assortment of jangling pails, mops and brooms, so that she mechanically took down her hat and coat and started home.

To-night she would not stop at Mabel's. On second thought, better to run in for a few moments, face the music, and get it over. Thanks to her own poise, and self-control, they did not know she still cared, thought her interest in Doctor McDonald growing so that they had begun to accept the fact that the affair was serious.

"Oh, hello, Judy. Did Ruth Jean tell you the news?" Mabel was trying to take off the baby's coat while he bounced up and down like an animated pump handle.

"Yes. Isn't it fine?" She was proud of her straightforward look.

"He's driving through—going on to Hollywood. Something about screening some of his stuff. Doesn't that sound important? And"—she bent over the baby—"bringing his girl. My word, Judy, can you imagine your mother or mine letting us drive across the country with our beaus, engaged or not engaged?"

"I should say not. Proof that we're outmoded, Mabel." She was as cool as she could have wished.

Ruth Jean fixed the two with her solemn round eyes.

"Maybe," said the small oracle, "she's got married to him by this time."

"Maybe she has." They both laughed.

Judith rose to go, but stopped at hearing Joe come into the drive. She would wait to see Joe, too, a minute. She felt strong; now that the first ice was broken she would be all right permanently.

"Hello, Judy."

"Hello, Joe." How poised she was.

"Hear about Hal?"

"Yes—isn't it lovely?"

Mabel separated the baby's mouth and one of the chair's tassels. "Joe and I sort of sketchily planned this noon just what we'd do for them. We think, on account of their driving in that way sometime in the afternoon of Saturday, we'll have just a small dinner for six or eight of us. Then on Sunday we'll get father's bigger car and all drive to Millard to dinner at the Chief. Maybe Hal might want to make a few calls over there where his mother's people used to live. Then Sunday night we'll have an informal buffet supper here with perhaps twenty—as many of the old crowd as we can scrape together anyway—and a few of the newer people would like to meet him. He's leaving early Monday morning, he says. About the small dinner, Judy. Shall we have Doctor Mcdonald for you?"

"*No,*" said Judith in a frantic refusal, "*Oh, no.*" And it had happened.

With no control of her emotions, the thing was said. With words no more important than those simple ones, she had done the damage. It was as though a curtain had been pulled aside and she stood naked and ashamed before her two best friends. Pink and embarrassed and sick with distress, she knew that they had suddenly seen what she had intended no one to see—merely by saying she could not come to a dinner for Hal with Doctor McDonald. For years she had laughed with Joe and Mabel at Hal's foolery in the papers, saved comic strips for them which they might have missed, discussed freely his rise to popularity, lived the constant pretense that he was nothing more to her than a good friend of the old days—and now this.

"Oh, well," Mabel set the baby down and said quickly to fill the embarrassing gap: "I tell you—we'll just wait a day to see what our plans are, for sure, whether we'll do that way or . . . " Her voice trailed off vaguely.

And Judy went home sick with the hurt in her heart and the wound to her pride.

At home she told her father and mother with elaborately assumed cheerfulness that Hal Dening was coming home and bringing his girl—at which her father launched into a chuckling tale of reminiscences involving the youthful Hal and some contraband watermelons; but with the uncanny knowledge of mothers, Mrs. Marsh kept a discreet and suspicious silence.

During dinner the phone rang. It was Mrs. Clement Waldo Stryker, and she was summoning Judith to a called meeting of the division heads of the Mayville Community Ladies Welfare Club. This meeting was to be at 8:30 at her home, and the dictum was absolute.

Mrs. Clement Waldo Stryker was the mayor's wife—old Clem having held office for twelve years and bidding fair to hold it another dozen, for one went right on voting for him term after term, realizing that one's ballot was not so much for old Clem as it was vicariously cast for his wife. Mrs. Stryker was the head of so many of Mayville's organizations that, in truth, if Hercules had appeared in Mayville and cut off one of them, in good old mythological fashion, two new organizations would have appeared to take its place, and both heads would have been Mrs. Clement Waldo Stryker.

It seemed now that Mrs. Stryker had just learned of the coming visit to Mayville of Hal Dening and, half incensed at the six hours' delay in being apprised of it, had forthwith decided that there should be a welcoming dinner for him at seven o'clock on Saturday night at the new community building. As she elucidated over the wires, there the new building stood, all completed, so that it seemed as if providence had taken a hand and sent them Mayville's distinguished son just in time to introduce the two to each other as the populace looked on.

In vain Judith began an explanation that Hal was to be Joe and Mabel's guest; that they were planning a small dinner party; that he was bringing a girl friend, so the time did not seem auspicious——

It fell on deaf ears. Mrs. Stryker was the official greeter of the town, and on this particular occasion held no intention of allowing her place to be usurped.

Judith went stubbornly to the committee meeting. It seemed so silly to have a dinner of that type—so small-townish. If Hal were coming alone! But the girl—what would she think? The best they could do would be one of those hospitable noisy village demonstrations. A dozen women in Mayville could have given a very creditable little dinner that would not have been glaringly defective from a social standpoint. They were not all back-woodsy. But a huge conglomerate gathering! It was a horrible thing to perpetrate on Hal and the girl. She began to see everything through the eyes of the strange girl who was coming with him, and the metamorphosis was not pleasant to contemplate.

The Mayville Community Ladies' Welfare Club was divided, through the chief's armylike leadership, into four divisions, each headed by a chairman and Mrs. Stryker—and the greatest of these was Mrs. Stryker. The four were Mrs. Otto Schneiderman, Mrs. Hattie Durkin, Mrs. Ralph Hitchcock and Judith.

Judith was the last of these to arrive, for she had taken time to go around by Mabel's and tell her what Mrs. Stryker was putting across, willy-nilly. Mabel had capitulated, as one must before the Mesdames Strykers of the world; had said that she didn't want to be selfish, and if Mrs. Stryker really felt that Hal should be given some kind of ovation by the town——

"Yours not to wonder why—yours but to do or die." Judith had congratulated herself on her self-possession. Perhaps by adhering strictly to this renewed poise she could counteract any impression she might have given Joe and Mabel earlier in the day.

As she mounted the stairs to remove her wraps in Mrs. Stryker's guest chamber, she could hear the other ladies in conversation—specifically the voice of Mrs. Hattie Durkin remarking acridly: " . . . embarrassing to be an old girl he ditched."

"Hold on to yourself, Judith," she said under her breath; "consider the source."

For Mrs. Hattie Durking, head of Division II, was the town's human flea, not a wasp whose sting is formidable, but a mere flea, which is "a wingless, blood sucking creature with extraordinary powers of leaping." From one person to another Mrs. Hattie Durkin darted, sticking her tiny proboscis of gossip into one, piercing the outer texture of his sensibilities, while her thin lips smiled and her small beady eyes shifted cannily toward her prey.

"Oh, hello, Judith," she said now. "You'll be glad to see Hal—you were such old friends." Then she bit Mrs. Ralph Hitchcock, whose husband's business had failed: "Hal will see changes in *your* life, Etta." And she enjoyed the victim's momentary irritation at the puncture.

They all went downstairs to begin plans for an event which Judith loathed with every fiber of her being.

Mrs. Stryker, having figuratively donned her general's uniform upon first hearing of Hal's coming, was ready with her bombardment. She made her assignments immediately.

Mrs. Otto Schneiderman was to have charge of the food, a very sanguine procedure, for Mrs. Schneiderman's theory of life was that earth held no sorrow that food could not heal; her motto, "A bird on the table is worth two in the hen house"; her prayer, "Give us this day our daily bread," contained no spiritual interpretation. So she came like a warhorse to the Battle of the

Menu. One would have thought, to hear her talk, that Hal had never known a square meal since he shook the dust of Mayville from his nimble feet. She was all for vegetable soup, chicken pie, noodles, oysters, roast beef, rolls, cabbage salad, fruit salad—

Judith looked at her through the eyes of the girl who was coming. She seemed to be able to visualize that girl—dark and tall and slender, and the last word in modish attire. She could imagine her soft smile, guarded but supercilious; hear her laugh with Hal later. She could bear anything better than to think that Hal would laugh with her.

Mrs. Otto Schneiderman was concerned with the food to be consumed, Mrs. Ralph Hitchcock was torn by social problems; where Hal should sit; where the toastmaster, the girl; the order in which speakers and singers should be honored in the seating problem. Would the Rev. Arthur Caldwell be hurt if the Rev. Benjamin Hass were asked to give the invocation? Should the girl have a corsage at her plate?

"After all," said Mrs. Stryker pompously, "the dinner is for Hal. We really don't know the status of the girl."

Mrs. Hattie Durkin immediately lighted and bit: "Good land, he's engaged to her, or he wouldn't have brung her"—and darted her small beady eyes at Judith.

She hated it all, did Judith: the deep discussions over trifles; whether to put raisins in the dark cakes or leave them out; whether to have the salad placed fresh on the plates as Mrs. Schneiderman wanted it, or embalmed in gelatin as Mrs. Stryker insisted.

Eventually all four, however, were assigned to their respective posts: Mrs. Otto Schneiderman for food; Mrs. Ralph Hitchcock for the program; Mrs. Hattie Durkin for publicity, tickets and finances; Judith for tables, dishes and decoration; with Mrs. Clement Waldo Stryker, in the language of Mr. Kipling, as he correctly, if unintentionally, described her, "sitting up in a conning-tower bossing three hundred men."

Out of a chaos of plans and suggestions, ludicrous, feasible and impossible, there slowly and painfully evolved a program for the occasion. She who can handle a small town community affair could be ambassador to the Court of St. James's. Tickets were to be sold to the public.

"He belongs to every man, woman and child in the community," Mrs. Hitchcock had said, with ready emotional moisture in her eyes.

Mrs. Hattie Durkin had leaped. "I'd say he belongs to his girl," she cackled, and shot Judith a furtive glance.

The dinner was to be at seven, or as nearly afterward as it was possible for Mayville's beauty and chivalry to assemble. The high-school orchestra was to play. The Rev. Benjamin Hass was to give an invocation before they were seated. Although it took physical bravery and a goodly portion of tact, Mrs. Otto Schneiderman was to be held down to three courses of food.

Mrs. Walter Merrick, who had studied music in Chicago, was to sing. "To render" sometimes meaning "to inflict," the Methodist men's quartet was to render a piece. Hannah Thompson Emmett was to read an original poem. Mayor Stryker was to make the official welcoming speech in behalf of the town. Joe Edminston was to give an expurgated summary of Hal's boyhood, after which résumé, and appropriately, as atonement follows confession of past sins, the Rev. Arthur Caldwell was to pay tribute to Hal's later and supposedly less lurid life.

This assortment of literary, musical and spiritual contributions to Hal Dening's welcome was good as far as it went, but to Mrs. Hitchcock's emotional nature it did not go far enough.

"As I said before"—her sensitive chin quivered in comradely alliance with her warm heart—"Hal Dening belongs to every man, woman and child in the community, and I repeat 'child'—but notice that up to this minute not one of the little darlings has a part in the program. I want the little folks to have a share in this welcome, too. Judith, couldn't you train a group—some little flag drill or something of that kind?"

"No, I couldn't," said Judith, and cast about wildly for an excuse that would not wabble too noticeably. "I—we're beginning a new and hard number work Monday, and I always—always make a good deal of preparation for it."

And in as much as not one of the other four had ever taught, the frail little excuse limped past them without reproach.

Oh, she hated it all. If it were Hal alone! But the girl—it would be a ridiculous thing for her to witness. Why should these good, kind people, salt of the earth, as the Reverend Caldwell called them, work their heads off for three days to welcome Hal home, only to be laughed at for their pains? Yesterday she had loved all these home folks—well, almost all of them—tonight she hated them for proposing and expecting to carry out this wild small-town festivity, this village orgy, this—this wineless bacchanalia.

But it was always of the girl she was thinking. Hal would fit in anywhere. But that "rag and bone and hank of hair" who was coming with him; how could she understand the love and affection for Hal that was going into this ridiculous dinner? Hal, alone, would understand, but Hal was not to be alone. Men were so susceptible to the opinions of the girls with whom they were in love—and Hal was in love.

Thursday and Friday were lived through. On Friday afternoon Judith went to the woods with the school children for autumn leaves with which to decorate the freshly plastered sides of the new barnlike room called by courtesy the banquet hall.

Saturday dawned mild and warm and sunshiny. October's Indian summer was welcoming Hal, too, with the haze in the distance that he loved, and the smell of fall-turned loam and wild haws and bonfires coming over the town on the wings of the autumn breeze.

Just before noon Judith made her angel-food cake—a huge fifteen-egg affair that in its completed white perfection soothed her pride for the space of a few moments. In the early afternoon she went down to the community building and set her tables. At home again she bathed, and dressed for evening in a soft gray-blue mull the exact shade of her eyes. At five o'clock she took her cake in its basket and started back to the community building.

Because there was no car at Joe and Mabel's she stopped for a brief moment, half in fear that the couple would come before she could get away. She found Mabel tired and irritable with the nervousness that comes from preparing to entertain a stranger. Ruth Jean was practicing monotonously "one . . . two . . . one . . . two." The baby was nibbling a piece of paraffin, so Judith extracted it from his mouth and cuddled him for a few moments. "*She* may not like children," she thought, and for no special reason had a fleeting hope that she would not.

All the way down to the dinner she looked at the town through the coming stranger's eyes: the small park with its simple little fountain—once she had been proud of that newly acquired fountain; the wide country-lane streets, with the trees nearly meeting overhead—once she had reveled in their soothing shade; the hodgepodge homes—square frames, bungalows, cottages, red-brick two-storied ones—once they had looked pleasant and adequate because they housed old friends; the community building itself, now a huge, gray-stucco affair, its architecture merely inverted soup tureen—once she had worked hard for that building, given school programs to earn money for it, been proud of its completion. Today she saw nothing but through alien eyes—and a small Midwestern town through alien eyes is sometimes not a lovely thing.

She went up the walk to the south door. Box-elder bugs swarmed over the whole side, the warmth of the Indian summer day having brought them out of their fall hibernation. They clung to the gray of the stucco like an army of Reds carrying their flags under each wing. They irritated her, as though they too were merely small-town bugs, as though city bugs might have flaunted more modest colors, been better behaved.

She went directly into the kitchen with its new pine built-in tables and sinks. The room seemed too warm with the heat from a range, so she took her cake on into the far end of the cool plastered furnace room and placed it on a shelf near a partly open window, covering it securely with a snow-white tea towel.

Back in the kitchen she encountered Mrs. Clement Waldo Stryker, her portly figure incased in black satin, jet earrings against the pink smoothness of her fat cheeks, just now a huge apron swathing the satin dress. How grotesque! How the girl would laugh at the combination. Where besides a small town did one ever encounter such an association of servant-and-hostess ideas and clothes?

Mrs. Hattie Durkin came in. She darted a swift glance at Judith with her little shifting eyes. "Judith, you and Hal was such old friends—you should have et with him instead o' workin'."

Judith felt the bite, pretended it hadn't stung, said casually, "Oh, somebody always has to put over a social affair."

The helpers were arriving—the two women hired to pare potatoes. Everything was so confusing in the kitchen that Judith slipped into the large dining hall, where her tables stretched their forms down the room like block-long white sheeted panels. The tablecloths were of a dozen varied patterns. Mrs. Schneiderman's Irish damask ones overlapped Mrs. Hattie Durkin's mercerized ones. The flowers were home-grown, the vases a heterogeneous collection borrowed from high and low. All the leaves that the children had brought could not hide the bareness of the newly plastered walls. There were not anywhere near enough new chairs for the crowd, and now the high-school boys were noisily stumbling in with a jumble of drugstore chairs, funeral parlor chairs, Mrs. Merrick's early-American, Mrs. Stryker's modern-Jacobean and Mrs. Hattie Durkin's painted kitchen ones.

The high-school girls who were to wait on tables arrived in fifteen-year-old breathless excitement over the coming of the romantic couple. Judith fixed salads. A million little quivering pyramids of pale green gelatin arose from their pale green lettuce beds, giving specific proof that Mrs. Stryker, still wielding her scepter, had won in the salad argument.

That majestic personage was now engaged in giving everyone orders. "As soon as I give the signal, start in to arrange the second course. As soon as the second course is being removed, start cutting cakes. It must all go off like clockwork."

Judith had a wild notion that the whole affair was being conducted from the trenches; that this was just before the zero hour, and soon they were all to go over the top. How she would have loved to laugh about it with Hal, imitate Mrs. Stryker's bombastic orders and Mrs. Schneiderman's perturbation over the amount of provender. She could see the way Hal's mouth would have drawn up at the corners and the wicked grin give way to contagious chuckles. Oh, would the girl have a sense of that same deep humor, understand that delicious whimsy?

It was nearly time now. People were in the "parlors," freshly plastered and decorated with the autumn leaves and the G. A. R., Spanish-American and World War flags. She could hear laughing, talking; through the constantly swinging doors catch glimpses of the town's merchants and professional men, farmers and laborers, a cosmopolitan group of men, and such wives, sisters and daughters as were not actively engaged in the food belt.

Three high-school girls stuck their heads through three swinging doors simultaneously to shrill: "*They're here!*"

The members of the Mayville community Ladies' Welfare Club forgot their cues, ignored their field marshall and crowded to the swinging doors to peek at the guest of honor and his young lady. Mesdames Durkin, Schneiderman and Hitchcock all went out to shake hands with the returning hero and his sweetheart headed by no less a personage than their bellwether, Mrs. Clement Waldo Stryker.

Judith knew she should have trailed along, too. But she could not—not with the eyes of the town upon her. She had been a traitor to herself at Joe and Mabel's and now she could not trust the unreliable person she had thought to be her placid self. It seemed suffocating here in the kitchen. In a few minutes she would be all right, but just now her heart was pounding so hard that its noise was in her ears, the pulsation of her throat was so apparent that she put her hand there to still its beating. Suddenly she turned and slipped into the cool quiet of the furnace room, colliding, as she did so, with Joe, who had just deposited an ice-cream freezer therein.

"Oh, Joe—sorry!" she said. And finished lamely, "I have to see about my cake."

And then to fool herself, pretending to herself to prove her point, she walked over to the far end of the room where the cake sat, to unveil its white perfection.

And stared. Some four hundred box elder bugs were toiling their way patiently up the treacherous iced sides like so many hearty Alpine climbers. Several dozen, having gained their objective, peered out from frosted crevices at the top. The gayest adventurers of them all, a few clumsy fellows, flew flappingly up from their highly original investigation of the dark shaft of the center hole. From the open window a long line of happy fellow soldiers of fortune were hurrying cakeward.

It seemed the last straw on a breaking camel, the paramount horror of a hideous nightmare, the final drop of a three-day deluge of small-town stuff. She clenched her fists in her nervousness. Angry tears came to her eyes, so that she pinched her tongue with her teeth to keep back the hysteria. She was ashamed of Mayville, ashamed of everyone in it and everything they did. She was going to slip out of that far outside door and leave the—

Because she heard a door open behind her and saw a shaft of light she turned.

"Hal!"

"Judy!"

"How did you —"

"Joe told me you were in here, crawling into the furnace."

After a lifetime of longing for him, years of dreaming it all out, days of the anticipation of meeting him again, all she could think to say was, "Oh, Hal, my cake's ruined with a thousand box-elder bugs." Thus do we meet life's deepest crises.

"What's a bug or two between friends, Judy?" Hal was grinning in that never-to-be-forgotten way, with the corners of his mouth drawing up, and holding out his arms.

Before she could think, before reason had time to command, and only foolish sentiment directed, she was in those arms and Hal had held her close and kissed her. Like a flower to the sun, or the tides to the moon, she had gone, before she remembered how or why she had let herself go. After all, Hal was modern, probably kissed indiscriminately these days if he chose. She had always been a little old-fashioned about it. Well, she still was. More small-town stuff, maybe, but it was the way she felt.

"Oh, Hal! I'm sorry. I shouldn't have—nor let you."

"And why not, Judy-Prudy?" It was the first time she had heard that old nickname for years.

"Well—the girl——"

She was laughing in embarrassment. After all, she shouldn't attach any importance to the very natural thing of that friendly greeting—except for the fact that it had seemed so much more than friendly!

"The girl? What girl? Whose girl? Why a girl?"

"Why—the girl you brought." She looked up at Hal, startled. "You did bring her, didn't you?"

Hal threw back his head and laughed long and merrily behind the furnace in the plaster-smelling room. "My girl's eighty-one—grandma. I told Joe I was bringing her, but it seems that my penmanship isn't all that it might be, and in my hastily scribbled note the word 'Gran' looked like 'Grace,' and Joe and Mabel were all set to welcome a real fiancée. You should have seen their faces when I helped little old Gran out of the car." Then he pulled Judith close again. "Lord, Judy, you're sweet and dear. I don't know why we've wasted any——" He broke off to say hurriedly, "I'm dropping grandma off here to visit and I'm taking you on to the Coast with me. Will you, Judy? Marry me before Monday morning and drive on to the Coast with me?" And without waiting for an answer: "How do you get married around here now, anyway? Do you have to tack up a notice in the post office, or does old preacher Hass announce it from the pulpit along with prayer meeting and choir practice? . . . I get married so seldom these days."

Judy was laughing. Was she always to laugh now? "Oh, Hal—I couldn't."

For the first time he was serious. "There's no one else? None of these new men? If there is——"

"No, there never was anyone but you." Doctor McDonald might have been in Tasmania. "But—I mean—not Monday. Why, I couldn't. I'm a teacher. We're—we're taking up new number work Monday morning."

"So am I. I'm subtracting grandma and adding you and dividing my income and"—Hal would—"we'll talk about multiplying later."

Joe opened a door, stuck his head around the furnace and emitted an ancient small-town joke: "Hey, folks—sorry to interrupt, but we can't start things out here without the prodigal calf."

And Hal had to go. He kept Judy's hand a moment, kissed the soft pink palm. "Aren't you coming in to sit with me?"

"Heavens, no, Hal; go on—hurry! I'm chairman of Division IV of the Mayville Ladies' Community Welfare Club."

"My word—and to think I once also glimpsed the sultan of Turkey." And Hal was gone.

And Judith, her heart shouting to the four winds that she was going away with Hal, had to go back into the kitchen to hand out quivering green-gelatin pyramids through an aperture in the wall.

The kitchen was now a mass of moving, hurrying, perspiring members of the Ladies' Community Welfare Club obeying the orders of their chief. When the last of the second course had gone the way of the opening in the wall, the order was on to start the cakes. Judith cut a layer cake of mulatto hue, chocolate filled and chocolate covered; Mrs. Hattie Durkin, next to her, cut an albino-complexioned one of lemon origin.

"My! Hal's swell, ain't he?" was her opening wedge. "And did you hear it was only Grandma Dening he brought?"

"Yes—oh, yes," said Judith, so very, very happy that it was only Grandma Dening he had brought.

Mrs. Hattie Durkin prepared to light. "But he's goin' to get married, though. Pa asked him, and he laughed and told pa 'soon,' and pa just had time to tell me when I was comin' back in."

"Yes, so I head, too."

Having lit, Mrs. Hattie Durkin prepared to bite. "You're hardly good enough friends with Hal now, I suppose"—she darted her little eyes sidewise toward Judith—"to know who she is? I been wonderin' who he's goin' to marry." She did not care especially who the girl was. She merely wanted to puncture human skin as she hopped lightly from one person to another. "You wouldn't know, I suppose?"

"Yes," said Judy, sweetly confidential; "they say an old girl of his that he once ditched." And she sawed away serenely on a tough, if bugless, cake.

The swinging doors to the banquet hall opened and shut constantly like the doors to heaven. And Judith knew herself to be a peri, one of those elfs of Persian myth excluded from paradise until they had paid penance—and the penance was abject humility before the god of friendships because of disloyalty to her own.

Through those swinging portals she could hear the Rev. Benjamin Hass praying for Hal's immortal soul—Hal, who had given clean and wholesome joy to a nation. She could hear Mayor Stryker welcome

Hal home and give him the key to the city—Hal, whose inquisitive nose had poked itself into every culvert and cranny of the village before he was ten. She could hear them laugh uproariously at Joe's homely exposé of Hal's checkered boyhood career, and hear the Rev. Arthur Caldwell smooth it over so the Lord would not take Joe's report seriously and think too ill of Hal.

She could see a long unfurled manuscript in the hands of Hannah Thompson Emmett and guess at the literary value of the home-grown poem. She could catch glimpses of little old Grandma Dening beaming with pride as though to say, "Just look at the man I paddled him up to be."

She could hear the high-school orchestra, rather top-heavy as to brass; could hear Mrs. Walter Merrick sing in her best Chicago voice "Home ag-a-a-in . . . home ag-a-a-in . . . from a faaaw-rin shore," and the slightly discordant but lusty Methodist quartet render, "There zno pla sli kome."

Her work done, she stepped through the swinging door in time to see Mrs. Ralph Hitchcock's little darlings welcome home Mayville's distinguished son in their own blithe way. Mrs. Hitchcock, with emotional moisture in her eyes, and much after-school practice, had trained a group of kindergartners to go through a little drill, at the close of which they were, with startling surprise, to form suddenly with lettered cards held high above their heads the touching tribute:

WELCOME HOME, HAL!

In her most enthusiastically hopeful moment Mrs. Hitchcock had underestimated both the startling nature of the procedure and the efficacy of the surprise. Measles having somewhat disrupted the *entente cordiale* during the practice, and substitutes at a late hour having taken the places of a few of the original cast, there was now, as the drill was ending, a bit of confusion in the assembling of the component parts of the surprise greeting. A few of the late recruits, including the exclamation point and the comma, who had not rehearsed at all, becoming confused concerning their respective positions, and fearful of being left out altogether, were elbowing, not to say fighting their way into the display with more zeal than discrimination. For suddenly, to Mrs. Hitchcock's red-faced mortification and the company's raucous hilarity, the greeting stood forth in all the simplicity of its hospitable invitation:

AW, HELL! COME HOME

Judith laughed with the others until she cried. Hal was shouting like a schoolboy. The effect was disrupting to whatever shreds of formality might have clung to the event. Happily it was the last thing on the program, for no other participant could have been taken seriously.

Chairs were pushed back—modern Jacobean, early-American, the funeral parlor ones and the soda-fountain ones and the yellow-painted ones. People were crowding around Hal, shaking hands with him, laughing, adding their own extemporaneous speeches to Joe's summary of anecdotes concerning the town's prize mischief-maker. A sort of jovial pandemonium reigned supreme. The kindergartners, released from their devastating responsibility of welcoming the home boy who made good, were trying their hands and mouths—at the various deserted orchestra instruments, with ear-splitting results—all but the exclamation point and the comma, who were surreptitiously finishing the left-over ice cream. In their patrician way the Irish damask table-cloths were as guilty of being awry as the plebeian mercerized ones. Crumbs of homemade cake lay soggily in green puddles that had once jauntily looked the world in the eye as salad pyramids. A thousand dirty dishes awaited washing by a tired membership of the Ladies' Community Welfare Club. A box-elder bug in a jolly exploring mood sailed back and forth across the scene, piloting his red-painted airplane impartially from table to table.

It was all small-town stuff put on by small-town people in a small-town way. But Judith, whose heart was singing, felt only a warmth of affection toward them all. Hal would understand the sincerity and kindliness that had prompted the whole event. Only a strange girl with critical alien eyes would not be able to understand. And there was no strange girl with critical alien eyes. Just Judith Marsh with tender love-filled ones.

Juno's Swans

"Juno's Swans" (*Cosmopolitan,* 1935) is the second of the Emma-Jo and Angie stories. The magazine liked the two stories so well they asked Aldrich to write more of them with the intention that they would become a series much as the Masons and Cutters had been; however, she wrote only this one and "How Far Is It to Hollywood?" (*Cosmopolitan,* July 1934). Aldrich was under a contract to *Cosmopolitan* in which they guaranteed to purchase five of any six new stories she might send them. The two Angie and Emma-Jo pieces fulfilled a part of that contract. (The others were "The Silent Stars Go By," January 1933; "Low Lies His Bed," January 1934; "Another Brought Gifts," January 1936; and "The Drum Goes Dead," January 1938; all of these are Christmas stories.)

Aldrich had written "Josephine Encounters a Siren" in 1922, a story similar to "Juno's Swans," which *The American Magazine* published in its December issue. That was Josephine's story in the series that later became *The Cutters* (1934). Aldrich's empathy with the rejected little girl is apparent; this is once again a story in which the reader gets the sense of Aldrich's "climbing into another's skin and figuratively buttoning it around" herself, as she expressed the importance of becoming the character about whom she was writing.

George Landy, Aldrich's and Appleton's Hollywood agent at one time, took the two Angie and Emma-Jo stories to Samuel Goldwyn, who expressed some interest in filming one of the stories, but nothing came of the efforts.

Emma-Jo Thomas bent her fat little body over her desk and looked across at Angie Bryson sitting two rows away. Her round pink face plainly asked of Angie: "How do you like *that?*" And Angie without so much as moving her lips telegraphed back: "Grand." Some friendships are like that: wordless, significant, all-embracing.

Miss Clarkson, the music instructor, standing in front of the pupils, had just announced that the grades were to give an operetta some evening in the last week of June. It was a perfectly lovely operetta, Miss Clarkson was telling them in the vivacious voice that Emma-Jo sometimes thought too sugary. Miss Ray, the real teacher, now sitting over at her big desk, always talked to them in an ordinary way as though they were her own age, but Miss Clarkson, who came twice a week, made her voice gay and excited and a little babyish unless she grew provoked at something, and then it sounded mad and natural. This afternoon she was making it as sweet as a flute and very enthusiastic.

"There are several parts that will take a great deal of practice," she was saying—"starring parts."

Emma-Jo, gazing across at her chum again, distinctly saw Angie look self-conscious. It was a foregone conclusion that Angie would have one of those starring parts. She always did. There was not the slightest trace of envy in Emma-Jo's loyal heart, for Angie could sing in a clear true voice, and—to Emma-Jo's uncritical mind—could act better than any of the four girls in "Little Women." Miss Clarkson was saying that the operetta was called "The Forest Child's Dream," which even more definitely settled matters in Emma-Jo's mind, for it followed that Angie would be either the Forest Child or the Dream.

There were to be squirrels and birds and flowers and butterflies, and it all sounded tremendously exciting to Emma-Jo and the other feminine listeners. But as usual, there was noticeable a most exasperating lethargy among the less deadly of the species. Not one of the boys seemed to be getting up any temperature over the potential impersonation of squirrels, birds and butterflies.

Miss Clarkson was working the girls into a perfect lather of anticipation, but the boys remained bored, as with a weary surfeiting of much participation in grand opera. Jimmie Landers even formed his lips and tongue into a realistic, if merely pantomimic, representation of the noisy offering known as the raspberry. And when Miss Clarkson said in a sprightly tone that some one was to be a funny, funny grasshopper and illustrated the jumping, Herman Stutz laughed out loud, but not mirthfully.

It exasperated Miss Clarkson to such an extent she was moved to say that unless they exhibited a little more interest she would not have *one* of the boys in it. Afterward she told Miss Ray *that* statement would bring them around to a show of interest if she knew her Applied Psychology. But Miss Ray, who thought that Applied Psychology was nothing more or less than applied common sense, merely laughed and said that she never paid any attention to that unenthusiastic attitude, that it was a familiar masculine trait and employed merely as a mask.

School having been dismissed with no more definite information on the future musical soirée, conversation by the Misses Bryson and Thomas, en route home, consisted largely of speculation over the coming event. A block down the street their close communion was interrupted by the approach of old Mr. Moseby, the father of their own Mr. Moseby, the superintendent. Old Mr. Moseby had once been a college professor, but this last year he had lived in Huntsville with his son's family. He stopped now, leaning on his cane and looking down his long red nose.

"Well, well," he said cheerfully, "here are the two little inseparables again—Rosalind and her Celia. Do you know who they were?"

Emma-Jo volunteered the guess that they might be some of his relatives. But Mr. Moseby said no, they were friends in a play called *As You Like It,* written by Shakespeare. And did they know him?

"My father does, I think," said Angie brightly, adding modestly that railroad conductors knew most every one.

"I do declare!" chuckled Mr. Moseby.

Emma-Jo was ashamed that Angie had said that, for somehow she had a feeling that the man was dead. People who had written books were usually dead, and at home there was a long row of books with this one's name on them. When Cousin Mel's little boy Georgie came to dinner he had to sit on *King Lear,* but when the little Johnnie came, it also required the services of *Hamlet* to connect Johnnie with his food.

"Yes, you're like Rosalind and Celia." The old man was enjoying himself.

The names sounded rather nice. Not long before, Angie and Emma-Jo had been Greta Garbo and Mae West, but their impersonations had ended so disastrously that they never mentioned the two now.

The little girls were getting anxious to move on but Mr. Moseby, with time hanging heavily on his hands, had more to say about Rosalind and Celia. In a voice like a radio announcer he quoted:

> " . . . we still have slept together,
> Rose at an instant, learn'd, play'd, eat together,

And wheresoe'er we went, like Juno's swans,
Still we went coupled and inseparable."

At that the two edged politely away, Angie muttering under her breath, "The old bore." But Emma-Jo rather liked it, especially the part about Juno's swans. She said it out loud several times, enjoying the way the syllables slipped over her tongue like cream pudding. To be sure, her personal interpretation was slightly original, inasmuch as she thought Juno was merely a poetical way of referring to the month of June.

She even remembered it the next day when she looked across at Angie two rows away. The nice, gay month of June was here with its roses and operetta. She and Angie were like that Rosalind and Celia.

Her heart swelled with friendship for Angie. Angie was a swan. *She* was a swan. *Juno's swans.*

But even as Emma-Jo was having her pleasant and rather poetical thoughts of friendship—even then, the serpent was creeping into her Eden. For the door opened to admit Mr. Moseby, the superintendent, and a strange girl.

All eyes—raised surreptitiously above books—were upon the two. Mr. Moseby was explaining something to Miss Ray, and Emma-Jo could hear part of the conversation. The new girl was the niece of Mrs. William Rider. She was from Capitol City and she was to be in school for the rest of the term. Her parents had been called away East, and because she was obliged to come and stay with her aunt, she must finish her grade here.

To say that the newcomer was pretty is a fractional truth. She was a vision. She was dashing. She had on a tan-colored pleated skirt and a vivid green silk sweater, turned-down tan hose, tan-and-green sports shoes, and two green bracelets. Her hair was the fluffiest canary-yellow bob, her lips were bright red, her eyes large and blue. She stood at ease in front of the room and looked the pupils all over, tapping one sports shoe impatiently and biting her full red lips. Emma-Jo in her excitement telegraphed repeatedly to Angie. But Angie, gazing in fascination at the stranger, was not at the keyboard.

When Mr. Moseby left, Miss Ray told the pupils that their new classmate's name was Faustina Farr. It kept running through Emma-Jo's mind like a song. Faustina Farr! It sounded frosty and sparkling and as pretty as "Juno's swans."

Faustina Farr, in spite of hailing from Capitol City, did not recite noticeably better than the others, but she succeeded somehow in giving the impression that this whole thing called education was beneath her, and a little silly.

At recess time, play on the feminine side of the grounds lagged noticeably; there seemed nothing to do but surround Faustina Farr in a constantly widening circle, from the equidistant center of which the newcomer told the perimeter of girls a great many interesting things of a statistical nature, largely about herself. She said there were as many pupils in her building in Capitol City as in this whole two-by-four town. She said that she was asked to be in practically every entertainment there, that she had crooned in the Elks Club and that she had been prevailed upon to broadcast torch songs from three different stations. She casually remarked that she had colored bracelets to go with every dress she owned and admitted to owning many dresses.

She offered gratuitously the following items: that her photograph had won a prize at an exhibit of pictures, that sometimes she was called a "child prottigy" and that almost every one thought she should be in the movies. Her last observation, as the bell rang, was concise, terse and critical—namely, that she didn't know whatever she could do in this little stick town for several weeks.

It depressed Emma-Jo. She looked up and down the street where the pleasant old elms and maples met overhead and wondered what they could offer so rare a guest by way of entertainment. And then she remembered. *The operetta!* But some presentiment of coming trouble must have possessed her, for as the girls turned reluctantly away from the Charmer, she flung a plump little arm around Angie in vague motherly concern.

When school was dismissed, Miss Faustina Farr cast her large blue orbs over the feminine contingent. In search of a companion en route home, she discarded all comers but Angie, and Angie, as fascinated as elated, went with her. But when Faustina asked Angie who the funny fat little person was trailing behind them, and Angie, with the same nonchalance a rooster might have used toward a worm, said: "Oh, that's just a neighbor of ours, Emma-Jo Thomas," the world and the solar system crashed about the funny fat little person.

The second evening, after Faustina had laughed at everything Angie and Emma-Jo had once thought lovely; had burst into mirth at the thought of cutting out movie actresses and pasting them in a book; had gone into a mild form of hysteria over the idea of making jewelry out of flowers; nay, more, had been joined in this ribald outburst by Angie herself—Emma-Jo took her troubles to that source of all wisdom, her mother.

Mrs. Thomas told a tearful little daughter she was sorry for her, but not to care—that if *that* was all Angie's friendship had meant, it wasn't worth anything. She told her a great many other things—that friendship was like a sheltering tree; that real friends stick to one at all times; that she who cannot stay by a friend through all experiences is no friend at all. But Emma-Jo's stanch little heart did not move one iota against Angie—only against the serpent which had beguiled her.

Faustina proved to be everything that stolid little Emma-Jo was not. She knew the latest slang. She knew the latest songs. She attracted masculinity. She could play the piano with dash; rather sketchily, to be sure, and with much blurring of chords, but for getting over the ground there was not her equal in Huntsville. It all captivated the heart of Angie, so that where'er went Faustina Farr, there went Angie Bryson. And Emma-Jo trod the lonely path of exile.

Old Mr. Moseby, meeting Emma-Jo one day on the street, asked what had become of the other little girl, and when Emma-Jo made an evasive answer, even he sensed something wrong.

But after all, there was the operetta. Life, even in its darkest aspects, does not withdraw all its allurements.

Operetta practice was on in full swing. And it was all and more than Miss Clarkson had so sportively predicted for it. Its authors had been most lavish in their presentation of characters. There were to be robins, butterflies, sparrows, a mocking-bird, squirrels, a brown thrush, an old witch, goldenrod, a gardener, a cuckoo. . . . Practically everything that ever grew, climbed, crept, ran or flew in the forest was to be impersonated, excepting poison-ivy and wood-ticks.

Five of the leading parts fell to pupils in Miss Ray's room. Brown Thrush proved to be Angie Bryson. Mocking-bird was Faustina Farr. It might have been a matter for open debate as to why the talented ladies who wrote the operetta had placed a mocking-bird in a pine and birch forest, but no doubt they were more musical than arboreal and avifaunal. The gardener was Jimmie Landers; he who had once raised only raspberries was now to have a garden in the clearing. Cuckoo was Herman Stutz who had once laughed without merriment, proving again that he who laughs first, laughs last.

And wonder of wonders—the old witch was none other than Emma-Jo Thomas in person! This dazzled Emma-Jo limitlessly, for she was the kind of child who seldom stars. All her young life she had been relegated to the back row of the chorus of daisies or made a member of the peasantry; and now she was to be the old witch with a tall pointed hat, a yellow cape and a long crooked stick with which—like a ringmaster—she was to command all the inhabitants of the forest. She was almost ill with nervous excitement at the glory of it. Not once did she stop to think that her part was all talking—no solo work! For alas! Emma-Jo was no more musical than she was mathematical.

That was a queer thing she could never tell any one. She wished people knew how musical she felt inside her. She could hear lovely tunes in her head, but when she sang them they were not quite recognizable. And lovely words were always repeating themselves over and over in her mind. To say "Minnehaha, laughing water" made her flesh feel quivery; and "By the shining Big-Sea-Water stood the wigwam of Nokomis" made tears come to her eyes. She may have been dumb in arithmetic but she leaped to meet her reading lessons as the tides leap to meet the moon. Poetry rippled over her like the curling waves of Lake Crystal at the picnic grounds. When Herman Stutz or Jimmie Landers read poems in their slow halting way it was as painful to her as piano discords to a musician.

But now she had a great deal of talking to do and it was all in poetry—at least Emma-Jo called it that although Miss Ray was well aware that it would never have been chosen for an anthology.

From that time on Emma-Jo Thomas was a disciple of poesy. No longer did she talk as she had been wont to do. She became a sister to the Goddess Thalia, her habitat Parnassus. Day after day she drank of the water that flows from Helicon's harmonious stream to the fountain of the Muses. Because Angie no longer played with her, she made of her poetics a solitary game in her own back yard. With her long stick, an elm understudy to the hickory one at school, she would point and say in impromptu fashion:

"O lilac bush, I'll change you now
Into a lovely *lady*
And when you la la-la la-la
You'll find it nice and *shady.*"

At her mother's simple request to hand her the broom, the poetess would say:

"Here *is* the broom that sweeps the dirt
And I will bring it *to* you
So *sweep* the porch and *sweep* the steps
And la la-la la *do* you."

"The operetta is making Emma-Jo poetical" her mother said. "The operetta is making Emma-Jo screwy" her father contributed.

But if Emma-Jo had not known this new diversion she would have been far more wretched than she was. Even so, she had periods of deepest little-girl misery, for it is not pleasant to see one's twin swan sailing off with another.

Every day at school was rehearsal day now. More and more was arithmetic shunted to the background. More and more did poetry come to the front. The sciences seemed to have decamped almost entirely in favor of the arts.

The operetta became one's whole object in life. But all the time the forces that were later to be so disrupting were forming like cyclonic clouds on the horizon.

To Emma-Jo the music was lovely, especially one waltz song called "The Summer Song." It made her feel like dancing whenever she heard the lilting tune. She could feel herself float about in exact time to it, but when she surreptitiously tried it, her fat little limbs refused to float. The spirit was willing but that too, too solid flesh was weak. This delicious melody was the highlight of the operetta. And Miss Clarkson said it was to be sung either by Brown Thrush or Mocking-bird.

It is easy to be seen that what happened, then, was distinctly the fault of the two composers who had collaborated on the operetta. For after all, it could not have occurred if they had just made up their minds which character was to sing "The Summer Song." But they had left the decision poised in the air. "To be sung either by Brown Thrush or Mocking-bird" was plainly printed at the top of the page.

Because Faustina Farr was Mocking-bird and Angie Bryson was Brown Thrush, it followed that the prettiest song of all was to be sung either by Angie Bryson or Faustina Farr. Faustina asked Miss Clarkson right before every one if she could sing it. Such brazenness appalled even Angie who was no modest violet. Miss Clarkson parried by saying in her twittery voice that she would have to confer with Miss Ray.

Emma-Jo could plainly see that "confer" meant to argue. She tried not to listen; it was almost like reading a letter which did not belong to you. But from her front seat she could hear snatches of the conversation. She knew that Miss Clarkson was wanting Faustina—something about "the Riders liking it." And just as distinctly she could hear Miss Ray say something about "unfairness to regular pupils." Twice she heard her say very low, "*so* affected."

Emma-Jo made a mental reservation to hunt up the word in the dictionary the moment she got home. She said it off and on out loud all the way there so she would not forget it, but inasmuch as there was a slight discrepancy between the word Miss Ray had used and the word "effected" which Emma-Jo looked up, she found that it merely meant "to be performed, accomplished, achieved," which, of course, was nothing against Faustina.

But even so, each night Emma-Jo prayed consistently that Angie might be chosen. She and Angie might not be chums any more, but friendship was a sheltering tree. So when Miss Clarkson said Brown Thrush—Angie—was to sing the song, Emma-Jo, realizing the efficacy of prayer, turned her eyes guiltily from Faustina's angry countenance as one who has prayerfully maneuvered the whole thing.

The operetta was to be on Thursday night. Miss Ray said they were to come back to school on Friday morning merely to get their books and promotion cards. Sometimes Emma-Jo caught her breath in the gripping fear that she would not be promoted—that the ogre, Arithmetic, would hold her back with his clutching hands. But a glint of hope would invariably shine in the distance. After all, she always *had* been promoted, some unseen force had seemed always to push her from class to class. It was as though those friends, Reading, Writing and Spelling, with whom she was on speaking terms came to her aid each time and would not permit the ugly stranger, Arithmetic, to harm her. But it was going to be terrible not to know the worst until Friday morning.

Rehearsals went on. The last one was held on the big stage of the Community Building, where the voices sounded hollow and unnatural.

The Community Building was new and smelled of plaster. The curtain was a huge velvet thing that ascended somewhere to the heights of heaven and hung suspended from the stars. It was interesting even to Emma-Jo, but the little awe-stricken kindergartners, who were sparrows, could not take their fascinated eyes from the faraway spaces among the rafters so that Miss Clarkson kept rapping for their attention.

This last practice was called a dress rehearsal, and practically everything went wrong. The squirrels kept singing off key. Angie failed to take the first notes of the waltz song with the orchestra. The gardener went on at first without his rake and, hurrying breathlessly back with it over his shoulder, raked off the blue jay's top-knot and a goodly portion of scalp.

The cuckoo, proving himself to be inordinately fond of cuckooing, had to be squelched vigorously and limited to a minimum output. A little sparrow, while gazing open-mouthed up to the vast space among the rafters, tripped over a fellow sparrow, which had the marvelous and mechanical effect of sending the whole row of little brown birds down like dominoes.

It was all disheartening. Miss Clarkson was upset, nervous and cross—and there was not the slightest warm twitter to her voice. Miss Ray was nervous, but not cross—merely caught in the spell of a great grim silence. It was as though she were saying: "Let fate do its worst. Nothing could be more terrible."

Faustina snickered audibly and said in an undertone that the Capitol City teachers would have just *died* to see all this. Altogether, it made Emma-Jo feel a vast and awful responsibility, though she herself was letter-perfect.

At supper time she sat down with substantial food before her, at which she pretended to nibble because her mother was insisting, but it was sawdust on her protesting palate. She had a bath; she was dressed. And she was one of the first to arrive at the Community Building.

In almost no time it was all noise and confusion behind the scenes. Miss Ray, pretty and smelling of apple orchards, "made up" the witch. When Emma-Jo turned her plump pink face up to her teacher so seriously, Miss Ray suddenly said: "Emma-Jo, it's a shame to make your sweet little face into an old witch." And then she did a very peculiar thing. She bent and placed a quick warm kiss on Emma-Jo's forehead, for quite suddenly it had occurred to Miss Ray that, after all, dumbness in arithmetic is a very slight evil in this world. She said, "Emma-Jo, you've been so nice in school all year, I'll hate to have you leave me."

Emma-Jo's heart was bursting with happiness. That was the answer to the question about promotion. She was to go on. It didn't seem possible after all those wrong answers about "If a train . . . " and "If a farm . . . "

People were coming in; there was a constant noise of chairs and voices and shuffling feet. The denizens of the forest took turns in peeking around the edge of the curtain; Herman Stutz stuck out his head and cuckooed so often that by the time they were ready to begin, his own part of the program was virtually over. Emma-Jo caught a hurried glimpse of her mother and father, her brother Bob and his girl, Mr. and Mrs. Rider, and old Mr. Moseby. It was going to be wonderful to show all these people how she could turn children into birds at the wave of her stick.

Faustina laughed at the excitement of the others. She said you ought to be in a broadcasting station once if you thought this little hick-town program was anything so hot.

But she could not hurt Emma-Jo to-night. Something very queer hung over Emma-Jo—a sense of the unrealities of the everyday world, the realities of the play. It was not possible that they were from the families of Thomas, Bryson, Stutz, Landers, *et al.* It was the forest folk who were real. The spirit of the play was gripping Emma-Jo. If raindrops had fallen from the rafters high overhead or lightning flashed across the stage, it would not have surprised her.

It was going to be a wonderful occasion, and the grandest part of all was to be that lovely waltz song of Angie's. Even if she and Angie were not chums any more, she retained her old pride in Angie.

The high-school orchestra was playing "Over the Waves." It may have been a little top-heavy as to brass, but to Emma-Jo it was the perfect symphony. Then Miss Clarkson was tapping her baton, which was the signal for the great heavy velvet curtain to lift—and there was Marian Reynolds sitting on the log in the forest, saying:

"Oh, dear, oh, dear, I'm lonely here
In the forest by the hill."

That was Emma-Jo's cue. Emma-Jo's heart was beating painfully. Her throat was so dry she wondered if she could swallow. She walked into the forest with her stick, and a voice that seemed to come from far away mechanically said the very thing it should have said:

"Ho! ho! my dear! It seems so queer
That you should lonely be.
With all the woods so full of friends
For you to hear and see."

Strangely enough, everything went off rather well. That unfortunate rehearsal was but a memory. The little girl saw all the things in the forest she should have seen, and left unseen all the things she should not have seen. The robins sang; so did the squirrels and the butterflies. And Emma-Jo commanded and changed things at the point of her stick so successfully that it gave her a sense of overwhelming superiority.

It was nearing the end of the play now—time for the lovely summer song, the waltz song, that Angie was to sing. Emma-Jo stepped back under the trees next to Faustina Mocking-bird. And then the most terrible thing happened. Emma-Jo thought she was in a dream, an awful breath-destroying nightmare. At the first orchestral notes of the swinging melody Faustina said in an undertone: "Watch *me!*" Emma-Jo could not believe her eyes; before the chords which were to be Angie's cue to take her place, Faustina had gone forward to the edge of the platform and stood ready to sing the first notes of the song. Faustina Farr, in her grown-up crooning voice, was starting to sing Angie's lovely summer waltz song!

No one in the Huntsville schools had ever done such a terrible thing, but Faustina Farr from Capitol City had the nerve to do it. She was going away early the next morning and probably didn't care what happened.

Emma-Jo could not look all ways at once—at Miss Clarkson, who looked terribly surprised but went on swaying her baton; at Miss Ray, whose face was redder than anything; at Angie, who had taken one step forward and then back—so she concentrated on Angie. Angie's face was red, too, and she looked ready to cry. Emma-Jo had seen Angie mad a hundred times, but she couldn't remember seeing her look hurt. It was as though the iron statue of Mr. Hunt who started the town would have looked that way.

All this, happening in the space of a moment or two, set Emma-Jo's mind working far faster than usual. Responsibility sat heavily upon her. She, the old witch, must do something for Angie.

To understand what followed, one must delve into the realm of heredity. Emma-Jo's mother had been the coolest member of the neighborhood the time the Landers' house caught fire. Suddenly, Emma-Jo was her mother. Emma-Jo's grandmother, left alone on the farm once, had stayed up all night in the barn because a horse thief was about. At this moment, Emma-Jo was her grandmother. Emma-Jo's great-grandmother had once torn away the mud chinking in her log cabin, thrust a rifle through the hole and dared an Indian to come on. Just now, Emma-Jo was her great-grandmother. Stolid little Emma-Jo Thomas was suddenly all her courageous pioneer forbears. She was Right! She was Law! She was Justice with her Scales! She was Truth-Forever-On-Its-Throne.

She could command all things in the forest. A great strength was upon her. She strode forward with her long crooked stick.

"Stop!" she said in a clear high voice, so dictatorial that Faustina broke off on the syllable, Miss Clarkson's baton wavered, the orchestra died away on a lingering note.

The audience, thinking it part of the operetta, sat unmoved. Had they not been seeing a small fat witch making sudden transformations all evening, just by swinging her stick? Little did they know history was being made.

Emma-Jo in her short life had never made an extemporaneous speech before an audience. The chances were she never would again. But now she made one. Out from somewhere—for who can tell whence spring all the little lilting rhymes of the poet?—came the words. Not for nothing had Emma-Jo Thomas conversed for weeks in verse.

Thinking it out simultaneously with her speaking, she said:

"Mocking-bird . . . your song is heard . . .
But brown thrush now must *sing* . . .
Good-by, farewell! . . . Good-by, farewell! . . . "

There was a perceptible pause. Fate juggled poor little Emma-Jo Thomas in its cruel hand. But the Muses had not forsaken their child. It came:

"You *must* be on the *wing*."

And miraculously the thing was done. Emma-Jo Thomas' Big Moment was over.

It was too much for Faustina. She had a bewildered, beaten look as though her colossal nerve had at last deserted her. Miss Ray's face was as red as old Mr. Moseby's nose, and she might have been cast in bronze as "Amazement." Miss Clarkson also was the personification of perplexed surprise. All the birds and the flowers and the animals were wide-eyed with the peculiarity of the thing they had just witnessed. Only the little brown sparrows, gazing in open-mouthed fascination into the vastness of the rafters high overhead, remained immune to any bewilderment over a change in the program.

Faustina walked back under the trees. Angie, returning to normalcy, stepped out to her legitimate place on the stage. Miss Ray, cast in bronze, felt the blood start to flow again in her veins. Miss Clarkson's baton came up. The orchestra picked up the scattered notes of the waltz song. The little old witch slipped back to her place. Angie sang her song.

Then the grand finale with all the beasts and birds and flowers of the forest bursting into a wild revel of song, intoxicated with the thought that this was the last of the school year, the cuckoo adding a half-dozen raucous calls for good measure—and the operetta was over.

Immediately all was confusion. Emma-Jo stood alone, dazed, all her recent strength gone from her like a cast-off garment; stood there until Angie came flying through the milling crowd to throw both arms around her.

"Emma-Jo, how *could* you *do* it? Oh, Emma-Jo, you're my friend—my best friend for all my life." But such affectionate emotion was not natural to Angie. Immediately she was saying: "That *old* Faustina—that old *meanie*—that *old*—"

And then Faustina herself was coming by, her red silk coat over her arm. She tossed her yellow head, addressed Emma-Jo Thomas pointedly and without restraint. "You think you're smart, don't you? You little—little *cluck* of a *fat* hen!"

But Emma-Jo was wrapped in the warmth of Angie's arm and sustained by the glowering face of Angie turned Faustina-ward. And in that friendly shelter she knew she was not a fat hen nor yet the cluck of a fat hen. She was a swan—a graceful swan—and so was Angie. Inseparable friends! Like that Rosalind and Celia! Twin swans in the lovely month of Juno!

The Heirs

This very short story is a masterful piece of description of the main character; as has been noted, Aldrich's depictions of older people are excellent.

The theme of "The Heirs" seems to have disturbed Aldrich. She examined it first in 1923 with "The Cashier and the Little Old Lady" (*McClintock's Magazine,* January–February) and again in January of 1931 in the *Delineator* with "It's Never Too Late to Live." She returned to it again in 1949, distilling the idea still further and sending it to *Colliers,* who published "The Heirs" as one of their short, short stories in the 10 September issue. As noted in discussing "It's Never Too Late to Live," Aldrich must have known of such individuals and found it impossible to comprehend how a wealthy man could keep his wife so in fear of penury and so unnecessarily enslaved by physical labor. Here, however, Emmaline Smith has the last laugh on them all.

Old Emmaline drove up in front of the county courthouse, climbed out of the buggy and tied her horse to the one hitching post left in town. Her husband used to say he hoped that post would stay there as long as he lived, for you wouldn't catch him putting good money into a car. Well, Pa had been dead a year now, and here was the old post as stout as ever.

Emmaline started up the long walk which led to the entrance of the big brick building. It had a weather-beaten look, but so did old Emmaline. She was slight of build and as brown and brittle as the elm leaves falling now in the courthouse yard, but her eyes were black and bright. Her bony hands clutched a shabby purse whose broken clasp was held together by a rubber band. Her sunken lips worked ceaselessly on the sunflower seed she was chewing. Her withered face had a bewildered look, and with reason.

For in the next half hour the judge would announce whether Emmaline was capable of looking after her own affairs or was in need of a guardian. *Competent. Incompetent.* Lawyer Marks had explained them to her with patient care.

It all went back to Pa's will. She could say that will, word for word, like a child speaking a piece. It didn't sound a bit like Pa's talk, but that was because Lawyer Marks had written it: "Inasmuch as I deeded a farm to each of my children, namely Edward Smith and Ivy Smith Langenmier, at the time of their respective marriages, I hereby give, devise and bequeath to my beloved wife, Emmaline Smith, the home farm and all my other remaining property, both real and personal, with the right to sell, reinvest, or use as she may wish."

To my beloved wife. Old Emmaline had been more moved by those words than by the outright gift of the farm. Pa had never used language like that in his whole life. He probably didn't really say it then, either; but he hadn't made Lawyer Marks take it out, so he must have liked it. At so slight a fire did old Emmaline try to warm her heart.

Eddie and Ivy were stepchildren, but she had cared for them since their mother's death when they were eight and ten respectively—first as the hired girl and then as their father's wife. And now they were middle-aged and had brought suit to have her declared incompetent.

The hearing had been yesterday, and when it was over, the county judge had said he would take it under advisement and render his decision this afternoon at two o'clock. Lawyer Marks had told her not to come to town, that he would drive out and tell her the decision; but she had come anyway. She guessed she was just as interested in it as the rest of them.

As she trudged up the long walk, she thought over all that had happened yesterday. It still amazed and confused her. The things the children had said on the witness stand! The lawyer asking Eddie: "What would you say as to her mental condition?" And Eddie, not looking toward her: "Well, I would say it was poor." And the lawyer asking him to tell any incidents to the court, with Eddie saying she walked a lot in the woods, gazing up in the tops of trees—that she rocked all the time on the porch, staring into space—that she had grown so neglectful of her work she hadn't even set a hen last spring.

She could have told them it was the first time she ever had a chance to watch the birds in the timber—that she never before had leisure to rock on the porch—that she decided not to set any hens when she figured up and found she'd set about twelve hundred of the squawking things. But when the judge talked to her later, she had felt just stubborn and wouldn't give any explanation.

Ivy had gone on the stand, too, telling about Emmaline giving money to the church circle. "More at one time than Pa ever let her in his whole life," Ivy had said. Then she told about Emmaline buying all those new things. You could hardly get into the house for all the purchases standing around, Ivy had told the judge—a new couch, dining-room table and chairs, a bedroom set, three rugs not even unrolled yet, new dishes still in their excelsior. "Why, at the rate she's agoin', she won't have anything left." Here the judge had interrupted Ivy and told her to stick to what she had observed. *She won't have anything left for Eddie and me,* was what Ivy really had meant.

Emmaline was in the courthouse now and walking down the hall. Yesterday she had felt timid. Today she knew right where to go. It made her feel important. This was the room. Eddie and his wife came in and took seats on the other side. Neither one looked her way. The children's lawyer came in; then the court clerk.

Lawyer Marks nodded to her, but he looked surprised and maybe a bit cross. And there was Ivy waddling in, late and hurried, coughing asthmatically. The judge came in and took his seat. The room grew quiet. Old Emmaline snapped the rubber band on the purse and chewed her sunflower seed.

What was that the judge was saying? Incompetent. Now which one was that? It was the guardian one. Oh well, she had almost known from the first that was the way it would turn out.

They were all gathering around the desk now and there was some fussing with papers. It reminded old Emmaline that she had a paper of her own. She removed the rubber band from the purse and took out a long envelope. Then she stood up, her lips quivering nervously. She walked through the group to the judge and handed him the paper. His eyebrows shot up and he asked "What's this?"

"The deed," she said. "The deed to the farm. See, it's all drawed up legal—before a notary. I was deedin' it to the children. Givin' it to 'em, the way Pa said in his will—'the right to sell, reinvest or use as she may wish.' I was goin' to live in the little tenant house. I didn't need the big house or the farm, neither one. I got a little money o' my own—egg money, that is—and the cash Pa left me in the bank I was aimin' to keep. Them rugs and furniture and dishes Ivy was tellin' about was for furnishin' the cottage. I was plumb enjoyin' gettin' 'em together all year."

The silence in the room was so deep that only Ivy's breathing could be heard. Emmaline's black beady eyes darted toward her and Eddie, both standing there stupefied.

"But all that was when I was still right in the head," she volunteered cheerfully. "Now—" she looked at the judge again. "Now it ain't legal, is it? The property's got to be held in trust for me as long as I live, ain't it?"

The judge cleared his throat. "Yes," he said "that's correct."

Emmaline's bony fingers reached over and picked up the paper. She tore it through once and dropped it in the wastebasket. Then she turned and walked past the lawyers and the middle-aged children, out of the courtroom's heavy silence.

The Great Wide World of Men

Aldrich wrote almost exclusively of small towns and their inhabitants, which makes this story somewhat different, for it is one of her few in a specifically urban setting. Aldrich was very clear on the fact that cities were only clusters of small towns called neighborhoods and that the people in cities were very much like those in small towns. "The Great Wide World of Men" (*Woman's Home Companion,* May 1950) has the same types of people found in her rural stories, for, as she commented in "How I Mixed Stories with Doughnuts" (1922), wherever there are folks "who live and work and love and die . . . there is stuff of which stories are made."

In this story, Aldrich pays her respects to her unassuming pioneer family when she has Mr. Cuddy express his disgust with the "biggest snob" in town, a woman who thinks she is more socially acceptable than he, even though his "folks [were] some of the best-known settlers here in pioneer days, [with] everybody in the county knowing 'em and making our place their headquarters." Aldrich had little use for snobs, and both in her personal and in her professional life she was known for her warmth in dealing with people from all walks of life.

Another personal note in this story is the description of the little boy whose "face shown with the born fisherman's rapture, that soul-stirring emotion with which a certain percentage of the human race is happily endowed." Aldrich was so endowed and spent as much of her summer as possible fishing at the Minnesota lake where she had a cottage.

In 1948 Aldrich wrote a Christmas story called "Star Across the Tracks," which was published in the 25 December issue of the *Saturday Evening Post*. The characters were Harm Kurtz, Ma Kurtz, and their children; they lived on Mill Street. Harm was a local yardman/handyman who worked for three families who lived on High View Drive. In writing "The Great Wide World of Men," Aldrich has used basically the same characters and similar settings but with different names and different events.

In 1948 Aldrich had been living in Lincoln, Nebraska, for a little over three years, having moved there from her Elmwood, Nebraska, home of almost forty years. "Star Across the Tracks" and "Great Wide World of Men" are two of her last three fiction pieces, all written in Lincoln.

Mr. Mort Cuddy, lunch pail in hand, got off the bus which had lumbered its way out to the city's finest residential district.

The big bus carried few passengers that far, for High View residents rode in sedans, convertibles and station wagons. But Mr. Mort Cuddy was a regular thrice-weekly patron. Every Thursday he worked at the Dr. Dean home. On Friday he went to the Butterbaughs. Saturday belonged to the Horners. For several years he had been a yard man in summer, a handy man in winter and a mainstay in all seasons for these families. Without Mr. Cuddy, the Deans, Butterbaughs and Horners might have been buried alive in unshoveled snowbanks, or compelled to peer out on High View Drive through jungles of undergrowth.

Today as Pa Cuddy walked away from the bus he felt a boyish response to spring in the air. It was in the yellowing of the willows and forsythia, in the swelling maple buds and in the smell of the wet grass. Springtime! Planting time! Fishing time! Pa felt in lighter-hearted mood than he had for many wintry months.

He planned to clean up Mrs. Dean's tulip beds the first thing. She was the only of the three women out here who let him alone. Not knowing the slightest thing about vegetation, she gave him his own way. Mrs. Horner was a member of the garden club and thought she knew all there was to know about horticulture, agriculture and plain culture, so she bossed him constantly. Mrs. Butterbaugh had been raised on a farm and knew more than the other two put together but she wasn't noisy about it—a real lady.

But today was the Dean job. He might not even lay eyes on Mrs. Dean all day. That was all right with him for he didn't like her. Sitting at home with Mamma in the Mill Street kitchen after his day at the Deans', he would sneer: "Biggest snob in High View. Head up and nose quivering like a rabbit's. Throws me a word or two like it hurts her."

The episode of the front door had always rankled. He had attempted to hand her a potted geranium but she had told him coldly to take it to the rear. "And my folks some of the best-known settlers here in pioneer days, everybody in the county knowing 'em and making our place their headquarters! She ain't no call to be snooty with me even if she does live on High Falutin' Drive.

"Well," said Mamma philosophically, "I guess all rich folks ain't snobs and all poor ones ain't humble. The snobbiest woman I ever knew was that Mrs. Pierce that lived down past the mill and poor as Job's turkey."

The day Mrs. Dean had entertained her bridge foursome there had been an unusually acrid report to Mamma. "There I am, down in the pansies and standing not six feet away and her pointing me out and telling the other women what I'm good for and can't do to suit her, like I'm deaf or behind bars in a zoo."

"Well, what did you want her to say?" Mamma could be acrid too, on occasion. "Ask you to come on in the house and play something five-handed with 'em?"

Mamma always kept Pa on an even keel. When he was down, she bolstered his morale. When too far up, she took the wind out of his sails.

Pa liked the doctor, though. When Mrs. Dean was on her high horse the doctor might say quietly, "Just overlook it, Mr. Cuddy. She's nervous."

That was something Pa couldn't understand. It seemed that women on High View Drive were nervous about things that Mamma would have laughed off.

"My, my!" Mamma often said, more in amazement than envy. "If I could have somebody do my cleaning and then could set and look out on them grassy lawns with the spray whirling, I'd never feel nervous." This with a glance out at the old sheds, the chicken yard and the geraniums guarded by sticks and wire.

The Dean house was before Pa now, set in its greening lawn. It was long and low, gray stone, blue trim, big picture windows.

It hugged the curve of a natural elevation, snuggling into its clumps of juniper.

There was a reason for the Deans to have built this kind of house. They had a little crippled boy and the one floor and the wide spaces allowed Ronnie Dean to roll his wheel chair easily from room to room.

Pa was fond of Ronnie. A cheerful little soul and a lot like his dad. He often told Mamma and his daughter Ollie and his son Dan about Ronnie's doings and the funny things he said. Once he had to go into the boy's room to fix a window. "You shoulda seen it. Pink things everywhere like a girl's. And looked to me pictures was painted right on the walls."

"Murals," Ollie had said. She worked in the Butterbaugh department store and knew practically everything that Pa didn't.

"And you never saw anybody so crazy about fishing. He pores over the magazines and they let him send for about anything he sees advertised. He's got rods like a millionaire. And I wish you could see his tackle box—more funny bugs with horns and feathers! If there was fish in the back yard he'd sure catch some, for every sunny day he comes out there and practices casting. 'Mr. Cuddy,' he'll holler, 'my lure's caught up in that tree again.' "

Mamma had been all interest, as she always was about the three well-to-do families in the big High View houses. Not one of the three women would have known Mamma if they had passed her on the street and yet she knew that Mrs. Butterbaugh slept late in the morning, that Mrs. Dean wasted enough food to keep a family and that Mrs. Horner wore long flannel nightgowns in winter, Pa having seen them on the line.

So, with her deep curiosity over their activities, she had asked, "What real fishing luck has the little fellow ever had?"

"That's the funny part," Pa had said. "He ain't never been."

"Never been fishing when he's so crazy about it?"

"Not once. They're always promising him a long trip far away to some big lakes."

Mamma had clucked her disapproval. "A little boy don't need no big lake. All he needs is a line and a hook and a worm and a creek. I wish we could take him with us over to Spring River come Sunday. You ask her on Thursday."

Pa had shrugged. "Not me. I'd as soon ask the governor. Rather."

"It won't hurt to ask."

"Not her. Not that snob."

Mamma had set her lips in a straight line. "*You ask!*"

This was Thursday. This was the day Mamma had said to ask. Emerging from the garage with his garden tools, Pa saw Ronnie propelling himself down the broad terrace. It gave him a warm feeling of friendliness toward the little fellow, always watching for him on Thursdays.

"Hello, Mr. Cuddy. I got a new lure."

Pa approached the subject on his mind as one tiptoeing toward a firecracker with lighted match in hand.

"We're going fishing on Sunday, Ronnie."

The boy's face shone with the born fisherman's rapture, that soul-stirring emotion with which a certain percentage of the human race is happily endowed. "Where you going? Who's going with you?"

"Over to Spring River. Mamma's going and Ollie and Dan and Dan's girl."

The chair rolled closer. "Tell me more, Mr. Cuddy."

"Oh, we'll drive over there in Dan's truck and take our dinner in a basket and we'll fish."

"What'll you catch, Mr. Cuddy?"

"A nice catfish or two, I hope. Maybe bullheads. Maybe just soft old carp and have to throw 'em back."

He glanced furtively toward the house and lighted the firecracker. "I wish you could go along with us."

"Oh, Mr. Cuddy! Could I?"

"You sure could if your folks would let you." The fuse was sizzling. And then Pa blew on it to hasten the moment of combustion. "You might ask. Wouldn't hurt to ask."

The explosion was terrific. "Mommy, Mommy!" the little boy was shrieking, his chair rolling over the bricks at its best speed.

Mrs. Dean came running out on the terrace. No doubt her moment of fright made her more vehement, for when he asked breathlessly if he could go fishing with the Cuddys, she said sharply, "Of course not."

"They'd take me. Mr. Cuddy said they would."

Mrs. Dean gave her yard man a look that contained no gleam of delight.

"Mr. Cuddy is going and Mrs. Cuddy is going and Dan Cuddy is going and Ollie Cuddy is going and Dan Cuddy's girl is going." Some little-boy instinct made him draw out all their names, as though the crowd were very large and so more protective. "Couldn't I go too?"

"No, Ronnie, you couldn't."

"Why not?"

"Because they're not your own people. *We're* a family—and *they're* a family." The words were simple and wholly true but the way she spoke them made the classification seem absolute and insurmountable.

"But they want me to be in their family that day. Don't you, Mr. Cuddy?"

His mother ignored this and added sweet patience to her voice. "Now, Ronnie, we'll take it all up later."

"But I don't want to take it up later. I want to go fishing with Mr. Cuddy."

"Listen, Ronnie. Spring River isn't much more than a creek. People who can't get away to the lakes just *have* to go there if they want to fish. But *we* can go to the lakes some day. When you've come home from the hospital again we'll plan to take you where the fishing is really good. We'll hire a guide and go away out on the big blue lake in a nice launch."

"But I don't want to go there. I want to go fishing with Mr. Cuddy."

"And besides, there aren't any good fish in that little muddy stream."

At this Ronnie blew up as though he had been a blow fish himself. "There are too, good fish, aren't there, Mr. Cuddy? There are good big old catfish and good big old bullheads and even some of the carp might be good . . . "

At five o'clock Pa Cuddy scraped the dirt from his garden tools, washed his hands at an outside faucet and caught the down bus, vaguely aware that he had left a smoldering fire behind him but unaware how great the conflagration was. For he could not know that when the doctor arrived home his wife began telling him that Mr. Cuddy, of all things, had wanted to take Ronnie fishing and that all day long Ronnie had pestered her to go and when the doctor said, "Well, why not?" she was provoked at him too.

"In the first place he's a grubby old man who says, 'There ain't no harm in that.' "

"Well," said the doctor cheerfully, "there ain't no harm in that, is there?"

But Mrs. Dean would not smile. For a time there was polite argument and then some not so polite.

"See here." The doctor turned on her. "He's trying to be a normal boy. If everything were all right, he'd be tearing all over the neighborhood with other kids. He's never been away from us excepting those times at the hospital. You hover over him like a jittery hen. If the operation is successful or even helpful, he'll get out in time and adjust himself to people. If it isn't . . ." The physician gave way to the father and he paused a moment. "If it isn't, he still has to get out in what someone has called 'the great wide world of men.' "

"But that isn't with people like the Cuddys," she flared back. "No illiterate yard man is going to get chummy with my son. I feel like dismissing him for good, after creating all this disturbance."

"Phooey!" said the doctor. And Pa Cuddy would have loved this: "Don't be a snob."

On Friday Pa Cuddy put in his full day at the Butterbaughs'. Just before quitting time Mrs. Butterbaugh came out to say that Mrs. Dean wanted him to stop on his way to the bus. When he turned into the Dean driveway she was hurrying toward him.

The interview was short. If Ronnie was all right Saturday morning he could go with them. "His father"—her voice had the cutting edge of sarcasm—"wants him to get out into the great wide world of men."

Pa said that queer thing over to himself on the bus and, with no great gift of intuition, knew the decision was not to her liking.

"No, don't you go along," the doctor had said. "My mother took me to a party once. She wasn't invited but she stayed. I remember how I secretly resented it. The Cuddys are a good respectable family. These descendants of the early settlers here in the state have a kind of pioneer aristocracy of their own—probably sorry for us that we're not native-born. And it's pretty decent of them to want to bother at all with Ronnie and his big chair. Dan's a steady reliable driver. And he knows cars—he works in a garage."

Sunday morning was mild and muggy. Three days of unseasonably warm weather had pulled out the willow leaves and pried open the plum buds. Mamma got breakfast, washed the dishes, fed her chickens and packed the lunch baskets. Ollie tried on three different outfits and manicured her nails. Pa dug fishworms and Dan went after his girl.

The Deans' big car, custom-built for the wheel chair, came down unpaved Mill Street bringing Ronnie and his three rods and twenty-seven lures to the little brown house behind its picket fence. Mrs. Dean had his lunch in a white basket, not quite tied with ribbons but dainty with rosebud napkins over the top.

"He must eat his own," she told Mamma. "That is, if you can get him to eat. He's not always hungry. There's a custard and there are some chicken sandwiches—just the white meat, for we have to be so careful of his digestion." She was outwardly gracious but her voice was the voice of a martyr.

Ronnie, excited beyond measure, was not interested in the nuances of the human voice. Nothing like this had ever happened to him before. "You can go now, Daddy and Mommy."

"Yes, let's go," said the doctor. "Let the kid have the fun of starting out on his own."

Mrs. Dean told him to be courteous to everyone, reminded him never to touch anything dirty and said all the things mothers say to their offspring when breaking home ties.

"I know just how you feel." Mamma was all understanding. "Don't you worry none. We'll never take our eyes off him."

Mrs. Dean turned a bit stiffly to Pa. "When can I look for you?"

Pa snapped open the old silver watch which had been his father's. "We'll have him on your doorstep at five o'clock."

"Yes, he'll be tired. Five at the latest. Will you promise me that?"

Strangely enough, Pa answered with spirit. "When I say anything, it *is* a promise."

The Deans left. Simultaneously with their departure there came, through several displaced boards in the back-yard fence, three little boys.

"What's cookin'?" the redhead called.

"Hi, Rooshie," Dan called to the red-headed one. And "Hi, Jim and Jake," to the two little Negro boys.

Immediately they were surrounding Ronnie's chair and were asking, "Who are you? What you settin' in that funny chair for? Can't you walk? Why can't you?"

Satisfied that Ronnie was really lame, they stood about watching so wistfully that Mamma, whose heart was as expandable as a sponge, asked them if they would like to go too. Rooshie was off like a shot to get a bamboo pole but the two little Negro boys' answer was to scramble into the truck and produce from their pockets fishing lines wound on spools with hooks protruding from them.

Ronnie gazed in fascination at the little boys. No preparation. No lunch. No asking. And with tackle all ready in their pockets. He had never known that life could be so simple.

There was much noisy discussion over riding arrangements. It turned out that Pa, as special guardian of Ronnie, was to sit on the one seat with Dan, so they could have the boy between them. Ollie and Dan's girl sat on boxes. The three camp followers argued over which one could sit in the wheel chair. Mamma, in a kitchen dress with a wide straw hat tied under her second chin, was a centerpiece in a stout rocking chair of her own. The motion of the chair and the truck together made a sort of double-jointed swaying which would have rendered seasick anyone less robust than Mamma.

They drove out on the long highway in the warm spring weather. Over the rumble of the truck Ronnie's high-pitched voice kept up an unending chatter. "What's that machine there for, Mr. Cuddy? Did you see that funny cow, Mr. Cuddy?" Dan and the girls flung wisecracks back and forth, the three little boys with monotonous regularity pushed one another out of the wheel chair and Mamma rocked with fine disregard for the laws of equilibrium.

Several miles out, they turned onto a dirt road moist from the spring thaws; newly flowered cherry blossoms spilled over a fence and the winter wheat made vivid green rugs on the floor of the countryside; then into a woodsy road, so narrow that the undergrowth scraped the sides of the truck. There was the smell of water and then the little stream flowing high between its banks.

Dan braced Ronnie's chair against a fallen log. "To keep you from being pulled into the water by a huge muskellunge," he explained to the big-eyed boy.

There followed the business of worms and minnows, of bobbers, leaders and all the absorbing preparation for the great unknown.

In time Dan caught a good catfish; Pa, two smaller catfish and some bullheads; Dan's girl, an unwanted carp; Mamma, Ollie and the neighborhood boys, several bullheads. Ronnie had no fish at all.

The others did all they could for him. Someone exchanged a pole for his expensive rod. They substituted worms and minnows for his many-colored lures. They put his chair in various strategic spots on the bank. Nothing happened. Always his bobber lay sluggishly on the water. At each catch of the others he expressed polite elation for the lucky one but as the morning wore on, it grew noticeably harder for him to show his pleasure.

"That's the way they are, Ronnie, contrary and bull-headed," Dan told him. "That's why they named 'em bullheads."

Mamma, whose approach to the Deity was always very direct, grew so perturbed that she secretly prayed for the boy's luck to turn. But it remained unchanged and, in addition to that unhappy situation, when it came time to eat they found that his basket had been left behind.

"You mean I don't have no lunch?" Ronnie asked.

Mrs. Dean had been right. Already the Cuddy language was insidiously creeping in.

By afternoon, with no catch at all, Ronnie was showing such dejection that Pa suggested he carry the little boy on his back downstream to see the sight Dan had reported: beavers at work on a dam.

Everyone went excepting Mamma, to whom self-propelled transportation was something of a hardship. When all had disappeared into the timber, Mamma, having had no help from Providence, decided to take matters into her own earthy hands. She reeled in Ronnie's line and then she pulled the stringer of fish out of the water and removed one of the bullheads. It was lively and flopped about slimily, but she carefully worked it onto Ronnie's hook and threw it back into the stream.

When the crowd returned, full of talk of beavers and a raccoon, with the girls squealing their dismay at having a little black-and-white animal cross their path, Mamma was sitting in her rocking chair, looking like a sleepy cat.

"My bobber!" Ronnie shrieked. "It's under water."

Excitedly, but with the practiced hand of one who had pulled in many a fish from a High View lawn, he landed the bullhead.

Everyone was immensely relieved. Jim and Jake and Rooshie turned cart wheels. Ma said it was by far the nicest bullhead she had ever seen in all her born days. Pa said it just beat all how Mamma could have been right there and never noticed that bobber going under.

There was so much excitement that no one had paid attention to the creeping shadows. Now they became aware of the dark clouds looming above the trees. There was hurried preparation to leave. During the ride through the woods the gloom deepened. Out on the dirt road they had an open view of the coming storm, greenish-gray clouds rolling up the skyways over the prairie country. Lightning forked through the wind-blown mass and the distant thunder growled constantly.

Dan, guiding the truck over the moist rutty road, had no gay banter now, was intent only on getting them all home. Out on the main highway he drove faster, dexterously weaving in and out of other hurrying cars, while Pa's arms steadied Ronnie.

As they drove into Mill Street, the blackness deepened. After the others were out, Dan took his girl to her home and Mamma herded the little boys into the house. And then it broke—the fury of wind, lightning, rain, hail and crashing thunder.

Pa went at once to the phone to tell the Deans of their arrival but there was only the hollow sound of no connection.

"Something must have happened to it," Mamma volunteered.

"Transformer burned out," said Ollie, who knew practically everything that Mamma didn't.

The rain slapped down in noisy sheets and the lightning cracked its yellow whip over the little house.

There came intervals of the storm's seeming abatement and then it would break again in full fury. During one of the moments of easing, Pa looked at his watch. "Getting toward five," he said. "I'm going up there."

Mamma was provoked. "You've no call to." She kept her voice low on account of Ronnie. "She wouldn't turn her hand over for you."

But Pa, paying no attention, put on Dan's army raincoat, drew his cap down low and started into the storm.

Mamma stood at the window and watched him go up the muddy street, his wiry body bent into the wind. That was just like him, faithful to his duty. Always did things better for someone else than for himself. Let him be his own boss and he mismanaged and floundered. Like running the farm they once owned that had come from his folks. They had lost it because Pa, as hard-working as he was, couldn't plan right. Same sun shone and same rain fell on it as on the Kupkes' next to it. Same drought came on it. And now the Kupkes in these prosperous times owned both of them and Pa was doing odd jobs around town. Mamma sighed and turned back to the room where the four little boys were waiting for her to read to them.

Part of the small shelf of books was taken by a huge volume titled Etiquette for All Occasions. She took down the one next to it, a boys' storybook that had been presented to Dan on his eighth birthday.

At any time Mamma's reading was a bit on the unpolished side and now in the semidark of the storm and her worry about Pa being out, she was scarcely at her best.

There was reason to worry. Pa caught a tardy bus sloshing its slow way along Washington Street, but the bus went only a few blocks and then stopped in its tracks. Pa wasted no time getting out on the sidewalk, breasting the wind and rain. Branches lay everywhere and occasionally he had to skirt large ones. At times the lightning appeared so close that he would stop, involuntarily throwing an arm across his face.

It seemed an endless fight, that buffeting up those long streets. No human stirred, nor dog, nor bird. Only Pa.

High View Drive and finally the low stone pillars at the Dean driveway. Another onslaught of hail in the midst of the cold rain and, head down, Pa was making his way toward the rear entrance when the big front door was flung open. "Come this way," Mrs. Dean called, so that he remembered that old rebuff.

He stepped gingerly into the tiled vestibule and took off his cap. Rivulets ran from it and from his old corduroys.

"What's happened?" Her face was white, her hand at her throat.

"Why, nothing," Pa said. "Not a thing. Ronnie's fine. Snug as a bug. We got home just before the storm broke. Ma's reading to him. Kid stories," he added, as though she might have suspected crime tales.

"Then why did you come through this awful storm?"

"Why, it's five o'clock," Pa said simply. "And I said I would."

For a moment Mrs. Dean looked into Pa's weather-beaten face and then, surprisingly, burst into tears, so that he was embarrassed and shuffled from one soaked foot to the other. "I'm sorry." She gave her head a quick shake and smiled at him. "Just emotional, I guess, from the reaction. I was so worried, not knowing where he was. I've been imagining him scared and soaked and under the trees in all this terrible lightning. And the doctor away on an emergency. I tried to call you. And then to have you come all the way through the storm to report and relieve me. Mr. Cuddy, you're one of the most loyal people I've ever known."

She began bustling about to make Pa comfortable. She made him take off the dripping coat and get into a smoking jacket of the doctor's. She wanted him to take off his shoes too but Pa demurred. He wasn't very sure how Mamma's darning had stood up under stress of the day. So she put the Sunday papers down on the floor for him to walk on and had him come out to the kitchen while she made coffee. She had him sit in the breakfast nook with its curving leather seat and brought him a tray with silver on it.

When the coffee was ready she said cheerfully, "I'll have some too. I've been so upset it will do me good."

She was making ready to sit down opposite him, so he hurriedly took the spoon out of his cup and put it in his saucer. Mamma's Etiquette for All Occasions had come into its own.

Mrs. Dean—sitting at the table with him—drinking coffee—chatting sociably. He couldn't wait to get home to tell Mamma.

The storm was dying away with farewell grumbling. The doctor came. All three got into the big car and drove down to the Cuddys', picking their way through the storm's debris. They had to leave the car at the corner and walk through the dripping weeds.

Mamma met them at the door, a finger on her lips. "They dropped off when I was reading," she explained. "I guess I ain't no great shakes of a reader."

The doctor and Mrs. Dean tiptoed into the room and over to the couch where a clean pieced quilt was spread over their sleeping son. He had a faint smile on his face and several streaks of dirt, not faint. On a chair at his side a little bullhead, with marvelous vitality for all its frequent catching, swam around in Mamma's dishpan, bumping its nose daintily against the tinny side. As though the gazing called the boy back from sleep, he suddenly opened his eyes and stared dazedly. Then he shouted, "Daddy, Mommy—*I caught a fish!*"

At the outburst, the other little boys wakened and sat up suddenly.

Startled, his mother asked, "Why, who are these?"

"My friends," said Ronnie proudly.

It was then that she noticed the lunch basket and lifted its rosy coverings. Before she had time to say anything, Mamma volunteered sorrowfully, "We forgot it."

"Forgot it? Why, what did he eat?"

"I don't just remember. But about what the others did."

"I remember," said Ronnie glibly. "I remember everything: two pieces of chocolate cake and some candy beans and a chicken leg and some potato salad and a deviled egg and a liverwurst sandwich and a doughnut."

"And gooseberry pie," added Rooshie.

His mother was gasping but the doctor laughed. "If he's had no ill effects by this time, there won't be any."

Dan came home, slithering around in the Mill Street mud. Dan's little truck could rush in where limousines feared to tread.

Pa said he would carry Ronnie on his back to the corner where the car was parked. When the Deans objected, Ronnie hooted his derision, informing them he had been miles and miles on Mr. Cuddy's back to see beavers and raccoons and skunks.

The doctor wheeled the chair through the wet weeds. Dan carried the tackle box and Ollie, the discarded lunch. Rooshie and Jim and Jake each had a rod and Mrs. Dean brought up the rear with a pail containing the day's catch, still active. Only Mamma remained at the gate. "If I got stuck," she said by way of apology, "Dan would have to go after the wrecker."

Pa deposited Ronnie in the car. The doctor and Dan lifted in the chair. Mrs. Dean got in with her fishy charge and the doctor took the wheel. It was all over—the day of truck riding and fishing—of treed raccoons and transient skunks—of unsponsored lunches and freedom of the spirit.

"Good-by, Mrs. Cuddy," the little boy shouted back to the woman at the gate. "Good-by, Dan. Good-by, Ollie. Good-by, Mr. Cuddy. Good-by, fellows. Don't forget you're coming up to see me tomorrow." He was still pumping his arm up and down when he leaned out of the car and called back: "I had the best time I ever had in my whole life."

"Well," said Pa Cuddy to no one in particular, "looks to me Ronnie got out in that great wide world of men, all right."

Working Backward

"Working Backward" (*The Writer*, November 1950) is vintage Aldrich trying, as she so often did, to help beginning authors and to give them encouragement. She talked to writing classes at the University of Nebraska in Lincoln, she answered questions from students who visited her home to ask about her work as a part of their own writing assignments, she responded to query letters from hopeful writers about the intricacies of the writing field. And she wrote articles ("How I Mixed Stories with Doughnuts," 1921; "Advice to Writers of the Future," 1924; "The Story Germ," 1941) to help others along what she called "a stony path" to publication. This is the last of those articles and was written from the perspective of a woman who had been writing and having her work published for over fifty years.

A number of years ago I wrote an article for *The Writer* titled "The Story Germ." Several young writers were kind enough to tell me it was helpful to them. In that article I stressed the point that plots for stories seldom come to one in their entirety, but that, given some small situation or dramatic moment or distinctive human trait, one can work out a story based on that little happening or emotional period or outstanding characteristic.

With the editor asking for another article I can think of nothing more practical than to follow that lead with a detailed account of how one can work backward in developing a short story. Any similarity between this article and the former will harm no one, for those who read the other, written so long ago, no doubt have become sure-fire authors by this time or have given up the literary ghost.

People who have had no experience in writing often hold the idea that turning out a story must be the easiest thing in the world. A story reads smoothly. The people in it seem natural. Events move forward in regular and interesting sequence. It comes to a surprising or satisfactory climax. And there you are. Nothing could be easier. Or so they think. But they do not know with what knitting of brows, chewing of pencils and discarding of wordage that easily read story is constructed. For more often than not, it is the outgrowth of some little happening, too small in itself to constitute a whole story, which has become one after intensive work.

Over many years of writing I have evolved two methods for the development of short stories. For a character story—one which stresses the person rather than the plot—I begin by getting mentally acquainted with that fictitious character, dwelling on his appearance, traits, mental processes and emotional reactions, until he takes upon himself the semblance of such reality that automatically he moves into action. In this way "The Man Who Caught the Weather" was constructed; a story which was rejected by twenty-eight magazines before it was purchased by the old *Century Magazine.* It was chosen for the O. Henry Award volume of that year, has been used in several anthologies, syndicated, resold to a British magazine and read on various radio story hours. I insert that item for the benefit of young writers who lose their courage over a second or third rejection and who, like the ship wrecked brother, "hearing, may take heart again."

The second method—which is the line this little article is taking—is the constructing of a story from some dramatic incident or interesting contrast between two settings or ideas, and working backward from that point. With fine disregard for the law of gravity, I start with the capstone of the structure, slip another stone under it, and another one under that, until solid ground is reached.

Naturally the story which I shall use as an illustration should be read in its entirety if a detailed analysis is to be understood. It was in the 1948 Christmas number of *The Saturday Evening Post* and titled "Star Across the Tracks." Also it is to be found in my book "Journey Into Christmas," a compilation of short stories. Bearing down heavily on the Christmas atmosphere, it has the simplest of plots, but even so, it entailed a great deal of planning, for the little plot grew out of a mere setting upon which this backward method was used.

Very briefly, the story is this: An old day laborer is the yard man for three families who live in a fine residential district of a midwestern city in which there is a city-wide contest for the best outdoor Christmas decorations. The old man assists his three families in putting up their elaborate decorations, but wins the first prize himself with a simple nativity scene at his own little home across the tracks.

The origin of the story was this: On a Christmas night we were taking one of my sons to his train after his holiday visit with us. Our city had gone in extensively for outdoor decorations and as we drove from our suburban section we passed any number of elaborately decorated yards. There were lights in brilliant landscaping effects, picturesque Santa Clauses, and life-sized reindeer, expansive and expensive. At the station we found the train had changed time, and there would be quite a wait, but not long enough to drive back home. It was a mild evening, in contrast to some of our mid-western holiday weather, and we drove leisurely through a section of town beyond the station where the Christmas touch was evident, if on a less extravagant scale. Then we came to it: a hay-filled manger, evidently made from packing-boxes, by the side of a small cottage, a white-robed figure bending over it and lighted with a single faint glow.

The son, who was a young newspaperman, said: "There's a story for you, Mother. That's right up your alley . . . elaborate decorations up town and this little manger scene here across the tracks."

Now any incident which brings laughter or tears, or which calls forth one's sympathy, anger, admiration, in fact, anything which touches the emotions has the germ of a story in it. The sight of the crude manger and the white pasteboard figure here by the little house, far away from those brilliantly lighted ones, touched us all. And I knew, as my son had suggested, there *was* a story in it waiting to be developed if it could be worked out.

But a story is more than a scene and more than the contrast between two settings. There is nothing static about it. Something must happen. Characters must come to life. People must live and move across the pages of the magazine so that the reader lives and moves with them. A few days later I was starting the mental machinery by which a story could be evolved from the small germ of that little manger across the tracks. *And working backward.*

In other words, the climax was to be that the simple scene by the cottage would win a city-wide first prize away from all that uptown splurge. But as almost all stories change from fact into fancy, even though based on reality, instead of the mere manger of boxes, I find myself visualizing a shed with open front to the street, a cow and team of horses munching on the hay, pigeons fluttering on the roof, a star overhead, and the Babe and Mother in that stable setting. (Immediately I am thinking this is a bit incongruous in a city which prohibits stock in its limits, so make a note to state casually, early in the story, that this is the only section where stock can be kept.)

Now, the people who live there—in the story, of course—who are they? What do they do? Some old man and his wife, hard working and obviously with a religious trend. Almost at once I have named them: *Mr. Harm Kurtz* and his wife. Pa Kurtz and Mamma. For fictitious characters immediately named come more readily to life. The rest of the family, if any, stays vague, for I may want to create characters to fit the story needs.

Mr. Kurtz will be a day laborer. Why not connect him in some way with one of those big highly decorated homes? At once he becomes the yard man for three of the well-to-do families, and they are named, too, so they will begin to seem real: the Scotts, the Dillinghams and the Porters. I see them in their homes with Pa Kurtz helping to put up all those brilliant lights, then see Pa going home to his small house across the tracks on an unpaved street, telling the day's happenings to Mamma and fixing up his own shed, with its cow and horses, for the nativity scene. But something there doesn't ring true,—the incongruity of Pa Kurtz, tired to death of the whole thing, coming home and entering into the decorative contest. No, it will be Mamma with the religious bent who arranges the stable scene.

And here is a knotty problem: our midwestern climate so cold at times, and a shed for stock standing open toward the street? One can't state an incongruity and let it go at that, if one's stories are to ring true. Each step must be the natural outgrowth of that which has gone before. So for some reason the one side of the shed has to come off temporarily. Why not have Pa Kurtz yank off the boards in anger? Mamma has chided him for the old shed looking so decrepit. She is expecting Christmas company and her pride will be hurt. Immediately, I am creating a daughter coming home with her little boys, and Mamma is saying: "Just as plain as I'm standing here I can remember your telling Carrie you'd have the new lumber on that old shed by next time she comes." At that, Pa flares up with: "I'll have that new lumber on by the time Carrie comes if it's the last thing I do." And he begins yanking off the siding, exposing the manger, the cow, the horses, the hay. That problem over, I'm trying to think what can be used for the Mother Mary. A mannikin from a store would be just right, but one doesn't simply go into a house and bring out a mannikin.

I digress here to say that nothing is so irritating in a story as the parenthetical statement. As a judge for one of the monthly reading club's books, I recently read a submitted manuscript which was rather good, had it not been for that amateurish dragging in by the hair of the head, so to speak, of properties and people which never had been presented to the reader until the moment they became useful. So, to have a mannikin handily in the house, I create another daughter, Lillie, who works in a department store, and immediately the store belongs to one of those well-to-do families, thus making the little plot more compact.

In order that it will not escape me, I write that part at once, even though the story is not under construction. "Lillie was a whiz with the needle. She made her own dresses at home and tried them on Maisie the mannikin. That was one of the store's moronic-looking models which had lost an arm and sundry other features and Lillie had asked for it when she found they were going to discard it. Now she hung her own skirts on Maisie to get their length. That was about all the good the mannikin did her, for Lillie's circumference was fully three times that of the model."

So, early in the story I plant the mannikin and when the time comes for Mamma to want something for the figure of the Madonna, there is no incongruous break.

There must be a star above the shed, and because Pa is only a grouchy onlooker, not entering into the decorative scheme at all, I create a son, Ernie, who is a mechanic. Lillie says to him: "Mamma wants you to fix a star up over the stable. Mrs. Dillingham gave an old one to Pa." I am writing this also before starting the real construction of the story: "Ernie had been a fixer ever since he was a little boy. Not for his looks had the River City Body and Fender Wreck Company hired Ernie Kurtz. So, after his warmed over supper, he got his tools and a coil of wire and fixed the yellow bauble high over the stable, the wire and the slim rod almost invisible, so that it seemed a star hung there by itself."

And now I have the causes and effects of several movements in the story to come: Pa home from helping with all those elaborate decorations . . . Mamma chiding him about the dilapidated shed . . . his yanking off the boards in anger . . . Mamma seeing how like the Bethlehem scene the old stable looks . . . going into the house to get Lillie's mannikin, draping it with sheets into the form of the Mother Mary, saying: "I ain't doin' this for show like Pa's families he's been helpin'. I'm doin' it for Carrie's little boys. Something they can see when they drive in . . . something they'll never forget, like's not, as long as they live."

This much will suffice to show the working backward method sometimes used by writers. By working that way I have created a substantial reason for every stone which is going into the structure. Now I can begin to work from the first, putting in the atmospheric descriptive matter, conversation, all the human touches a story needs: the arrival of the children for Christmas . . . the drive up through the fine residential sections of town . . . the family's utter enjoyment of the elaborate lighting effects there, with no thought that their own scene is more effective . . . their wagering among themselves as to which of the big houses will get the prize . . . hearing over the radio the next day that their own has won it . . . the hundreds of cars driving down the little unpaved street on Christmas night . . . the open shed . . . the horses pulling at the hay . . . the cow gazing moodily into space . . . the pigeons on the ridge-pole in a long feathery group . . . white Mary bending over the manger . . . and overhead the star.

And then to end on some substantial Christmas thought. With Mamma asking Pa why he can't get to sleep and his saying: "Keep thinkin' of everything. All that prize money comin' to us. Attention from so many folks. Children all home. Folks I work for all here and not a bit mad. You'd think I'd feel good. But I don't. Somethin' hangs over me. Like they'd been somebody real out there in the shed all this time. Like we'd been leaving' 'em stay out there when we ought to had 'em come in. Fool notion . . . but keeps botherin' me."

And then Mamma gave her answer. Comforting, too, just as he knew it would be. "I got the same feelin'. I guess people's been like that ever since it happened. Their consciences always hurtin' 'em a little because there wasn't no room for Him in the inn."

This resumé of the constructing of a story plot has been written for beginning writers, as experienced ones will have worked out their own methods. There is little enough one can do to assist another in the writing line, for it is a lone wolf business if ever there was one. But sometimes a frank personal experience from one who has been at work in it for a long time will strike a helpful note. I know, for thirty-five years ago I was a beginner, avidly searching for all the helps in constructing, and advice for short cuts I could read. Occasionally I ran across some of the helps. But never a short cut could I find.

The Story behind *A Lantern in Her Hand*

Through the years, Bess Streeter Aldrich sent several short stories about a bank cashier and his customers to *McClintock's*, the house publication of O. B. McClintock's banking supply company in Minneapolis, Minnesota. Although McClintock paid very little for these pieces, he and his family provided Aldrich the land on their lake where she and her children built their summer cottage. In 1929, the year following the first publication of *A Lantern in Her Hand* (1928), McClintock wrote Aldrich saying that he had been so moved by the prologue of *A Lantern in Her Hand* that he wished he could have published it in his magazine. She appreciated his comments about the novel and wrote "The Story behind *A Lantern in Her Hand*" for *McClintock's*, where it was published in October of 1929.

In late 1951, the editor of the *Christian Herald* wrote Aldrich asking her for an article about the genesis of *A Lantern in Her Hand*, for interest in it had remained high through the 23 years since its first publication. The *McClintock's* article had been written a year after the novel's publication, and she returned to it to refresh her thoughts, then changed and expanded it; it is this later version from the *Christian Herald* (March 1952) that appears here. However, Aldrich omitted from the second article this portion that defines much of her philosophy of writing and also explains why so many readers felt Aldrich must have been a part of those early years on the prairie: "I think a writer's subject must possess him, body and soul, while his work is going on. He must be steeped in it.

He must gather more material than he will use—read and feel and think of a thousand details that he will eventually discard. Only then can he become a part of those times and at one with the characters."

When the editor of *Christian Herald* asked me to write the story behind the story of "A Lantern in Her Hand," it seemed an easy assignment. Here at my desk several weeks later the task does not look so simple. For the roots of a writer's work in creating characters often go deep into the garden soil of his own life. So the article must contain something of my childhood, for it was then that I began, all unconsciously, to gather material for this book.

The child of middle-aged parents, I was the last of a family of eight, born after they had moved from their Iowa farm into the college town of Cedar Falls, so I was not a farm child and never knew at first hand any of the experiences in the story. There was a great deal of talk and laughter in that childhood home, for many relatives were always coming and going, uncles and aunts who had been sturdy pioneers there on the Cedar River when the state was new.

My grandfather, Zimri Streeter, had arrived in Blackhawk County with his big family in 1852, when there was no railroad west of the Mississippi and the crossing of the river was made by ferry boat. He built a sturdy log cabin, sheltered his neighbors during an Indian scare or two, and turned the virgin sod. Dipping into the politics of the new county, he was elected to the first legislature after the capital was moved from its territorial status in Iowa City to the little new Des Moines. Because of his dry wit he was called "the wag of the House," and undoubtedly he was a reactionary, for there is an old letter still in existence which says he believes he "did more settin' on unwise measures than anybody in the House."

A dozen years later, at the time of the second Lincoln election, he was appointed by Governor Kirkwood to go down into Georgia and bring back the Iowa soldiers' votes. He was sixty-four years old then, and when he got back to Atlanta he found the city burning, all communication to the north severed, and he had to march along with Sherman to the sea. There is a story to the effect that in all the hardships he had to undergo, sometimes foraging for food from the fields, his only complaint when he got back was that he had lost his hat.

All these tales of hardy old Zimri floated around my childish ears whenever his rather garrulous clan got together.

Mother's family came to the county two years later than father's people. At eighteen she drove one of the teams all the way out from Illinois. Sometimes she would recall the scenes of that trip: the ferrying across the Mississippi, the horses and oxen plunging up and down the bridgeless creekbeds, the tipping over of one of the wagons with the eight precious sacks of flour slipping into the water and the feather pillows floating down stream like so many geese, while the younger children chased after them with hilarious laughter. She would tell the happenings merrily as though there had been no hardships at all. The camping on the edge of the woods, the sounds of the night winds, the odors of the prairie grass—all these she pictured so clearly that I could almost see and hear and smell them myself.

So the pictures she drew for me verbally became a part of my knowledge, even though they had happened so many years before I was born. And with no possible foresight on my part of how they were to be used one day in stories, they seemed to belong in my own memories.

Mother was a high-minded woman, a lover of good literature even though her own schooling had ended in a log schoolhouse. She was a person who found joy in little things—to whom a cloud floating across the blue was a poem—to whom the twilight chirp of robins was a prayer. In those early days of hard work after starting the new home with my father, she must have been torn between her love of the finer things of life and the menial tasks her hands were forced to do. And being so torn, she did what many another pioneer woman did: she lifted her eyes to the hills while her hands performed their humble labors.

When she was in her eighties, she once related some pioneer experiences about the snow sifting through the chinks of the cabin and making grotesque figures on the bed quilts. In a moment of sympathy I remarked that we daughters were sorry her life had been hard in her pioneering days, that it seemed unfair that we now should live in an easier era with all its modern conveniences. She looked at me with an odd little expression and said: "Oh, save your pity. We had the best time in the world."

I thought of it many times after she was gone—that I would like to do a story of that type of woman. Other writers had depicted the Midwest's early days, but so often they had pictured their women as gaunt, browbeaten creatures, despairing women whom life seemed to defeat. That was not my mother. Not with her courage, her humor, her nature that would cause her to say at the end of a long life: "We had the best time in the world."

So my desire was first, to catch in the pages of a book the spirit of such a woman, and second, historical accuracy. Almost before the outline of the book was formulated, I named this main character Abbie Deal, a name which seemed from the first to fit her. The fictitious character, Abbie Deal, might have lived anywhere. She might have traveled into the Mohawk Valley in another era. She might have gone with her husband into the wheatlands of Dakota, onto a Montana ranch, into the orchard country of the northwest. But the natural choice of settings was the Iowa and Nebraska backgrounds known to me.

Probably the question most often put to me in the twenty-three years since Abbie Deal was pictured in "A Lantern in Her Hand" has been, "Was she your own mother?" The answer is *yes* and *no.* With all the above introduction to my mother's character, it is easy to see that she was with me in spirit all of the time I was at work. But in the physical realm, that pioneering in Nebraska, she was not Abbie Deal. For mother never came to Nebraska until she was in her seventies, when she moved here with us to live out her days. And as I never lived in Nebraska until after my marriage, whatever knowledge I have of the pioneer days has been obtained from old people who did live there in an earlier day. Some of them were still living when the book was written, none of those who helped me are now alive. It was only the authentic historical material that I lacked for the story, as those childhood memories of my own hardy forebears gave the keys to the pioneer character.

Three books of mine had been published previously and I was under contract to my publishers for another one when I came to the decision to do that pioneer mother story which had been dormant in my mind for so long. Because one of the previous books, "The Rim of the Prairie," had pictured a pioneer couple among its cast of characters, the editor of the *Nebraska State Journal* asked me to give a talk over the radio on "The Pioneer in Fiction." Twenty-five years ago that was something of a pioneering event in itself, and I remember how my family all trailed over to a neighbor doctor's home to hear me, his radio being the only one in town. At the close of that rather nervous talk into the unfamiliar mechanism, I asked all those listening who had any anecdotes concerning the early days here in Nebraska, and who were interested in having them incorporated into a novel, to send them to my home. Expecting perhaps a half dozen or so responses, I was amazed to see the letters, newspaper clippings, scrapbooks and diaries which almost swamped me. In addition to this, there were the interviews with many old people closer at hand.

For fourteen months I worked among that material sent me and the notes from the interviews, the actual writing took only five months. The necessity for the lengthy preparation was the rambling nature of those letters and interviews, as they jumped blithely from one subject to another and one year to another without regard to sequence of events, making one huge jigsaw puzzle. So it took that long to prepare anecdotes and events in their correct succession of time. So thorough had been this sorting into containers for each year of the story that when the actual writing began I could pick up any chapter and work on it, be it fourteen, five or eleven. A certain reward for this rather painstaking process is the fact that the book has been used for years as supplementary reading in history classes, through an educational edition with questions at the end of chapters.

"A Lantern in Her Hand" was written to please no one but my own consciousness of the character of many of those pioneer mothers. It was written in the so-called "mad twenties" when most of the best-selling books were about sophistication, flaming youth, or far-flung countries. There was some youth in it, but not of the flaming type. There was no sophistication, for Abbie Deal was of the soil. There was not even diversity of scene, for Abbie was only a homemaker.

"Lantern" seemed destined to be lost in the wave of the popular type of the times. That it has made new friends each year since that day might be a bit of a lesson for young writers. *Regardless of the popular literary trend of the times, write the thing which lies close to your heart.*

The Outsider

This is the last story that Bess Streeter Aldrich wrote. She sent it to the *Christian Herald* in November of 1953 where it was published in May of 1954. The story opens with the officious, humorless type of woman whose "high mission in life is to correct other people's mistakes." This kind of individual was contrary to the Aldrich ethos and personality, for she believed in helping others if they wanted help, but she did not tell them what to do. Other stories in which such "efficient" characters appear include "Nell Cutter Gets Back on the Job" and "Nell Cutter's White Elephants." Aldrich also depicted this type of person as one of Abbie Deal's daughters-in-law in *A Lantern in Her Hand* and *White Bird Flying.*

Aldrich knew Memorial Day in small towns, for she had lived in several. In Elmwood, graves were decorated the day before Memorial Day, as they are in this story. The day itself was a time when former servicemen put on their uniforms, the band played, and youngsters decorated their bikes. Then the ex-servicemen, the band, the children, the residents, and neighboring farm families paraded from the center of town to the cemetery where someone, usually a veteran, made a speech about the servicemen buried there and recalled other deceased members of the community. After the talk and a few other formalities, there was a salute by the firing squad. A bugler played "Taps." From the far edge of the cemetery, another bugler echoed "Taps," and then silence. After a few moments the crowd broke the hush, and friends began to gather in groups to visit and to celebrate the lives of those who were buried there and to anticipate the joys of lives just beginning, much as they do in "The Outsider."

Bess Streeter Aldrich had attended many Memorial Day ceremonies in Elmwood, where, in earlier years her husband, Spanish-American War veteran Captain Charles S. Aldrich, had often been the speaker.

Aldrich had had what was believed to have been successful cancer surgery in June of 1951. She may or may not have known that the cancer had returned when she wrote "The Outsider," but it had; she died a few short months (in August of 1954) after its publication.

Whatever personal considerations were behind her writing of this story, Bess Streeter Aldrich was witnessing a scene she knew well and of which she would, in a few short months, again be a part.

Mrs. William Stander walked briskly through the breezeway into the garage, opened the wide doors and backed her car onto the driveway. One could have told in those few moments that Doris Stander was energetic and independent. The very click of her heels and the swift movements of her body would have spelled efficiency to any onlookers. What they could not have known was that she wanted everybody else to be like her, that her high mission in life was to correct other people's mistakes. And today she was looking forward to correcting the mistakes of a whole town.

As the car turned into the street she glanced back approvingly at the low stone house. She and Bill had owned it thirteen months now. After twelve years of city apartment-house living it was nice to have moved here to Postville and gone into business for themselves. Bill had done very well too, she thought. Of course part of it was due to her own efforts. For she had lost no time in entering into the small town's activities. Right now she was on her way to meet some of the members of her Civic Club. And although they did not know it, she was going to point out something for their own good. Tomorrow was Memorial Day and if Doris Stander knew anything at all it was that a great deal of success in this world depends on timing.

Halfway down Sycamore Street she pulled up at the curb in front of a small white house. A young girl stuck her head out of the door. "Aunt Millie's already gone," she called. "You're the third one that's stopped for her. But thanks anyhow."

Doris nodded and drove on. How everyone carted that old woman around—an ancient person in out-moded clothes, but one of the most popular people in town, "Aunt Millie" to old and young!

She drove on down Sycamore, turned into a side street, then onto a gravel road which ended abruptly at the cemetery gates with the word "Hillside" wrought into their iron filigree. Inside it was very lovely. The day was warm and windless. Peonies were in full blossom on almost every lot. White syringas sweetened the air and a few early roses spilled onto the driveways. Far across the graves she could see the cenotaph on a gently sloping rise of ground. There were little knots of people here and there and voices came clearly across the stillness.

She located her own group of women, parked the car and joined them. They had finished decorating the graves of past members and were settling themselves on the grass inside a low privet hedge. Aunt Millie was there, sitting on a cement bench, fanning her warm face with her hat. "I'm hostess," she greeted Doris. "Come on in and have a seat." She waved a hand toward the tombstones enclosed by the hedge. "These are my folks." She said it in the cordial tones of an introduction, and added cheerfully: "So many of us here now." She looked lovingly at the graves, the very old ones and the newer ones and the tiny one of a grandchild upon which the grass had not yet started to grow.

There was some conversation pertaining to the finished work of decorating, but at the first opening Doris said, "I'd like to talk to all of you a few minutes. May I?"

There was pleasant assent and she began at once. "Because you've honored me with the presidency for next year, I'm taking advantage of it to talk to you about something that has been on my mind all year."

There were questioning murmurs and she warmed to her subject. "I want so much that you understand me. It's not that I mean to be critical, only helpful. As you know, Bill and I were scarcely settled this time last year but we came out to Memorial Day exercises here in the cemetery anyway. I wonder if you could possibly know how they seemed to an onlooker?" She paused for the coming effect.

"Please don't be hurt if I tell you that I was *shocked.* I had been used to services in a big city cemetery where everything was so beautifully conducted. Do you know what this one seemed like to me? A *picnic.* A regular *country picnic.* I know it's awful to put it that blunt way, but I wouldn't be helpful unless I was frank and that is the way it impressed me. Everyone was chatting, laughing, talking loudly, calling across graves to each other. Children were playing among the tombstones. Only a few people were listening to Judge Cutshaw. Oh, it was such a shock! Maybe you didn't realize it. Maybe you had been used to it that way. Maybe it was just that *one* Memorial Day. Please forgive me for saying it, but it seemed there was a complete lack of awe and reverence."

There were a few gasps and a crooked smile or two. But Doris went on imperturbably. "It just came to me forcibly that when I knew you better I'd call it to your attention. Well, I know you all now and like you, too. I thought maybe if I spoke about it, you could see it the way I did and begin to rectify it. Oh, I know reforms don't take place over night." She would be magnanimous. "It's too late to make changes for tomorrow. But because you were all in the spirit of the coming Memorial Day, I thought now was the best time to bring it up."

A grandchild of Aunt Millie's came up at that moment, a small straw-haired boy carrying a little toy known to children as a squawker. He whirled it round and round in his little hand so that it buzzed raucously near the Postville Civic Club. All unaware that he was a living illustration of the talk which Mrs. William Stander was giving and seeing everyone looking his way, he gave it another series of vigorous whirls. Several women frowned and someone giggled nervously. Aunt Millie smiled at him across his baby brother's new-made grave.

As though the incident gave fresh impetus to her task, Doris went on brightly. "You see, I've been in so many of the lovely cemeteries of our country and have seen the reverence displayed there. I've been in Sleepy Hollow where the Hawthornes and the Emersons and the Alcotts are buried. And Mount Auburn where Lowell and Longfellow sleep. There is a feeling of awe as one enters them, so that one scarcely speaks above a whisper. Then there's Arlington . . . such quietness and reverence broken only by taps and the other military sounds . . . and the old Bruton churchyard at Williamsburg where early Virginians lie. I simply can't imagine the laughing and talking that go on here in any of those cemeteries. You'll find nothing but awe and reverence there. I know you will accept what I've said in the spirit in which it is given, one of helpfulness rather than criticism."

She moved over with her back against a young aspen tree as a sort of gesture that she was through now and let the chips fall where they might. There were several murmurs of "Maybe you're right." But then Aunt Millie spoke up.

"I am sure you meant well, Mrs. Stander. Reformers usually do. But I can't agree with you."

Everyone was startled. There was no quarrelsomeness in Aunt Millie. But now she was openly disagreeing.

"I know just how it must have appeared to you, a newcomer. It *does* look like a picnic. Children *do* play around. We *don't* listen very well to Judge Cutshaw, but maybe," she laughed, "that's because he's made the same speech every year for a quarter of a century. But when you were talking I kept thinking of the way the cemetery got started, the way it grew, and I knew you couldn't understand. No outsider could."

All eyes were on Aunt Millie as she went on. "It doesn't have famous people in it like Sleepy Hollow and Mount Auburn, and it isn't kept up by the government like Arlington. It has just got our old friends and neighbors and it's kept up by a handful of folks descended from the old settlers.

"My mother used to tell me about the first one buried here, close to ninety years ago. He was a little Pendleton boy, not much older than Dickie here, dead from snake bite. His father made the little coffin and some of the pioneer women lined it with a pieced quilt. Julie Pendleton, the mother, kept saying that she couldn't stand it to see him put on the open prairie where there were no trees. Wanted him laid in the shade somewhere, the way it had been back home. There wasn't a tree in sight excepting one big cottonwood up there on that slope." Aunt Millie was pointing to the rise of land where the cenotaph stood. "Just one tree as far as the eye could see, probably come from seed dropped by a bird half a century before, so it was sort of a landmark. 'Go six miles straight south of the cottonwood tree,' the settlers would tell strangers. It's been gone for over fifty years but I remember it well. The land there belonged to Henry Echardt and he told Julie Pendleton she could bury her little boy near his tree.

"Well, come Fourth of July and the settlers wanted to do something extra, so they brought their dinner baskets up there where the one tree stood. Julie sat under the cottonwood all day and she ate her lunch right there, and Mother said they would see her put her hand over on the grave sometimes and stroke the cut-off prairie grass. Comforting to her, you might say.

"Then an old Mr. Jones died. Like all the rest, he'd come overland with his sons in a covered wagon. And the Jones sons asked Henry if they could put him under the tree by the little Pendleton boy. So that fall they built a little fence around the two graves to keep the coyotes out, and the tumbleweeds piled up against the fence and the snow drifted over it and nothing molested the dead. Then in the spring a young woman died in childbirth and they took down one side of the fence and enlarged it and buried her there, too. By then Henry said he'd just give that corner of his land for a regular burial ground. And it was needed all right. Graves accumulate fast in a new wild country. Children died from diphtheria because antitoxin had never been discovered . . . a settler from lockjaw because there wasn't such a thing as tetanus serum . . . and all that slope of the hill got covered and after some years they bought more land from Henry. Now the third new section over there has a lot of graves in it. More people out here now than over in town."

She paused. "But for a long time back in those old days people brought baskets and got together for visiting near the old tree. Then after awhile the trees they'd planted in town got big enough and nobody brought baskets out here anymore. But I guess what you call irreverence might have got started on account of the tree and never stopped when we got a little park in town. Like you say, children play around the tombstones and folks laugh and talk a lot. But I never thought of it as lacking reverence. I wish I could explain to you that it's something deeper. This reunion that people have out here Memorial Day—it does something to the folks who have lost their loved ones. It's like the ones sleeping out here still belong, are still a part of their families. I stood by Rachel Acton just a few months ago when they brought her boy home from Korea and she said 'Aunt Millie, it's comforting to think he can lie right where he played.' Believe me, I do see how it must look to an outsider. I assure you sorrow is just as deep here and grief just as terrible. Only there's something here in this cemetery eases both of them. I've seen people bowed with grief and then up would come some of the warm-hearted friends to visit and it would take away a little of the lonesomeness."

Aunt Millie's eyes brightened. "There have been quarrels patched up here, too. Some of you remember how Joe Painter wouldn't go into Asy Flood's store for years. One Memorial Day with everybody visiting together, Joe rounded the cenotaph and ran into Asy and before he'd realized it, he's said, 'Morning, Asy,' and Asy had said, 'How are you, Joe,' and they stood there and talked. Maybe they talked too loud. Maybe they laughed too loud. I don't know. But when we laugh and talk and visit across the graves of those we loved, it's as though the ones sleeping here are still a part of our lives, as though there wasn't any death at all, as though life is everlasting—still unchanging, and going on."

There was a little outburst of clapping hands which ceased as soon as it began. After all, Doris Stander must not be hurt. But Doris Stander was not hurt, merely temporarily sidetracked. There would be other reforms to push in the fall.

Aunt Millie stood up. The little grandson came and leaned against her. "We must go, Dickie." She put her hand on the boy's head. "Where's that loud toy of yours?"

"I put it there." The boy pointed to the grave of his baby brother. The red-painted squawker lay inside the white syringa wreath as though it were a symbol of something warm and human connecting the noisy living with the quiet dead.

Sources and Permissions

Sources

"Ginger Cookies," *Ladies' Home Journal* 37 (January 1920): 25.

"Across the Smiling Meadow," *Ladies' Home Journal* 37 (February 1920): 20+.

"Last Night When You Kissed Blanche Thompson," *The American Magazine* 90 (August 1920): 28–30.

"How I Mixed Stories with Doughnuts," *The American Magazine* 91 (February 1921): 32–33+.

"The Man Who Dreaded to Go Home," *The American Magazine* 92 (November 1921): 46–47.

"What God Hath Joined," *The American Magazine* 94 (September 1922): 46–49+.

"The Victory of Connie Lee," *The American Magazine* 96 (October 1923): 21–23+.

"The Weakling," *The American Magazine* 99 (February 1925): 46–49.

"The Woman Who Was Forgotten," *The American Magazine* 101 (June 1926): 50–52+.

"I Remember," *McCall's*, November 1926, 11+.

"He Whom a Dream Hath Possest," *The American Magazine* 103 (June 1927): 48–51+.

"The Man Who Caught the Weather," *Century Magazine*, July 1928, 304–10.

"Romance in G Minor," *Delineator*, February 1929, 11–12+.

"Pie," *Country Gentleman*, June 1930, 7–8+.

"The Faith that Rode with the Covered Wagon," *Christian Herald*, 9 August 1930, 6–7, and 16 August 1930, 8–91.

"Wild Critics I Have Known," *Bookman*, November 1930, 264–65.

"It's Never Too Late to Live," *Delineator*, January 1931, 10–11+.

"Will the Romance Be the Same?" *Physical Culture Magazines*, September 1931, 28–30+.

"The Day of Retaliation," *Ladies' Home Journal* 49 (February 1932): 10–11+.

"Trust the Irish for That," *Cosmopolitan*, March 1932, 48–51+.

"The Runaway Judge," *Ladies' Home Journal* 49 (July 1932): 17.

"Why I Live in a Small Town," *Ladies' Home Journal* 50 (June 1933): 21+.

"Alma, Meaning 'To Cherish,'" *Good Housekeeping* 98 (June 1934): 28–31+.

"How Far Is It to Hollywood?" *Cosmopolitan* July 1934, 66–67+.

"Welcome Home, Hal!" *Ladies' Home Journal* 51 (September 1934): 5–7+.

"Juno's Swans," *Cosmopolitan*, June 1935, 76–79.

"The Heirs," *Colliers* (Short, Short Story) 124 (10 September 1949): 32.

"The Great Wide World of Men," *Woman's Home Companion* 77 (May 1950): 22–23+.

"Working Backward," *The Writer* 63 (November 1950): 350–53.

"The Story behind *A Lantern in Her Hand*," *Christian Herald*, March 1952.

"The Outsider," *Christian Herald*, May 1954, 21+.

Permissions

"Alma, Meaning 'To Cherish,'" copyright 1934 by Bess Streeter Aldrich, renewed; "The Day of Retaliation," copyright 1932 by

Bess Streeter Aldrich, renewed; "How Far Is It to Hollywood?" copyright 1934 by Bess Streeter Aldrich, renewed; "It's Never Too Late," copyright 1931 by Bess Streeter Aldrich; "Juno's Swans," copyright 1935 by Bess Streeter Aldrich, renewed; "The Man Who Caught the Weather," copyright 1928 by Bess Streeter Aldrich, renewed; "The Mountains Look on Marathon" (here titled "The Runaway Judge"), copyright 1932 by Bess Streeter Aldrich; "Trust the Irish for That," copyright 1932 by Bess Streeter Aldrich, renewed; "Welcome Home Hal!" copyright 1934 by Bess Streeter Aldrich; "Will the Romance Be the Same?" copyright 1931 by Bess Streeter Aldrich, renewed, from *The Man Who Caught the Weather and Other Stories* by Bess Streeter Aldrich. Used by permission of Dutton Signet, a division of Penguin Books USA Inc.

"Working Backward," copyright 1977. Used by permission of *The Writer.*

"Why I Live in a Small Town," copyright 1933 by Meredith Corporation.

PORTER COUNTY PUBLIC LIBRARY SYSTEM